FIVE VOICES

FIVE VOICES

Kevin Conlin

For my wife, with love and thanks.

Author's Note

The last time an American was executed by hanging was during the winter of 1996. The condemned was dropped from a gallows built especially for him. Convicted before the state of Delaware had updated its method of execution to lethal injection, the murderer was given the rare opportunity to choose the method of his own demise. He decided on hanging, stating that he did not want to be put to death in the manner of a sick dog.

The elderly couple that he had murdered a decade-and-a-half earlier had lived and taken their last breaths about ten miles from the gallows.

Delaware is a small state, and people know each other. If you don't know someone personally, you surely know his brother, or at least his cousin. Associations that others would attribute to coincidence are generally considered a way of life in Delaware.

The following story is a work of fiction, and though a character in the story faces similar legal circumstances to two real-world murderers, this one is a product of my imagination.

Nevertheless, this story could only happen in Delaware.
-K.C.

PART 1: THE REPORTER

Friday, August 6, 1976

It's happening, and Joe Conway is the only one who is ready for it.

He watches as sixteen tiny children run through the hot sun toward the far gate of the enclosed tennis court, their small bodies hurrying awkwardly away from him. He knows they can't possibly comprehend why they are running toward an exit that they have never used, or know what they are running from. They are doing exactly as they have been told, following Joe's directions: Run as fast as you can. Do not look back. Do not stop until a grownup tells you to.

Joe turns to Shannon, the young woman who brought the children to the tennis courts for lessons this morning. She is still standing next to him, but he tells her she has to go with the children. He can see that she understands, but she tells him she doesn't want to go. She doesn't actually say the words; rather, she puts both of her hands over her mouth to keep the emotion from escaping. Joe knows she is, in fact, the only person who could possibly understand exactly what is in his mind right now. Though it is absurd at this moment, he notices how the hot wind catches her blonde hair. He tells her she has no choice. She must go with the children. Now.

He turns his head again. From the tennis court, high on a hill at the far end of the campground, he has a perfect view of the swimming pool area, where the chaos has unfolded beneath them. It's a hot day, even for August. At 9:24 A.M., it is already 91 degrees. But right now, the tempered pace that is so characteristic of a humid summer morning in Delaware has turned to panic-filled fury.

He turns back to Shannon. "I have to go down there," he says. His steady voice is soothing, even to his own ears. He is calmer than he should be.

"Go!" he shouts to Shannon, not in panic, but because he needs her to understand that now is the time. The woman now places both her hands on her

flat stomach, her sweaty palms leaving handprints on her red t-shirt. Joe allows his eyes to explore her for a moment before their eyes meet again. He nods his head, trying to assure her. "Everything will be okay," he says. She extends her right hand to caress his cheek before she turns to leave. He feels the sweat from her palm on his face, and he quickly takes her hand in his and kisses it gently. Then she disappears, running after the children.

Joe turns his head again toward the swimming pool where it is clear that someone has begun firing a gun. Children, counselors, and lifeguards are frantically trying to flee. It has probably only been thirty seconds since he heard the first echoes of what sounded like fireworks, but it seems much longer. He scans the distance between his position on the tennis courts and the fenced-in swimming pool. His eyes follow the trail down a long sloping hill to the baseball diamond, then to a small open field that leads to the swimming pool. He can be there in less than a minute if he runs fast enough. Then he feels his grip tighten on the tennis racket that he now remembers he is holding. He squeezes the grip as tightly as he can, allowing the pain to sharpen his senses. He breathes deeply and begins his sprint, hoping to summon up his blood, to feel the hard-favored rage that every man has the capacity to feel.

Joe Conway sprints into a world which few will ever experience, but far too many will be affected by. He has no way of knowing what his actions will create. He will never see the confusion, the heartache, the denial, or the love that will come from what he must now do. He runs harder as the ground levels out, and the picture of what is happening comes into focus. He runs into the fire, into chaos, into the screams.

Joseph Conway will never know the mystery he is about to create. He will never know the people who will solve that mystery.

He hopes they will know each other.

***

Friday, June 13, 1996

What Izzy noticed most about Abigail Conway's walk was

2

how it sounded. She had known for years that the woman was full of resolve, and now she could even hear it in the clicking of her footsteps as they made their way across the wood floor. In fact, it was practically the only sound that filled the space of the crowded gymnasium. When the slender, elegant, woman dressed in black walked through the entrance door behind the rest of the VIPs, there was a barely audible gasp from the hundreds who had gathered. Mrs. Conway had scarcely been seen in the twenty years that had passed since the murder of her husband, and as her high heels clapped against the gymnasium floor, Izzy Buchanan could almost feel the temptation among the crowd to stand and cheer for her, but nobody did.

At 48 years old, Abigail Conway was clearly in great physical condition. Emotionally, of course, she had to be decades older. Izzy was aware that years ago Abigail had made up her mind that the only way to keep the torment of her past from destroying her was to devote herself obsessively to her physical health and to that of her only child.

Of course, all eyes were on Abigail Conway today, not because of her pleasing appearance, but simply because of her presence, which was so very unexpected. As the woman made her way toward the makeshift stage, Izzy stole glances at some of the people in attendance, and she could see the wonder in their eyes as they all asked themselves the same question: *Was that really Abigail Conway?* She was easily the last person expected to be seen at this ceremony, though she had been formally invited each of the past nineteen years.

Walking close behind her was Governor Michael Springer, who had most graciously accepted the invitation every year. He was tall and thin, and he wore a perfectly tailored navy blue suit. He had a full head of brownish-gray hair. Like everyone else in the room, his expression was glum and serious. Unlike most in the room, he could turn that expression on or off at will, whenever the occasion made it necessary, as Izzy had observed many times.

Abigail walked to her seat next to the other guests of honor, two ten-year-old boys who stood politely to shake her hand. She smiled as she introduced herself and whispered a few words while simultaneously embracing them both, drawing a warm gasp from the audience. The governor quickly followed suit, hugging them both and even allowing himself a smile that rivaled that of the widow. Then he took his seat after she took hers.

From her folding chair in the media section, Izzy Buchanan observed everything and took note of most. As she watched the governor embrace this year's two recipients, she was positive that he didn't even know the boys' names. He didn't have to. The names would have been written on the paper that contained his speech, spelled out phonetically and highlighted so he could glance at them before he began speaking.

Izzy looked from the governor to the podium, where she spied the leather-bound folder, placed there by one of Governor Springer's two trusted aides. He seemed to be bringing two to all of his public appearances lately, which was one more than usual. This was regarded by local media as evidence that he would be making a run for the presidency in 2000, if he were to win a second term as governor, which was all but a foregone conclusion. After all, he had served two terms in Congress and was considered one of the Democratic Party's hottest prospects for national office. Even if he didn't win the nomination in 2000, he would certainly be on a short list for the Vice Presidency, or so said those in the know.

The governor's routine at this ceremony was the same every year. After being introduced, he would stand, face the cameras, and eloquently announce that these two boys, whom he would refer to as "fine young men," had been chosen as this year's recipients of the Joseph T. Conway Memorial Award. He would explain that this gave them an entire summer of free camping at St. Maria Goretti's Campground. The governor would then say a few words about how he remembered his old friend Joe Conway and still thought about him every day. He wouldn't mention it in his remarks, but the fact that Mike Springer was with Joe when he died always heightened the emotional impact of his presentation of the award. He would explain

4

why these two fine boys had been chosen, from among four hundred of their classmates, to receive this honor, and then he would patiently pose for pictures. This was an election year, and events like this were of immeasurable value. If events unfolded as expected, a photo of him with the widow would appear in all of tomorrow's newspapers, and video of the event would hopefully be featured on tonight's evening news.

After all were seated, Father Bill Johnston, the perennial master of ceremonies and also a friend of Joe's, stepped to the podium. The large, round Catholic priest had served as the trustee of the Memorial for the past nineteen years, the award having been his idea in the first place. He had done nearly all of the early legwork, securing promises of money from businesses, charities, and politicians to maintain the annual award. For such a worthy cause, the money poured in, making it possible to send not just one, but two children to St. Maria Goretti's for the summer. The criteria were simple: excellent behavior, an example of faith, and expressing in writing how he or she would carry the legacy of the hero Joseph T. Conway.

After warmly greeting the attendees and guests of honor and leading a short but emotional opening prayer, Father Bill began the presentation. Never a natural public speaker, he read from a piece of yellow paper, his deep voice booming through the gymnasium.

"This summer marks twenty years since that day when our friend Joe made the ultimate sacrifice. He had a choice to run for safety or charge after a man firing a gun. We all know the choice he made. And while it may have seemed like he carried nothing with him except for his beloved tennis racket as a weapon, that was not the case. Joe carried *God* with him. In some of his final words to those around him, he was heard to be praying for the strength to bring peace to a violent and evil situation. The killer had already ended nine innocent lives and was hoping to take every life at that camp that day, including his own. But Joe Conway stopped him. He was a man who, despite any of his own imperfections, rose up without hesitation and gave his life when the terrible moment - the

5

unthinkable moment - presented itself. That is what a hero does."

Only a minute into his remarks, Izzy had all but tuned out the words of the priest soon after he had started. She'd heard it all before. Today, she was far more interested in the reactions of the others on the stage, particularly Governor Springer, who, for now, was watching stoically as he waited to be introduced.

The crowd applauded as Father Bill pinched the skin beneath his chin, an unflattering habit he fell back on when he became emotional. In delivering the opening and closing remarks for each of the last nineteen of these ceremonies, he never once mentioned the name of the gunman, and he wouldn't today. Over the years he had referred to him sporadically as "the killer," "a psychopath," "an animal," and once even as "a manifestation of evil." Today he stuck to calling him the killer. The killer was actually named Evan Long, and he was at that moment residing in a small cell, fifty miles away from where the ceremony was being held, where he awaited execution.

The priest continued: "Joe's bravery that day came at a high cost. He left behind his soon-to-be-born daughter, Elizabeth." He paused at this, as if in prayer. Izzy watched as audience members darted their eyes back and forth across the stage, wondering if Elizabeth was in attendance. Apparently, she wasn't, though she had occasionally been seen at the ceremony in the past. Bill pinched his chin again and studied his notes. "And it is a special honor for me," he continued, "to be able to recognize the other brave individual whom Joe had to leave behind on that terrible day." He turned his massive body and faced the widow of Joe Conway. "Abigail," he said slowly as he leaned toward the microphone, "thank you for being here with us today."

The crowd erupted into applause as all came to their feet, with the exception of the members of the media and one man who had required a wheelchair since the day of the shooting. Abigail sat for a moment and smiled, then stood and walked to Father Bill, who devoured her in a massive embrace.

As the embrace ended and the applause faded, the audience

waited for Father Bill to continue. But he didn't. Instead, he walked back to his chair and sat down, leaving Abigail standing alone at the podium. Abigail Conway, who had scarcely been seen or heard from in public since the day of her husband's funeral, stepped forward to address the audience.

Izzy put down her pen and folded her hands neatly in her lap.

Abigail Conway was feeling it. Her heart pounded fiercely, and she tightened her fist to remind herself that she was in complete control. She breathed steadily, ignored the clicking of the cameras, and looked out over the assembled crowd. They were back in their seats now, many leaning forward as if already she wasn't speaking loudly enough. Abigail swiveled her head, trying to take in all the faces. There were people of every age, including the school children of St. Maria Goretti's who were there to see their friends awarded with a free summer of camp.

Looking to her left, she saw the group of print, radio, and television reporters occupying the section of bleachers that had been roped off for them. Many had to squint in the morning sun's rays that crept through the windows and hit their sections directly. All of them had their pens out and their recorders at the ready. Except for one. Abigail recognized the tall, slender, young woman at the end of the row of reporters. She was not taking any notes, at least not at the moment, and she did not hold a little tape recorder. She was dressed in jeans and a white blouse, with her hair pulled back in a ponytail, the sun glaring off the lenses of her dark sunglasses. The young woman sat with her hands folded neatly in her lap and with her press credentials hanging from around her neck. She wore the neutral, objective expression of a seasoned news journalist. Beautiful and professional. Abigail couldn't help but smile.

Mike Springer was wearing a respectfully content smile as he watched Abigail Conway take the podium, but he was seething inside of his perfectly tailored suit. *This was not the plan.* The governor had at first been delighted when he realized the widow of Joe Conway

7

would be attending the ceremony today. Not only was it entirely appropriate, but it would also mean great media coverage. Sheila, his new aide, was practically dancing with joy when she told him, in her hushed, urgent tone. Her energy was contagious. She could see the politics in everything, something Springer had always had difficulty doing. That was why he'd hired her. Keeping in mind the politics of Abigail Conway's heavy presence, he decided on the spot that he would sharpen the tone of his speech a bit, maybe even mention the new gun law reforms he had spoken of in recent speeches.

The fact was he wished the widow of Joe Conway ~~would have~~ had attended four years ago when he'd run for governor. He'd won the race by a wide margin, but not as wide as he would have liked. If he were to emerge from the realm of Delaware politics to make a national run, he knew he would need to be extremely popular, especially in a state the size of Delaware. He also knew that if things went the right way, his face would be plastered across every newspaper in the area next to the grieving widow, hopefully beneath a headline about the speech he was planning to deliver. He could already see the words: *Springer calls for tougher gun laws at memorial of campground shooting.* Sure, he was *supposed* to keep politics out of it, but this was an election year, and the fact that he had actually been present at the shooting twenty years ago gave him license to say just about whatever the hell he wanted. Everybody in the room regarded him as a hero, not one of *Joe's* stature, but a hero, nonetheless. After all, he was the one who had actually recovered the shooter's weapon after Joe had smashed the hard edge of his tennis racket into the back of Evan Long's head. It was Springer who'd ended up pointing the shooter's own weapon at him until the police arrived, while poor Joe lay bleeding to death from a knife wound. Joe couldn't have anticipated the knife.

But now things were quickly changing. Instead of the priest introducing the governor, as had been the routine for years, the elegant widow was stepping to the podium to speak. Springer's mind raced to come up with a plan. He'd been ready to give an emotional speech that would pull on every heartstring, full of sound bites for

8

the news. He would thank the priest for the heartwarming introduction, calling him "Bill." Then he'd launch into how personal an experience this was for him. It was for most people in the room, but everyone would know it was even more so for the governor since he had been only a few feet away from Joe when he died. There would be tears, including a few of his own. Then he would announce the two recipients of the award, embrace them, and pose for the cameras, hopefully with Abigail standing with them.

But now Abigail was going to *speak*. Springer glanced urgently in the direction of his aides.

The widow began: "Thank you, Father Bill. You've done so much for this foundation and for this award." Springer heard it in her voice immediately. She was a natural. Her voice was full of compassion and sorrow, and positive energy. No signs of nerves, even to his trained ear.

Seeing her turn to face him in mid-sentence, he widened his eyes a touch. "...and thank you also to Governor Springer for being here, once again," he heard her say. "Everyone here knows how much this day means to you, and how deeply you are dedicated to this award and to Joe's memory." Springer said nothing, but closed his eyes and nodded slowly, a grand and subtle gesture he had practiced thousands of times, a perfect half frown that simultaneously revealed his gratitude and his humility. He placed his hand to his heart and opened his eyes to look at Abigail. With perfect timing, he mouthed the words, "Thank you."

Abigail continued. "Unlike many of you who have come today, I was not there to witness what happened that day. But like some of you, I continue to know the feeling of loss that comes with the realization that a loved one is never coming home again. I know the feeling of loss that comes with climbing into an empty bed. My daughter, Elizabeth, was born one week after Joe died, and every time I put her to bed in the weeks, months, and years that followed that terrible day, I began to understand how unthinkable a feeling it must be to have a child that you will never put to bed again. This is one that is shared by nine sets of parents who lost their children that day. Some are here with us."

Springer's temper was beginning to get the best of him, as he deliberately wiped a tear. How was he supposed to follow this? He began reworking everything in his head. He would have to cut his words short, no doubt about it. He still had much he wanted to say, but the widow was destroying his opportunity. Nobody would want to hear from him after this.

"And for those of us who lost loved ones that day, we have the work of Father Bill and many others to remind us that the devastation could have been much worse. We know that Mr. Long's intention was to take the life of every single person at that camp that day." She paused and looked around the room as her words echoed into the silence.

Abigail looked out again at the many faces, eventually landing on a familiar one. The face offered the tiny hint of a smile, though the nearly invisible gesture would not have been interpreted that way by anyone other than Abigail. Without returning the smile, or whatever it was, Abigail turned again to the governor, then back to the assembled crowd and felt the warmness of that one face stirring inside her, trying its best to replace the monumental emptiness that had filled the last twenty years. These were the collected faces that would have never grown to young adulthood had it not been for the actions of her late husband. The memories they stored were countless: joys, heartbreaks, love, and life. Abigail did not say it, but she knew everyone in the crowd was thinking it.

She continued. "Joe felt joy every day he was director of Maria G's Campground, and I don't need to remind anyone how much he loved the sport of tennis and teaching it to children. And all of us can take some comfort in knowing that Joe's legacy continues in the two recipients of the award named in his honor." She paused to smile at the two winners. "Now, I would like to tell you a little bit about Jason Chatterton and T.J. Santiago."

10

Springer tried to keep himself calm, knowing now that he'd really have to think through his next move. Abigail was brilliant. She was wowing the audience with anecdotes about the two boys. She was calling the campground by the nickname the kids used. She was making them *laugh*. They were laughing at a memorial! He could hear the tension just pouring out of them. The audience was in love with her, and all he could do was play along. He wanted to leave.

But he didn't. He waited politely until she was finished. At the end of her remarks, and a rousing round of applause, the widow was kind enough to introduce him. It was finally his turn.

The governor took the podium. "Thank you, Abigail," he said with the sincerest smile he could muster. He knew it was a good one. "We are all so glad you could be here today." The audience again erupted into cheers. "And I know Joe is glad, too!" More cheers. He paused and looked at his notes. Realizing they were now all but useless, he instead looked back at Abigail and said in his most sorrowful tone, "I was with Joe when he died, Abigail." He looked back at his notes and allowed his voice to break just a little bit when he said, "But I know Joe was thinking of you when he left this world. He would be so happy to see you here today. He would be honored to know these two fine young men." He looked out over the audience. They had heard enough from him.

He glanced to his left to see his aides, Bob and Sheila, standing by the door. Bob's expression was intense. He didn't know what to do. Sheila's was angry. As she casually scratched her neck with one finger, she quickly slashed the finger across her throat. *Finished.* Opportunity lost. "Thank you," the governor said.

Izzy noticed the exchange between the governor and the new girl. *Well done, Abigail*, she thought.

Once again, Abigail saw the attractive young reporter in dark glasses on the end of the row of media. She saw her stand as the audience finished clapping. The reporter scribbled something on her notepad, then turned to her right and walked to the exit just as

11

the governor nodded to Father Bill. Abigail scanned the row to see that several reporters had begun to murmur to each other over the sudden exit of one of their colleagues.

She smiled again.

***

In the surprisingly small office of Warden Andrew Wood, Izzy sat alone, going over her notes from earlier in the day. After a few minutes, as promised by the polite uniformed woman at the main desk, Izzy began to hear the strong, heavy footsteps of the warden of Delaware State Prison. She stood as he came through the door.

He was an impressive-looking man who wore a perfectly maintained uniform that fit tightly over his tall, muscular physique. He had dark skin and piercing brown eyes that sat beneath his shaved bald head. He looked curiously at Izzy.

"Warden Andrew Wood," he said as he extended his huge right hand.

Izzy took his hand and said, "Izzy Buchanan."

He smiled dryly as if his suspicion had been confirmed. "*You* are Izzy Buchanan?" he asked.

"I am," she said. "You were expecting someone else?"

"I apologize," he said as he maneuvered his body around his desk to take his seat. "There is no polite way to say this, but I thought 'Izzy' was a man's name."

"No apology needed," Izzy said. "That happens to me a lot. Thank you for meeting with me. I know your schedule is very busy."

"It is, but I don't mind," he said. "In fact, I'm eager to know what this is all about and what it is you're up to."

"I beg your pardon?"

The warden smiled as he chose his words. "Well, my secretary tells me an award-winning journalist wants to meet with me to discuss my prison and some of our inmates. I walk into my office to find a girl, looks no older than twenty, who can't know much of anything about prisons. So I am suspicious."

"First of all, I have won a few awards, but your secretary is probably referring to the Remsburg Award. I placed second in that. It was a pretty big deal."

"Congratulations," the warden said flatly. "Now why don't you tell me what you want with me?"

Izzy understood. The warden was all business. She decided to just say it. "I would like to interview Evan Long."

She watched as the Warden's face went blank. She had expected that. He would be surprised. Then the warden broke into laughter, which she had not expected. It was genuine laughter, deep and involuntary.

"I wasn't trying to be funny, sir," she said.

"I am sure you weren't," he said. "But that boy is scheduled to be executed in a week."

"So?"

"So a lot of things. First, I only approve an interview if the inmate agrees to it," he said. "And Long has gotten interview requests from everybody from the New York Times to the local supermarket flyer. He says no to all of them."

"He might say yes to this one."

"Why would he do that?" he asked.

"I don't know, but he told me he might."

The warden's face dropped again. "You've had contact with him?" he asked.

"Yes, through the mail," she said. "He says he might be interested in the story I'm writing."

She watched as the warden drew back in his chair, closed his eyes, and pinched the space between them. He exhaled deeply and said, "There is a chance you are in over your head, Ms. Buchanan."

"How so?" Her tone was defiant, and he took notice.

"Many reasons," he said. "Security, for one. He does an interview in the days leading up to his execution, and he could get all ramped up. We have him in a routine, you see? Change that routine even slightly, and all that gets thrown off. It could make our jobs a lot harder."

13

Izzy thought about that. "That's not a good enough reason to deny an interview, in my opinion," she said. "What's your next reason?"

The warden shook his head in disbelief before he continued. "I have the boy's rights to consider. He's still filing appeals. He talks to you on the record, and that could muck things up pretty good for him."

"He and his lawyer should decide that," Izzy said. "Not you."

"You're right about that," he said. "And if it's up to his lawyer, believe me, you won't get near him."

"I'll take that chance," she said. "What else?"

The warden sighed in exasperation. "You know, I really expected you to be a man," he said.

"That's like me saying I expected you to be white," Izzy said.

The warden laughed loudly again. "Fair enough," he said. "But this is true, Ms. Buchanan. As warden, there are certain things I have control of, not because I like control, or because I don't want people to know the truth. I have control because of my experience and my history of making good decisions."

"Congratulations," Izzy said.

The warden's eyes widened in amused disbelief. "Are you really mocking me now? Trust me. That will get you nowhere."

"You did it to me," she said.

"So I did, but remember who's asking whom for something here. I am in a position of authority."

"You think the press has no authority?"

"I didn't say that," he said. He took a deep breath and shook his head. Izzy could tell he wanted to put this part of the conversation behind him. "Look, the boy is very stubborn, okay? I'm telling you he has a story to tell. If you were to actually speak to him, he'll want to tell you all about how he was bullied as a kid, how he's sorry for what he did, how he's found Jesus and prays for his victims every night — *out loud*, I might add. Then he'll want you to

14

feel sorry for him because he's choosing to be executed by hanging, like we *want* to hang him."

"How do you know all this?" Izzy asked.

"Because I know these people. I've spent time with them," the warden said. "These guys on death row love to talk about how far they've come." He closed his eyes for a moment then lowered his voice almost to a whisper. "But the thing with Evan is, that is *all* he'll tell you. If you try to challenge him on something, he will clam up, or call for a guard to come take you away. He's very much an adolescent that way. He will not let you control the conversation."

Izzy thought about this. The warden had a point. In the few letters that he had answered, he only wanted to say things on *his* terms. He never answered any of her questions. There was no back and forth, other than when he had said he would consider granting an interview. If he had answered her questions in his letters, there would really be no need for an interview. That's why she wanted one. She wanted to sit across from him, challenge him, and get a picture of the 39-year-old Evan Long as he awaited execution.

"And there's one more thing," the warden said. "Far too often, I find that reporters have an agenda. They want to interview these guys for the sole purpose of making them look good while making the people who come here to do their jobs look bad. Make my officers look bad. And Long is a special case, as you know. He'll want you to tell the world he's a martyr, the last man to be executed by hanging. I don't need that kind of distraction leading up to this thing."

"That is not what this is about, Warden," Izzy said. "I promise you that."

He took a deep breath and looked at her. "Now why should I believe you?" he asked. "It's happened to me before. Reporters come in here, smile, shake my hand, and tell me how much they respect me. Then they go off and write about how these men have changed their lives, and we're just incarcerating a man who's become a good person. How we're *killing* this good person. They have an *agenda.*" The warden sneered. "And if I can stop that from

15

happening, Ms. Buchanan - if I can stop you from trying to impress your sociology professor by writing a story that's sympathetic to a mass murderer, I will, because that is something I can control."

Izzy saw the beads of sweat that had formed on the warden's forehead. She considered her options. It was impossible to conduct a face-to-face interview with someone on death row without approval from the prison warden, even if the prisoner was willing to be interviewed. She decided this was the right time to show her hand.

"Warden, I don't have an agenda," she said. "How about this? May I tell you something about myself that might change your perspective a bit?"

The warden's eyebrows raised as he leaned back in his chair again. "Let's hear it," he said.

***

The Flat Rock Tavern was Abel Ryan's favorite pub on Main Street in Manayunk, a lively neighborhood on the west side of the Schuylkill River in Philadelphia. He quickly settled into his usual table in the corner next to a window that looked out at the busy street. Only 3:30 on Friday afternoon, there were still plenty of tables available. As was usually the case on Friday afternoons, the stench of stale beer emanated up from the floor, a result of the Thursday night beer specials that Abel never engaged in. He unfolded his fresh copy of the *Daily News* and smiled when a waitress named Jackie removed the empty ashtray and slapped a cold Dogfish Head draft on the table along with a menu.

"Just beer, Jackie," Abel said,

"That's different," the waitress said, picking up the laminated menu.

"Last day of school," Abel said. "Gave us all hot dogs and chips after field day. Not hungry."

Jackie looked out the window dreamily. "I used to love that day," she said. "I miss it."

"I still get it," Abel said. "Every year."

16

Abel looked at Jackie, who now appeared genuinely sad. "What is it?" he asked.

"Life was so simple when we were kids, wasn't it?" she asked.

"Sure."

Jackie smiled again. "I'm sorry," she said. "I don't know anything about your childhood."

"It's okay," Abel said. "It sounds like yours was simple."

She laughed. "It was," she said. She looked at him again. "Yours wasn't?"

Abel didn't answer, choosing, instead, to slowly shake his head while wearing a friendly grin. It was a gesture he had practiced hundreds of times over the years, his way of telling whomever he was speaking with that he would like to change the subject. Abel was a private person, and Jackie knew that. It had been a year since Abel had come to know the pretty young waitress at the Flat Rock, and in that time they had made small talk every Friday. He offered bits of information. He was a teacher. He'd lived in Delaware. He was twenty-nine years old. He liked the music of U2. It never went beyond that.

Jackie, on the other hand, had been an open book. Abel had been educated on every boyfriend, fight with mom, and dead pet that Jackie had experienced in the last five years. Abel enjoyed hearing the details but rarely shared any of his own.

Jackie got the message. "Well, I hope you stay for an extra beer then." Then she leaned and whispered, "And a shot of whatever you like. Happy last day of school."

As she walked away, Abel suddenly became aware of the person sitting at the other end of the bar. The young woman caught his gaze and smiled. Suddenly nervous, Abel felt himself turning red. The woman, with whom Abel was now purposefully avoiding eye contact, had blonde hair pulled into a ponytail and wore a navy blue V-neck t-shirt that revealed just enough to catch someone's attention, at least Abel's. He surmised that she must be waiting for someone else to arrive.

He turned back to his *Daily News* and took a long pull of his beer, trying to forget about the awkward exchange. Summer vacation had begun and Abel wasn't going to be distracted from getting a nice Friday afternoon buzz. He had just completed his seventh year teaching social studies to eighth graders at St. John the Baptist Elementary in Manayunk, where he'd moved eight years ago from Wilmington, Delaware, a town that had very little in common with Manayunk.

From the start of his teaching career, he had made a habit of finding places to drink beer, and sometimes bourbon, while reading the newspaper on Friday afternoons. For about a year now, that place had been the Flat Rock. He traveled almost always on foot, which many did in Manayunk since parking was a perennial nightmare. Abel enjoyed being alone among crowds of people. He had no interest in the solitude that came with the small towns and suburbs. That kind of boredom was torture. Likewise, he had no interest in joining many of his colleagues for their weekly happy hours, especially on the last day of school. He had done that one time and found that it was nothing more than a three-hour session of bitching and moaning about the underworked principal. When the principal showed up, they switched to bitching about the pain-in-the-ass parents, and when that got old, they would start talking about the people who got up to go to the bathroom. Abel had seen and heard enough.

When he realized that not only did the Flat Rock serve Dogfish Head, but that the teachers he worked with never went there, he became a regular. The wings weren't bad either. So the routine began. He was more than happy to read his newspaper and flirt with a pretty waitress. The more he drank, the more daring he became in his interactions with her. She never seemed to mind, but eventually the place would get too crowded for him. He'd quietly pay his bill and tell Jackie he would see her next Friday.

But Abel was beginning to sense that this afternoon was different. Even though he had moved on from the embarrassing moment involving the blonde across the bar, apparently she had not.

Every time he glanced up at her, there she was glancing back between sips of her coffee. She would occasionally even smile at him. *Was it possible she was checking him out?* Abel dismissed the thought. The woman was far too attractive to be picking up men in bars on Friday afternoons. She had to be waiting for friends.

When Jackie came with a refill, she leaned in again and whispered, "Looks like you have a fan."

Abel shrugged. "I doubt it. How long has she been here?"

"Ten minutes before you. Ordered coffee."

"She's meeting someone," he said.

"Nope," Jackie said. "I asked her. And look, she's even reading the same newspaper as you. You already have a lot in common. Why don't you send her over a drink?"

"No," Abel said.

"Come on. This is how people get together. I'm sick of seeing you in here alone all the time."

"I like being in here alone."

"I'll take care of it," she said, ignoring his protest. "You just sit there." She hurried away before he could protest.

Izzy Buchanan sipped her coffee and bided her time, pretending to read the *Daily News*. She had planned this meeting weeks ago, and so far, all was going exactly as she had planned. She would let Abel finish his second glass of beer, and then she would get to work. By then he'd be easier to crack. It was the start of Abel Ryan's summer, and he would be delighted to talk to a pretty young stranger. Abel was better looking than she had expected. He was average height and build, but she was picking up on an urban sophistication that she found appealing. His brown hair had enough length to be a little messy, but was neat enough to look professional in a classroom setting. He had just enough scruff on his chin to be noticed.

"Excuse me," the waitress said. Izzy looked up from her newspaper.

"The gentleman across the bar would like to buy you a drink."

19

Not part of the plan, Izzy thought. *He wasn't supposed to hit on me.*

"He would?" she asked

"Of course," Jackie said. "He's a very nice guy."

Now quite unsure of herself, Izzy scrambled for what to do next. "What's he having?" she asked.

"He's drinking Dogfish Head. A pretty strong IPA. You probably wouldn't like…"

"I'll take that," Izzy said.

The waitress raised her eyebrows. "Whatever you say," she said.

"And please take it to his table. I'll join him."

Jackie smiled and nodded.

Izzy made eye contact with Abel and smiled brilliantly, like he had just made her day. He smiled back. He looked nervous.

Change of plans. Go with it.

Abel swallowed hard as he realized that there was now a tall, beautiful, woman approaching his table. He felt his palms getting sweaty. He sipped his beer, trying to hide his nervousness. Jackie came between them and plopped a fresh beer on the table where the blonde would sit. She turned to Abel and winked before walking back to the bar. He was not amused.

"Do you mind if I sit?" the woman asked, her voice sounding much younger than he'd expected.

"No, I don't," Abel said.

"I'm Izzy," she said as she took the seat across from him. "Thanks for the drink."

"Izzy?" Abel asked. "Like the guitarist in Guns N' Roses?"

The woman smirked. "Short for Isabelle. Do you like Guns N' Roses?"

"I'm not even sure they're a band anymore, but yeah. I like them."

"I don't," she said.

This was going well. "Nice to meet you, Izzy. I'm Abel." He looked at her glass. "You like Dogfish?"

She looked puzzled for a moment before she answered. "When I'm in the mood for a beer," she said.

20

"They brew it in Delaware," Abel said, quickly realizing that this fact was probably thoroughly uninteresting to the woman across from him.

Her eyes brightened. "I'm from Delaware. I go to Brandywine U."

"You do?" he asked. "I went there."

"Really? When did you graduate?" She sipped the beer, and Abel couldn't help but notice the effort it took her not to wince at its bitterness.

"Finished about eight years ago," he said. "What year are you in?"

"Junior this coming fall," she said.

Abel glanced around the bar. "Are you even old enough to drink that?"

"Almost." She smiled and took a sip.

Strange, Abel thought. This girl was not even old enough to legally buy a drink, but here she was in a near-empty bar in Manayunk on a Friday afternoon hitting on a 30-year-old.

"So what can I do for you?" he asked, hoping to figure out what this was all about.

She got that puzzled look again. "What do you mean? Aren't we just talking?"

"I doubt it," he said.

"Why?" she asked.

Abel sighed. "For a lot of reasons. First of all, you've been pretending to read that newspaper for the last half hour. It happens to be the same one I'm reading. Now you're pretending to like this beer just because I'm drinking it. Meanwhile, there are a thousand bars within minutes of the BU campus where you could be swilling down Coors Light for two dollars a pint, and having some guy your own age pay for it. But I'm guessing you don't even drink beer."

"Why?" she asked.

"Because you don't look like a beer drinker, especially *this* beer."

"It's good," Izzy said.

21

"I know it is," Abel said. "That's why I'm drinking it. But you obviously don't like good beer. And you had no idea what else to order, so you got this. You should have just asked for more coffee."

"Very good," Izzy said.

"And not to mention the obvious."

Her eyes narrowed into a question. "What?"

"Girls that look like you don't hit on guys like me, especially in a bar like this on a Friday afternoon. It would have to be much later in the night and you wouldn't be drinking coffee."

"Okay, okay," she said, holding up both palms slowly. "I'm busted."

"So what do you want?" Abel asked.

She paused. "What do you think?"

He downed the last of his first beer and said, "Can you just tell me? It's the last day of school, and I'd like to get drunk in peace and go home." Abel had decided not to be charming. He picked up the free shot of bourbon and downed it quickly.

"You get drunk alone?" she asked.

"Sometimes. Do you care?"

"I don't care," she said. "But I'll bet your head of school would object."

He took a long pull of beer from the second glass. "How much do you know about me?" he asked.

"Not that much," she said.

"You know where I work and where I drink," he said.

She reddened a bit, then smiled. "I know a lot about you."

Abel was losing his patience. "Who are you?"

"My name is Izzy," she said smiling.

"Who are you?" he asked again.

"I'm a reporter, and I want to talk to you."

"A reporter from Brandywine University wants to talk to *me*? About what, the last day of school?"

Her smile disappeared as her expression changed from amusement to concern. She looked in his eyes and said, "No."

Abel held her gaze for a moment then glanced away. He took another drink of beer. He said nothing.

Then he watched as her perfectly manicured fingernail crept slowly across the table to the newspaper that Abel had been reading. The finger pointed to the headline of the article Abel had been trying to avoid, the one he knew he would eventually have to read. He sighed heavily and took another drink.

Then she said quietly, "I want to talk about the last day of summer camp."

Abel put down his drink and glared at the one who had finally found him. He hadn't seen her coming, and he was angry because he *should* have. He'd been tracked and lured by a pretty face. Caught after almost twenty years on the run. Ambushed.

Izzy carefully studied the man across from her. She had succeeded in catching him off guard. Her plan had worked to perfection, so far, even after the interference from the waitress. A smile, a drink, an interview. But she didn't feel good about it. Abel Ryan, obviously stunned, stared back at her, and Izzy could see the story behind his eyes. It was a good one. In hiding and on the run from the public for years, he had to have many stories to tell. But the one she wanted - the *only* one she wanted - was the one that started it. She didn't care about the changing of names or addresses. He had attended high school and college under different names, but he was now Abel Ryan of Philadelphia, information Izzy had worked hard to obtain. Rules had been broken and values had been compromised, but she had found him. Now, she wanted his story. She needed to know what he had seen that day, and why he had tried so hard to keep from telling anyone about it. This was *her* story.

Abel ordered another beer from Jackie, who had suddenly lost all of her conversation skills.

"How did you find me?" Abel asked quietly.

"I just kept looking," she answered.

He shook his head. "Nobody knows I come here."

"Can I ask you some questions?"

Abel shook his head. "I've got a few for you, Izabelle."

"It's Izzy. Go ahead."

"How did you find me?" he asked again.

"I told you. I just kept looking."

He wasn't nearly satisfied. "And…"

"And what?"

Abel leaned forward. "Reporters have been looking for me for twenty years. Good reporters. *Experienced* reporters. My parents saw to it that none of them would ever get to talk to me. No matter how hard they tried, my mom was always two steps ahead of them, and my dad would scare the hell out of them. No reporter has ever even gotten close to finding me, much less talking to me."

"Until now," she said with a smile.

He scoffed. "And along comes a pretty-faced reporter from a college newspaper, and I'm supposed to talk?"

"You were a reporter once," she said. "Aren't you impressed that I found you?"

"It doesn't matter that I'm impressed," he said. "Truth be told, I'm even more impressed that you know I was once a reporter."

"I write for the same newspaper you did," she said. "And I've read your stuff. It was pretty good."

Abel could feel his temper rising. "Pretty good?" he said.

"I didn't mean it as an insult," she said. "I saw your photos, too. They were really good."

"I was an excellent reporter *and* photographer," he said. "I would have done it professionally, but…."

"Being in the spotlight isn't your thing?"

He nodded. Then he saw her glance toward her side where she held her purse. "Are you recording this? Turn that thing off," he said.

"I just want to be sure I get everything right," she said as she stopped her tape recorder. "I would hate to misquote you after all these years."

Abel raised both hands. "I have not given you permission to interview me. This is *not* an interview. Anything I have said to you is off the record." He threw a twenty dollar bill on the table and stood to leave.

She stood with him and quickly took him by the hand. He saw her eyes, full of raw nerve. She would not let him go. Jackie the waitress took notice, as did the few patrons at the bar. "Everything okay, Abel?" she asked.

Abel ignored the question. "What do you want from me?" he asked the girl.

"Just information," she said. "You don't want to speak on the record, fine. Can we just have a conversation? I would like to tell you what I'm writing about."

"I've spent my life avoiding much bigger journalists than you. What makes you so special?"

She took a breath and reached down for her glass of beer. She took a long drink of it, winced at the taste, and then finally said, "I'm the one who knows that you were the last person that Joseph Conway spoke to before he died. And I know what you told his wife. I know about the ice cream stand. You told her, 'In front of the ice cream stand in Avalon.'"

Izzy had been hoping not to have to use Joe Conway's last words, but Abel Ryan wasn't giving her a choice. He had stood to leave and was in danger of disappearing out the door. She needed to get his attention, and for him to understand that she was already neck-deep in the story, not just a nosey reporter looking to get her name out there. She thought he would respect her for that. Eventually, she would tell him everything.

Abel felt as though he'd been injected with a fast-acting poison. He had just heard the words he had never in his life expected he would ever hear again. For years he had tried not to think about the message he had been tasked with passing to Joe Conway's widow. It was a horrible memory. A ten-year-old boy taking the clammy

25

hand of a young woman dressed in black as she held a newborn infant. He had pulled away from his mother's own tight grip to get close and whisper the words he had been ordered to pass along. He had pulled away from the widow before she could respond, but not before he could hear her gasps and cries as he was hurried away. Twenty years later, he could still hear that cry. It was joy and sadness, combining into a horrible cacophony of grief. To this day, he didn't know what the words meant, only that they must have been deeply meaningful to the young couple. He glanced at the smooth side of his forearm and sat back in his chair.

He knew the widow of Joe Conway had never spoken publicly about the events that took her husband's life. And here was this woman named Izzy, a journalism student who was too young to buy a drink, who seemed to have a knack for knowing things that no one should know.

"Do you know the rest?" he asked, reaching for her glass. "What else did he say?"

She nodded.

"Tell me," he said. "Then I'll talk to you." He quickly finished her beer.

She looked at the table and frowned. "I'm sorry."

He looked away, toward the bar but at nothing in particular. He couldn't believe what he was hearing. He had only heard this combination of words twice in his life: first when Joe had said them as before he rushed away to stop a crazed killer, and second when he repeated them to Abigail Conway at his funeral. Until now he had known he would never hear them again. He looked back at the reporter. "In front of the ice cream stand in Avalon. I'm sorry," he muttered as he sipped at her beer, hearing the words out loud for the fourth time in twenty years. "Do you know what they mean?" he asked.

She shook her head slowly. "No."

"I'll talk to you," he said. "But I want answers, too."

"Okay," she said quietly.

"How did you know all that?"

26

"She told me."

"His widow told you?"

She nodded.

"How did you get her to talk to you?" he asked.

"Pretty much the same way as I did you."

"You met her at a bar and pretended to flirt with her?"

She smiled. "No. I told her I would not quote her; just background info."

Abel considered this. "That can't be all there is. You must have done something else. How did you even get to talk to her?"

"I can't give away all my secrets. I have a long career as an investigative journalist ahead of me."

Abel shook his head. "Well, you must be some kind of reporter."

"I am an excellent reporter," she said. "But I also explained to her what I was writing. She wanted me to get it right."

"And she didn't tell you what the words meant?" he asked.

"She wasn't even sure herself," Izzy said. "She had ideas but didn't want to share. It was too personal."

"That's understandable," Abel said.

Izzy nodded sadly.

Abel shrugged and began to make his way toward the exit. "Tell me what you're writing, and then I'll talk to you. But I want to go back to my apartment. The booze there is already paid for."

"Is there coffee there?"

"Yes," he said.

"Can I smoke there?" she asked.

"Absolutely not."

As they walked out together, Abel glanced back at Jackie. She looked back, trying to read Abel's expression. She would want all the details next Friday. Of course, he had no idea how he would explain this.

27

"Tell me what you're writing," Abel said as they hit the sidewalk. The late afternoon sun was bright, and the street was beginning to swell with people.

"My specialty is revisiting big stories from the past and uncovering facts that were missed at the time they happened. I find new facts and bring them to light."

"Your *specialty*? You're still in school. Don't you think you should establish yourself first?"

"I've already done that," she said. "I wrote a story last year that placed second nationally. There were thousands of entries and mine was the best. I should have won."

"What was it about?" he asked.

"An accident that happened thirty years ago on the Brandywine campus. A boy fell from his dorm room window and died."

Abel stopped walking. He remembered the story. "I saw that," he said. "You were written up in the alumni newsletter."

She grinned. "Good story, huh?"

"They didn't reprint it in the newsletter," he said as they resumed walking.

"Of course they didn't," she said. "The conclusions of the article were embarrassing to the school, but they still wanted their alumni to know that one of their own was one of the best in the country. But I'm sure you found the article and read it."

He stopped again. "Is that how you found me? You knew I received the alumni newsletter."

"I don't reveal my methods."

Abel was impressed. He started walking again, beginning to sweat in the hot early June sun. "Yes. It was a good story," he admitted.

"It was an excellent story," she said. "It should have won."

"No, you shouldn't have," he said. "I read the one that did win. It was better."

She stopped and turned to look at him. She delivered a cold, blue-eyed stare that Abel could hardly believe she was capable of.

28

"And what was so great about it?" she asked harshly. "I was *not* impressed."

Despite her demeanor, Abel had to try to keep himself from laughing. "You weren't impressed?" he asked. "This was a graduate student who discovered her economics professor was a Nazi. Not some modern day skinhead Nazi, he was an actual member of the Nazi party. He participated in the Holocaust and was hiding from the authorities! You weren't impressed?"

She sighed in frustration and resumed walking. "Holocaust stories are too hard to compete against," she said dismissively.

Abel had many things in mind that he could have said back to her, but he decided it wasn't worth it. Her story was good, and he remembered it well. She had found and interviewed every police officer and first responder who arrived at the scene the night Robert Arnold fell to his death thirty years ago. It was no small task. Most of them had very little to say about the incident, which had been a huge story. However, she did find one retired police officer who had been a rookie at the time of the accident. He had taken statements from students who had lived on the floor above where the accident had happened. A few years after that fateful night, Kelton had been passed over for promotion. He left the campus police with a chip on his shoulder, later joining the Army National Guard and retiring with a nice pension. He was more than happy to retell everything he remembered, and what he told Izzy was far different from what had been reported at the time.

Without putting it in so many words, the University had been glad to let the public assume that the boy had been reveling in drink when he started roughhousing with a few of his buddies. Things got out of hand and, as one thing led to another, he went through the safety glass window and fell to his death.

This version of the events was called into serious question when Izzy Buchanan, a sophomore undergrad working on a journalism degree, interviewed the retired Colonel Scott Kelton, who recalled that several witnesses made a point to tell him that the young man in question had actually had nothing to drink at all and that he was not

29

engaged in roughhousing of any sort. Yes, there had been drinking and guys with beer muscles had indeed been throwing their weight around that night. But Robert had had an exam the next day and refused to partake in any of the partying, except to lean with his back against the large bedroom window while he conversed with a group of highly intoxicated and very attractive young ladies. To the best that three of the girls could recall, the window began to give way very suddenly and Robert was falling before he even realized what was happening.

Officer Kelton reported what the girls had said to the detective in charge, who took these statements into account, along with all the statements from the party-goers in the main room of the apartment. They had reported a lot of drinking and a lot of roughhousing. After examining all of the windows in the building, it was determined that poor Robert could have only gone through the window if he had hit it with great force. Case closed.

That is until Izzy Buchanan did some digging and discovered that during the remainder of that same academic year, every single window in the building had undergone extensive maintenance. Officer Kelton even remembered the name of the contractors who had done the work. He had been so haunted by the experience that he checked the building every day. He still remembered seeing the white trucks emblazoned with "Ruggiero Construction" on the side. He had asked a few of the workers what they were up to. They had always responded, "Just routine maintenance and cleaning." That is until Paul Ruggiero, retired owner and operator, answered the telephone at his house in Palm Beach and told the young reporter what she wanted to hear. "A lot of those windows had decayed considerably. There wasn't much danger, but freak accidents tend to happen. We were told to keep quiet about it at the time, but it's been thirty years, so what the hell? You might as well know the truth."

And then the truth was out. Izzy had sprung a huge story on the academic community and made a name for herself, even in professional journalism circles. Brandywine University offered all the requisite denials and attorneys for the family of Robert Arnold indicated they were not interested in revisiting the matter legally, though there were whispers that private arrangements had been made for certain members of Scott's family to receive special scholarships. These rumors were never confirmed or denied. Izzy had dug and dug, and brought out the ugly truth.

"You should be proud of that," Abel said. "It was a good story."

"I am," Izzy said. "I'm always proud of my work, because I know it's good. I don't do hard news or sports because I don't want my stuff in the papers the next day. I investigate, and I write. I don't cut any corners, and I never settle for writing *so and so could not be reached for comment.*"

Abel considered this. He knew what he was about to say was going to send her into a fit, but thanks to the beer, he said it anyway. "You could have gone a little further."

This time she did not stop or turn to look at him. She quickened her pace dramatically and stormed up the sidewalk. Abel stopped and watched.

"I'm going inside," he called. She stopped and looked back, anger in her eyes. "This is my apartment building," he said. "Come inside and I'll give you a lesson in journalism."

Izzy inhaled deeply to allow her anger to subside. *No time to waste on emotion.* Abel unlocked his apartment and stepped aside to let her enter. She was conflicted and scrambling to choose a direction. On one hand, she was thrilled to actually be talking to the last person that Joseph Conway had spoken to before he was killed. No reporter had ever come close to being where she was right now. On the other hand, she was used to being the one to catch the subject of an interview off guard. She had managed to do this today with Abel Ryan, but he quickly turned the tables on her. He had read her stuff, and he had even read the story that beat hers for the Remsburg Award. On top of that, he had the nerve to tell her the story could have gone deeper. Going deep was what she prided herself on. Finding the answers to questions no one thought to ask before she did. She was good at it. And here was someone who had been out of journalism for a decade telling him she should have gone deeper.

Izzy was not quite as upset as she was pretending to be, but she was agitated. She had wanted to give him some power, let him feel like he was in control of the conversation. Any decent journalist knew the value in this, like letting your subject drive his own car during an interview. It is amazing what even shy people will say when they are behind the wheel of a car. So this had worked. Abel was actually talking to her. But she worried he might have a little too much control. If he were going to start criticizing her work, this could be a problem. If there were one thing that Izzy was passionate about, it was her skills as an investigator and a writer, and she was not prepared to have a 30-year-old social studies teacher stare down his nose at her. She would play along, but she wouldn't like it.

Abel went to the kitchen and fixed himself a cocktail and offered Izzy a drink. She politely declined, raising her to-go coffee cup that she had stopped for halfway through the walk from the bar. Abel dropped an REM C.D. into his impressive stereo system. The apartment was decent, Izzy thought. Not too bachelor pad, but not too old man either. The walls were adorned with framed posters from classic films including *The Godfather* and *Casablanca*. He must have purchased them at an antique shop. The space reflected time and effort, but not obsession. Izzy asked again if she could smoke, though from the cleanliness of Abel's one-bedroom apartment, she had a feeling it was never going to happen.

She was right. "Don't you know smoking is on its way out?" he asked. "People are smarter than that now."

She rolled her eyes. "It can come in handy sometimes."

Abel raised his eyebrows.

"In an interview," she said. "Smoking with your subject often gets them to open up. It creates a bond. But it backfires if they can tell you're faking. So you have to be good at it."

"That's why you were pretending to drink with me? You could have at least ordered a *light* beer."

She smiled. "I don't know anything about beer. I can't pretend at that. I do know how to smoke though."

"It's better to live till your nineties."

"You sound like my mother," she said. "But you'd be surprised at how many exclusives I've gotten because I ducked out for a cigarette at the same time as some stuffy politician or elusive police detective."

Abel waved her off. "Just don't do it around me," he said. "I choked on second-hand smoke my whole childhood, and I never will again."

He took his drink to his seat, a large easy chair that was obviously his favorite. She sat on a sofa across from him.

"So, you were going to give me a lesson on journalism," she said.

He sipped his drink. "You don't need a lesson. You're a good writer."

"But…"

"But there are some other people I would have interviewed."

She smirked. "Like who?" she asked.

"Did you ever think about interviewing the guy who cleans those windows?"

Her eyes narrowed. "Why would I do that?"

Abel placed his drink on an end table and leaned forward. "Think about it," he said. "It was probably the same guy doing it every time. The guy who cleaned it before the accident was probably the same guy who cleaned it right after. That had to be hard, or at least interesting. And a guy like that who goes up ten, fifteen floors to clean something isn't some teenager. He's been doing it a while, so he probably has a family, kids of his own. I'll bet he'd have had some interesting insight thirty years later, if you could find him."

Izzy sat back and sipped her coffee. "I could have found him," she said. "If I'd have wanted to, that is."

Abel continued. "Those are the kinds of people I like to hear from, the ones who see the dirt and grime and tell me all about it, so I can tell the rest of the world."

33

"I see what you mean," she said. "But it wasn't that kind of a story. I was investigating the cause of the accident. It wasn't supposed to be some kind of a retrospective."

"Fair enough," Abel said. "But you never know. It's in the way you use the story. You could have opened with it. Start with a quote from a window guy - 'I been cleaning this window for fifty years...but this ain't just any other window...' You know what I mean?"

She thought for a moment, then nodded. "You think that would have made mine better than the winner?"

"It would have made your story better, but I doubt it would have won," Abel answered. "They locked up a Nazi because of that story. He will die in jail because of the work that reporter did. It's hard to beat that. Your story was good, but nobody is going to jail over it." He rested back in his chair. "Good journalism uncovers the truth. Great journalism makes things happen. *Consequences.* Good and bad."

She took it all in. "Well, this story is going to be the best," she said. "There is no way this does not win an award, lots of awards."

Abel sipped his drink and looked at her. "So what's the story? Will you tell me now?"

Izzy's eyes darted around the room and allowed a smile to creep across her face as she searched for answers, one for herself, and one for Abel. "I'll tell you," she said as she stood from her seat. "I have read literally hundreds of stories and interviews about what happened that day - parents, politicians, cops, survivors, their relatives. And they are all the same." She looked at Abel and smiled, waiting for him to ask the question.

"And what makes yours different?" he asked.

Holding both her hands in front of her face as if holding an imaginary book or newspaper, she said, "It's going to be firsthand accounts from a select few of the survivors. Only people who were there when it happened. No grieving parents, no cops, no widows. Only the people who were there.

Abel scratched his chin. "What else?"

Izzy cleared her throat before she spoke. "Here's the thing," she said, lowering her voice. "There are only five witnesses to the shooting who have never once spoken on the record. They range from young children at the time, to retired people now. And the way I see it, they all must have a story. They all have something new that people will want to know."

Abel sat up a bit as she continued.

"All that other stuff has already been done. People who want to see this law passed or to remember this person... we've gotten all that, and we get it every year on the anniversary. What we don't have enough of are the perspectives of the witnesses, especially *these* witnesses. And these were key players, people who were really involved."

Abel smirked. "*Key players?*"

"You know what I mean. They were people who I think would really have a lot to say, if I ever got them to talk. And I *will.*"

"And I'm on that list?" Abel asked.

"You were," she said. "But now you're talking to me."

Abel waved a finger as he put down his empty glass. "Put me back on the list," he said. "I'm not speaking on the record, for now at least. And what about Abigail Conway?"

"What about her?"

"She's never spoken about it. Is she one of your five?"

Izzy exhaled in frustration. "She wasn't at the shooting. And she spoke this morning. Are you paying attention to me?"

"I'm sorry," he said. "It's the alcohol. She spoke this morning?"

"Yes, at the memorial for Joe Conway. Don't you watch the news?"

He shook his head. "I read it the next day. I wonder what she said." He stood and walked to the kitchen to get himself another drink. Izzy noticed he was slightly off balance.

"I was there," she said, raising her voice to be heard. "But I left early. She was incredible. She's still beautiful. She spoke

35

without notes, and she spoke about the two winners like she really knew them."

Abel returned with another cocktail for himself and a new cup of coffee for Izzy. "The two summer camp winners," he said. "I always thought they should have made it into an academic scholarship, instead of just free summer camp."

Izzy shook her head. "Abigail and the priest that started the award decided to keep it as a summer camp. They think Joe would have liked it that way. He loved being in charge of that camp. Did you know Abigail still picks each recipient herself?"

"I knew that," he said as he took a sip. "What else did she say?"

"I didn't pay much attention to her. I was mostly looking for the other people on my list. They weren't there."

"Oh? Then why did you say she was incredible?"

Izzy's eyes lit up. "Because nobody was expecting her to speak. And Governor Springer always has this long speech prepared, especially in an election year. He was all prepared to go on and on about these two kids he never met, and the need for more gun control, and school safety and everything else. Instead, Abigail gets up and talks about the two boys like she really knows them, and then she introduced them! He didn't know what to do when she was done! I mean, how was he supposed to follow that?"

Abel laughed. "I take it you don't like Mike Springer."

"Not especially," she said. "He just can't help but turn the memorial service into a political event. But today he couldn't because he was upstaged by the one person who could upstage him. It was great to watch."

"I'll bet," Abel said. "How long did he talk?"

"Only a few minutes," she said. "He would have gone on, but one of his people cut him off. It was a smart move. What are you supposed to say after Abigail Conway?"

Abel sat back in his chair and looked contemplatively at nothing in particular. "I was with Springer," he said, his voice slurring. "Right after the shooting started."

Izzy leaned forward and looked intently into Abel's increasingly watery blue eyes. "Tell me," she said.

Abel took a long drink from his glass, wincing as the taste of the whiskey hit. He took a deep breath and exhaled. Izzy caught a whiff of the booze he had just swallowed.

"He was my camp counselor. I loved him back then. All the campers did." He stopped and took another drink.

Izzy watched as Abel's eyes slowly explored the room. "You loved him back then," she said quietly. "And now?"

Abel took another sip. "Not especially," he said.

The booze was hitting Abel now. That fabulous, familiar haze was coming over him like a warm blanket. His thoughts were getting more and more jumbled, and the music was beginning to sound better as the whiskey did its job. But he wasn't enjoying himself. He was getting mad. He was starting to have thoughts of his mother and his dead father. And his brother. Abel felt he had to get a hold of himself before he lost control. But he was getting angry, and this beautiful young reporter was just looking at him and talking. And smiling. He wondered if she had even heard what he'd just said because she had not reacted to it. She didn't ask a follow-up question. She didn't even write it down.

"Are you recording me?" he asked.

"No."

"You're interviewing me, and you're not even going to write down what I say?"

"I'm not here to interview you under the influence," she said. "That would not be good for the story."

"People are more truthful when they're drunk," he said.

"Sometimes," she said. "Sometimes they're full of shit. It's hard for me to tell which I'm getting."

"Well, I'm drinking," he said. "And I don't plan on stopping."

"Maybe we should talk later?" she said.

"I'll probably be drunk later, too," he said.

37

"Tomorrow then?"

"Sure."

He felt her poke his knee. He looked up to see her standing over him. He was surprised.

"You *will* talk to me about this, right?" she said. "Even if it has to be off the record?"

He looked at the woman who sat across from him. The sun was getting low in the sky and the horizontal rays crept up her neck and chin. Without answering, he downed what was left of his drink and stood to leave.

"Where are you going?" she asked, taking his hand again.

He stopped and looked at her hand, enjoying its cool touch. He slowly turned his wrist and lifted his gaze to meet her clear eyes. "I need to lie down," he said. "How long can you stay?"

"As long as I'm welcome, I guess."

"Make yourself at home," he said as he stepped toward his bedroom. "We can talk later, but I want a few answers from you first."

He shuffled down the short hallway, banged through his bedroom door, and fell into his unmade bed.

***

Mike Springer climbed into the black Dodge SUV that was his official transportation. A veteran state trooper took the wheel and his two aides settled onto the soft leather across from him. He looked at both of them with disdain. They knew why, but they waited for him to say it.

"Why wasn't I prepared for that?" he asked.

Bob Casarini, a seasoned lawyer who had worked for politicians since he was in law school, spoke first. "Sir, she always gets invited. This is the first time she's come in twenty years. There's no way we could have known."

Springer's eyes hardened. "I *pay* you to know!"

"Governor," said Sheila Avery with a smile, "I don't think anyone knew she was coming. Besides, now we have you supporting the widow in public." She was much younger than Joe, and far more cunning. Her smile settled him.

"I guess that's the important thing," he conceded. "But the way she went on about those kids..." He shook his head. Then he drove a finger into the seat. "I needed this day," he said. "I needed this speech. Evan Long's Pardon's Board is in six days. Execution is in a week. I need to be on record about the guns." He looked at Bob. "What's next?"

"We're thirty minutes from the capital," he answered. "We'll call a press conference - away from those kids and away from the widow. You'll make your speech then take a few questions."

Springer shrugged. He hated questions. But he loved speeches. He looked at Sheila, who nodded her agreement. "Make the call," he said. "I want Philadelphia media there, not just the locals."

Sheila patted his knee. "We'll take care of it, sir." He winked at her and dug his speech out of his pocket. He would have to re-work a few things.

"Old Abby Conway," Springer muttered. "I never thought I'd be upstaged by her."

Sheila leaned in to clarify. "You were *ambushed,* sir."

***

Izzy made herself comfortable on Abel's sofa. She took her notebook from her bag and began writing what she had learned, starting with the fact that Abel hated Governor Mike Springer, even though it had been Springer who had ultimately disarmed the shooter, Evan Long. At least that's what all of the official reports said.

She considered this. Izzy knew that Joe Conway had spoken his last words, meant for his wife, to Abel only moments before he charged at the shooter and struck him in the head from behind with the hard wooden frame of his tennis racket. Conway's charging and striking the shooter was public knowledge. Izzy had learned of the last words privately from her own investigation. The blow to the head had knocked Long nearly unconscious, and he fell to the ground, loosening his grip on the semi-automatic pistol he had been using.

Mike Springer, who had followed closely behind Joe, quickly grabbed the weapon before Long was able to recover. As he did this, Joe had managed to pin one arm behind the shooter's back. It seemed as though they had him under control until the shooter reached under his belt with his free hand and produced a combat knife. In one motion, he turned his body into Joe's and drove the knife into his stomach. Joe held onto him as long as he could, but the shooter soon pushed himself free and charged at a nearby child. Jacob Suddard, a ten-year-old boy who bravely thought he could assist, died quickly after the shooter slit the boy's throat.

It was then that Joe, now bleeding profusely, willed himself to deliver one more blow to the shooter's head, this time with a baseball bat that had been carried by Mike Springer. Springer had dropped the bat next to Joe when he moved to retrieve the killer's weapon. Joe picked it up after Evan Long stabbed him and broke free. This second strike to the head had rendered the shooter unconscious and with a fractured skull that would require two surgeries to repair.

Joe fell to his knees after seeing that the shooter was now fully incapacitated. He began to move toward the already dead Jacob, but before he could, his body fell limp and he died in a pool of blood. By now, two teenage camp counselors and a forty-year-old maintenance man had arrived and were attempting to revive Joe and Jacob. The maintenance man, a veteran of the Korean and Vietnam Wars, announced that the two had "bled out," and that it would be better to attempt to help the other victims who were still alive. One child, who was physically unharmed, screamed and grabbed hold of the maintenance man's leg and begged him to keep helping Jacob. He was taken away from the scene by the two counselors. Mike Springer, a twenty-five-year-old law school student who had seen himself as a future criminal defense attorney, held the gun on the motionless, but still breathing, body of Evan Long until the police arrived. When Evan Long was taken under arrest, a note was found inside his jacket that indicated his intention to take his own life after he had killed as many others as possible.

The two teenagers who had tried to revive Joe and the youngster had been interviewed on television and spoken to many reporters and authors. One was now teaching math in a school in Lower Delaware, while the other was the owner of a lucrative landscaping business and was rumored to take bets on football during the season. The maintenance man had recently retired from the public school system but occasionally did work at the campground when it was needed. He had never spoken publicly about the shooting, and he was on Izzy's list of five. Any information she had on him she had gleaned from the statements of the teenagers and later confirmed by public records.

As for the identity of the screaming boy whom the counselors consoled, Izzy could now reasonably assume that it was Abel Ryan. He had been right there at the scene and could have possibly been frustrated with Mike Springer who, rather than try to help his friend Jacob, continued to point the weapon at Evan until the police ordered him to drop it. However, that was only a theory.

Interestingly, Izzy had spent weeks poring over information on every single child and adult who was present that day, and she had never found a single reference to a child named Abel Ryan. She later learned that this was because his parents had taken the drastic step of changing his name. After tediously accounting for the name of everyone who was present that day, the only name left was that of a Norman Jefferson. His name was recorded by police as a witness and filed away with the rest of the case materials. After that, the boy seemed to disappear completely. Izzy assumed that Norman Jefferson must be the man she now knew as Abel Ryan.

Strangely, when several of the camp employees had been interviewed, a few of them had mistakenly first thought that it had been Norman, now Abel, who had been stabbed to death. Izzy could

41

only guess the reason for this was the chaos created by the horrible circumstances of the day, combined with the fact that the one counselor who knew Norman and Jacob best, Mike Springer, was not talking to anyone other than the police.

Many times, Izzy had tried to imagine the events from the points of view of all who were present when the shooter was taken down. Tonight she tried her hardest to see it from Abel's. In the years since the shooting, Mike Springer had never once publicly stated that he had disarmed the shooter, though others, including the police, had stated that he had. Mike Springer had never once acknowledged doing anything heroic that day, instead lavishing all manner of praise and respect on Joe Conway and little Jacob Suddard. He would one day run for public office, always pushing a platform of ending gun violence and creating tougher penalties for violent criminals, all the while remaining a compassionate liberal. He would eventually be elected and re-elected to the United States House of Representatives, and later governor. Governor Michael T. Springer, survivor of the St. Maria Goretti's Campground shooting, had never spoken a word about what he had actually witnessed that day. This put him third on Izzy's list. Other than to make a few vague statements about the heroics, evil, and lifelong damage that had been done, Springer had never spoken a word about that day.

And now she had learned that Abel Ryan, also a survivor, hated Mike Springer. He was going to tell Izzy why. As she considered these facts, she began to feel that rare but familiar tingle in her spine.

She had a story.

***

Evan Long waited for the small black and white television to switch off. He had no control over it. Television was an earned privilege. He settled back on his cot and stared at the ceiling. It was his evening ritual, part of the endless effort by inmates, especially those on death row, to stimulate the mind. Tonight would be easier than most. He blocked out the screaming that always ensued after

42

T.V. was switched off. Inmates going to the bars to converse, complain, or simply scream to be heard. He didn't bother with that anymore. His thoughts were on Abigail Conway. He smiled as he thought of what the widow must think of him. And that fat priest always putting on that brave and compassionate face. Every year the same message - God loves us, even during tragedies. It was okay to be angry, he always said. But don't let your anger consume you. Then the priest would sit down while that fool politician spoke about ending violence and remembering his old pal, Joe Conway. Evan often fantasized about one of those inept reporters shoving a microphone in the priest's fat face and asking, "Does God love Evan Long?" They never asked him that.

The priest never mentioned Evan by name, always calling him "the killer." Evan imagined the priest sitting, quietly contemplating how "the killer" would burn in hell on his execution day. Evan watched as the priest would occasionally smile at the thought. But Evan knew the truth. And today he even saw the priest smile as he whispered in the widow's ear. They were discussing his eternal damnation, no doubt. Then they sat and watched the fool politician ramble on about justice, the same politician who had been pointing Evan's weapon, his hands and knees shaking in fear, at him when he woke from being knocked out by Joe Conway.

Evan closed his eyes tightly and decided to forgive them all. He loved having that kind of control, that kind of *power*. Then he opened his eyes and looked down at his list and found the next name. He couldn't pronounce it out loud, but God would know whom he meant. Then he closed his eyes again and began to pray intensely for the soul of Nick Keomanikhoth, who died almost twenty years ago, at the age of eleven.

***

The only thing that woke Abel from his sleep was the need to piss. At thirty years old, he was beginning to find it a little harder to sleep through the urge, especially after having drunk himself to sleep. He

43

rose from his bed, still wearing the clothes he had worn to work, and made his way to the bathroom. Halfway through relieving himself, he remembered the girl. *Was she still here?* He glanced at the small digital clock on the sink. 10:30 at night. He finished and wet his hair before stepping into the living room.

She was there. She had followed his directions and made herself at home. Izzy Buchanan was sitting upright on his sofa, casually scribbling on a notepad. He stood in the archway that separated the short hallway from his living room.

She was surprised when she saw him. "I didn't hear you walk in," she said. "Sleep well?"

"Well enough," he said. "I'm sorry. I didn't expect to drink that much."

She smiled and said, "It's the last day of school." Then she tilted her head and looked at him curiously. "Do you have a drinking problem?"

Abel smiled. "Only during the summer," he said. "From September through May, I'm straight and narrow, except on weekends. But from June through August, there is a better chance than not that I am intoxicated."

She put down her pen and notebook. "Even in the morning?" she asked.

"No. I don't usually start until the afternoon, at least."

"*Usually?*"

He scoffed. "Is this an intervention?"

"Do you drink by yourself?"

"You already know I do," he said, getting agitated.

"I had an aunt who was an alcoholic. She died when she was fifty. It was a nightmare for my whole family for as long as I could remember. I'm just concerned."

Abel stepped into the living room and sat in the reclining chair next to the sofa. "I'm sorry to hear that. But don't worry about me. I just like drinking in the summertime. I don't need to. I can stop whenever I want. However, I prefer to stop after Labor Day. And don't be concerned. You don't even know me."

44

"You don't have to convince me," she said. "I was just asking."

He shrugged. "In that case, I'm going to get a beer."

"You just woke up."

"I'm joking," he said, stepping into the kitchen. "I need coffee."

"I need to eat," Izzy said.

"Me too. Let's go."

They took a booth at Nino's Pizza, three blocks from Abel's apartment. The place wasn't busy at this hour, and the service was prompt. The pizza was greasy and tasty, the way Abel liked it after he'd been drinking. Izzy liked it too.

"I didn't get to eat like this growing up," she said.

"No?"

She shook her head as she chewed. "Pizza was a rare experience, and eating at this hour was unheard of."

"Your parents were strict?" Abel asked.

"Not overly," she said. "But my mom was a fanatic about eating healthy."

"How did she feel about smoking?" Abel asked through a full mouth.

Izzy shrugged. "Practically disowned me when she found out."

"Good. So would I."

Izzy put her pizza aside and took a drink of her soda. "Do you want children someday?" she asked.

Abel looked at her with suspicion as he flagged down their server to order a beer.

"I'm just making conversation," she assured him. "People get so paranoid when they know I'm a reporter."

"That's because I *was* a reporter," he said. "But I believe you when you say you're making conversation. I'm just being cautious," he said. "And yes, I think I'd enjoy having a family, but I'm in no rush."

"Me neither."

Abel was amused. "How old are you, twenty? Why are you even thinking that?"

"I'm 19, and it's good to have a plan."

45

Abel finished his slice and took another from the pie that rested between them. "So what is your plan for this story, Izzy? Is that your real name?"

"Yes," she said. "And I told you my plan. You're the first of five. I need to get all of you before Evan Long's execution."

Abel scoffed. "You know that's in a week."

"He has one more hearing before the Pardon's Board, then that's it."

Abel nodded, remembering the conversation now. "Yes," he said. "His lawyer is trying one more time to say he's crazy." Abel glanced around the restaurant, his eyes focusing on nothing in particular. Then he said, "It sounds like a good story. It might even win you that award you're after, especially if you uncover something new. Tell me who you're going to interview."

"Okay," she said, and Abel could hear the excitement creeping into her voice. "Mike Springer."

Abel put up a hand. "You think you're going to interview the governor of Delaware?"

"He was just *Mike* when the shooting happened."

"I remember him from back then," Abel said. "He was friends with Joe Conway, at least I think he was. He was in law school."

Izzy checked her notes. "Twenty-five years old at the time," she said. She looked at him with a curious expression. "You were 9 years old and you knew he was in law school?"

"It's all he talked about. You'll never interview him."

"I will interview him."

"Good luck with that," he said. "But why him? The public gets plenty of him in the media. Don't they?"

"Yes they do," she said. "But he is apparently the one who disarmed the shooter. And there are rumors he may run for president in 2000."

"He did take the gun. I was there," Abel said. "That's nothing new. Why bother talking to him?"

"Because *he* has never talked about what he saw or did that day," she said. "He disarmed the worst mass killer in the state's history, and he has never said a word about it. I want to know why."

Abel's beer arrived and he took a sip. "That's fair," he said. "That's good journalism, but he'll never talk about that. Unless he decides he can use it to run for president next time around." He took a drink of his beer and thought about it. "He'd have a decent shot. He's known around the country. Even if he doesn't win the nomination, he could still be picked as a VP."

Izzy pushed her notebook aside. "Do you know why he has never spoken about the shooting?"

Abel looked at her. He was beginning to recognize her body language. She was all business now, as she leaned forward, her eyes fixed on his. Abel took another sip of his beer. "Yes, I do," he said. "Who else do you plan to interview?"

Izzy was sure she had hit it. She saw it in the newly sober man's eyes. She had gotten to the point of impact. There was a reason Mike Springer had never made any comments about his disarming of Evan Long twenty years ago, and Abel knew why. He might be the only person in the world, other than Springer himself, who knew. It worked logically, she thought. Joe gave the message meant for his wife to Abel. He then attacked the shooter, Evan Long. Mike Springer, who was with him, disarmed the shooter after Joe incapacitated him. Abel was right there when it happened. He knew. And Izzy was sure that Abel would eventually tell her. She would have her story, and it would be incredible. But he was drinking again.

"Who else?" he asked again. "And don't worry. I'm not getting drunk again. I'm just having one."

"I didn't say anything," she said.

"I saw your look. I know that look."

"Do you get that look a lot?"

"Who else are you interviewing?"

"A groundskeeper named Will Janicki," she said.

Abel remembered him. "The maintenance guy. That makes sense. He's never been interviewed?"

Izzy shook her head.

"Who else?" Abel asked.

"A camp counselor," she said. "Shannon Maher."

"I remember her, too," he said. "Ms. Shannon. Mostly worked with the youngest groups, five-year-olds. She'd probably be about 40 by now. What's special about her?"

"She's thirty-nine," Izzy said. "And what's special is that she was probably one of the last to see Joe before he went after the shooter." Izzy lowered her voice for emphasis. "She has never given an interview. I have a source that said she wouldn't even cooperate with the police."

Abel considered this. "I can't imagine why. Where was she when it happened?"

"Details are sketchy on that, but several witnesses, most of whom were five years old at the time, say she was on the tennis courts with Joe and a group of children when the shooting started."

Abel nodded. "That makes sense," he said. "Joe gave tennis lessons."

"Some remember him yelling at them to run. Others say she told them to run as fast they could, and then she hid with them in a ditch by the main road."

Abel took a sip and nodded. "The road is a long ways away. The shooting probably ended by the time they got there. Where is she now?"

"It took some digging, but I found her living in Charleston, South Carolina."

"Interesting," Abel said. "I guess she had to get away. I came all the way to Philadelphia."

Izzy smiled. Philadelphia was only a thirty-minute ride from Wilmington, Delaware. "She would probably be the last person to talk to Joe before the shooting started. Who knows what he may have told her? She could have heard something that upset her so much she had to disappear."

48

"That's intriguing," he said. "Is she married?"

"I don't think so, possibly divorced."

"Who else?"

She took a breath and said, "Evan Long."

Abel put his beer down. "You're joking."

"He's never been interviewed."

"He's on death row."

She nodded.

"He's psychotic."

"How do you know?"

"He killed eleven people, nine of them children."

"That was twenty years ago," she said. "Think like a journalist, not a witness."

"I was fifteen feet away from him," Abel said. "I saw his eyes. He's psychotic."

She sighed. "So what if he is? That doesn't mean I shouldn't interview him."

Abel ran a hand through his hair and took a long drink of his beer, which was almost empty. "When do you plan to interview him?"

"Later this week," she said.

Abel laughed. "Evan Long has not given an interview since he was arrested. He has never said a word to anyone since the shooting. What makes you think he'll talk to you?"

She smiled. "You're talking to me."

He laughed again. "There was beer involved. Besides, you'd have to get permission to interview him, right?"

"He has already consented to an interview," she said. "All I need now is permission from the warden, and I'm working on that."

"Long has a pretty busy week ahead. A pardon hearing and an execution."

"Exactly," Izzy said. "If he ever had something to say, this would be the week to say it. Now or never."

Abel shook his head. "No way the warden allows it. Long's attorney will see to that."

"I have a plan."

49

Abel wanted another beer, but he was growing weary of the concerned looks he kept getting from the woman sitting across from him. He hated that look. He had to acknowledge that she was impressive. She had a confidence about her that contradicted her age and experience. He'd been confident as a young reporter, but this girl had something else. She was *courageous*, something he had never been. Izzy had ventured out of Delaware to find him in Philadelphia. She had settled in for the day and evening with her subject, whom she had never met. Even though he had proven to be unpredictable, she had gotten him to open up about his past more than any other journalist, just by insisting on accompanying him. She had used her beauty to her advantage, but she didn't have to. She could have roped him in some other way if she had wanted. And he knew the journalist in her was actually hoping he would order another beer. It would get him talking again. When the waiter came back, he asked for the check. They finished up and started walking back to his apartment. It was nearly midnight.

Main Street in Manayunk was crowded with bar hoppers as Izzy and Abel made their way toward a side street that would take them to his apartment. This was a crowd that Abel usually didn't encounter since he tended to get his drinking out of the way early so he could spend the night in his apartment watching movies, usually by himself.

"Where did you park?" he asked.

"I didn't," she said as she lit a cigarette. "I took the train from Wilmington. You don't mind if I smoke *outside*, do you?"

"How are you getting home?" he asked. The trains were finished for the night.

"Do you feel like giving me a ride?"

"To Delaware? I don't think so."

"Can I sleep on your sofa?" she asked.

He stopped walking and turned to look at her. "You barely know me," he said. "You shouldn't go sleeping on strange men's couches."

She smiled. "You're not that strange, Abel."

50

He shook his head. "You're brave, you know that? You'd risk your life for a story, wouldn't you?"

She bit her bottom lip and stared intently at him. "Wouldn't you?" she asked.

Abel shook his head. "Nope. I never would have. That's one reason I gave it up. I was good at journalism, but I didn't care enough to keep doing it." He began to walk again until Izzy stopped him with a hand on his forearm.

"So you went into teaching," she said.

"That' right," he said.

Izzy stepped closer and spoke in almost a whisper. "Would you risk your life for your students?"

Abel curled his lips. "Yes, I would," he said. "For any of them."

Izzy looked in Abel's eyes for a moment, and Abel had the feeling she was trying to see if he really meant what he said. Then she turned and kept walking.

Abel followed her back to his apartment. The noise of the drinking crowds dwindled as they ascended the concrete steps that took them to Abel's street. When they got to his apartment, Izzy took the couch while Abel took three beers out of the fridge and went back to his bedroom. "Help yourself to whatever you need," he said.

"Are you really going to drink all those tonight?" she asked.

"Yes," he answered. "It's the last day of school, and I'm celebrating."

"Until Labor Day. I know."

"I have *The Godfather* on VHS in my bedroom."

"Some celebration," Izzy said.

"Would you like to join me?"

Izzy raised her eyebrows.

"We can watch it out here," he said.

"Can I get drunk with you too?" she asked.

"You're too young," he said. "But sure, I don't care."

"I'm joking. Go watch your movie. Can we talk more in the morning?"

"Okay. Make yourself at home," he said. "I'll get you a pillow and blanket."

"Thanks."

Izzy found the right remote control and switched on the television, keeping the volume low. She could hear the muffled sounds of the movie in the next room as she searched for news. Her bedtime routine was to check local and national news, in that order. The local news had long since ended, so she found CNN. The local news was national.

There was Governor Mike Springer. He was on the steps of the capitol in Dover making bold pronouncements about the need to end gun violence. His hair was perfect and his face was full of color and vigor. Probably makeup, Izzy thought.

They played a short video of his remarks about the need for greater gun regulation, driving home his personal experience, and the loss of his friend. Izzy was about to change the channel when they played another segment of him referring to Evan Long. Springer chose his words carefully, refraining from calling him a "sick maniac" or a "psychotic killer" as he had in the past. Both terms had been used in court in attempts to bolster his attorneys' claims of insanity, which would make him less likely to be sentenced to death.

"Today, Evan Long sits in an eight-by-twelve-foot jail cell on death row, just a few miles from here. He is awaiting justice for the crimes he committed twenty years ago. And while that justice will never bring back our loved ones..." He bowed his head and frowned. "...or our friends, we can only hope that finally bringing justice to the one who committed cold-blooded murder will serve as an effective deterrent to others who may wish to do the same. After he is finally brought to justice, the fight will go on to be sure that those wishing to commit murder do not have access to deadly weapons, and those that are convicted of such crimes are promptly sentenced to death, and that sentence is carried out."

Izzy switched off the television. It was an interesting political position the governor was taking. He had always come out very

52

strongly against assault weapons, a stance that pleased his mostly Democratic state. However, he was now posturing for the death penalty in a very positive way, on national news. This had to be a play for the presidency.

Izzy felt a little sick to her stomach. It could have been the pizza or the coke, neither of which she was used to. Or it could have been because Governor Mike Springer was hoping to get elected president by using the St. Maria Goretti's Massacre as a springboard.

She took a breath and promised herself that she would remain as objective as a person in her position could. As she reclined on the sofa, preparing to sleep for the night, she made a note to herself to tell Abel what Mike Springer had said.

But she would wait until he had a few drinks.

Saturday, June 14, 1996

The sound of the shower woke Izzy, and it took a few moments for her to remember where she was. Once the cobwebs cleared, she glanced at her watch and saw that it was 7:35 in the morning, earlier than she had expected. She stretched and sat up on Abel's couch and glanced around at the apartment. She stood and walked to the kitchen to make coffee, only to see that Abel had already made a cup. It sat in the one-cup coffee maker, already with cream. She assumed it was for him, so she moved it aside and made another.

She jumped when he came bounding into the kitchen, his bare feet hardly making a sound. "I can't drink it while it's hot," he said. He then grabbed and opened a granola bar and took his coffee to the living room. "Help yourself to anything," he said as he switched on the television. "There's yogurt in the fridge and granola bars in the cabinet."

"Thanks, just coffee," she said, hearing the lack of sleep in her voice. "You're up earlier than I thought you'd be."

"I don't like to waste a Saturday morning."

"I got your newspaper from under the door."

53

"Thanks," he called.

"I need to look and see when there's a train to Wilmington," she said.

He waved a hand as he switched channels. "I'll drive you back," he said. "Just tell me when you're ready."

"I'm ready. Can we talk in the car?"

He turned to look at her. "Last night you made it seem like you were willing to spend weeks up here to get me to talk. Now you're rushing me to drive you home?

"I didn't bring a change of clothes. Besides, now I know where to find you. I can get up here anytime I want."

"Well, I'm not ready to drive, or talk. Drink some coffee and have a granola bar. I need fifteen minutes."

"Okay," she said.

***

Governor Mike Springer sipped his black coffee while he lounged in his home office, going through his private emails, as had become his Saturday morning ritual. He deleted most of them right away. Most of the major networks wanted to talk to him about the election cycle, including his own race for reelection in Delaware. He let Bob and Sheila deal with these.

When he came across the email that had "Izzy Buchanan" in the subject line, he paused and tried to remember why the name was familiar. Unable to recall it, he placed a call to his secretary, Mary Rita, whom he knew would be sitting by her computer and phone. She knew the governor's ritual well, so she always cleared time on Saturday mornings between 8 and 9 to take his calls. Sometimes he called a lot, and sometimes the phone was silent. The governor was oblivious to her great consideration but was always fond of her dedication. Their relationship was perfect, he always thought, truthful but professional. The two had worked together since long before highly-paid assistants came into the picture.

She answered on the first ring. "Are you trying to remember who Izzy Buchanan is?" she asked without saying hello.

"Stop reading my mind," he said. "Who is she?"

"She's a reporter from Brandywine U."

"Okay," he said. "A college newspaper. You're going to tell me why I should let her interview me?"

"Of course I am," she said. "The girl placed second in a national journalism contest last year. You called her personally to congratulate her."

Mike closed his eyes and it came back to him. "The kid who fell from the window. I do remember her. She didn't take my call. She wants an interview?"

Mary Rita paused before answering. "She does, but..."

"Get to it, Mare. What does she want?"

"She's writing a story about the shooting."

"I don't talk about that," he said abruptly.

"I know you don't," she said.

"So why did you send me this?"

"Because her story sounds interesting. May I tell you about it?"

"Go on," he said.

"She's going to interview only people who were there and who have never spoken publicly about it. You are one of only five."

"So you're thinking I should talk to her. Why?"

"Here is what I am thinking," she began. Springer could hear the careful stepping in her voice. "You're probably going to run for president..."

"Mare, don't make me hang up!" he barked.

"No, listen," she insisted. "This story will be by an aspiring journalist from your home state and your alma mater. It will look like you're doing her a favor. Plus, you'll be in the story with four other people. This way it doesn't look like you're deciding to speak to a major news agency about the shooting just so you can get national attention and spout off on gun control legislation. You're doing a local girl a favor. And we know it will be good. The kid can really write."

55

Springer squeezed the space between his eyes. "I don't know," he said. "They'll see right through it."

"Doesn't matter. The story will be picked up nationally and you'll sound great. *Reluctant hero who wants to make a real difference.*"

He considered this. "I am no hero, Mary Rita," he finally said. "And I don't want people to see me that way. The heroes from that day are all dead."

"I know, Governor," she said quietly. "And I didn't mean to put it that way. But this could get you some national attention, especially after yesterday. Think about it."

"I don't know," he said again. "There's a lot that happened that day. And there are many reasons I don't want to talk about it."

Mary Rita was ready for this. "But the biggest reason you don't want to talk about it is that it would make you look like you're exploiting tragedy for political purposes, right? Well, this gets you off the hook."

"I've done some slimy things," he said. "We both know that. But I can't pretend to be a hero."

"You'll just be talking to a reporter, Mike," she said. "You'll be one of a few others who has finally broken their silence. It won't just be a story about you."

He thought for a long time. Mary Rita waited patiently. "Call her," he said. "Have her meet me at the office today."

***

Izzy pushed her feet into the floor of Abel's immaculately clean Honda CRV as he weaved in and out traffic.

"Let's talk," Abel said.

"Great," Izzy said as she reached for her notebook.

"No," he said. "I know I told you I would talk, so I will. I just want to be clear on what my role is going to be, and about what your intentions are."

"What do you want to know?"

"I've led a very private life up until now," he said. "My parents saw to that. They changed my name, moved me around, taught me how to avoid the media, if they ever found me..."

"I'd like to know why," she said. "I don't really get the secrecy. It's not like you were a celebrity. You witnessed a horrific event. The publicity wouldn't have lasted forever. Why so secretive?"

"There's a lot to it," Abel said. "It starts with my parents being weird, but they had their reasons."

"I need more than that," she said.

"You'll get it. But I am also hoping to keep my life as normal as possible, no matter what I tell you, okay? This is a good idea you have, and I think it will make a good story, but I want to go back to my life when it's over."

Izzy was relieved to hear this. She had been hoping to win his cooperation by presenting him with a good story idea. It appeared to have worked. "I'll make a note that some names have been changed," she said. "I hate changing names, but I'll do it. I'll call you something else, whatever you want."

"I guess that's okay," he said. "But I know someone will figure it out, even if you use a different name."

She thought about this. "How?"

"They just will," he said. "Once you hear all I have to say, you'll understand."

Izzy let that sit for the time being. She knew there had to be a reason, or many reasons, for Abel's secrecy. Then she remembered something else he had said. "And what did you mean by figuring out my intentions?" she asked.

"I'm sure I don't have to tell you that there are a lot of politics at stake here."

She shook her head. "Like?"

"First, an execution that's supposed to happen in a week. Your story is likely to bring out the crazies on all sides of that issue."

"No," she said. "This close to an execution, the crazies are already out. *Burn in hell* or *turn the other cheek*. This story won't take a side. And I don't care if they execute him or not."

"I'm sure the story won't take a side," he said. "But a lot of people do care if he's executed, especially in Delaware. This is going to stir emotions."

"I understand that," she said. "It probably won't be published until after he's dead, anyway."

Abel nodded. "Well, I want Evan Long dead," Abel said with perfect calm as he switched lanes and pulled onto the Blue Route. "I hate violence, but I do believe in the death penalty in some cases, including this one. If you say this isn't an anti-death penalty story, then I believe you."

"Fine," she said. "Anything else?"

He laughed. "A lot else, actually. How about the Second Amendment?"

Izzy wasn't expecting this. "What about it?"

"I support the Second Amendment," Abel said. "But a lot of people don't. I happen to think that journalists should stay neutral on topics like this. So if you were planning to write a piece that's going to advance an agenda, either way, I'm not going to cooperate."

She sighed in frustration. "I am not looking to advance any agenda. I just want to write a good story that will share the stories of people who have held them inside for twenty years. At best, maybe some new details will come out. I hate guns and I hate the death penalty. I don't have the personal perspective that you have, but I have my views and I intend to keep them to myself while I write this, okay?" She turned her head and looked out the window. She hoped he could see she was annoyed.

"That's another thing, Izzy," he said. "Exactly why are you writing this? Is it really to win an award? This is a pretty big deal to a lot of people, and a lot of people will find it quite unsettling - myself included - that you're using what happened that day as a means of earning yourself national recognition."

Izzy shook her head slowly as she continued to look out the passenger side window. "Jesus, where was all this righteousness last night? You make me sound like a horrible person."

"I just need to know why I'm getting into this," Abel said. "Last night was different."

She turned back to look at him. "Well, obviously you're not doing it to make me famous. You have your reasons, and I have mine. It's true that I have personal reasons for wanting to write this story, but they are not all selfish ones. I believe in finding the truth. Maybe I get an award for it, maybe not. I don't think Harper Lee turned down the Pulitzer for exposing racial injustice in the South, and she certainly didn't turn down the money. I'm writing this whether you cooperate with me or not. Just decide now, ok? Save me the trouble."

She turned back to the window and neither spoke for a long time.

Abel focused on the road. It was an easy drive to Wilmington, and the silence made it easy to think. The woman next to him had a great idea for a story. She was talented, relentless, and brilliantly manipulative, but she was too young to see that the story was rife with politics. Maybe she was right in that she could keep her opinions, and all manner of politics, out of it. But that wouldn't stop others from insinuating theirs, especially the sitting governor of Delaware who had his eyes on the White House. Gun control and the death penalty - two issues that were not going away.

There had been a time when Abel had eagerly looked forward to the execution of Evan Long. He had even marked it on his calendar every time a new date had been set. That was years ago. The execution had been delayed so many times that he eventually gave up waiting. However, this past spring when it seemed it was just about inevitable, Abel began to take notice again. It was then that a friend had asked a painful question. Thomas Patel, a young priest at the school where Abel taught, asked him if he could ever forgive Evan Long. The answer was easy: *absolutely not.*

"I don't want to forgive Evan Long," he had told the priest. "I want to forgive my father."

"Forgive him for what?" Tom had asked through his sagacious Indian accent.

"For turning to booze when times got tough," Abel had answered. "For losing his job. For abandoning us by drinking himself to death."

The priest had nodded slowly and offered very simple advice: "Forgive Evan Long first, then forgiving your father will be easy."

He couldn't imagine doing either.

"Can I ask you one question?" he said to Izzy, breaking the long silence.

"What?"

"The execution is in a week. You've got five people who you want to interview, and you want to talk to all of them before Friday. Why did you wait so long?"

"A couple of reason," she said. "First, I didn't realize there were five until about a month ago. I thought it was just two or three. Second, I think with his execution looming, people will feel more pressure to talk. Like it's now or never. And I wanted it timed with the twentieth anniversary. I think people will be more truthful and willing to share when all things are considered."

Abel thought about this. "That's not bad," he said.

They drove again in silence.

Izzy was trying to settle on a plan of action. Initially, she had planned on inviting Abel to lunch and allowing him to drink himself into a rant again. However, this exchange had changed everything. He was challenging her motives and even questioning her understanding of the politics surrounding the issue. *Jerk.* Not only was she keenly aware of the tinderboxes that were gun control and the death penalty, but she was also aware that Abel had made his views on these issues quite clear years ago in his weekly columns in the Brandywine U News, and they seemed not to have changed a bit. Izzy had actually struggled with the idea that Abel may not be seen as a reliable witness. She thought the NRA might actually drool over a witness to a school shooting who was against gun control, and Izzy didn't want that to come as a result of her story. She was also aware that Abel was patiently but happily awaiting the execution of Evan Long, which she viewed as nothing short of barbaric.

She considered changing the plan entirely to just giving Abel a straight interview. He could answer the questions he liked, and refuse the ones he didn't. If he never told her his problem with Mike Springer, she would simply pursue a different angle. She hated to throw away that kind of source, but she was not about to risk the story. She turned to him again, watching him as he drove. His hair was pleasantly disheveled, and he wore a day's growth on his face. He carried the relief of someone whose vacation had just begun. Even his reddened, hungover eyes were relaxed. The only thing that betrayed any tension was his vise-like grip on the steering wheel. Abel was simultaneously stress-free and full of angst. He had something to say.

Her pocket pager vibrated. She looked down, expecting to see her mother's phone number on the screen, but instead saw one she did not recognize. "Can you pull over someplace?" she asked. "I need to make a call."

Abel pulled off I-95 and drove to a nearby Shell station to let Izzy make her call. Without the fog of the alcohol that had affected him the night before, he was becoming even more unsure of whether he should cooperate with this story. However much he liked the story's idea, he knew the danger of digging up ghosts, both living and dead. But so did she. She had blown the window accident story out of the water. It was provocative without being gossipy, and it was respectful of the boy who had died, as well as his family. But this was different. Murder of children was different. And as smart and aware as Izzy seemed to be, she was not there when it happened. He was there. A child. And he could feel something telling him that he needed to speak for the other children, somehow. He was in it for that.

From the car, he could see her talking on the payphone. It was obviously an important call. She nodded as she scribbled information onto her notepad. When she hung up, she kept her hand on the phone and looked intently at her notepad, as if she were trying to make a decision. After making up her mind, she picked up the phone again. This call was more casual. A boyfriend? Maybe a parent?

Izzy hung up the phone and rushed back to the car.

"Jesus Christ!" she said as she climbed in.

"What?"

"Take one guess who that was."

"The president."

"Close," she said.

"What?"

"Can you drive me to Dover?" she asked.

"Why?"

"That was Mike Springer's office," she said breathlessly, waving both her hands as if she was fanning flames on her cheeks. "He wants to talk to me in two hours!"

"You're joking," Abel said.

"Can you drive me to Dover? I don't have much time." Dover was about forty-five minutes farther south from Philadelphia than Wilmington.

"I guess," he said. "Are you ready for this? He could be the next president."

"I know!" she said, putting up a hand. "I need to think. And make notes. You just drive."

"Yes, Ma'am," Abel said.

Izzy tried to gather her thoughts. "I really need to get a cellular phone," she said.

They were quiet as Abel drove. Traffic was light for a Saturday morning and Abel coasted along I-95 and merged onto Route 1 South before he informed his passenger of their ETA. "We'll be in Dover in about 25 minutes," he said quietly. Izzy ignored the update and continued scribbling on her notepad.

Abel stole a glance at her list of questions. "Make sure you let him talk," he said carefully, knowing she would not react well to the advice. She answered with a glare.

He shrugged. "It just looks like a lot of questions. That's all I'm saying."

"They're back up questions," she said.

"I know," Abel said. "But you should consider starting with a curveball."

Izzy stopped scribbling. "What do you mean?"

"I mean start with a question from completely out of nowhere. He's prepared himself to answer questions about the shooting. Whether he's going to give you real answers or just a bunch of bullshit, he's already got his answers rehearsed, right?"

"Right," she agreed.

"So start by asking him about the Lewinsky scandal. He stumbles through it. It takes him a second or two to get over the irony that a knockout college coed is asking him about an affair between a powerful man and an intern. He stumbles through an awkward answer, tries not to blush, and when you finally start asking him questions about Joe Conway, he's relaxed and much more willing to talk openly."

Izzy laughed, and Abel was glad to see her happy. "That's funny!" she said. "Did you learn that in journalism school?"

"Nope," Abel answered. "I picked that one up in the field. It backfires every once in a while though. If you take that kind of risk, you need to be prepared with a 'Get the hell out of here! No more questions!' But Springer is too smooth for that. It will just throw him off a bit."

They drove a little further in silence, then Abel said, "Just think about it."

"I will," Izzy said.

Izzy took a deep breath and exhaled as Abel took the exit for Dover and turned toward the governor's office. She was glad for this opportunity. She had not expected it so soon, and she was still wearing yesterday's clothes. Doubtful that Springer would notice - men typically didn't - but she did not feel prepared. Her encounter with Abel had been planned for weeks, and he was a school teacher. This was a politician, a *governor*, and she had been given two hours' notice. She glanced sideways at Abel, who was scanning the street signs for the capitol building.

She was glad to have him along.

***

"Who the hell is Izzy Buchanan?"

Sheila Avery was out for blood, and she was making it as clear as possible to Mary Rita, who carefully looked up from behind her computer screen, which sat on top of her immaculately kept desk.

Mary Rita was surprised. "Thanks for coming in on a Saturday, Mary Rita," she said sarcastically. "It's not part of your job, and you really didn't have to."

Sheila gritted her teeth and stepped toward the older woman. "It isn't your job and you most definitely should not have!"

"What's the problem, Sheila?" Mary Rita asked.

Sheila stared right through her, her eyes burning with rage. "The problem is that the governor has an interview scheduled to start in thirty-two minutes with a reporter named Izzy Buchanan whom I have never heard of."

Mary Rita scoffed and looked back at her screen. "Mike was fine with it," she said.

Sheila drew a deliberately deep, harsh breath and moved a step closer to the desk. "*Governor Springer* will be running for president one day soon. And every meeting he has goes through me!"

Mary Rita's eyes never left the screen. "I've known the governor for a long time, Sheila," she said dismissively. "If he tells me to bring someone in for an interview, I do it. I don't need to ask you."

Sheila waited a few seconds, letting her eyes explore the space in front of her. Everything had its place, and everything was clean. She

64

bent toward the floor and yanked a thick power cord from its outlet, immediately shutting down Mary Rita's computer, as well as her perfectly placed desk lamp. Then she leaned forward, placing her sweaty palms on the stunned woman's desk. Mary Rita's eyes, which finally showed concern, followed Sheila's hands, then looked at her face.

Then in a cold whisper, Sheila said, "It's my job to see to it that the governor never gets blindsided, so I don't care how long you have known him. No fucking reporter interviews this governor without my fucking knowing about it!" She had actually sneered, stripping her teeth just a touch as she said the words. Mary Rita said nothing, but Sheila could feel her eyes watch her as she slammed the office door.

***

Raymond Woodson was sitting across from the worst killer in the history of the state of Delaware. Three feet away from him, across a small metal table that was bolted to the floor, sat Evan Long. He wore an orange prison jumpsuit and large, awkward eyeglasses, both prison issue.

Twenty summers ago, he had walked onto a campground on a Friday morning and murdered nine people with a semiautomatic pistol, and two others with a knife. His plan to take more lives, including his own, had been thwarted by the bravery of one man, and the fast action of two others. He was arrested at the scene of the crime, then taken to Wilmington General Hospital where he was treated for two traumatic blows to the back of the head and a broken nose. After an overnight stay, he was taken to Delaware State Police Troop 6 in Newark, where he was processed, fingerprinted, and placed in a holding cell. In the twenty-three-hour-period between the murders and the fingerprinting, he had not said one word to anyone, not even to the medical personnel who had treated his injuries and reset his nose. He had not even acknowledged to the arresting officers that he understood his rights under the law.

Because of this, he was reminded of them continually each time an officer attempted to ask him a question.

He did not speak a single syllable until a well-dressed attorney named Raymond Woodson walked into the holding cell after dinner time Saturday evening and informed him that he was his court-appointed lawyer.

"Mr. Long," Woodson had said in a tone that demonstrated that what he was about to say he had said a thousand times or more. "I am your state-appointed attorney and anything you say to me is strictly between us, unless you ask me specifically to speak on your behalf. The police can never use anything you say to me against you in court. So please be as direct and honest with me as you can. I am here to protect your rights before the court."

At that moment, Long looked Raymond Woodson in the eyes. It was the first time the nineteen-year-old had made eye contact with anyone since he had been arrested. Then, from behind the bandages and raccoon eyes that came from his nose injury, he quietly said, "I did it." Raymond told his client he understood. He then explained that by pleading guilty, he could avoid the death penalty. The Supreme Court of the United States had only recently allowed states to resume executing its worst offenders, so Raymond was sure that the state of Delaware would be eager to use it in this instance.

Raymond recalled the expression on the young killer's face as he silently contemplated his options. After a good deal of thought, he said, "I don't want to plead guilty."

Raymond had gotten the message. He was looking at a nineteen-year-old man who did not want to spend the next seventy years in jail.

"I understand," Raymond had said. "But if you are convicted and sentenced to death, I will insist on exhausting every possible appeal to keep you from being executed." Raymond had always been appalled by the death penalty, and he was not about to assist Evan Long in committing suicide. "If you give up *any* of your appeals, you will need to find a new lawyer to represent you. If they sentence you to death, I will never stop fighting for your life. Do you understand?"

Evan Long did.

The trial had been predictable. Raymond had emphasized his client's young age, his difficult upbringing, and poor mental health. According to Evan, who never took the stand to testify, his mother had told him that his father had abandoned her during her pregnancy and that he had never intended to be a part of their lives. Evan was eight years old when he learned this, and he would never even know his father's name. His mother had struggled to earn money to care for him, and she had suffered from severe depression, eventually taking her own life when Evan was only twelve. He had discovered her body in her bed next to an empty bottle of sleeping pills. After that, he bounced around from group home to foster home, not having any known family in the area to turn to for help. He never spent more than six months under the same roof. Despite these obstacles, caseworkers, group home employees and residents, as well as foster caregivers had all spoken on the record about the friendly and curious nature of the Evan Long they had remembered. His former teachers, all of whom Raymond had met with, had all shared the same sentiment, finding it shocking that he could have done such a thing. A few even agreed to testify at his trial.

Raymond also had Evan examined by a psychiatrist, who testified that Evan was clearly suffering from depression, as well as some form of dementia. He could not make an entirely accurate diagnosis due to Long's lack of cooperation, but he made it clear that he was not at all sure that Evan could understand the charges against him, participate in his own defense, or understand that what he had done was wrong.

The attorney for the state, of course, countered every argument effectively with experts of his own. He presented an overwhelming amount of evidence and a parade of eyewitnesses. The case was airtight, and none of the jurors believed that Evan Long was at all confused about what he had done, especially considering the suicide note he had written before his actions at the campground that day. In less than three hours, the jury had found Evan Long guilty of eleven counts of first-degree murder, and fifteen counts of attempted murder.

During the sentencing phase of the trial, Raymond raised the same concerns about Evan's age, background, and mental health. Only one of the twelve jurors had been moved enough to recommend life in prison. The other eleven voted for execution. The Honorable Joseph Northrop followed their nearly unanimous recommendation and sentenced Evan Long to death by hanging, which was still Delaware's only method of execution in the newly revived death penalty era.

Nearly twenty years later, Raymond Woodson, of the Law Offices of Woodson and Sabbath, former public defender, now high-priced attorney, continued to be Evan Long's one and only lawyer. The work was now pro-bono, and Raymond only continued to attend to the case out of a sense of obligation to a client who had flatly refused many times to be represented by any other attorney.

Most of their meetings took place over the phone. Today's meeting was a somewhat special one. Evan Long was scheduled to be executed in one week. Raymond wanted to prevent that from happening and would need to meet with his client in person to convince him to cooperate with the efforts that were being made to save his life. He knew full well that Evan Long, though not overly interested in spending the next fifty years in prison, was always willing to go along with just about anything that broke up the boredom of solitary confinement on death row.

Raymond was dressed professionally in a suit and tie, even on a Saturday, as he always was when meeting with a client, paying or otherwise. Besides, there was always the possibility a reporter would show up outside the prison asking for a comment. As always, Raymond would simply smile and give a quick wave with his left hand. "My client has no comment," he had said at least a hundred times over the years before climbing into his car. His client never had a comment.

"Should we start with a prayer?" Evan asked his attorney.

68

"Whatever you want," Raymond answered as he shifted uncomfortably on the steel bench.

Evan Long began to pray aloud, the words rolling off his tongue as if he were reading from a prayer book:

"Loving God, we humbly ask you this morning to bless this meeting, and make it a productive one. We ask that you make it one that will celebrate the glory of your son, Jesus Christ."

"Amen," Raymond said.

Evan continued:

"And we humbly ask your forgiveness as well. Forgive me for the terrible things I have done, especially those things that robbed innocent children of their lives. Forgive my attorney, Lord. For even though I am eternally thankful for his help in these grave matters, I know that he needs your forgiveness for the lifestyle he has led and continues to lead..."

"Jesus Christ, Evan. That's enough," Raymond said.

"I'm praying for your soul."

"Pray for your own soul, okay?"

"I do."

Raymond exhaled impatiently. "It's Saturday. I have other things I could be doing. I'm glad you found Jesus, but I'd like to get to work."

"I'm not judging you, Raymond," he said. "But it is my duty as a Christian to pray for you."

"You'll have plenty of time for that after I've left."

"My time is running out."

Raymond stomped his right foot loudly. "Not if I have anything to do with it," he said. "You'll have the next fifty years to pray for me when I'm done with this. Just cooperate with me, okay? I think you've had enough fun for the day."

Evan smiled. "Okay, Raymond. Tell me what I need to do."

Raymond plopped his files on the table and grunted angrily. *There were so many better ways to spend a Saturday.*

***

Abel was standing behind Izzy as she was wanded by a Capitol policeman. He noticed how she continued to take deep, nervous breaths as she held out her arms to allow the handheld metal detector to do its work. Abel tried not to stare as he delighted in seeing Izzy raise her arms and spin around, though he had a feeling the police might be enjoying the view as well. His suspicion was confirmed when it was his turn and he was subjected to far less scrutiny.

Even though it was Saturday, there was still a full team in place. Three polite, but serious men in uniforms saw to it that nobody got into the building carrying a weapon. Izzy thanked them and collected her tape recorder and keys from the conveyer belt that carried them from the x-ray machine. Abel followed behind and did the same.

Abel could tell Izzy was nervous. She hadn't shown any of this kind of energy when she'd confronted him the day before. He was nervous for her. What would the governor say? It suddenly occurred to Abel that if the governor were to recognize him, it could spoil everything. He might change his mind and keep quiet another twenty years. Abel dismissed the thought as ridiculous; he looked nothing like the ten-year-old boy who had witnessed Mike Springer at his worst twenty summers ago.

"You must be Izzy Buchanan!" Izzy heard the loud, friendly voice coming from a corner of the cavernous lobby, echoing through the empty space. Izzy scanned the room and saw that a woman, maybe 30 years old, was quickly approaching her with an extended hand. She was smiling broadly, and she held an expression that portrayed nothing but absolute welcome. Izzy extended her own hand to the well-dressed woman and they shook hands. Izzy recognized her as the governor's new aid.

"You're here to talk to Governor Springer, right?"

"Yes, I am. And you are?"

"Sheila Avery," the woman said pleasantly. "I work for the governor. I just need to see your identification."

Izzy looked at her. "Why?"

Sheila smiled again. "It's a routine security check," she said.

70

Izzy looked back at the security team. "Isn't that what they just did?"

Izzy fixed her eyes pointedly on those of Sheila Avery. After a few seconds of harsh silence, Izzy decided nothing was going to happen until she produced identification. Finally, she reached for her wallet and handed Sheila her Delaware driver's license. Sheila took the card in her hand without looking at it. Then she turned to Abel. "And yours, please?"

Abel instinctively reached for his wallet. However, before he could, Izzy's hand was gripping firmly to his, holding it in place. "Now, why would you need to see his ID?" she asked. "He isn't part of the interview. He just gave me a ride."

Abel watched Sheila prepare to return fire. Still smiling, but eyes narrowing, she said, "It's routine security."

Izzy turned back to the police officers and said, "Excuse me, Officer?"

The oldest of the three, who seemed to be in charge, answered, "Yes, ma'am?"

"You gentlemen look like you know a few things about security. Is it routine for the driver of an interviewer to have his driver's license checked?"

The officer chuckled. "I'm not familiar with that, ma'am," he said. "We check everyone for weapons here, but the governor may have his own procedures."

"Officer, have you ever witnessed the driver of a reporter getting his ID checked when he wasn't even going to be…"

"That will be enough, Ms. Buchanan," Sheila said, still friendly as ever. "We don't need to bother them. I'll be right back with this." She waved Izzy's license in the air, turned, and disappeared into the same corner of the lobby from which she had appeared.

"What the hell was that?" Abel said.

"It's bullshit is what it was!" she said.

"She's checking you out," Abel said. "I'm sure it's routine."

"No way," she said. "This was not supposed to happen. They don't run the identification of everyone who interviews a politician." She looked at Abel. "She's trying to intimidate us."

"It worked on me," Abel said.

"Not me. I don't care what she wants. I'm not taking any shit."

"I'm picking up on that," Abel said.

"Why the hell is she checking ID's?" Izzy asked out loud, but Abel assumed it was to herself. She bit her lip as she thought. Abel noticed.

"I don't believe this!" Izzy said, feeling her palms begin to sweat.

"What's the big deal?" Abel asked. "She checks your license to be sure you're not a terrorist, and you get your thirty minutes with Springer. So what if she checks you out?"

Izzy turned her attention back to Abel. "I don't *want* anybody checking me out! Who the fuck is she?"

"Ma'am," said one of the policemen. "You're going to have to watch your language."

"I'm sorry, Officer," she said. "I just get a little upset when my rights are being abused."

The officer shrugged. "Just watch what you say."

At that moment, Izzy saw a man dressed in jeans and a sweatshirt quickly making his way through the security area. At the same time, she heard the friendly voice of Sheila Avery again.

"Bob," Sheila called from across the lobby. She was actually using Izzy's driver's license to beckon him to her. Bob did not look happy to be there. Izzy watched as Sheila handed the license to the man, and the two quickly retreated into an office.

Izzy looked at Abel, who seemed to be getting more nervous by the second. "You can wait outside if you want," she said.

"It's okay," Abel said. "I just don't like confrontations."

"You were a reporter," she said.

"I *was* one. Then I was a photographer. Now I talk to children all day. There's a reason for that."

72

Izzy sighed. "I just want this interview. I don't care if you wait outside."

"I'm fine," Abel said.

They waited in the lobby for ten long minutes. Izzy scribbled notes furiously while Abel passed the time examining paintings of former governors and the portraits of fallen police officers. When the two finally emerged from the office, Izzy was ready with her pen and notepad, brandishing them as weapons.

This time the man in the sweats did the talking. He was older than Sheila, and he carried an air of importance, one he did not have to work on demonstrating. "What publication are you with?" he asked in a friendly tone as he handed Izzy her license back.

"I mostly write for the Brandywine Review," she said. "But I am an independent reporter."

"I see," the man said. "Well, I'm sorry you came out here today, but I'm afraid there isn't going to be an interview with the governor."

Izzy began writing in her notepad as she spoke. "And why not?" she asked.

"Governor Springer has a lot of things going on today."

"I see," Izzy said, taking down every word. "Then can you tell me why he personally invited me here today for an interview?"

The man smiled and watched as Izzy scribbled. "It was a mix-up. His scheduling secretary was unaware that he had already made a prior commitment when she invited you."

"Actually, Mr..."

"Casarini. Bob Casarini."

"Actually, Mr. Casarini, Ms. O'Neill did not invite me. She made it perfectly clear over the phone that *the governor* was personally inviting me. In fact, those were the exact words she used. 'Governor Springer would like to personally invite you to speak with him.'"

"She was wrong. The governor has some important meetings he has to attend."

"Ms. O'Neill specifically told me his afternoon was free," Izzy shot back. "In fact, she said that it was a rarity for a Saturday during an election year."

The two stared at each other, neither close to budging. Abel began inching toward the door. Izzy took his arm in her hand without looking. She didn't want either of them to retreat.

Sheila finally spoke up, still smiling. "The governor is not available. But thank you for coming. These men will see you both out." Her dark eyes narrowed as she gestured to the police.

Izzy kept looking at the older man. She had decided he was the more reasonable of the two. "It's just an interview, and I know he's free. What's the problem?"

He was about to speak when Sheila spoke again. "I think you know what the problem is." She gave Izzy a once over and said, "And a word of advice, dear: don't wear yesterday's clothes when you're interviewing a governor."

Izzy glared at her.

"The governor is looking to the future, ok?" Bob said, trying to bring the confrontation to a swift end. "He doesn't want to talk about events that happened twenty years ago. He never has."

Izzy was unfazed. "Actually, Mr. Casarini, I was going to ask him his thoughts on the Monica Lewinsky scandal." She turned back to Sheila. "But maybe I should ask for *your* thoughts first."

Sheila's face flushed for the first time, and her eyes betrayed her rage. Izzy knew that if it had been a different place and time, Sheila would have lunged right at her and tried to rip her limbs from their sockets. Izzy would have gladly taken her on.

Just then, the deep voice of the officer in charge announced an end to the hostilities. "Right this way, folks," he said with friendly authority. "These two officers will show you to your car."

"We'll show ourselves. Thank you, officer." She turned to face Joe. "And please tell the governor I'm disappointed that *he* had to break *his* invitation. I'll try to find a way to word that nicely in my story. And I'm sure you speak for him when you say 'he doesn't want to talk about the past.' I'll quote him on that."

Bob didn't take the bait. "Have a nice day, Ms. Buchanan," he said kindly, then added. "And good luck to you."

74

Izzy couldn't help herself. She jabbed a finger at him. "Trust me," she said. "The last thing I need is luck." Again, she took Abel by the arm and began walking quickly toward the entrance. Two of the officers followed closely, despite Izzy's assurance that they would see themselves out.

They exited the building and made their way toward Abel's car. Neither wanted to speak with the police so close behind them. As they entered the car, they both heard the deliberate noise of one of the officer's clicking his pen. He was writing down Abel's license plate number.

"Why are you doing that?" Izzy asked.

"This is state property, ma'am," he said. "We have every right to take down all…"

"That's not what I asked," she shot back.

Before the officer could answer, Abel said, "Izzy, please just get in the car."

She looked at him. Abel just gestured urgently toward the car. He had had enough for one day.

***

Fifteen minutes after the meeting began, Raymond was gathering his things and preparing to leave. "So, you know what to do on Thursday, right?" he asked his client.

"Yes," Evan answered. "Act like I'm Loony Tunes"

"Just be yourself."

"Thanks a lot," Evan said pretending to be insulted. "You don't think I'm really crazy; do you?"

Raymond stopped collecting his things and looked at his client. "I don't think you're crazy," he said. "But only a person who is mentally ill would do what you did. And we don't punish the mentally ill with death."

"Maybe I'm just evil, Raymond. Maybe I'm the antichrist," Evan said playfully. "Couldn't that be it?"

"No!" Raymond shot back, nearly shouting. He poked a finger at Evan. "Something is wrong with you, inside. When Dr. Cras conducts his examination, he'll find the same thing."

Evan closed his eyes. "We have been through this so many times," he said. "One shrink says crazy; the next says sane. Do we really have to do this again?"

"It's bought you fifteen years, and counting," Raymond said as he stood to leave. "And this particular shrink is a stone atheist. So talk about Jesus as much as possible."

Evan shrugged. "Praise Jesus."

"That a boy," Raymond said. "I'll see you Thursday."

***

It was approaching eleven A.M., and Abel was halfway through his second bourbon. He was sitting across from Izzy at a restaurant two blocks from the building from which they had just been escorted.

"You clearly have a problem," she said, exhaling smoke from her second cigarette.

"So do you," he said.

She shook her head. "I've got lots of problems, but not like you have," she said.

Abel drained the rest of what was in his glass. "I don't have a drinking problem. And you're twenty years old. You don't have problems. Trust me."

Izzy ignored his words. "I can't believe what happened back there."

Abel raised a hand to get the waiter's attention. When he caught Izzy's glare, he said, "I'm switching to beer. Don't worry."

She rolled her eyes.

"And by the way, Izzy, this little story of yours just got a whole lot bigger, in my opinion."

"How's that?"

"Easy enough to see, isn't it? A governor avoiding a college newspaper reporter who's writing a story about a shooting that

76

happened twenty years ago. That's a story. Better yet, *a Governor who might run for president.* It's huge if you want it to be."

"It may be a story," she said. "But it won't win me any awards. I'm not doing all this to write a story about avoiding the press."

Abel ordered his beer, then looked at her. "That's not it," he said. "Think about it. He's all set to give an interview on a Saturday morning. Empty building. Nobody around. All of a sudden, his little shadows come in to save the day."

"That woman was obnoxious."

"She may have been," Abel said. "But she did her job. Now do yours."

"What do you mean?"

"Go find out what the hell she's so afraid of. "

She thought about this for a long time. Abel sipped his beer and stared at the empty street. The waiter brought the lunch they had ordered, a cheeseburger for him and a grilled chicken sandwich for her. Abel dove into his immediately. Izzy kept thinking, staring into across the restaurant. Finally, she looked back at Abel.

"You know what it is they don't want him to say, don't you?" she asked.

"I have a good idea," he said.

She groaned. "Well, can you please tell me?"

He nodded his head while he tapped his finger on one of the empty glasses. "It'll take a few more of these."

She sighed again. "Then order another one! This is getting old."

Abel took a bite of his fries. "I'll tell you all about it, Izzy. I promise."

"When?"

"Soon," he said as he took a drink of beer. "But you need to tell me something first."

"Like what?"

"You're not being straight with me," he said. "There's something you're not telling me."

She glanced around the restaurant. "What are you talking about?"

Abel pointed his chin toward the street. "Little Miss Smiley Face back there, the obnoxious one. She said something."

"What are you talking about?" she repeated.

"I was a damn good journalist," he said. "And I trust my hunches."

"I don't understand."

"Yes, you do. That woman said that you knew what the problem was."

"I don't know what you're talking about."

Abel put his burger down and looked at her. "If we're going to be sharing secrets, Izzy, we start with you. She wasn't worried about the governor. She was worried about you. Why?"

Izzy shrugged. "She must have read my last story."

Abel just looked at her. "Bullshit," he said. "Tell me what she knows."

She stared back at Abel for a few seconds before she shrugged. "It'll all come out, eventually. Everything does."

The food came. Abel sipped his beer, and Izzy wrote in her notebook.

***

The governor was fuming mad. "What the hell is this, Sheila?"

"Please calm down, sir," Sheila said breathlessly. "I can explain."

"Then explain!" he shouted. "And close the door!"

Sheila closed the governor's office door, and she and Bob Casarini took seats around a small conference table. Springer stayed on his feet, too angry to sit.

Nobody spoke. Even though Sheila had been ordered to explain, she and Bob just looked at their boss. They both knew from experience that he would have more to say, and it was easier to let him do his shouting now, rather than be interrupted as they tried to speak.

78

"So which one of you is going to explain why I had to cancel an interview with a college newspaper reporter?" His voice was a touch calmer now.

Sheila tried first. "Sir, I..."

Springer interrupted immediately. "And explain for me why I am having to console my scheduling secretary of ten years because one of my staffers cursed her out for doing something I told her to do?"

Sheila looked at the floor. Bob looked at Sheila.

"That was me," Sheila said. "I was just..."

"She told me that one of my staffers said, 'Nobody schedules a *fucking* interview with this Governor without telling me first.' Is that the kind of language that you think is befitting my senior staff?"

Sheila exhaled loudly, looking like she was trying to find the right words. "Sir, I was upset because..."

"Well, you got her upset! We may have a damn lawsuit on our hands. The woman goes to church every day. Not every Sunday, every *fucking* day. And that's the language she has to hear from you?" He turned quickly and walked to the window. "Just what I need."

"Sir," Bob said. "Aside from the way Sheila spoke to Mary Rita, we do have some important information to share with you." Recognizing Bob's tone, Springer turned toward him and gave him his attention. He could always tell when Bob meant business.

"What is it?" he asked.

"Please have a seat, sir," he said. The governor sat down and Bob continued. "Governor, the reporter who came to interview you this morning was not just any reporter."

"I'm aware of that, Bob," he said impatiently. "I remember the story she wrote about the kid who fell from the window. I trust her reputation."

Bob nodded his agreement. "She has an excellent reputation, sir. The problem is that Sheila uncovered some other interesting information about her this morning when she ran a simple background check."

Bob was still using that tone. Mike was starting to get the picture. He placed his hands on the table and looked at Sheila. "What is it?"

Sheila took a breath and said, "We believe she may have an agenda, Governor."

"Why?" he asked.

There was a knock at the door. "Open," the governor shouted. The door opened and the police officer in charge of security stepped inside, holding a piece of paper.

"What is it, Bill?" the governor asked. "We are in a meeting here."

"Yes, sir," he said. "It's just that Ms. Avery asked me to bring this information as soon as I got it."

"What is it?" Sheila asked.

Tom cleared his throat. "I ran the plates of the car those folks were in. Pennsylvania 259…"

"Thanks, Bill," she said as she stood and extended her hand. "I'll take that."

Tom handed her the piece of paper and stood in the door.

Sheila looked at him. "That will be all," she said.

Bill didn't move. He looked to the governor. Bob lowered his eyes.

"Thank you, Bill," the governor said as he glanced at Sheila. "That will be all."

"Yes, sir," Bill said, and officiously exited the room. Mike let the moment sit before he let her off the hook. This was, after all, his office.

"Anything important?" he finally asked, pointing to the paper.

Sheila looked at the paper. "The car is registered to Abel Ryan and - this is interesting - he changed his name several years ago. In fact, he changed it a couple times.

"Let me see," Mike said as he reached for the paper. Sheila handed it to him.

Springer felt his face go pale as he read the names on the paper. He handed it to Bob and slowly stood. He stepped toward the window.

"Do either of these name mean anything to you?" Bob asked.

The governor stared out onto Caesar Rodney Street. He thought a long time before he quietly said, "One of them does, yes. It's a name I haven't heard in a long time." Then he took a breath and turned back to Bob and Sheila. "I can't believe this is happening," he said as he turned back to the window.

***

"So what's your next move?" Abel asked. He was in the passenger seat, in no condition to be driving. A very sober Izzy was at the wheel. She'd been unwillingly pressed into driving due to the amount of alcohol Abel had consumed while they ate lunch. She was annoyed, and she'd told him so. Lack of self-control was something she simply couldn't tolerate or understand.

"Sorry that you have to drive," Abel said, without sounding even slightly remorseful. "I get a little carried away this time of year."

"So I've heard," she said. They rode in silence.

She was weighing her options. As she drove north on Route 1 toward Philadelphia, she considered the man sitting next to her. Based on his success as a teacher, she didn't think he was really a horrible drunk, though she had suspected it at times. She had barely known her aunt on her mother's side who had died young due to her addiction, but her mother had described the experience as hell on earth for the entire family. But Abel claimed that his fondness for overindulging in whiskey and beer only lasted through the summer months. Izzy had no reason not to believe him. And the truth was she didn't care much about Abel's health outside of the context of the story she was working on. What she needed to know was how reliable he was. Would he make a good source? Could he help her even more than that? He seemed likable enough, even when he was inebriated and his confidence seemed to swell. After a great deal of consideration, Izzy decided she could use him.

"I want you to help me with this story," she said.

Abel, who had been staring out the window, close to sleep, turned his body toward her. "Isn't that what I've been doing?"

81

She smiled and said, "Yes, but I'm wondering if you would like to collaborate, in addition to being a source. Be a journalist again."

"What are you talking about?"

"I have three things I'm thinking," she said. "The first is your experience. I am a good investigator and a good writer."

"Yes, you are," Abel said. "A great writer."

"Thanks. What I don't have is a lot of the know-how that you picked up along the way. You seem to have a better idea as to who is important, and what should be asked. Like the window-washer guy. I would not have thought of that. I said the smoking thing, but I just made that up to justify it to my mom."

"Those are all skills you pick up along the way, Izzy," he said. "You'll get them very soon. Faster than I did."

"I know," she said. "But I don't have that kind of time now. I need those skills for *this* story. Not my next one."

Abel scoffed. "Well, we're not even in agreement as to what this story is," he said. "To me, you've got a nationally known governor whose people are afraid to let him talk to a college reporter. To me, *that* is the story."

"That's all part of it," she said. "You have that bigger picture perspective that I need. I'm too hyper-focused on what I want. I don't plan to change the story - not a chance. But your skills and perspective could really help me."

Abel sighed. "What else?"

"I need a photographer," she said. "I can take pictures, but yours will be better."

"I don't even have a camera anymore," he said.

"I do. Nikon. It's nice."

"What else?" he asked.

Izzy swallowed hard. Her nerves were acting up a tiny bit. Maybe it was the fact that she was cruising up the interstate on her way to Philadelphia, a drive she had never made on her own, and from the looks of things out her window, there was about to be a rainstorm.

"Okay," she said. "The other thing I am thinking is your personal connection to this case. I think..."

"You mean what I know about Springer," Abel said.

"Yes, that," she conceded. "But everything else, too. You were there. I feel like you can point me in directions I otherwise wouldn't even consider."

Abel turned back to the window. Small drops of rain were beginning to appear on the window. "Izzy, I'm not nearly the journalist you think I am. And I'm way too involved in the story to be objective."

"I know," she said. "I'll do all the writing. You're taking pictures and providing background, and being interviewed. That's it." She let Abel keep looking out the window for a while as she drove. The rain was picking up. Finally, she said, "I just want your help. I don't need it, but I want it. I think that with both of us, this story can be very special."

Abel watched the rain. The bourbon and beer were still with him, and he knew this was no time to make a decision. He had spent years running, first being pulled by parents, then on his own – always hiding his past.

Abel could still hear the shots, and the screams, and the sirens. He had sometimes thought about connecting the dots on some of the events he was unclear about. As a child, he had known that he should never ask his parents about it. As an adult, he busied himself so as not to think about it. When he wasn't busy, he drank.

And here was Izzy Buchanan - too smart for her lack of experience - too attractive for Abel not to be distracted by it. At the moment, the alcohol was making him think all kinds of things about her, none of which were good for a news story. "I'll think about it," he said, trying not to slur his words. "But my journalism career ended a long time ago."

"Well, think about it quickly, okay?" she said. "I have an interview tomorrow morning with Will Janicki."

"The maintenance man?"

"Right."

"Good for you," Abel said.

"Then tomorrow night, I'm getting on a train and heading south. I won't be back until Tuesday."

"Where are you going?"

"Charleston, South Carolina, to interview Shannon Maher."

Abel turned to look at her. "Is she expecting you?" he asked.

Izzy shrugged. "I don't know why she would be," she said. "I have an address, and I'm going to knock on the door."

"Expensive trip," he said. "Especially if she tells you to go to hell."

"I have the money."

"That's still pretty ballsy. Knock on somebody's door twenty years later? Good luck with that."

He turned to the window again. Abel had grown to hate confrontations, and journalism was full of them. Difficult phone calls and awkward questions. People telling him to screw off. He had had enough. He loved taking pictures, and he loved writing, but that wasn't even half of what it took to be a decent reporter. These days, the only confrontations he had were with parents who were angry about grades or their kids getting demerits for chewing gum in class. He hated those too, and he cringed whenever he thought of them, but they were few and far between.

"Yes," Izzy said. "It's pretty ballsy, but I'm ready for it."

It was starting to rain steadily, and Abel was getting tired. "Call me when you get back from interviewing Shannon. I'll tell you my decision when you get back, okay?"

"No way," she said. "If you're going to help me, I want you there for these interviews."

"In Charleston?" Abel asked. "I'm not ready to go to Charleston tomorrow."

Izzy raised a hand to stop him from talking. "Just think about it," she said. "I'll take you to your house, and then I'll take a train home while you sober up and think it over." She let her words sink as she drove. It was raining hard by then, and Izzy was concentrating on the road. "I could use your help," she said as seriously as she could.

Abel stared out the window. "I'll think about it."

Friday, August 6, 1976

Mike Springer stumbles into the employee room at St. Maria Goretti's Campground. He is late usual. He is quite hung over from the night before, which happens at least twice a week. It is summertime and nobody cares, least of all his friend Joe, who is sitting at the big table sipping coffee and reading a newspaper. The night before, Mike and a small group of counselors stole away from their charges and hit the town. Unlike Joe, he is required to spend nights at camp, with the exception of weekends. This morning, he is irritated with Joe, who was a no show at last night's gathering.

"What the hell happened to you last night?" Mike asks as he punches the clock. "We waited for you." It is 9:06 A.M.

Joe looks great. No bloodshot eyes. No messy hair. He looks up from his newspaper as he sips his coffee. "Sorry, I got busy," he says, wearing a smirk Mike has seen a thousand times. "I couldn't make it."

Mike places his timecard in the slot, finds a chair and collapses into it, placing his right hand over his forehead. "You said you were going to meet us on Main Street," he mutters. "We waited for you."

Joe looks amused as his friend complains. It is their fifth summer working together, and they have had countless mornings like this. On many of them, Joe was the one who was hung over. Many more had both of them suffering through dehydration, headaches, and lack of sleep. Fun times. "I couldn't make it," Joe says again, glancing at his watch. "Looks like I missed a good time."

"You did," Mike says. "Shannon was there."

"Shannon came out? Why?" Joe asks.

"Because she thought you were coming," he says. "You said you were."

"I know," Joe says. "But my plans changed. It happens."

Mike stops rubbing his eyes and looks at his friend. "You need to start thinking of other people," Mike says. "You had plans with me, and we need to talk."

Joe stands at the table. He stares at Mike for a second longer than usual before he speaks. "And just what do you and Shannon have to talk to me about? Is there a counselor rebellion brewing?"

Mike closes his eyes and massages the space between his eyes. "Shut up, Joe," he says. "It's nothing like that. It just feels like you've been somewhere else all summer."

"What are you talking about?"

"You know what I'm talking about," Mike says.

Joe turns and steps to his locker. He opens it and grabs his tennis racket. He is about to slam the door shut when he notices a small piece of paper taped to the inside of the locker door beneath the photos of him and his wife. He pulls the paper from the door, unfolds it, and reads the contents. He exhales and turns back to Mike. "It's been a good summer," he says. "For everyone. I'll try to get out more, okay?"

Mike shrugs. "Summer is almost over. And maybe it's been good for you, but the rest of us have had a long, boring, stinking hot summer."

Joe closes his locker and looks out the window. "No different today," he says. "Supposed to get up to ninety. Make sure the kids keep cool. Lots of water."

"Yeah. Yeah," Mike says, annoyed. "We're going to the pool first thing."

"Well, drink some yourself, Mike. You look like hell." Joe looks at his watch. "Let's get moving," he says. "It's after nine."

Mike stands and runs a hand through his hair. He takes a deep breath, trying to somehow shake off what he did to himself the previous night. His group of ten-year-olds will know what he's been up to. He looks again at his friend. Joe looks perfect - white tennis shorts, dark blue St. Maria Goretti's T-shirt. His body is lean and toned. He has already worked up a good sweat from his early morning warm up.

"You look like a goddamn superhero, Joe," he says. "No wonder you've had such a good summer. Your wife dress you?"

Joe doesn't acknowledge the comment. "Your kids are waiting," he says.

Mike realizes his friend is in no mood for jibes, and there is no time. He turns and starts to leave. "You in the air conditioning all morning?" he asks on his way out the office door.

Joe shakes his head and smiles. "Tennis lessons in a few minutes," he answers. "Had to reschedule because of the rain yesterday." He smiles and says, "Group one."

Mike shakes his head. "Have fun, boss."

Saturday, June 14, 1996

Governor Mike Springer ran his right hand through his hair. It was thinning, but the drugs had helped, as had the coloring. He would not have minded being gray, or bald, or both, but the massive billboards with his name on them every election year thought otherwise. He would eventually need hair plugs. He often wondered how Joe Conway would look if he were alive today.

In the summer of 1976, Mike was twenty-five years old and about to finish law school. Joe was thirty, but had a way of seeming both younger and older than he really was. An avid tennis player, he had the body of a college athlete. Being married with a child on the way, he had the wisdom and practicality of a man ten years older. Joe had been a natural leader, able to deal with bickering, hell-raising college-aged staff on the one hand, and demanding, overbearing parents on the other. Mike marveled at his friend's skills. He would have made a good politician, or advisor to one, anyway.

Yet even with all of his responsibilities, he was almost always willing to join in on the late night revelries of the summer camp staff. Mike remembered the bonding that had gone on among the staff those summers and the three-month-long unbreakable friendships that came every year. A new, younger group arrived each summer, with only the occasional counselor who returned for a second or third year. Mike was an anomaly, staying on for five years. The only real mainstay had been Joe Conway, who spent six summers at St. Maria Goretti's, and probably would have spent twenty more.

Mike could still recall hearing Joe tell his story of how he came to be the director of St. Maria's. Joe's private life was almost never a topic of discussion, so Mike was all ears when Joe had decided to start sharing on a rainy Thursday night over a pitcher of beer. Joe had been born and brought up by the high society of Philadelphia. A tennis star since practically birth, he had attended and played for the University of Pennsylvania, an Ivy League institution that unfortunately did not allow its students to major in tennis. The sport was all Joe cared about. When he graduated, five years after he had started, he walked away with a degree in English. He was close to the bottom of his class, but his father, a Penn graduate himself, often reminded him that this was still more valuable a degree than one from most other universities. Not quite talented enough to play on the professional tennis circuit, he decided to put his degree to work by giving tennis lessons to children in Philadelphia. It was a noble occupation, but one that didn't sit well with his parents. They pushed their son towards many professions that would tolerate an English degree, but he wasn't interested in any of them. It wasn't a question of money, which no one in the family needed. Joe was more concerned with doing something that would give his life meaning, and he wasn't finding anything outside of a tennis court that fit the bill.

That same night, Joe had even shared with Mike his desire to serve in the Vietnam War once he had finished college. However, his parents dismissed the idea outright. Their opposition to the war, combined with their desire to keep their son out of harm's way, meant that they would "completely disown him and cut him off" if he even dared go near a recruiting office. When Mike asked his friend if he had worried about being drafted, Joe shook his head dismissively and said, "My parents wouldn't allow that either." Mike didn't ask any more about it.

Eager to get their son out of Philadelphia and into a respectable job, Joe's parents began listening up at cocktail parties, hoping to find something that would keep him occupied. When they heard there was a priest who was building a campground that would cater to underprivileged children in Delaware, their ears perked up. It was simple from there. Joe's father called a meeting with Father Francesco Antonelli. He offered to donate a huge sum of money that would cover the completion of the campground, complete with state-of-the-art tennis courts. The only thing Mr. Conway asked was that his son, Joe, be "strongly considered" to be the camp's director. Father Antonelli explained that while he had already hired a director, a parishioner who had managed many such ventures in the past, Joe could certainly act as her assistant until she saw fit to move on, which should be soon. The deal was done. Joe started at St. Maria Goretti's Campground in the summer of 1971 as assistant director and tennis instructor. Two years later, as expected, he ascended to the role of director, a job that suited him perfectly.

Mike had loved working for Joe. They quickly became close friends, almost always going for beer after camp closed for the night, and occasionally making a night of it. When Joe got married, with Mike walking among the groomsmen, this practice slowed a bit, but not much.

Joe's memorable tenure as Camp Director would last three days shy of three summers, ending with his death at the hands of Evan Long. Mike would watch his friend bleed to death while he pointed a .38 caliber handgun at Evan Long.

But twenty years later, what Governor Mike Springer remembered more vividly than the gunshots or the blood, or that warm handgun, was the horrific sight of a ten-year-old boy standing over the dead body of Jacob Suddard, begging Mike to help him, then glaring with contempt as his body was covered with a sheet. That same glare was there a week later at Jacob Suddard's funeral. For all the governor knew, that same boy still wore that scowl to this day, only he wore it under the name of Abel Ryan.

The governor reached for the phone on his desk and began to dial Sheila's number but changed his mind and dialed Bob's instead. When Bob picked up, Mike said, "Let's meet tomorrow outside the office. My house will be fine. Have Sheila join us, and we'll get started at 9. In the meantime, I need you and Sheila to find out everything you can about those two. You have contacts. Use them."

The next presidential race wouldn't begin for another three years. Mike hoped to be a household name throughout the country by then. He wanted to become known as a hero for gun law reform throughout the country, a label he would use as a springboard to the presidency, or possibly V.P. At the very least, he could fill a cabinet position before his own time came. However, none of these things would be possible if he failed to win reelection as governor of Delaware this year.

He hung up the phone. Something would have to be done about Abel Ryan and Izzy Buchanan.

***

Abel stood in his small bathroom and studied his reflection in the mirror. It was a ritual he engaged in nearly every time he had to make a difficult decision. He looked deep into his own eyes, examined his own motives, and usually found that he trusted his own judgment. Today, he wasn't so sure. For as long as he could remember, he had been taught that the past was a horrible and dangerous place to go. Look forward, into the light. It's what Jacob would have wanted, or so his parents said.

These were sober thoughts for a sober subject. He picked up the phone and dialed the number he had scribbled on the small paper stuffed in his pocket. Izzy answered on the first ring.

"It's late," she said. Her voice sounded scratchy with sleep. "Are you sober?"

"*Too* sober," he said.

"Are you going to help me?" she asked.

"What kind of help are you looking for?"

"The truth," she said, her voice becoming clearer. "And a good photographer." Abel could hear her sitting up in bed.

"You might not like what you find," Abel said. "There are reasons people don't talk for decades. None of them are good."

90

Abel stood, still looking in the mirror while he waited for her to speak. He imagined how she looked as she sat curled in bed, cradling the phone to her ear the way women do. He tried to push the images from his head. They would only cloud his judgment.

"Let me worry about that," she said.

"I don't think you will worry about it. That's what I'm afraid of."

"What do you mean?"

"We're not researching history," he said. "There are things we are going to learn that nobody has ever heard before."

"That's what I want," she said. "And it sounds like you're on board."

He sighed. "I am."

"Why did you change your mind?"

He looked in the mirror. "I owe it to someone."

Izzy didn't say anything.

"I'll be your photographer," he said. "And I'll give you all the background information you need. You can interview me and quote me. Just use a different name. That will at least buy me some time."

"Meet me tomorrow morning at nine, and be sober," she said. "Thank you."

She gave him an address and they hung up. Abel turned to look at the clock in his kitchen. It was almost one in the morning. He got undressed and went to bed.

PART 2: SCREAMS

Sunday, June 16, 1996

Will Janicki was sitting on his front porch, newspaper open, a full coffee cup next to him.

Izzy introduced herself and Abel as they ascended the cement steps to his porch.

Will smiled and put down his newspaper. Izzy studied him as they drew closer. He was a nice looking older man, with the rugged handsomeness of a man who had spent his life doing physical work and had only recently begun to relax. He had a full head of gray hair and thick gray eyebrows that framed his deep blue eyes. His hands were big and rough and protruded from strong, wiry arms. His two-story home bore the signs of a handyman - an added garage, screened-in porch, and immaculate landscaping that could only be the work of the owner. Everyone shook hands.

"Would either of you like coffee?" Will asked. "I just brewed a whole pot."

Abel did. Izzy didn't.

Will went inside, leaving Izzy and Abel sitting on wooden patio furniture. The home was situated near the top of a hill in the Pike Creek area just outside of Newark, Delaware. From where they sat, they could see the top of the scoreboard and stadium seats at Kirkwood High School, only a couple miles away.

"You can see the whole school once winter comes and those trees drop their leaves," Will said as he opened the door and handed Abel a steaming cup. "I worked there thirty-five years," he said. "Feels like I still do, having to look at it all the time." He sighed and looked at the view. "But I don't mind. It's nice to look at."

"Yes, it is," Abel said as he fumbled with Izzy's camera.

"Do you live alone here?" Izzy asked as she prepared her notepad.

"Yes," Will said with a touch of resignation. "Katie passed away three years ago. Cancer."

"I'm sorry," Izzy said.

He frowned pleasantly. "Thanks. Kids are grown. Families of their own now. You work your whole life to retire. You get the house just the way you want it, and then…" He looked around again, never finishing the sentence.

"Well, I appreciate your talking to us," Izzy said. "It's very kind of you."

Will smiled again. "I never could say no to a pretty face."

Izzy blushed. "We were on the phone, Mr. Janicki."

"You're pretty on the phone, too," he said. "Who could say no to you?" He looked suspiciously at Abel. "You're a photographer?"

Izzy spoke up before Abel could answer. "Yes, he is. Abel is also assisting me with research and background information," she said. "He was present at the shooting that day."

Will raised his eyebrows and looked more closely at Abel. "How old were you?"

"Ten," Abel said.

Will shook his head. "A hell of a thing, wasn't it?"

"Yes, it was."

"I've never spoken to anybody about it, except Katie." He gestured toward the house as if she were still inside. He sat back down in his chair, took a deep breath, and slowly shook his head. "I was in Korea in '52," he said. "I barely made it out alive. I stayed on in the reserves, mostly doing maintenance on vehicles. Then they sent me to Vietnam for two tours during that whole mess. That was the Sixties, by then. He shook his head again. "I saw a lot of bad stuff over there, but that campground was the worst I ever saw." His eyes shifted to Izzy as he noticed her pen moving. He smiled. "Part of me forgot you were a reporter. You didn't come to hear me talk about war stories though."

Izzy stopped writing and looked at him. "I'd like to hear it all," she said.

He shrugged and looked from Izzy to Abel, and back to Izzy. "Where should I start?"

"Were you born in Delaware?" Izzy asked.

William Janicki was born in Georgetown, Delaware in 1930. Georgetown is located in the bosom of Sussex County, the southernmost of the state's three counties, the area known to people in the northern part of the state as "Slower Lower." He went to high school at Georgetown High, then trained as an electrician. Too young to serve in World War II, he jumped at the chance to join the Army, once he heard about the war in Korea. After a year serving as an infantryman, he was badly injured when a Chinese grenade landed next to him. Rather than take cover, Will frantically searched through the snow so he could throw it back at the enemy. Fortunately, he was looking in the wrong place, as the grenade had ricocheted off a rock and landed several feet away. The ensuing explosion knocked him unconscious, and several pieces of shrapnel landed deep in his left shoulder. His treatment and recovery were long and painful. By the time he had fully recovered, the fighting in Korea had stopped.

He returned to Delaware and met Katie, who was studying to be a teacher at the University of Delaware. After she graduated, they married and moved north to Newark and both took jobs at area schools. She taught third grade at Bear Elementary, while he joined the building and grounds staff at the newly built Kirkwood High School. They had two children, both girls, and had begun to settle into family life when the Vietnam War started. Will's obligations to the Army Reserve forced him to return to South-East Asia. However, this time his duties were strictly to supervise the maintenance of vehicles. "This was fine by me," he said. "At that stage of the game, I had a family. Having a wife and two children cured me of the desire to get shot at."

Upon returning to Delaware from his second war, he found that not only was his job still waiting for him, but that his boss had retired, and the school's principal had seen fit to make Will the new Head of Building and Grounds, a position he held until his retirement. "Principal was a good guy," Will said. "He had a soft spot for veterans. A couple of the guys were fuming mad when he promoted me over them. He just told them to stuff it."

94

One Sunday morning in 1972, after attending 9 A.M. mass, Father Francesco Antonelli, an oblate priest who'd been born in Italy, approached Will and asked him if he would mind lending his talents to the maintenance of a new summer campground he had opened. Will knew the priest had been working tirelessly for nearly a decade to open the campground that would serve the needs of children from all economic backgrounds. It would be only a few miles from where Will lived, and he would only need to be there a few hours a day in the summers or as emergencies arose. Will couldn't say no. "At that stage of the game, I figured God had gotten me through two wars and gave me a wife and two healthy kids, so taking care of that campground seemed like the least I could do."

Will worked at the campground over weekends in the spring and a few days a week in the summer, never accepting any payment, even after Father Antonelli offered him a small salary. His refusal of pay allowed for the priest to hire a part-time assistant to help Will throughout the summer, and the job became that much easier.

"It was easy work," Will said. "And I always enjoyed being there. Well, almost always, I guess." He stood from his chair and looked at his two guests. "Why don't we take a ride over there? Maybe I'll think of more to say if I'm looking at it. I'll drive."

"Good idea," Izzy said.

The interview was already going better than Izzy had expected. She had considered many ways to gently coax Will into taking them to the campground. If they didn't work, she was prepared to come right out and ask if he could take them there. Having heard his comments about his inability to say no to a pretty face, she figured she could talk him into just about anything. But she wouldn't have to. She was relieved and was about to smile at Abel when she caught his concerned expression. He was clearly *not* relieved, or even happy about the prospect of returning to the campground. Izzy had not considered this until now.

She looked at Abel and saw the anxiety in his eyes as they walked toward Will's truck. As Will climbed into the driver's seat, she tried to make eye contact with Abel, but he wouldn't let her. He stared straight ahead, like a child waiting in line, terrified to board a rollercoaster for the first time, but not wanting to show how afraid he was. She tried to gently take his hand, but he pulled it away quickly. Now feeling a bit uneasy herself, she stepped into the truck after him.

Abel felt his stomach tighten. He had not been to St. Maria Goretti's Campground since the day of the shooting. There were many weekends and idle summer days when he had considered jumping on the highway and making the short trip to Newark to revisit the spot where Jacob and many others had taken their last breaths. It would be good to pay his respects, something he felt he had never adequately done. Now, Will Janicki was offering to take them there to show them what he remembered.

He realized now that he didn't even want to look at Izzy, who he wished had at least asked his opinion before she so eagerly agreed to jump in Will Janicki's truck. He knew it was the right move - let the subject lead the way, keep him talking, let him drive. He just wished she had at least asked for his input, if nothing else to show they were on equal footing.

They piled into the front, and only, seat of Will's pickup truck. "It rained yesterday and it gets muddy at the campground," he explained. "So I'd rather take the truck. I hope you don't mind squeezing in."

"It's fine," Izzy said. She took the window, with Abel in the middle.

It was a short drive to the grounds, and Will explained that he would often leave the truck there and make the walk from his house as long as there was no rain in the forecast. In fact, he said, he had walked to the campground the day of the shooting. "I never even thought of that until now," he said. "It's funny, the things you remember... at this stage of the game."

96

Abel tried not to fall into Izzy's lap as Will turned the truck into the campground entrance and stopped at the front gate, which had been locked for the weekend. While Will got out to unlock the gate, Abel heard Izzy ask if he was okay. He ignored her, his eyes never leaving the windshield in front of him. Will hopped back in and continued driving down the steep, sloping entrance road of the campground. "I still keep a key," he explained. "They'll call me occasionally to help them fix something." He explained that when the campground had been built, Father Antonelli had gratefully accepted the volunteered time of many different contractors, and each one did things his own way. "Believe me," Will said. "Every air conditioner, generator, and toilet in this place has its own unique personality. There aren't many people who understand that." Will shook his head and chuckled. "Father Francesco is a great old guy, but he made this place harder to maintain than the space shuttle."

Abel was surprised. Speaking for the first time since he entered the truck, he said, "Do you mean Father Francesco is still alive?" Father Francesco had been ancient when even Abel attended camp.

Will laughed. "I don't think that guy was ever young! In fact, he just turned 90, and he is still out here every day working on something." Will scanned the hills in front of them. "He took that day really hard," he said quietly. "I know a lot of parents lost their kids that day, but this place is *his* baby, and he's never been the same since."

"What's changed about him?" Izzy asked.

Will twisted his lips in thought. "He's more suspicious of people since then," he said. "He used to chat up everybody that ever came through these gates. Grab their hand. Kiss the ladies' cheeks the way those old Italians do. No more though. He looks people over now. Head to toe."

As the truck proceeded up the winding road, the entire campground was silent and still. "Tomorrow is the first day of camp," Will said. "Volunteers have been busting their butts to get it ready. They still would be, except Father Antonelli is very strict

97

about Sundays. No work on Sundays." He chuckled. "You wouldn't believe the stuff he made me wait until Monday morning to do: flooded bathrooms, broken air conditioners..."

As Abel took in the campground for the first time in twenty years, he could feel the anticipation of the summer to come. Gleaming backboards and nets stood at the ends of shiny blacktopped basketball courts; pristine picnic tables sat in perfect rows; freshly-painted kayaks were stacked neatly by the lake, and shiny lifeguard stands overlooked the enormous blue swimming pool. This camp was waiting for the throngs of children to parade down every trail, tear up every field, and sneak into every corner to find mischief or spread gossip. Despite its history, it was still a marvelous place.

Will kept driving until they came to the bottom of the hill, turned left, and continued up a steep incline as the road wound around to what looked like the back of the grounds. Abel vaguely recalled most of what he was seeing. He immediately recognized the sleeping cabins, which housed about half of the camp attendees. Sleeping over was optional, and most parents would decide week-to-week whether their children would spend the night. Abel had always enjoyed sleeping over. As they drove past, he took note of the fenced in basketball courts and the large outdoor dining area. Details were gradually coming back to him. He saw the large open field where counselors would pitch tents and have cookouts once a week. It was always a great time, and he could smell the campfire burning as he recalled those precious nights. He and Jacob had always looked forward to it.

They drove past the snack bar, which backed up to the swimming pool, and Abel began to feel his stomach tighten again. He could easily imagine the crowds of children clamoring for a place in line while their counselors, who were also children, yelled at them to wait their turns. The girl behind the counter would feverishly try to serve each child as the line grew longer and longer. Abel would wait patiently to buy a double chocolate chip cookie and a grape juice - the same thing every day. Eventually, Joe Conway would show up, and help the overwhelmed snack bar girl, cracking jokes and getting the prices wrong, always in favor of the camper. The children would laugh and make their own jokes right back at him. "Did you come to help your *girlfriend*, Joe?" they would shout, making the poor girl blush.

"Eww!" Joe would shout back. "Why would my sister be my girlfriend?" The children would erupt in laughter.

Abel smiled, then shuddered at the memory.

Izzy had been silent since the truck had entered the gates of the campground. She was trying hard not to focus on the awkwardness she was experiencing with Abel, who had flatly ignored her when she had asked if he was okay. They would have to discuss it later. What they were seeing now was simply too important to let the rest become a distraction.

The truck came to a stop at the top of a hill at the far end of the campground. "Have you been here before?" Will asked Izzy.

She shook her head, but then said, "Once, I think. My mom brought me here to swim when I was little." She vaguely remembered attending a pool party with her mother.

Will nodded. "Well, I thought this would be a good place to start," he said as he pointed out his window.

"The tennis courts," Abel said as he looked past Izzy. A set of three fenced in, red, cement tennis courts stood at the very end of the campground. "I came here five summers and I don't think I was ever on them."

The three climbed out of Will's truck. The sun was getting hot now as it rose high in the sky. Abel and Izzy followed Will.

"Father Francesco was really proud of these when we had them built," Will said. "He managed to snag a generous businessman from Philadelphia who loved tennis and had some money he needed to get rid of. Naturally, Father Francesco had a friend in the business who could do the job for half of what it would have usually cost. So he had these beauties built, and the rest of the money went to getting more kids in here the next three summers."

99

They walked slowly toward the courts, stopping when they came to a plaque that was neatly placed on the locked gate. All three read it silently.

JOSEPH T. CONWAY TENNIS COURTS
DEDICATED TO THE HONOR AND MEMORY OF THE
MAN WHO SACRIFICED HIS LIFE FOR THE CHILDREN HE
LOVED AND CARED FOR
DEDICATED JUNE 11, 1977

"They were actually built in 1973," Will explained. "But Father Francesco had them rededicated in Joe's honor the year after the shooting."

Izzy watched as Will carefully unlocked the chains that secured the entrance. Then he pushed the opened gate as far as it could open and locked it to the fence. He noticed Izzy watching. "We've done it this way since '76, for this gate and for the pool. You understand, right?"

She did. Evan Long had used the chains and padlocks on the pool gates the day of the shooting. He had brought two padlocks with him that day. He had first walked to the back of the swimming pool, where a rear gate backed up to the woods and a trail leading to the lake. He used the chain on the rear gate, and one of the padlocks he had with him, to lock it. He then walked around to the main gate and locked that one the same way. The lifeguards had been in the habit of unlocking the gate, then arranging the chain so that it wouldn't hang freely. Evan Long had known that this was the procedure and used it to his advantage. With two of the three gates locked, he walked to the entrance of the third, where he stood and opened fire on the campers, counselors, and lifeguards. Under Will's new system, a person trying to lock people inside would have to first cut the chain free of the fence, presumably with bolt-cutters, which would be easily noticed in time for someone to raise an alarm. This was one of several precautions taken after the shooting. They were

100

all done strictly for peace of mind, Will explained. Realistically, everyone knew the events of that day would never be repeated.

Izzy noticed that as Will pushed open the gate, there was not even a squeak. He stepped through and Izzy and Abel processed in after him.

The three of them walked to the edge of the first court and stood near the net. Izzy and Abel stared in awe at the beautifully kept surfaces and nets. They looked up and down the high chain link fences as well. There was almost no wear and tear anywhere - not a single crack in the surface, or a single piece of webbing missing from the net. It was evident that people had worked hard over the many years to keep them in perfect condition. Will sighed with satisfaction. "We like to treat these courts like our own little church," he said, his voice much quieter now. "If they're going to be in Joe's memory, they're going to be perfect."

Abel took in the view and wondered why he had never come to the tennis courts as a child. The grounds looked magnificent from this spot. Every part of the camp, and the hills beyond, could be seen from there. He could even make out the shape of the majestic Delaware Memorial Bridge on the horizon. Abel could see for the first time that the campgrounds were framed by the main road on one side, the lake and tennis court at opposite ends, and the woods on the other. It was an almost perfect square, situated on a sloping piece of land.

Will pointed to the ground with his right hand. "So this is where Joe was when the shooting started. He gave tennis lessons three times a week. He was up here with maybe fifteen kids and a counselor." He pointed to the baseball field about two hundred yards down the sloping hill. "When he heard the shooting, he ran out the gate we just came in. He took his racket with him. He crossed the baseball field there. There was nobody on the field at that stage of the game, but there were two counselors, a guy and a girl. They were having a smoke on the far side of the dugout where nobody at the pool could see them. That was typical of the counselors back then. When most of the kids were at the pool, they would take turns."

Abel glanced at Izzy, who just looked and listened. She had yet to say anything, or even write anything down since they had been on the grounds. Abel was expecting her to ask Will some questions. When she didn't, he decided to. "Did those counselors see Joe running toward the pool?" he asked.

Will nodded. "They did. Their names were …." He had to think for a moment.

"Allison Witherow and Mike Springer," Izzy said, surprising both of the men. "Allison saw him running and yelled that there was a man with a gun. She later told police that she asked him to stop and hide with them behind the dugout, but Mike did not corroborate this." Abel noticed that Izzy's voice was different now. It was a trance-like rhythm, as if she were under hypnosis. "Mike told police that he remembered Allison screaming that they had to call the police, which they couldn't do; the closest phones were at the pool and at the lake, on the far side of the camp. Joe told them he was going after the intruder. Mike and Allison told him he would get himself killed if he did. The man had a gun and was shooting. "

Will looked at Izzy. "That's right," he said somberly. "You've heard this before."

"I've read all the police reports," Izzy said. "Mike Springer spoke to police but to nobody else."

They all kept looking at the baseball field. "What else did they tell the police?" Abel asked.

Izzy continued, never shifting her gaze from the baseball field. "Allison's recollection was that she said she would run to the lake to call the police but would have to go the long way around since the shortest distance was through the swimming pool area. Mike said someone had to have already heard the shooting and called the police by now. Their stories never quite matched, but the police said that was not out of the ordinary for a case like this.

"However, where their stories match exactly is this: Mike told Joe that if he was going to go after the shooter, he would go with

102

him. Joe said to Mike, 'Okay, get a baseball bat.' At that point, Joe ran full speed toward the pool. After a second of hesitation, Mike ran after him, stopping in the dugout to pick up a baseball bat. The last thing Allison saw was Mike and Joe as they both ran toward the pool, Joe several feet ahead. After that, she stayed hidden behind the dugout, where police found her an hour later, terrified and weeping."

"You've been researching this for a long time," Abel said.

Izzy nodded, still looking at the field. "Yes, I have," she said. "Mr. Janicki..."

"Call me Will."

"Will, were counselors allowed to smoke behind the dugout?"

Will scratched his head. "I guess not," he said. "But things were different back then. If it was outside, and there were no kids around, nobody minded."

Izzy nodded. "Did Joe ever go back there?"

"I don't remember ever seeing him there," Will said. "Plus he'd been a big tennis star in college, as I recall. I don't think he ever smoked."

Izzy turned toward Will, taking her eyes off the field for the first time. "Can you tell us what happened up here?" she asked.

Will looked at her blankly for a moment before it registered. "Oh, of course," he said, turning back to face the center of the courts. "Joe was up here with a group of the youngest kids and their counselor. The details of what happened are sketchy here because the kids were so young, but what the police think happened was that Joe and the girl who was their counselor..."

"Shannon Maher," Izzy said.

"Right, Shannon Maher," Will said. "Joe and Shannon heard the shooting and told the kids to run." He pointed to the far exit. "They ran out that gate with Shannon. There is a short trail that leads through those woods and out to Old Pike Creek Road. The police found the children, and Shannon, in a church parking lot about an hour later. Someone had seen them on the side of the road and picked them all up." Will looked back to Izzy and Abel. "Now, I'm

103

guessing you already know this, but those details came from the kids and that driver," he said. "Shannon wouldn't talk to the police or anyone else. She never has to this day, as far as I know."

Izzy nodded. "I did know that. The only accounts of what happened on the tennis courts came from five-year-olds. Just about every one of them told a different story." This was true. The stories the children reported at the time and ever since had varied remarkably. The only common thread among the accounts was that Joe was there on those courts with them and Shannon Maher when the shooting had started.

"Maybe old Shannon Maher is waiting for someone to knock on her door and ask her to tell her story," Abel said. Izzy smiled and looked back at the field. Will chuckled uneasily.

"I'll bet Ms. Maher has a story to tell," Izzy said. "I'd like to hear it."

Will looked at both of them and asked, "Are you ready to see the pool?"

Abel looked at Izzy. He watched her smile fade away as she turned to look at him. Her eyes now showed genuine concern as if she were apologizing for not asking him earlier. She stepped carefully toward him and took his right hand. "Are you ready to go back to the pool, Abel?" she asked.

***

Everyone looked exhausted. Mike Springer, Bob Casarini, and Sheila Avery sat around Mike's kitchen table sipping coffee, trying to wake up. They were not meeting this morning to talk strategy. This meeting would be about politics - dirty, underhanded, below-the-belt politics.

The governor looked across the table at the folder Bob had open in front of him. Then he looked at Sheila and waited. Confused, Sheila looked at Bob, who nodded toward his open folder. Finally getting the message, Sheila produced a folder of material herself and laid it open on the table. Mike studied the contents of

104

each from a distance. Neither Sheila nor Bob had actually shared the contents of their folders with the governor. The two had been working feverishly through the night finding as much information as they could about Abel Ryan and Izzy Buchanan. They had started with their contacts in the state police, which led them to contact other agencies around the country, including the Pennsylvania State Police, the Federal Bureau of Investigation, and the Internal Revenue Service. The information was not easy to gather, especially on a Saturday night into Sunday morning, but this is why Mike had hired Bob so many years ago, and why Bob had hired Sheila a year ago. Not only were they skilled political strategists, but they were also relentless diggers. They were capable of finding every piece of information about a person that could possibly be found. Then they could exploit that information for the gain of whomever they saw fit, in this case, Governor Mike Springer.

Mike was casual and detached as he sipped his coffee and peered across the table. In this kind of operation, he did not want to seem overly interested. "So you both have enough to move forward?" he asked.

"I believe we do, sir," Bob said.

Mike shrugged. "This is my home, Bob. Call me Mike." He looked at Sheila. "That goes for you too."

They both nodded.

Mike looked at Bob. He looked older than he usually did. He probably had not slept all night, but he had been down this road before. For such an honorable man, Bob Casarini had seen a lot of dirty politics.

"Who first?" the governor asked.

"We'll start with the male," Bob said, purposefully avoiding the use of a name. "He has a sister," Bob said.

Mike's eyebrows raised. "A record?"

Bob shook his head. "Not exactly, sir. But she's been breaking the law for five years, from what I can tell."

Mike sighed. "How?"

"She doesn't have a job," Bob said. "Her husband works and she stays home with their two young children."

"And?"

"And she's been depositing about $400 a week just about every week for the past five years."

Mike was interested. "Drugs?"

Bob scoffed. "No. I think she's watching somebody's kids."

Mike looked across the table from Bob to Sheila and back. He was confused. "Help me out here, Bob."

Sheila took the lead. "She's not paying taxes, sir," she said. "And worse, she may be running an unlicensed daycare."

Mike took this in for a moment without saying anything. Finally, he dropped his pen on the table and ran his right hand through his hair. He leaned back and said, "Jesus Christ, Bob. I asked you for dirt. This is a woman trying to make ends meet by babysitting."

"She hasn't paid income tax for five years, sir."

"And I'll bet her oldest is six, right? She needed the extra money after he was born and they couldn't pay a daycare. So she commits that horrible crime of making money and not paying taxes."

The governor was annoyed, but his advisors were persistent. "It's against the law," Sheila said. "And if we need to, we can use it."

Mike leaned forward and squeezed the space between his eyes. "Yeah, her and Al Capone," he said. "Anything on the girl?"

"Well," she said. "It turns out her mother is quite wealthy."

Mike shook his head and sighed again. He was becoming more frustrated. "I know we're Democrats, but being wealthy is still not illegal," he said.

Sheila coughed and angled her chin inward as she looked across at the governor. Body language was everything in this situation. "You know this girl," she said suggestively. "She writes under an alias. You know her mother."

Mike looked across at Sheila and tried to ascertain what it was she was trying to communicate. There were things he didn't want

106

her to say, and they both knew that. However, Mike couldn't figure out what it was Sheila didn't want to tell him.

He looked from Sheila to Bob and back several times while they silently allowed him to put the pieces together. Finally, it dawned on him. "You've got to be kidding," he said.

Sheila shook her head.

Mike leaned back in his chair again and exhaled heavily. "Jesus Christ," he said. "Her family has donated to my campaign. A lot."

"I know, Mike," she said. Mike had to smile at that. It was amusing to hear her call him that. "Her *family* have been big supporters but not her specifically."

Mike raised his eyebrows. "So what?" he asked.

"Well, her mother's made donations to a lot of special interest groups," Sheila continued. "Some that I think the public would be very interested in knowing about, if she were to create a controversy."

"Who's she donated to?" Mike asked.

"Mostly to conservative candidates around the country, especially to pro-gun rights people. And she supports the NRA financially, though she's not a member."

Mike shook his head and found a far corner of the kitchen to stare at. "This girl's mother is donating money to the NRA? You're kidding."

"It points to an agenda, Mike," Bob said. "Her daughter is a college journalist with no paying job, so her mom must be supporting her financially. If we can assume she and the mother are on the same side, we have an agenda. We can't cooperate with this story. In fact, I think we need to either stop it, or discredit it before it's published."

Mike ran a hand through his hair again as he tried to process everything he had learned. He looked at the two of them. "Is that it?" he asked.

Bob shook his head. "The male is a Catholic school teacher who might've messed around with a former student, though she was of age at the time. We could use it if we have to."

107

Mike shook his head slowly. "So, we threaten to charge a young mother with tax

evasion, or we threaten to expose a woman who is *legally* donating money to the candidates and charities of her choice. If that doesn't work, we go after a teacher for not breaking the law."

Bob smiled at the governor's assessment and shook his head. "*You* don't do a thing. However, *we* do all three," he said. "Odds are we don't end up actually following through on any of them. Just the suggestion might be enough. She's very young, and he's weak. They'll back off."

Mike exhaled and considered this. "But donating to the NRA?" he said. "Come on, Bob."

"It could be a trap, Mike," he said firmly. "The male wrote a few op-ed pieces about guns when he was in college. The girl isn't being straight with you, either. This whole thing could be an attempt to embarrass you. So we play the cards we have and dismiss this thing as an attack by gun nuts. Worst case scenario, we get it pushed back until after the election."

Mike looked at Bob curiously. He hadn't shared anything about his experience twenty years ago with him. "What is it you're worried about?"

Bob pointed to the folder in front of Sheila. "The girl is a good writer with some credibility, and the mother has money. If they wanted to, they could snow you on your gun stance. You've got credibility, but so do they. I say we go after them all."

Mike looked at the empty pad of paper that sat in front of him on his kitchen table. He took the last sip of his coffee and stood to get more. He returned to the table and sat back down. He looked across at the other two, who were waiting patiently. "No," he said. "You can work the boy's sister. Use that. And go ahead with the former student. But the mother is off limits, at least for now."

"Yes, sir," Bob said. He was a good soldier, despite his obvious disappointment.

"For the girl, it might be enough that we know who she is and what she wants," Sheila said. "She's hoping for a bright future."

108

Mike thought about this. "You might be right," he said. "She's just a kid. In fact, if that poor girl digs deep enough on this, she might realize that *she* never wants this thing to see the light of day." He chuckled. "Though I heard she was pretty determined. And impressive."

"Yes, she was," Bob said.

Sheila's nose went in the air. "I wasn't impressed," she said.

Mike sipped his coffee and said, "It's safe to say she wasn't that impressed with you either, Sheila."

Sheila smirked.

Bob waited a moment before he said, "Mike, I have to ask. Is there anything specific we should be keeping from this girl? If she were to ..."

The governor stopped him before he could finish. "You don't have to ask that, Bob."

Bob was insistent. "Look, sir, you told us to do the digging. You're clearly worried about something. I just want to know what it is we are trying to keep from going public. Whether this girl gets it, or somebody else does. It seems like there could be a lot of different elements at work here."

"There are," Mike said. "And none of them are good for anyone, especially someone who's up for reelection." He sighed. "What am I worried about? I'll tell you if and when I have to, okay? As for now, do what you have to do."

"We're on it," Sheila said.

"Go get them," he said as they all began to stand. "Somewhere outside the office. Outside of Dover, if possible. Shut this thing down."

"We will," Bob said. He looked at Sheila. "I'll talk to the girl?" he asked.

Mike watched as Sheila's eyes turned fiery. "No way," she said. "You take him. I want the girl."

Bob raised his right hand to calm her. "You will do better with Abel, believe me. You and that girl are toxic. I'll take her."

109

She was about to protest when she felt the governor stepping in. "He's right, Sheila," he said with finality. "You talk to the guy. End this thing."

She gave Bob one more glare before stomping out of the kitchen. She was good at glaring.

***

Abel allowed his two companions to walk ahead of him. He was not in any hurry to return to the swimming pool, or to the spot where he had hidden while Evan Long committed eleven murders.

He had appreciated how Izzy had asked him if he was ready to return to the pool. That was collaboration, which she seemed to be getting better at. He thought of her story about the boy falling from the window, and how she had returned to that same room with the boy's parents. It was so many years later, and the words and tears began to flow from them as they stared at the window. Maybe the experience had made Izzy especially aware of the sensitivities involved with returning to a place where a terrible event had happened, he thought. Izzy Buchanan knew what she was doing, at least as far as reporting went. She had work to do as a collaborator, but that was probably brand new to her.

He watched her as she walked beside Will Janicki along the paved trail. It had been a dirt trail twenty years ago. Abel could remember walking it as a little boy, and his eager eyes were always on the gate to the pool. But today, he noticed the trees beyond, and the view of the lake, things that had escaped his observation as a child. He also doubted that back then he would have noticed a woman like Izzy Buchanan walking the trail ahead of him. Today, he could not help but notice. He watched how she turned to ask Will a question, and how she deftly handled the pen and notebook, nodding politely as she scribbled.

When they had all arrived at the gate to the pool, Abel was surprised to see that the concrete wall was gone. It was the place where he had hidden as the chaos unfolded around him. It was one

110

of the things he had remembered most. He began to hear the screams again, the ones he heard before he fell asleep each night, unless he was too drunk to hear them. However, standing in that place and hearing the chain of the pool gate rattle as Will unlocked it made him remember the horrific screams of children and the sound of gunfire echoing across the hill behind him. He now recalled that at first, he thought the shooting was coming from behind, and it was not until Jacob had pulled him to the other side of the wall that he had found relative safety.

He took a breath as he drew closer. There was a lot to tell Izzy about this place, but he would let Will tell the story for now.

He wanted a drink.

Izzy watched Will as he patiently waited for Abel to catch up to them. When he did, Will pointed to the large engraved wooden sign above the gate to the pool. "Father Francesco's idea," he said. "He can be a little dramatic, but it is appropriate, I guess."

The sign read *Pool of Eternal Childhood.* Will explained that the previously unnamed pool had been christened in memory of the dead a year after the shootings. He sighed and said, "A lot of kids got robbed out of growing up here, the counselors too. They were all kids." He glanced at Abel, then looked at Izzy. "This is where it all happened. What can I tell you?" he asked.

Izzy took a breath. "Why don't you tell us what happened from your perspective?" she said. "I may interrupt to ask a question or two."

"Of course," Will said.

"But before you start, Will, there is one thing I'd like to ask you," she said.

"Go ahead."

"You said that Shannon Maher has never spoken publicly to anyone about the shootings."

He nodded. "That's right. Nobody knows why."

"Yes," Izzy said. "But isn't the same true for you?" She watched for his expression to change, but it didn't. She continued. "You gave statements to the police, but declined all requests from media, even years later when new security measures were being put in place here in the camp, almost certainly by you. There were stories about them in the newspapers, and you were mentioned in those stories. But you always declined to comment."

"*Definitely* by me," he said.

"Excuse me?"

"Those new security measures. They were *definitely* put in place by me."

"I see. Once the trial started, you were never called to testify in court. You never told your story in a book or a magazine. You've never once spoken at a memorial service, even though you are well-spoken and highly respected, and I know you are invited every year and have even attended on occasion. You have not spoken about this in twenty years."

Will looked at Abel, whose eyes were fixed on the spot where a concrete wall had once stood. He looked back at Izzy. "So you want to know why?" Will asked.

"I do," Izzy said. "And why are you choosing to talk to me now?"

He smiled, "Well, I can't say no to a pretty face."

Izzy did not blush this time. "You already said that."

Will thought for a moment, then pulled open the gate to the pool, chaining it to the fence as he had at the tennis court. "Please understand," he said as his face grew longer. "I don't mean for this to be about me." He gestured to the grounds around the pool as if it were still strewn with the bodies of the dead and injured. "It's about them. I don't want to distract from that."

Izzy waited. Abel walked next to her.

"I've been through a lot this past year," Will continued. "I retired from my job to take care of my wife. Right after that, she died. At this stage of the game, I have so much time to myself, and I work around the house, or I come here and do what I can. But I spend so much time just thinking." He turned and looked into the pool. "*Thinking,*" he said again, almost in a whisper. "Now, they're going to execute that boy in a week." He shook his head and turned back to Abel and Izzy. Izzy was not taking notes. "I'm sorry," he said. "I'm having trouble finding the words."

"It's okay," Izzy said.

"I guess you just called me at the right time," he said. "I was ready to talk."

***

Warden Andrew Wood checked himself in the mirror of the staff bathroom, being sure his uniform was in perfect order. He knew his colleagues wondered why their warden took extra care of how he looked when he had to speak to death row inmates. No, he wasn't trying to impress any mass murderers. The answer was simpler than that. He was in the business of prisons, and there was no prison business more serious than death row. So when he went there, he was dressed for the occasion. Besides, something about seeing a man who was facing death made him want to look as official as possible.

He looked good, he thought. The first African American Warden of the state prison, Warden Wood had always insisted on his staff looking like professionals, and that started with him. His shave was close on his face and head, his badge and shoes were shined to perfection, and his shirt and pants were pressed and starched just enough to flatter his impressive, once-chiseled, physique. The man he was about to speak to would, in all likelihood, be dead in five days. One more hearing before the Pardon's Board had been scheduled for two days prior to his execution. In actuality, it was closer to one day, as the Board would meet on Thursday afternoon, and the execution was scheduled for very early Saturday morning, just after midnight. They would undoubtedly be discussing his mental competence. The warden always wondered how any man could be mentally competent two days before he was scheduled to die, but none of this was up to him. Andrew Wood's job was to act on behalf of the state. He would make sure Evan Long was safe, fed according to the state's mandated nutrition standards, that he received thirty

113

minutes of private recreation per day, and that he had access to his lawyer and spiritual advisor, if he so desired. Then in five days, as the first order of business that day, he would see to it that Evan Long died quickly for the crimes he had been convicted of committing.

The warden left the bathroom and made the short walk to the death row section, where seventeen men kept residence, most still years away from meeting their fate. He nodded politely to the corrections officer who sounded a required alarm and unlocked the main cell door that led to the twenty single-cell eight-foot by nine-foot chambers that made up the death row section of Delaware State Prison.

"I should be about ten minutes," the warden told the officer. "Meeting with Long."

"Yes, sir," the officer said, making a note of the time in his record book. He would have the warden sign it on his way out.

The warden took a breath and walked to the second-to-last cell on the right, where he found Evan Long. He was sitting upright at the small metal table, reading a book. Both the chair and the table had been welded to the floor. Evan Long did not look up from his book.

"Long," said the warden. "We have some things to discuss."

The inmate acknowledged the warden with one finger but kept reading. Evan Long, he had learned, was one who liked to maintain the illusion that he was in control. His making the warden wait was a subtle way of maintaining that. Wood waited patiently, one of the few courtesies he reserved for those on death row, at least the ones who behaved themselves. Evan was a small man. He had arrived at the prison nineteen years ago standing five feet, eight inches and weighing one hundred fifty-three pounds. Today, he weighed three pounds fewer than that, and his formerly firm body had disintegrated to become soft and fragile-looking. His orange jumpsuit hung loosely from his scrawny frame. He had lost almost all of his hair and what remained circled his crown in a white horseshoe. At thirty-nine years old, he would have passed for fifty.

After a moment, Long closed the book and looked at the warden politely. "*The Great Gatsby*," he said, as though the two had met by chance in a coffee shop. "I never read it when I was in high school. I never knew what I was missing."

"We have a few things to discuss," the warden said again.

Evan smiled. "I take it literature is not one of them."

"Your hearing is in three days," the warden said. "You will be taken from this cell to the parking lot and placed onto a bus that will take you to the courthouse in Dover. You will meet your lawyer there. You will get some time to meet with him privately before the hearing begins. You understand?"

"I'm supposed to be examined by a psychiatrist before that."

The warden nodded. "Dr. Cras will be here in the morning. You will meet with him in the conference room. That meeting is privileged. No recordings, but there will be a corrections officer with him for reasons of security. Nothing the officer hears will be recorded for any legal record. You understand?"

"You know I'm not dangerous, Warden," Evan said softly. "You don't need any officers with us."

The warden continued without comment. "I also need to offer you, again, the opportunity to meet with a spiritual or religious guide. Your records say you were raised Catholic. I would be glad to ask a priest or deacon to come in here to talk to you about..."

"The answer is no, Warden. It's been no for twenty years."

The warden frowned, his first break in character. "Evan, I know you are a religious man. I know what you read and the officers see you praying at night. Why don't you let me have someone come talk to you?"

"Warden, we have been over this," Long said, his blue eyes looking weary from reading and lack of light. "The only religious guide I need is the Bible. I never picked it up my whole life until they locked me up in here, and then it changed my life. I have a very personal relationship with the almighty, and I'd like to keep it that way. The answer is no."

"Okay, okay," the warden said.

115

"What else, Warden?"

Wood cleared his throat. "There is the matter of your last meal," he said.

"Fried chicken," Long said without hesitation.

Wood ignored Long's words and stuck to the script. "Let your lawyer know what you would like to eat on the day of your execution," he said. "Every effort will be made to meet your request, within reason. You understand?"

"I'll tell him," Long said. "What else?"

The warden frowned again, stepping out of character for the second time. "I want to talk to you about your execution," the warden said.

Evan stepped toward the vertical steel bars that separated them. "Shouldn't my lawyer be here for this?"

"I have already discussed this with your lawyer, as have you. I am still very concerned about the method of execution you have chosen."

Long scoffed. "I didn't choose anything, Warden. You know that."

"Yes, you did, Evan."

"Bullshit, Warden," Long said, drawing the attention of the guard at the main cell door. The warden nodded to him, indicating that he did not need assistance. Long lowered his voice and said, "The state sentenced me to hang, and I will hang."

Wood sighed. Evan Long was correct. He had been sentenced to death in 1977, just after the state of Delaware, and the U.S. Supreme Court, had given the go-ahead to resume executions for the worst offenders. However, no one in Delaware had been executed since 1946. Long's predicament was that he had been sentenced to death while hanging was still on the books as Delaware's only method of execution. That changed in 1986 when the state legislature switched the method to lethal injection. However, the new law stated that Evan Long, and the few others who were in the same situation, could choose lethal injection rather than hanging. Long simply refused to make the choice, leaving the Department of

116

Corrections no option but to build a gallows and prepare for a hanging. Warden Wood had hoped that the inmate would eventually change his mind. He was profoundly disappointed in Long's lawyer, who was much more concerned with getting the death sentence reversed than he was in counseling Long to choose the needle rather than the noose. It was not Wood's job to follow the case, but he was of the opinion that a reversal was highly unlikely. He knew a dead man when he saw one.

The warden looked gravely at Long. "Just take the needle, Evan," he said. "Leave this world with some dignity."

Evan took another step forward and spoke in a near whisper. "Warden, you know I respect you. You and your men have taken good care of me ever since you became a warden. Ten years now?"

"Eleven."

"You've been good to me. Better than I deserve. But I won't let them make me choose, Warden. You've got some good men here, and I don't like the thought of them having to hang me. I know you and your men have traveled very far to get this right. Do it wrong and I could be either decapitated or suffer a slow choke."

The warden nodded. There was a good deal of risk involved, and he and a few of his officers had traveled to the state of Washington, where they had recently carried out a successful hanging. The warden was confident they were ready to work when the time came. He would end up pulling the handle himself. But the needle would be infinitely less risky.

Evan turned and walked a few paces to the back of his cell, then turned to face the warden again. "I killed all those kids, Warden," he said. "I stabbed that tennis player in the belly. Hanging from that noose is what I deserve. And the only dignity I have left is that I get to leave this world in the ugliest way possible. And I shouldn't get to choose"

The warden swallowed hard and looked at Evan intensely. "My uncle's grandfather went that way, you know. The noose. He didn't die with any dignity."

Evan leaned his back against the cell wall, listening.

"They strung him up from a tree in western Mississippi," Wood said. "He didn't choose to hang. They just did it. But he never killed any kids. He didn't do anything. Just in the wrong place at the wrong time. But they stripped him naked, beat him, and strung him up while a crowd of people cheered. That's how the story goes, anyway." The warden took another deep breath and looked at the floor. "Dignity."

"I'm sorry, Warden," Long said. "It's not personal. I'm just doing what I think is right."

The warden looked at Long again. "Nothing is personal between us, Long," he said. "The only thing we have in common is our humanity and that book you read every night," he said as he pointed to the Bible which sat at the end of the small table in Evan's cell. "I haven't read mine in a long time, but I can tell you there are only a few ways to leave this world with dignity." He lifted his powerful hands and gently took hold of the vertical bars of Evan Long's cell. "But that's not why you're choosing the noose, Evan. I know why you want to hang."

Evan still said nothing. He just stared at the man on the other side of the bars.

"You're aiming to be remembered," Wood said. "The last man hanged in Delaware, possibly in the United States." A hint of disgust crept into his voice. "Nobody will ever know the names of the guys that have to do it. And most people won't even remember the names of the kids you killed. But everybody will remember Evan Long, the last man hanged. That's all you want, isn't it? You want to die with dignity, Long? Let those kids rest in peace. Take the needle, and you'll become just one more murderer who paid his debt."

Evan turned to face the small table. He slowly reached to pick up the list of names of the people he prayed for every night, most of them younger than twelve years old. "Warden," he said. "I'd rather discuss this with my lawyer from here on out."

Warden Wood put his hands back at his sides. The subject was over. "Whatever you want, Long."

Evan kept looking at the list. "Was there anything else we needed to discuss, Warden?"

"Yes, there is one more thing," he said.

Evan put the list down and looked at the warden. "Yes?"

"You have a few more requests for interviews. Shall I tell them no?"

"Is one of them Izzy Buchanan?"

The warden was surprised. Until now, the answer was always *no*. End of discussion. Now, Long actually knew one of the reporter's names. "You've heard this already?" the warden asked.

"I have," Long answered. "She's written me a few letters. She said she'd be asking for an interview right before my execution. Her story sounds interesting."

Wood couldn't believe what he was hearing. "You've never spoken to anyone out there for twenty years, Long."

Evan smiled thoughtfully. "That's what's interesting," he said. "There are five of us."

"Five of whom?"

"Five of us who were there and have never talked about it. She's trying to get us all to talk."

"And you want to talk?"

Evan stepped back to the bars. He examined the warden's face. "Yes, I do," he said.

The warden stepped away from the bars and looked down the hallway. "I don't believe this," he said.

"Can I, Warden?"

Wood scoffed. "I was just asking you as a courtesy, Long. I never dreamed you would say yes."

"But I'm saying yes, Warden. And now the decision is yours."

Long was right. As warden, he could approve or deny the interview for any reason. He looked at the inmate, trying to get a sense of what he was really thinking. It was not outside the realm of possibility that a man about to be executed simply wanted to see a woman up close one last time. He didn't want Long to get his hopes up; it could make for an especially ugly execution.

119

"It would be pretty rare to grant an interview the week of an execution, Long. A first for me. But I'll think about it. I'll have to tell your lawyer about it."

Evan nodded. "I understand," he said. "Just know, I've been a model prisoner, Warden," Long said. "You've been very good to me. I'll tell the reporter that."

The warden smiled and shook his head as he turned to walk away. He couldn't believe his ears.

Friday, August 6, 1976

Will Janicki places his key into the lock of the door on the auxiliary maintenance shed. He is surprised to find that it is already unlocked and slightly open. This annoys him because he suspects what is going on. The shed, known to the staff as "The Shack," has a small sleeping area with a bed, sink, and toilet. Will had always assumed the room was installed in case there was a job that took all night, and a maintenance man wanted to get some sleep without going home, so long as he didn't mind the smell of WD-40 and insecticide. Will had yet to see it used for that purpose, but he had witnessed many instances of camp staff making use of the room for other reasons. At least a few times a summer, he would find the door had been forced open. Upon entering, he'd hear the sound of one, or usually two, camp counselors moving about as they awoke unexpectedly. On two memorable occasions, he had walked in to catch a couple of youngsters deep in the throes of passion, not even aware of his presence until he ordered them to get dressed and out of there. He always hid his amusement, maintaining his stern expression even as they fumbled half-naked out the door. For this reason, he has requested several times that Father Francesco allow him to remove the cot permanently, but the priest has always dismissed the request. "It may come in handy some day," he always says.

Will's answer is always the same: "It's already come in handy, Father. For the wrong reasons."

This morning he coughs loudly as he enters, hoping to wake anyone inside before he catches a glimpse of anything unseemly. Fortunately, he finds that there is no one inside. He walks to the small cot and finds that it has been slept in.

A pillow has been arranged at the end, and there is a blanket he does not recognize. There is a large duffel bag and two empty Coca Cola bottles on the floor next to the bed. He does not check the contents of the duffel, assuming it belongs to one of the camp counselors. He straightens up the mess and leaves the shed.

It's a hot day, even for August. At seven in the morning, the humidity is already nearly unbearable. The campground is silent as most campers and counselors are still fast asleep. The only activity is in the dining hall where a few of the staff are arranging breakfast. Will adores this time of day. He knows within the hour, the grounds will be swelling with children and their young leaders, a different kind of joy altogether. At this early time of day, he takes in the majestic beauty of the hillside and listens to the frogs and birds as he makes his morning rounds. He walks to the trail that connects the swimming area to the tennis courts. Knowing that Joe Conway likes to warm up early on Tuesdays, he decides he will unlock the courts first. He begins the short but steep walk uphill. The humidity already makes it more arduous than usual, and he is already looking forward to the walk back.

Through the nearly silent hum that can only be heard on a summer morning, he hears footsteps and stops walking. They aren't close, but they aren't far. He glances at his watch. Two minutes until seven. Joe Conway never arrives before 7:30, and those aren't his footsteps, anyway. He hasn't heard a car pull up. He remembers the duffel in the shack. Someone has spent the night and is now walking nearby.

The echoing of sound off the hills makes it difficult to place the origin of the stepping sound until he hears the chain rattle. He spins around to see a man he does not know examining the lock on the fence that surrounds the pool. The man's back is to him, fifty yards away. Will charges full speed toward the stranger.

"The pool is closed," he shouts as he closes in on the man. "And so is the campground." The man is young, no older than twenty. He is small with long hair. He would look like a boy of fourteen if not for the facial hair. He is wearing khaki pants and a blue short-sleeved button-down shirt that's a little too big. He does not seem at all surprised or alarmed by Will's confronting him.

"I'm sorry," he says. He looks in Will's direction but not in his eyes. His voice is calm and detached, as if he has just woken from a long sleep.

121

"What are you doing here?" Will asks.

"Just looking around," the man answers.

"This is private property," Will says. "You need to leave now."

The man smiles and nods. He turns and begins to walk down the path in the direction of the camp entrance. He is no hurry.

"Hey," Will calls after him.

The stranger turns back around.

"Do you know somebody here?" Will asks. "A counselor, or a camper, or something?"

The man thinks for a moment, smiles again, and nods his head.

"Who?"

The man looks in the direction of the pool as he thinks again. "Actually, I know someone, but I doubt he knows me."

"How'd you get in there?"

"It was unlocked," he answers, and Will wonders if he forgot to lock it the day before. Then the young man's face sparks with realization. "I forgot my duffel," he says. "Can I get it?"

Will looks at the man suspiciously. He is conflicted as to what his next step should be. "Get it and get out of here," he says.

"Yes, sir." The stranger begins to walk toward the shack, having to walk past Will again.

"What is your name, son?" Will asks.

"Evan Long," the man says.

"Well, listen to me, Evan Long. You're not allowed to be here."

"Yes, sir."

Will wipes the sweat from his brow. "Are you on foot?"

The man is confused.

"Did you walk here?" Will asks.

"I walk everywhere."

"It's hot," Will says. "Do you have any water?"

The man frowns and looks at the ground.

"There's a clean thermos on the shelf inside the shack," Will says. "Fill it with water from the sink. The next time I see you here, I'm calling the police." He steps deliberately toward the man and looks him in the eyes. "You better believe I will do that."

122

The man smiles again. "I believe it."

Will watches every step the man takes as he walks back to the shack. When he emerges from the shed, Will notices that he has accepted the offer of a thermos of water. Will keeps watching as the man meanders down the long hill toward the campground exit. Will considers getting into his truck and following him. He even thinks about reporting the incident to the police. He does neither.

When the man is out of sight, Will shuffles for his keys and finds the one to unlock the pool gates. He unlocks all three, carefully wrapping the chains around the gates so they don't dangle. When he finishes, he begins the long walk up the hill toward the tennis courts.

By the time he makes it to the courts, he can see that Joe Conway has arrived at camp. He considers telling Joe about the strange visitor before he gets back in his truck to drive to the lake at the other side of the grounds, but he decides it can wait.

Sunday, June 16, 1996

"This is the spot where the first shots were fired," Will said as he pointed to the wet grass in front of him. Abel was surprised at this, thinking the shooting hadn't started until the gunman was much closer to where he had taken cover. The three of them were standing outside one of the two secondary pool gates. It was a spot situated on a small footpath that led to a shed with a public restroom. "Father thought about putting another small memorial right here but was persuaded that it was already enough to have the memorial at the entrance, and to rename the tennis courts and pool."

"Who persuaded him?" Abel asked.

"Board of directors," Will said. "They have the final say when it comes to new projects."

"And who's on the board?" Izzy asked.

"Mostly business people that belong to the various churches in the area. Investors. A few of them have been on the board since the place opened."

Izzy scribbled in her notepad.

123

"So it was probably right after Long locked this second gate that a counselor named Erik Pine came out of the bathroom. Nobody knows exactly what happened, but Pine probably asked the guy what he was doing, and the guy decided to start shooting. Erik was a bit of a tough guy, you know?"

Abel remembered Erik Pine. Tall and lean. Very loud. He led pretty much every group game and took every one of them way too seriously. Whether it was kickball or capture the flag, Erik wanted to win, and he rallied his team of twelve and unders mercilessly to do their best. Dropping a routine pop fly in kickball or whiffle ball was out of the question. And any camper who did so would incur his wrath. The rest of the counselors found it comical. Abel found it embarrassing, especially when he found himself on Erik's team. He had seen Erik earlier that day, and he had not known Erik was killed in the shooting until days later when he heard it on the car radio. Abel's father had quickly changed the station.

"So that was probably the shot I heard," Will said. He explained that he had been working on one of the kayaks at the lake. "So at this stage of the game, he has both gates locked," Will continued. "He keeps on walking right around to the main gate, knowing he has just about everybody trapped inside that fence." Will walked toward the main gate of the pool as Izzy and Abel followed. As they neared the main gate, Will pointed to the stone memorial that had been erected. It contained the names of all the dead, along with the text of the Prayer of St. Francis. "There was a wall here," he said. "Kids used to use it to play wall ball. That's where Joe Conway and Mike Springer took cover when they arrived from the baseball field. By now, Evan was standing here at the main gate, shooting. Mostly missing. But having a good old time, the sick fuck."

It was the first time Will had used any profanity, and Izzy made a note of it. Will saw her write it down and pointed to her notepad. "Please don't write that I said that," he said. Then he seemed to think about it for a moment, shrugged, then said, "Go ahead and write it. That kid was a sick fuck." He turned back to face the

124

memorial and continued. "There were two kids with Joe and Mike behind this wall, I think. Boys. They'd been playing wall ball instead of swimming, I guess." Izzy looked at Abel, expecting him to point out that *he* had been hiding behind that wall with Joe and Mike. However, Abel said nothing as he lifted the camera to take a picture of where the wall had been.

Will stepped over to the point where the wall once stood and made an outline of an imaginary one with his hands. "Nobody's exactly sure what happened at this stage of the game," he said. He pointed to the far side of the swimming pool. "I'm running along that path. Counterclockwise around the pool. I can already see the gate is locked. The kids are screaming and trying to force it open. One starts to climb the fence, but that makes him an easy target."

Will bit his lip. "I'll never forget that sight," he said, looking at Abel, as if he thought he shouldn't say it directly to Izzy. "In Korea, I saw a lot of men die, in a lot of horrible ways. But seeing that boy fall from that fence. That still keeps me up at night." He fumbled in his pocket and found his sunglasses, removed them from the case and put them on his face. His hands were shaking. "I went back to that spot a week later," he said quietly. "The police had sent people here to clean everything up." He looked across to the far end of the pool. "They never saw the blood up at the top of that fence. I got on a ladder and hosed it off myself." He inhaled and exhaled deeply. No one spoke.

Will coughed before he continued, his voice quieter now. "I kept running along that path that surrounds the pool," he said. "I went out of view as the path went behind the snack bar. He was still shooting, so I took cover back there. I poked my head out, waiting to see if he'd stop to reload. At that stage of the game, I thought I could at least help get the kids out of there when he stopped to reload, but I didn't realize he'd locked both the other gates. I stayed put behind that snack bar. I'm no hero." He turned to look at the monument. "Not me."

"Could you see him shooting?" Izzy asked.

"Not from where I was standing," Will said. "But I could tell it was a pistol. It turned out to be a .38, like the police carried at the time. He was carrying the rest of his ammo in a duffel bag. He had enough in there to kill everybody at camp if he'd been a better shot. "By now, I've called the police and I'm running in this direction. My truck is too far away from where I'm working to get to it." Izzy noticed that when Will switched his narrative to the present tense, his voice intensified, almost as if he was once again in fear for the lives of the children at camp.

He pointed to the imaginary wall. "Now, at some point, Joe comes running out from behind this wall and smashes the guy in the head with his tennis racket." He shook his head in disbelief. "A *tennis racket*. That's tougher than tough. But by now, the guy has already killed nine. Eight kids and one counselor. He's wounded at least ten, including a lifeguard. Poor thing has been paralyzed since she was seventeen."

"How could you tell it was a pistol before you saw him?" Izzy asked.

"I was in the Army," he said. "You never forget the sound of a gun being fired in your direction. Anyway, the shooting had stopped for a while - maybe ten seconds - and I thought maybe the guy had moved on, so I started running again. I turned the corner over there." He pointed to the near end of the pool, only a short distance from where they were now standing. Here's what I saw: Joe was laying on top of the shooter, bleeding badly from his side, but the guy was incapacitated. He'd taken a couple hard hits to the head. Joe's racket and a baseball bat were both on the ground, about ten feet apart. Mike Springer was standing over them, pointing the gun at him. His hands and knees were shaking pretty bad. I was still running, and it wasn't until I came to right here that I saw the Suddard boy. He'd been stabbed in the throat. Already dead." Will took another deep breath. "I went to him first, and I knew right away he had no chance. I moved on to Joe, and I saw he was bleeding out quickly, too. I took my shirt and tried to stop it. Long had been carrying a combat knife. He stabbed them both pretty deep. It turns

126

out his gun was out of bullets. Joe got him while he was trying to reload. With everybody screaming, he probably didn't even hear Joe coming up behind him." Will stepped carefully to the pool fence and looked inside. "This is about when I heard the first sirens. I decided I needed to get inside the pool area and see who I could help. But the other kid that had been behind the wall grabbed me by the waist and was screaming for me to come back and help the other boy. He kept telling me I had to help Jacob. But I knew it was no use. Jesus, it was awful. I just grabbed him by the back of his head and tried to pull him close to my side. Let him cry. There was nothing anybody could do. I tried to tell him to let me go inside and help the others."

Will stopped and waved his hand dismissively at the pool, all the important details had been discussed. "The police showed up. Took control of the situation as best they could. Eleven dead. Evan Long woke up before they put him in the ambulance, screaming that he was supposed to be dead, too. He'd planned on killing himself when he was done with everybody else. Joe didn't let the coward do it. Now he's going to answer for what he did." He looked at Izzy and shook his head. He had nothing else to say.

Abel and Izzy looked at each other, trying to decide if they had any more questions. Izzy gestured to the camera Abel was holding. He nodded. He had gotten the photos he wanted.

"Can you show us the lake now?" Izzy asked. "I'd like to see where you were when you heard the shots."

Will nodded. "Follow me," he said as he began to take a clockwise route around the swimming pool.

Izzy followed. Abel stayed behind.

An old memory had awoken inside Abel. It was the memory of a strong hand holding the back of his head, squeezing the back of his neck. It was the memory of his head being pulled into the sweaty skin of the man who told him that Jacob was dead and could not be helped. The awakened memory added to the still-piercing sounds of the sirens. The screams. It merged like an old, lost puzzle piece, perfectly with the thought of how he remembered the look in Mike Springer's eyes when Abel finally got up the courage to look at him.

He remembered the terrified, *guilty* look on the man's face.

***

Evan Long shuffled awkwardly down the short hallway to the conference room where he had met with his lawyer a day earlier. It was unusual to speak to him twice in two days. However, Evan assumed that he and his lawyer would probably be speaking a lot in the days to come. Evan was groggy, having been awakened unexpectedly by the guard on duty. With very little to do, and a clear conscience, sleep came easy for Evan Long during his time on death row. After waking him, Sgt. Dwayne Bond placed him in the required handcuffs and leg irons and led him down the hall to the conference room.

Sgt. Bond allowed Evan to seat himself at the table. "No time limit, Long," Bond said. "I'll be right outside."

Evan squinted as he looked around the small room. "There's no one here," he said. "Am I just waiting for him?"

The sergeant suppressed a chuckle, realizing he had not made himself entirely clear to the half-asleep inmate. He pointed to the phone.

Evan closed his eyes and shook his head in amusement. "My mistake, Sergeant," he said. "I should have known."

"Take your time, Long," Bond said. "The conversation is private." The officer stepped outside the room, closed and locked the door, and took one step back from it.

Evan Long and the men who guarded and protected him, and may soon kill him, had developed mutual respect over the years. The men appreciated his good behavior, while Evan appreciated their professional, and lately compassionate, treatment. Aside from a few hardliners over the years, Evan had been very impressed with the way he'd been treated. The men were never friendly, and never called

128

him by his first name, but they were always reasonable, even during the early years when he was prone to being irrational.

Evan picked up the phone. "Hello."

"Evan, what are you doing?" It was the highly-charged voice of his lawyer.

"What are you talking about, Raymond? I was sleeping."

"I just spoke to the warden," he said. "He told me you had consented to an interview." Raymond was practically shouting, but his voice was muffled. Evan figured he might be driving.

"I did consent. I've never done an interview," Evan said. "I didn't think it was a big deal."

"Evan, your hearing is Thursday!" Raymond shouted. "Anything you say in this interview can be used as evidence."

Evan was confused. "Well, I'm not going to say anything bad, Raymond. I just…"

"Shut up and listen to me, Evan. As your attorney, I am recommending you cancel, or at least postpone this interview. It can only hurt."

"Postpone the interview? I'll be dead in a week."

"Evan!" Raymond shouted. "That's what I'm trying to prevent!" He seemed to pull the car to a stop now, and his voice calmed. "You are not doing this interview, Evan. I won't allow it."

"It's not up to you, Raymond."

"Then I am going to recommend to the warden that this interview would pose a significant security risk to the courtroom and execution proceedings. I've known Andrew Wood for a long time. He'll see it my way."

"Raymond, I want to do this. There are things I think I need to say."

"Then say them to me. I can make a statement on your behalf. That's my job."

"That's not the same," Evan said.

"Evan, I can't protect you in a press interview."

"I don't want you with me."

Evan could tell Raymond was getting angry. He stammered, unable to find the words to say, finally managing, "I've never even heard of this reporter! Izzy Buchanan from Brandywine University? Who the hell is she?"

"She's written me a few letters," Evan said. "She has an interesting story idea. It's not just about me."

"Jesus Christ, Evan!"

"Please don't take the Lord's name in vain, Raymond."

"Evan, you have to reconsider this. If you don't, you'll have to find a new lawyer."

"You don't mean that."

There was a long pause. "You're right, Evan. I don't mean that. But this really is a horrible idea. Please reconsider. Think of all I've done for you, Evan. Do it for me."

Evan thought for a long moment. "I'll think about it, Raymond."

He hung up the phone and smiled, enjoying the feeling of control. He thought of Raymond, frantically pulling over to the side of the road to beg his client to see things his way. *Power.* He turned and nodded to the guard. He was ready to go back to his cell.

***

Abel took a seat next to Izzy at the small table in the camp employee room. It was a small room with a clock, refrigerator, coffee maker, and lockers. Some of the lockers were decorated with names of counselors and messages like "Have a great summer!" that they had presumably written to each other. The camp was set to open the next day, and the office was immaculately clean.

It felt good to get out of the hot sun and into air conditioning. They had toured the entire grounds of the camp, including the boathouse and the lake, where Will had gone step-by-step through where he was when he heard the shots. He showed them the phone he had used to call the police, which Abel had asked him to hold so he could snap a photo. Will had also shown them the auxiliary maintenance shed, known to the staff and others as "the shack," because of the young staff's tendency to sneak away from their sleeping quarters to "shack up," as Will had put it. "It was the Seventies, after all," Will had explained. "Every once in a while I'd have to chase a couple of the youngsters out in the morning. I'd turn my back till I was sure they'd left."

"Did you report them to Joe?" Abel had asked.

Will smiled. "Yeah, unless Joe was the one I caught." Abel watched as Izzy made a note of this, but he was surprised when she didn't ask any follow-up.

When they arrived at the employee room, Will put on some coffee and excused himself to use the bathroom. Izzy sat at the table and wrote feverishly in her notebook while Abel sat next to her.

"Getting anything good?" Abel asked.

"I think so," Izzy said. "Though I'm hoping you can help me clear a few things up later."

"I can," Abel said, and he sighed loudly enough for Izzy to hear.

Izzy stopped writing. "What?"

"What do you think about Will?" he asked.

"He's a reliable source," Izzy said without hesitation. "I believe he's telling the truth. Don't you?"

"He is," Abel said. "But it's the same truth he could have told five or ten or twenty years ago. Why aren't you pushing him on anything?"

Izzy bit her lower lip as she considered this. "Like what? You think he's not telling us something?"

"I'm sure of it," Abel said. "You don't wait twenty years just to recap the same story that's already been told."

Izzy looked around the room. "You're right. So what should we do?" she asked.

Abel leaned in close to her. "You should ask him again why he's waited so long to speak publicly about the shooting," he said in a whisper. "See what his reaction his. Go from there."

Izzy nodded. "Do you want to ask him?"

131

Abel's eyes widened as he drew away from her. "No," he said. "You'd better ask that. And don't be afraid to ask some follow-up questions."

Izzy's expression turned to offended. "What does that mean?"

"There are some stories here," he said. "He's talking about comparing his experience that day to what he saw in the war. He's talking about camp staff, including the Great Joe Conway, using the shed as a place to screw all summer. Why don't you ask about these things?" Then he added dryly, "*At this stage of the game.*"

"It's not that kind of story," she said, shaking her head dismissively. "This isn't going in a tabloid."

Will emerged from the bathroom and picked up the coffee pot and brought it to the table with three Styrofoam cups. He placed a container of sugar packets and a dish of creamers on the table as well. "This is as clean and neat as this room gets," he said as he poured three cups. "The summer staff will be in here tomorrow, ripping this place apart."

"Do you clean up after the counselors?" Izzy asked.

Will looked up at her in surprise. "Me? No way. Never did. The camp director makes them keep this area clean. If they don't, she does it herself. Always been that way."

"Who's in charge now?" Abel asked.

Will pointed to the first locker on the far end of the wall. "Katie Otto," he said. "Nice girl. Been here about ten years. This will be her third summer as director." Unlike the other lockers, it was not decorated. It only bore a small piece of masking tape with the word DIRECTOR written in black marker on it.

"Why no decorations?" Izzy asked.

Will took a seat and reached for the creamers. "The thing is, that was Joe Conway's locker, and he never had anything on the outside of it," he said as he fixed his coffee. "I guess they've kept it that way, you know, out of respect." He stood from his seat and walked to the locker. "But look at this." He fumbled through his pocket for a master key and used it to unlock the camp director's locker. "I don't

132

think she'd mind," Will said as he opened the locker door. He stepped aside so they could see the inside of the door.

There were two faded pictures taped to the inside. Izzy stood to get a closer look. Abel stayed in his seat and watched her. One of the photos was of a young man standing with his arm around a pretty young woman. Both were smiling, tanned with wind-blown hair. She was wearing a Sea Isle City sweatshirt, and Joe wore a Phillies t-shirt. The town around them looked alive as the night was getting underway. They were standing in front of what looked like an ice cream stand. The other photo was of the same smiling woman, now obviously expecting a child. She was wearing a yellow sundress, standing in what looked like a backyard.

"That's Joe and Abigail," Will said, exhaling heavily. "Abby was pregnant that summer. Their first and only. Joe must have taken that picture just before..." He stopped himself, trying to find the appropriate words. "He must have taken it just before that day." Abel stood to snap a photo, and Will carefully closed the locker, like he was closing a box full of precious mementos. "Abby gave birth about a week after the shooting," he said. "Joe just missed seeing his baby. It was one hell of a week for Abby."

"I wonder what became of him," Abel said.

"Became of whom?" Izzy asked.

"Joe's baby," Abel said.

Will walked back to the table and took his seat. "She had a girl, actually," Will said as he sipped his coffee. "Named her Elizabeth. But Abby was a private person. She still is." He looked at Izzy. "She's stayed out of the public eye ever since it all happened. The only reason I know that is because I cleared out that locker and took Joe's stuff over to the house." He looked at the locker again. "I saw the baby. I barely knew Abigail, but we cried together. She's a strong woman." He looked at the locker. "I just didn't have the heart to take those pictures down. I guess nobody ever has." He coughed and wiped his eyes.

The room was quiet for a time, the only sound coming from Izzy's notebook as she flipped a page and took more notes. Abel looked at

133

her face carefully as she wrote. She seemed to be moved by the revelations of the locker and the photos. Until now she had been impressively objective, sometimes even seeming to be more concerned with Abel's feelings. But Abel was surprised to see her wipe a stray tear from her left eye before she kept writing.

The silence was finally interrupted by the sound of approaching footsteps. All three turned to look in the direction of the door to the outside. Through it walked an elderly man dressed in black and wearing a Roman collar. Even for an old man, his steps were powerful. Will and Abel stood when he entered. Izzy did the same.

"Father Francesco," Will said. "I didn't expect to see you here today." Abel was amazed to see the old man he remembered from twenty years ago still standing, much less walking into a room and commanding attention.

"Nor I you, Will," the priest replied, in a thick Italian accent. "What is going on? You know I do not allow work on Sunday." His voice was surprisingly strong.

"I'm not working, Father," he said. "This is Izzy, and this is Abel. I'm showing them around. They're writing a story for the newspaper."

The old priest's face lit up as he turned to shake Abel's hand. "I am pleased to meet you!" he barked. "Sit down, Mr. Abel," he shouted. He took Izzy by the hand. "And Ms. Lizzy, a beautiful woman should *never* stand for a man, especially one as ugly as this one!"

Izzy smiled as she took her seat. "You aren't ugly at all," she said.

The priest pointed to Will. "I was talking about him!" he shouted, then roared with laughter. "Everyone sit!" he said pulling a chair for himself.

"I'll get you some coffee, Father," Will said.

"Wonderful, William. Thank you." He looked at Abel. "Will is such a good man," he said as he eased into his seat. He was a large man with big, heavy hands. Every gesture and movement was grand. "I could never have built this place without him. I keep telling him he is getting too old for this kind of work. He needs to enjoy his retirement."

"I'm trying to enjoy it, Father," Will said. "But every time a toilet overflows, you call me."

The priest shook his head and waved him off. "You are too old for this," he said.

Will scoffed. "You're ninety-one, Father. Why don't *you* retire?"

Father Francesco slapped the table with his huge hand. "Nonsense! I have a lifetime contract with the good Lord. I will retire when he is ready to take me home." He took a hot cup of black coffee from Will, thanked him, and placed it carefully on the table. "Now, you two," he said, becoming very serious. "I have just come from church. I trust you have done the same?"

"I went to early mass," Abel said.

The priest smiled. "Where, my son?"

"Good Shepherd in Manayunk," Abel said.

His eyes lit up with excitement. "I know this place," he said dramatically. "Very good. And what about you, Ms. Lizzy?"

"It's Izzy," she said. "I wasn't brought up going to church. I've only been a few times."

Father Francesco's face shrunk into grave concern. Everything the priest said or did seemed to be part of an opera. "My child," he said breathlessly. "You have God to thank for all the beauty in the world." He opened his arms wide as if the room where they sat proved his point. Then he extended his arms outward and joined his thumbs to make a frame of her face. "You must thank God for your own beauty. It is only through him that things in the world are so magnificent."

"I'll keep that in mind, Father," Izzy said.

"You must! Now tell me, have you come to write about this beautiful place?" He looked at Abel with curiosity. He glanced at Will, then back at Abel. He smiled. "You were a camper here, no?"

"I was," Abel said, quite surprised. "A very long time ago."

"I am ninety-one years old," he said, shaking his head. "You were not alive a long time ago! Your parents weren't even born a long

135

time ago." He looked closely at Izzy. He squinted, as he tried to place if he knew her also. "You were never a camper here," he said with authority.

"No, I wasn't," she said.

"But you have been here before, no?"

She laughed in disbelief. "One time," she said. "My mother brought me swimming here. I was…"

"You were four or five," the priest said. "Very tiny back then."

Izzy smirked with disbelief. "How could you remember that?" she asked.

"Your face, my child. It is unforgettable." He slowly turned and looked at Will. His pleasant demeanor was gone.

"Now, Mr. Will," he said slowly, a hint of suspicion creeping into his deep voice. "Tell me why these guests have come to our beautiful campground."

Will coughed. "They are writing a story about what happened twenty years ago. They…"

But the priest didn't let him finish. Izzy and Abel jumped as his huge fist came pounding down on the table. He shouted something in Italian. Abel assumed it to be profanity, or possibly a curse. The priest stood in one motion and stomped toward the door. Abel wanted to run out of the room. When he got to the door, the priest turned to Izzy. "You are a beautiful young lady," he said forcefully. "Like your parents before you. *Courageous*." He looked at Abel. "You are quiet, yes? Perhaps *timid*." he barked. "Not like that other boy, the one who followed that man into the fire," he said, jabbing a finger at Joe's locker. He looked at Abel with anger, then at Izzy. "You are digging up the past, yes?" he asked slowly.

"Yes," Izzy said without reservation, seeming to not be at all impressed with the priest's outburst.

He looked at her sternly. "This is not a good idea," he said, nearly in a whisper. "You will find things that should stay in the past. Prideful things. Things that will disturb the dead spirits of the innocent and the heroic. You will bring back the ugliness and death that once infested this place of God."

136

Abel watched Izzy's face. She didn't blink. "I'm writing the story, Father," Izzy said without hesitation. "No matter what I find."

The priest drew back as the opera continued. "Mr. Will," he said without taking his eyes off of Izzy. "You have shown these young ones the memorial, yes?"

"Yes, I have," Will said.

Father Francesco closed his eyes and nodded as if in prayer. "A holy place," he said. "A place full of evil and redemption." He walked to the window and gazed in the direction of the pool. "I pray there every day."

"Father," Izzy said, "Do you have an opinion as to whether or not Evan Long should be executed?"

The priest smiled, still looking out the window. "You are a strong one," he said slowly. "The words of an old priest do not scare you, not even one with a voice like mine." He picked up his coffee cup and took a sip. "You ask me what I think about the coming execution of one of God's children. A child who came to this holy place, bringing Satan with him." He turned to look at Izzy. "Do you believe in Satan, my child?"

"No," Izzy said.

"Do you believe in God?"

"Yes."

Father Francesco placed his coffee cup back on the table and raised his hands in front of him as if he was balancing an imaginary shelf. "There is not one without the other, you see? Without Satan there is no God," he said. "You cannot have the good without the evil. There is no love without hate. There is no war without peace. There is no lovemaking without murder. There are no new children brought to this earth without the promise of death." He sighed heavily. "There is a Satan. And this boy, this *Evan Long*, brought him to this place that day. There was evil here, and there was good here. The evil had its way, but only until the good was able to conquer him."

"But the good one died and the evil one is still alive," Izzy said.

The priest lifted his right hand and waved his finger at her. "But only for a time. Five more days, or five more decades. It doesn't matter. He has created a hell for himself." He pointed to his chest. "He has the devil inside of him. I wish to see the devil inside him die, not that boy. Not the *flesh and blood*. Evan Long must live a long time. He must find a way to kill that devil inside him." He shook his head. "But I don't know if he ever will."

"Would you be willing to help him?"

Father Francesco shuddered at the question. He turned back to the window and sneered. "I have been a good priest. I have gone into the prisons and celebrated mass with murderers and rapists. I have heard their confessions. I have forgiven them of their sins. But would I help that man make his journey back to God?" He shook his head. "I don't know if I could do this."

"Would you forgive him for what he did?"

"I don't think he is sorry for what he did."

"I didn't ask you that, Father."

Abel shifted uncomfortably.

The priest looked at her and smiled. "You ask brave questions, young lady," he said. "And you ask them boldly. There is much in store for you." He shook his head again. "Evan Long has never asked me for forgiveness. If he did, I would forgive him in the name of God's Holy Church. But I am only a man. I personally cannot forgive what I saw that day. Maybe this makes me a bad priest. Maybe my bishop reads that I say this, and he demands that I leave the priesthood." He waved his hand dismissively. "I am too old to worry about such things. I am only a man."

He walked back to the door. "I apologize for my earlier outburst," he said softly. "A gentleman should never lose his composure in front of a lady. You come to write a story, but not a good one. You write about the past. The ugly, evil past. I know of nothing good in this, but maybe I am wrong." He turned to leave. "I must go now." He raised his hand in blessing. "I pray that you find what you are looking for, my children," he said. "I pray that what you learn will not destroy you."

138

***

Mike Springer fumbled to find his cell phone. He could hear it ringing, but could not remember where he had placed it. He rarely received calls on the cell, so he never made it a priority to know where it was. He hated the damn thing. When he did get a call, it was almost always from Sheila or Bob to remind him of something he needed to say, or *not* say the next time he spoke to a reporter. When he finally found the phone in the desk in his home office, it had stopped ringing. Mike looked at the phone number of the missed call and tried to place how he knew it. It was familiar. He pressed the button to call back.

"Thanks for calling me back, Governor," a woman's voice answered. Mike immediately recognized the voice as Abigail Conway's. *Shit.*

"Of course, Abby," he said pleasantly. "I'm sorry I missed your call. It was really great to see you on Friday," he lied.

"You as well, Mike," she said. "I hope my remarks didn't throw a wrench in the works."

"What do you mean?" he asked.

"Come on, Mike," she said. "I know it's an election year."

"Stop it," he said, impressing himself with how sincere he sounded. "None of that's important right now."

"What *is* important right now?" she asked, sounding amused.

"What's important is that people got to hear from *you*, Abby. Abigail Conway,the widow of Joe Conway, spoke after all these years. That meant a lot, especially with everything that's going on. People care about you."

"Thank you for saying that," Abigail said. "I wanted to talk to you about that."

"About what?"

"About 'everything that's going on,'" she said. "I'm sure you've been asked to weigh in on the coming execution."

139

"I've decided to stay out of that talk. Too close to home." This was true. Mike wanted no part of the pending execution. He had even gone so far as to recuse himself from the pardoning process, announcing a year earlier that he would defer to the lieutenant governor in deciding if Evan Long should be pardoned, which he most certainly would not.

"*Please,*" she said, her voice as clever and disarming as it had ever been. "You've decided to dodge the issue because you don't want to sound like you're out for blood, especially to your liberal base."

Mike thought about this before replying. "Abby, we haven't spoken in over a year. Now you call me on a Sunday to give me a hard time about how I handle the media?"

"Yes," she said.

Mike had to laugh. "You're really something, you know that?"

"So are you, Mike," she said. "And don't think I was fooled by that face you were wearing on Friday. The last thing you wanted was for me to steal your spotlight."

He couldn't argue. He had always considered Abigail to be a friend, one that knew him too well. "Hey, in the long run, what you did was much more important, Abby. I'll figure something out." He meant it this time. "So, why *did* you call?"

"Well, as I said, I am sure you're going to be asked what you think about the execution."

"I already have, Abby," he said. "I tell them the same thing every time."

"*Justice for the families however the state decides to bring it about,*" she said, reciting his standard answer.

"That's right," he said.

"Can I ask you a favor, Mike?"

"Anything, Abby."

"There is a reporter who is writing a retrospective. Twenty years after the shooting. She may have already contacted you."

Mike felt the blood rush to his head. He took the phone from his ear and allowed his arm to fall to his side. He couldn't believe this

140

was happening. After a moment, he put the phone back to his ear. "What the hell are you doing?" he asked.

"I want you to let her interview you," Abigail said.

"No way, Abby. I don't want to be in that story any more than you do."

"She's already interviewed me, Mike. She needs you to tell your story."

Mike gritted his teeth. "This is not the time. I can't do this now," he said.

"What are you so afraid of, Mike?"

He struggled for words. "Abby, things happened that day. Things I wish I could do differently. I wish I could have... Abby, I..."

"It's okay," she said softly. "Mike, whatever happened that day. Whatever you did, or didn't do. It's not your fault."

"I know," he said as he gasped for breath, his voice breaking.

"The man whose fault it is going to be dead in a few days, at least he's supposed to be."

"I know," he said.

"It's his fault and nobody else's. I don't care what else happened that day. Do you understand, Mike?"

Mike exhaled deeply. "I understand, Abby," he said. "Things are just so complicated now."

"I know," she said. "You probably have your minions after her already, don't you?"

"Of course not," he said.

"Call them off," she said, ignoring the lie. "You have no chance of losing this election. You know that. And the presidential race is three years away. Would you rather be doing this then?"

"I'd rather not do it at all, Abby. I don't talk about that day, and I'd like to keep it that way."

"It is an important story, Mike. And she deserves to know the truth."

There was a long pause. "The *whole* truth, Abby?" he asked quietly.

"She'll find out, Mike. She knows what she's doing."

"But does she know what she's getting into?"

Abby didn't answer.

Mike sighed. "I'll think about it, okay? There's a lot to consider."

"Mike, you owe it to Joe. Besides, who would you like the media to hear the story from, me or you?"

"Abby, don't pull that. It's beneath you!" He could feel himself begin to sweat with anger. He took a deep breath. "I'll think about it," he said again.

He closed the phone and threw it back in the drawer. Then he slammed the drawer shut. "Son of a bitch!" he shouted.

***

Izzy and Abel found an empty sofa at Brew Ha-Ha, a crowded, trendy coffee shop around the corner from Will Janicki's house. Will had suggested they break for lunch, and they agreed. Will had said he needed some time to collect himself before finishing the interview.

Izzy ordered black coffee. She wasn't hungry and she had tons of notes to organize. Abel took a sandwich and a diet soda. Izzy scribbled while Abel ate.

She was annoyed when Abel asked her not to smoke. "It's a coffee shop," she said. "It's what people do."

"I'm trying to eat," he said.

She relented and put her cigarettes away. "Tell me what you think of Will Janicki," she said.

"Of what part?" Abel asked, biting into his turkey and Swiss.

"Of everything. Did anything surprise you?"

"You mean aside from the priest putting a curse on us?"

Izzy laughed. "He was pretty dramatic, wasn't he?"

"Italian," Abel said. "My mother's family is like that. Everything is drama."

Izzy smiled. She knew she would have to quote the old priest, even though her focus remained on the five witnesses. Her dilemma was knowing whether or not the priest was reliable enough to use as a source. She wasn't sure if Father Antonelli was a genius with an unbelievable memory, or a bullshit artist who had a special flair for making things seem more real than they really were.

"Are you going to quote him?" Abel asked.

Izzy affected her best Italian accent and looked at Abel with sinister eyes. *"I pray that what you find will not destroy you!* How can I not use that?"

Abel laughed. "That could be your lead."

Izzy sipped her coffee and ignored her hunger. Her goal was to regroup and get ready for the next round.

"That locker and those pictures," Abel said. "They were great."

Izzy nodded as she looked over her notes. "Amazing," she said. "That must have been the ice cream stand Joe was talking about, right?"

"Could have been," Abel said. "Did you ask Abigail what it meant?"

Izzy smiled. "She was funny," she said. "She said it was personal, but that she might share some day. It was cute, actually."

Izzy really had been genuinely moved by the photos for a number of reasons, mostly because she had seen them as the first reassurance that she should be writing this story. Until that point there had really been nothing new - a Governor whose people didn't want him to talk; a teacher who drank too much; a war veteran who had lost his wife. All were noteworthy elements to add to a good feature article. But that locker. Those photos. They could make that day come alive on paper. They revealed that there was still much to learn about what happened. Those pictures were the start of what Izzy had been hoping to uncover. And as Will Janicki opened that locker door and allowed her to look into the past, she was quickly overcome with that familiar rush of knowing she had a story. That exhilarating high that comes when a journalist has something that she knows no one else has.

Two photographs still taped to the inside of a locker twenty years later. Still taped to the same spot, not because they had been overlooked or because someone was lazy. They were still there because of respect. They were there to remember. They were there and would always be there because of what Joe Conway did, 20 years ago on a hot August morning.

A governor who wanted to talk, but couldn't. A boy who had a story to tell. Two photographs still taped to the inside of a locker. A story that needed to be told.

***

Will Janicki tried to keep his hands from shaking as he downed his third glass of water. He stood over his kitchen sink, looking into his backyard as he refilled his glass. He had hoped that by now he would have shared the truths that continued to haunt him, but the priest had interrupted things. Worried Fr. Antonelli would stick around all day, Will had suggested they break for lunch and meet back at his house. The reporter was fine with it. The photographer seemed to have other things on his mind. A drinker? Will had known a few of those in his time, the ones who needed it just to get through. Abel hadn't seemed like the type, but addicts often didn't.

They were due back any moment now, and once again Will wasn't sure he could go through with it. He closed his eyes and allowed his hand to reach for his ankle. As it gripped the cool metal, his hand stopped shaking. He stared at the loaded pistol and the hand that held it. Perfectly steady. He stared at the weapon for a long time. After a while, he felt a single tear run down his cheek.

His wits about him once more, he placed the pistol back in the ankle holster, where it had been all day. The doorbell rang. They were back. Before walking to the door, Will walked through the living room, stopping to look at a small photo of himself and his late wife. They were young and smiling, sitting on a sofa in a cabin in the Pocono Mountains of Pennsylvania. He couldn't remember who took the picture, but it had always been one of his favorites. Will had

144

convinced himself that he had lived two lives: one before the shooting, and one after. He had not been killed by Evan Long, but he had been nearly destroyed by him. The only thing that had kept him sane was his wife. He had been able to manage it with her. He looked around the house they had built together and at the photos of the children they had made together. Old memories that could have taken them both into the twilight, if only she had beaten the cancer. There was so much love that he knew would be wasted now. Poor, poor Katie who had been forced into a life of talking Will off the ledge so many times before she finally gave up her fight. Now she was gone, and all that remained were Will, the hard truth, and the pistol. He knew what he had to do.

He walked to the door.

Izzy walked ahead of Abel toward Will's front porch, where he was standing and waiting for them.

"Let's talk inside this time," Will said pleasantly. "Getting too damn hot out here."

"I agree," Izzy said as she followed him through the door. Abel followed.

"I just made some iced tea. Go ahead into the den and have a seat," he said, pointing to the small room to their right. "I'll be right in."

Izzy and Abel found room on the large sofa. Izzy glanced around at the well-kept living room and the dozens of knick-knacks and framed photographs. "You have a lovely home," Izzy called.

"Thank you," Will said, emerging from the kitchen with a full pitcher in one hand and three glasses of ice wedged between his side and his other arm. Abel stood to help him.

Izzy watched as Will poured the iced tea into the glasses. Something was different. He was talking very quickly as he offered them sugar and lemon. His hands were trembling a bit, and he seemed nervous. Izzy glanced at Abel, who seemed to notice the same thing. Will finally took a seat in a cushioned chair across the

145

table from them. He placed his trembling hands in his lap and took a breath.

Izzy decided to start. "Mr. Janicki," she said. "There are three questions I intend to ask all of the people I interview for this story. If possible, I'd like you to answer them in as few words as possible. May I?"

Will nodded. "Sure."

"First, what do you remember most about that day?"

"Screams," he said without hesitation. "It reminded me of combat. Korea. I've heard children scream in fear before. Hell on earth."

"Second, do you want Evan Long to be executed?" she asked.

He seemed to consider his answer. "Yes," he said. "But only because he is not repentant."

Izzy was taken by this answer. "Can you elaborate?" she asked.

Will's eyebrows raised. "Short answers. Your rules," he said.

Izzy shrugged. "Okay," she said. "But I might come back to that later."

"Whatever you need to do. What's the third question?"

Izzy wasn't satisfied, but she decided to proceed. "If you could, would you have done anything differently that day?"

She watched as the question seemed to hit Will like a hammer to the jaw. Without making a sound, he twisted his face and lowered his head into his lap, covering his head with his hands.

Izzy wasn't at all sure what to say next.

"Are you okay?" she head Abel ask.

Will lifted his head and looked at them. "Look, before I answer that, there are a couple things I want to tell you."

"I'm listening," Izzy said.

Will took a breath. "First, I have a few things to say about Joe Conway. Everybody knows what he did that day and all of that. I could not have done it, and I don't know anybody else that could have. But a lot of people don't know this, though. The guy was filthy rich." He looked at Izzy. "Did you know that?" he asked.

"Yes, I did," she said.

146

Will looked at her with a confused expression. "How?"

"I interviewed Abigail," she said. "She told me his parents were wealthy."

"That's right," Will said.

"And so what?" Izzy asked.

"I'm just saying, he didn't have to be running that camp and giving those tennis lessons; he just loved doing it," Will said. "He loved working with those kids. He could have taken his family away for the whole summer if he wanted, but he was at the camp every day at the crack of dawn. He was a great man *before* that day happened. Then he was a hero. I want people to know that, okay?" Izzy sensed an odd desperation in his voice.

"Okay," she said carefully. "Was there something else?"

Will exhaled loudly and squeezed his right hand until his knuckles cracked. "Yes," he said. "At this stage of the game, there are things that nobody knows." He paused, seeming to think hard about what he wanted to say. "Actually, two other people know this, and my wife *did* know it before she died. Aw hell..." He looked at the hardwood floor and bit his lip.

Izzy decided to help. "Who else knows?" she asked evenly. Her notepad rested on the table next to her pen.

Will looked up from the floor to meet her eyes. "Evan Long knows," he said. "But I guess he won't know much longer, will he?" He looked to his left. Izzy saw that he was looking at a photo that was hanging on the far wall. "And the other maintenance guy who was working that day. I told him." Will glanced around the room, and Izzy realized he was searching out photos of his wife to look at.

Izzy didn't ask the question. She could see that Will simply needed time. He squeezed his forehead in his left hand. He reached for his glass of iced tea, but when he lifted it from the table, it was shaking so much that he decided to leave it where it was. He looked helplessly at the two people sitting across from him. Abel shifted in his seat. Izzy was as calm as could be. She reached a hand across the table and placed it on the hand that Will had used to lift his glass.

Her hand was cool, and his was hot. Will looked at how her hand touched his. Izzy saw it in the man's eyes. He had longed to be touched. He looked longingly from Izzy's hand to the photo of his wife. He used a napkin to wipe another tear. His hands had calmed a bit.

"Take your time, Will," Izzy said as her hand squeezed his. "I don't have to tell anybody anything you say to us, okay?"

He shook his head. "That's not what you're here for," he struggled to say. "You want the details for your story. Otherwise, it's   a   waste   of   your   time."

"Not true," she said. "Trust me. I'll write the story no matter what you tell me. In fact, we can leave now, if you want."

"No," Will blurted out as he squeezed her hand. "Please don't. I want to tell you the rest. Just give me a minute. I'm not here to waste your time or mine." He took his hand from Izzy's and ran both through his white hair. "I agreed to be interviewed because I knew that I could not go on living without telling someone what I know. I used to cry myself to sleep three or four times a week thinking about it." The man's voice was deep and intense in a way Abel and Izzy had not yet heard. "Katie would rub my back. Pat my head. Tell me everything would be okay. Tell me it wasn't my fault." He reached for his iced tea again, then stopped. Izzy picked up his glass and took Will's hand in hers and helped him take a long drink. He thanked her and continued. "Well, she's not around to do it anymore. So I need to get rid of this thing that I've been holding inside me." He stood from his chair and reached into his hip pocket. He produced a folded slip of paper. He looked at it with disgust and dropped it on the coffee table. "Please open that and read it," he said.

Izzy took the paper delicately in her hands. Its age became apparent as she unfolded it. She saw the worn creases and worried she might tear it. Once it was open, she was able to read it clearly. It was written in pencil, in all capital letters.

YOU SHOULD HAVE STOPPED ME WHEN YOU HAD THE CHANCE. AND DONT CALL ME <u>SON</u>!

There was no signature. Izzy passed the note to Abel. She looked at Will while Abel looked it over. "Is that what I think it is?" she asked.

Will nodded slowly. He was still standing, now shifting his weight nervously from one foot to the other. He didn't say anything.

"You've never shown this to the police?" she asked.

Will closed his eyes and shook his head.

There was a period of silence while Abel and Izzy looked at each other. "Did you have the chance to stop him?" Abel asked.

Will nodded. Then he looked at Abel and spoke slowly. "I found that note a week after the shooting," he said. "It was stuffed inside a thermos I'd given him earlier in the morning. He and I had had a little run-in that morning. You see, earlier that day I found a bag in the shack, the auxiliary maintenance shed. I could have opened it, seen what was inside. Called the police. But I just left it there. I didn't even pick it up. I just figured Joe or somebody else had been in there with one of the girls the night before. But I was wrong." He closed his eyes and exhaled. "The worst massacre in the history of the state. One of the worst in the country." He tapped his chest with two fingers. "And *I* could have easily stopped the whole damn thing." He breathed deeply. "Every one of those kids would be alive today if it weren't for me. Evan Long would have been arrested. Joe Conway would have lived to see his baby. " He turned his head to look out the living room window. "Besides my wife, I'd only ever told one other person." He looked at Izzy. "But you'll write about it, and let *everyone* know, won't you?" he asked.

"Do you want me to?" she asked.

He nodded again. "Yes, I do," he said. "I need you to. But there's more I need to tell you."

***

149

Bob Casarini was startled when his cell phone rang. He had been staring at the gated driveway for more than three hours. He had already consumed two large coffees, a roast beef sandwich, and a bag of potato chips. He had also pissed twice into a soda bottle. It had been a long time since he had been on a stakeout, and he had not missed it.

"Yes?" he said quietly into the phone.

"Where the hell are they?" It was Sheila Avery, of course.

"I have no idea, Sheila," Bob answered. "That's why we're waiting outside their homes."

"Can't you call one of your cop friends and ask them to put out an APB or something?"

"Abuse of power, Sheila," Bob said. "Think about that. A multi-state manhunt for two private citizens who have done nothing illegal. Brilliant."

"We've already broken a few laws, haven't we?"

Bob gritted his teeth. "Sheila, we are talking on cellular phones."

"You're paranoid, Bob."

Bob ignored the comment. "Where are you exactly?"

"I am sitting in the same crappy coffee shop I was sitting in three hours ago. On my fifth cup," she said. "The bathroom here is disgusting."

"I am so sorry to hear that, Sheila."

"Sarcasm?"

"I have to go," Bob said. "I have another call." He pressed the green button to switch calls.

"This is Bob," he said.

"Go home, Bob." It was the governor.

"What?"

"You heard me. Cancel. Call it off. At least for now."

"What's the plan?" Bob asked.

"We'll figure it out."

Bob scoffed. "You mean *I'll* figure it out."

150

"That's what I pay you for, isn't it?"

"I'm sorry," Bob said. "Yes, that's what you pay me for. I'll call Sheila."

"Wait," the governor said. "Where is she?"

"She's camped out at a coffee shop outside the guy's apartment building. She knocks on his door every half hour to make sure he hasn't come in through a rear entrance, or while she's been in the bathroom."

There was silence on the other end of the line until Bob finally heard the governor say, "Leave her in place. Let her talk to him."

"Something I should know, sir?"

"We'll talk later, Bob. Make sure you talk to Sheila before you go to sleep. Then call me from your house phone."

"Got it."

They hung up. Bob started the car and put it in gear. He drove fast. He had to piss again.

***

"Now don't be alarmed when I do what I am about to do, ok?" Will said.

Izzy glanced at Abel. Each was trying to interpret the meaning of what Will Janicki had said, and how they should prepare for it. However, before she could even process the words, Will reached in one motion to his right ankle and produced a large handgun and placed it on the coffee table in front of him.

"Jesus!" Izzy gasped.

"What are you doing?" Abel blurted, standing where he sat, beginning to move away from the table.

Will raised both his hands in a calming gesture. "The gun is loaded," he said calmly, "but none of us is in any danger."

"What the hell is this?" Abel shouted.

"Just stay calm," Will said.

151

Izzy's eyes darted around the room as she tried her best to keep from panicking. She was looking for the nearest phone, or glass vase, or anything she might be able to use as a weapon.

"Everything is fine," Will said. "I just wanted to make a point." He extended an open hand to Abel's chair. "Please, sit back down. Nobody is in any danger. I have carried this with me every day for the past nineteen years. You can trust me."

Abel took his seat again. "It's a hell of a way to make a point," he said.

"You could have warned us," Izzy said.

"I   did   warn   you."

"You know what she means," Abel said.

"I apologize," Will said. "Just trying to make a point."

Izzy breathed deeply. "And what was your point?" she asked. Her nerves were beginning to settle.

Will scratched his chin and thought for a moment. He pointed to Abel. "What's in your pockets?" he asked.

Abel looked confused. "Just my wallet and keys."

Will nodded, then pointed at Izzy. "What's in your pockets?"

"Nothing," she said.

Will pointed to her purse, which sat next to her on the floor. "What's in there?"

"A gun," Izzy said.

Will looked astonished. "Really?" he asked.

"No, but you're scaring me," she said. "I wish I did have one."

"You mean for protection right?" Will asked.

"Sure," Izzy said.

"Okay, so you don't have a gun. What's really in there?"

"My wallet, a pen, address book, lipstick, breath mints, cigarettes, lighter, and a few personal items," she said.

"Great," Will snapped his fingers as if his point had been made.

"I don't get it," Izzy said.

"Neither do I," Abel said. "Why is there a gun on the table?"

Will carefully picked up the weapon and replaced it in his ankle holster. "The point is that I am the only one here with a weapon."

"So what?" Izzy asked. "I don't generally carry weapons on interviews."

"I need a drink," Abel said.

Will pointed over his shoulder toward the kitchen. "Help yourself to a beer," he said. "There's plenty in the fridge."

"He's joking," Izzy said. She looked at Abel. "We're working here." Abel didn't move.

Will looked at Izzy and smiled. "I'm impressed with you," he said.

"Why?" she asked.

"You have no fear," he said. "Maybe it's *because* you're so young, but you really are fearless."

"Why do you say that?"

"Let's start with how you treated Father Francesco," he said. "The man is a living legend. He walks around that campground like he's lord of the manor. But you weren't impressed. You were firing away at him with questions like he was just some kind of political hack."

Izzy smiled. "I've done a lot of interviews," she said. "Old men don't scare me."

"But they do scare a lot of people," Will said. "That's my point. And then I bring out a handgun and put it on the table. I watched how the two of you reacted." He looked at Abel. "What did you do?"

Abel thought for a second, then said, "I stood and prepared to run."

Will leaned forward in his chair. "Do you know what she did?"

"No," Abel said.

Will pointed a finger at her. "This girl, who's probably barely twenty years old, started looking around for something to clobber me with." He looked at Izzy. "Isn't that right?" he asked.

Izzy thought about it. "I looked around for a phone first, and then for something to throw at you. But I was looking for a chance to run too."

Will put his hands together. "That's my point. You're prepared to *do* something, while others would panic, run away, or do nothing."

"I've never witnessed a shooting," she said in Abel's defense. "Maybe if I ~~would have~~ ^had been present when eleven people were killed, my first instinct would have been to run."

Will nodded. "A fair point," he said. "All I'm saying is that you have the mentality of one who is prepared to act in situations in which many people would be indecisive or panic-stricken."

Izzy wasn't sure where Will was going with all of this talk, but she thought he was right in his characterization, at least of her. "Have you studied psychology or something?" she asked.

Will chuckled. "I didn't go to college," he said. "But I was in the Army, and since the shooting, I've read a lot and spoken to a lot of people who know a lot about the way people react to the unexpected. Some want to take action; some want to run; some instinctively protect the weak; others freeze and don't know what to do."

"What kind are you?" Izzy asked.

Will sat back in his chair and looked at the ceiling. "I'm not sure," he said. "You see, the first crisis situations I faced were in combat in Korea. And in those cases, I had people in charge yelling at me, telling me exactly what to do, so there really was no way to be indecisive. Plus, I'd been *trained* to act a certain way. That's what a lot of the self-defense stuff I've read says. You can train yourself to act decisively in a crisis. I don't know how I would've reacted if I had never been trained."

"Why have you carried that weapon with you for nineteen years?" Izzy asked.

Will looked at her curiously. "Listen to me," he said. "I worked at Kirkwood High School for a good thirty years, right?"

"I know," Izzy said.

Will chuckled. "Of course you do."

"Anyway, I made friends with an administrator over there. Ed King. We liked going hunting on weekends. He was a real gun enthusiast. Shooting ranges and all that. I wasn't really interested in that; I'd just come back from the war, so I didn't have much interest in shooting guns. But it turned out what I did with him, shooting ranges and such, really helped me deal with a lot of what I'd seen over there. Anyway, about a week after what happened at the campground, he came over to the house. He came in and sat right in this room and told me what we had to do. He said, 'Will, this is serious. There are too many crazies out there, and I'm sick of not being prepared.' I asked him what he meant. Then he reached into his wallet and pulled out one of these." Will pulled out his wallet and produced a small card with his picture on it.

"A concealed carry license?" Izzy asked.

Will nodded. "Eddy came to my house to tell me I had to get one, too. I thought about it for a while. I'm not a cop, so I wasn't sure I should be walking around with a weapon. But I just kept thinking that if somebody tried that again, I wouldn't want to be unprepared. Maybe I could save some lives, right? So that next week I did it. I applied for the concealed carry license, and I've carried a gun ever since."

"So you both were licensed to carry concealed weapons," Abel said.

Will nodded. "Believe it or not, just about anybody can carry a firearm, as long as it's not concealed. But most states require a license to carry a *concealed* firearm."

"I didn't know that," Izzy said. This was a lie, but she wanted to keep Will talking.

"Yeah it's true," he said. The tempo in his voice was quickening now. "But anyway, we both had our licenses to carry, and a couple days before school started, we went in to talk to the principal. Donald Haney was a great guy. We told him we needed to meet with him to talk about issues with the building or something. But when we went to see him, Eddy started talking about building security. That piqued Haney's interest, especially after what had happened at the campground. So as we were talking, Ed sort of eased open his jacket to show he was wearing a gun in a shoulder holster."

Izzy raised her eyebrows. "What did the principal do?"

Will smiled and shook his head. "Nothing. He went still for a second, and I saw his eyes get big, but then he just kept talking as if nothing had happened."

155

"Wow," Abel said.

"And then it was my turn, so I started telling Donald how much I agreed with whatever Ed was saying, and as I did, I put my foot up on the table like this." He casually placed his right foot on the coffee table, slightly exposing the holstered weapon under his pants.

"Did he react to that?" Izzy asked.

"This time, there was nothing. He didn't even blink," Will said shaking his head. "And we both got the message. So then we both took out our licenses and held them out for him to see, just for a couple seconds. He looked at them, but again, he didn't even flinch."

Izzy interrupted. "So this principal knew that he would have two men in his school who were carrying concealed weapons?"

"But he knew we'd been in the service," he said. "He knew that we were trained."

"I'd like to interview this principal," Izzy said. "Donald Haney you said?"

"Yes, but he's been dead for years," Will said.

"It's just hard to believe he was okay with this," Izzy said. "I wish I could confirm that."

"Not only was he okay with it, he moved our offices."

"What do you mean?"

"He had Eddy trade offices with a vice principal whose office was right by the main entrance. And he had me move into the office by the gymnasium entrance. They were the two most highly trafficked doors in the building."

"He liked it," Izzy said.

"Damn right he did," Will said. "He never said a word for another fifteen years. He's since passed away, and Lou's retired. But I know he appreciated the security."

While Izzy was busy writing, Abel asked, "Did you carry it at camp?"

Will looked at Abel and said, "I had it with me every single day I was there from that day forward."

"Did you tell Father Antonelli?" Abel asked.

Will scoffed. "He wouldn't let me carry a gun at that place in a million years. Even after what happened. Strict pacifist. He was a priest, after all, so you can't blame him. But he did appreciate some of the other stuff I did."

"Like what?" Izzy asked.

"At that stage of the game, I started having the counselors do all kinds of emergency drills. I brought in police officers to train them in reacting to a crisis. We did drills twice a month. Everyone knew what to do. Of course, a psychologist would say I was overcompensating for the mistakes I had made, but I didn't care. I wanted everyone prepared in case something like that ever happened again."

"Did anyone at the camp know you had a gun?" Abel asked.

Will nodded. "My assistant, Greg Burton. He's the other guy who knew about me finding Evan Long and his bag that morning. I'd recommend looking him up. He went on to work for the Department of Corrections. We still keep in touch. In fact, he works at the state prison now. We were very close."

"Why should I look him up?" Izzy asked.

Will scratched his chin. "He and I had very different views of things. You see, he got wrapped up in the peace movement in the 70s, even though he'd been in the Army, too. Got into the culture. Long hair. Sitar music. He was over most of it by the time he came to work at the camp, but he was still a big peace nut. I couldn't get him to carry a gun, but he never told anybody about mine. Interesting guy." Will paused and seemed to be thinking. "We became good friends. I only worked with him over the summers, but I always enjoyed it. He just had a very friendly way of saying things, even when he disagreed. He'd consider it a victory even if he just got you to *understand* his point of view. It really would be good for you to hear his perspective. Like everybody else, he was so angry about what happened, but he always said that Evan Long should not be executed. Don't get me wrong. He wanted him to suffer in jail. He just didn't want him executed."

Izzy knew this. "At the time Evan Long was sentenced, he told the newspapers he thought the shooter was 'disturbed' and that his life should be spared so that he could be rehabilitated."

Will looked at her. "You really did your homework, didn't you?"

"He's a prison guard now?" Izzy asked.

Will laughed. "Seems funny, right? A pacifist who's a prison guard. But he had it in his head that criminals need to be rehabilitated, rather than punished. Maybe that's what he tries to do."

Izzy leaned forward. "Do you think there's something wrong with being a pacifist?" she asked.

"Why do ask that?"

"You said we couldn't blame the priest for being a pacifist. Why would anybody *blame* him?"

Will looked at her and sighed with frustration. "Listen, if I had been wearing a gun the day Evan Long came to that campground, maybe he would be the only who died that day. Maybe *nobody* would have died."

Izzy squinted her eyes in confusion. "You were nowhere near him when he started shooting, and by the time you got there, Joe had already taken him down."

Will shook his head. "That's not the point," he said. "What if someone else had been armed, like one of the lifeguards, or a counselor? If Joe had a gun instead of a damn tennis racket…"

"You think lifeguards should carry guns?" Izzy asked.

Will threw his hands, clearly becoming agitated. "That's not what I'm saying. All I mean is that this whole thing could have been prevented if someone else there had been carrying a gun. A security guard. An off duty cop. Whatever."

"Maybe, that's true," Izzy said. "But it also could have been prevented earlier that morning, if you ~~would have~~ had looked in his bag, or   called   the   police."

"I know that, dammit!" Will shouted, startling both of his guests.

Everyone was silent. Izzy's pen was going crazy. Her

158

scribbling was all that could be heard in the room. When she stopped writing, she said, "When this story is published, Father Antonelli is going to know you carried a gun all those years. He'll know you saw and spoke to Evan Long that morning and that you could have prevented the shooting from ever happening. What do you think his reaction will be?"

Will breathed deeply, trying to calm down from his outburst. "I don't know," he said.

"Maybe you should tell him before the story is published?" Izzy asked.

Will stood from his seat. "To hell with that," he said. "After this story goes out, *everybody* will know that I'm to blame. That I kept it a secret all these years. And that's what I want. I've kept it in long enough. I even feel a little better now that you two know."

"Shouldn't everyone be blaming Evan Long?" Abel asked. "You never could have known what he was there to do. Nobody could."

"But I could have done more," Will said. "I could have opened that bag and looked inside. That was my job." He looked at Abel. "My wife would always tell me that. It wasn't my fault. Except when she'd say it, I would eventually believe her, at least long enough to fall asleep." He looked at her picture again. "Poor woman. I put her through hell over this thing for so long."

"It sounds like you've put yourself through hell," Abel said.

"Yes, I have. And I deserve it. I don't think I will ever forgive myself for what I did that day. For what I *didn't do.*"

"It was a mistake," Izzy said. "You didn't mean for anyone to get hurt."

Will scoffed. "Tell that to the parents of those kids," he said. "I've asked God for forgiveness so many times. But how can I ask those parents? Do I track them all down and ask them to forgive me? All their siblings? Everybody who was hurt by my failure to do something when I should have?" He looked at Izzy with desperation in his eyes. "Do you see what I'm living with?"

Izzy nodded. She didn't have the words to comfort him, the way another woman once had.

"Forgiveness is a tricky thing, isn't it?" Will continued. "I read in the papers all the time about the people who've forgiven Evan Long for what he did. I can't even forgive myself!" He shook his head. "Maybe after this thing goes public, I'll just..."

"What?" Izzy asked.

Will closed his eyes tightly. "Maybe I'll go visit Katie's grave one more time and thank her for getting me through it for all those years. Then..."

"Then what?" Izzy asked, her pen still moving.

Will pointed to the place at his ankle where his gun was holstered. "Then I'll probably just point this thing at my temple and pull the trigger."

Izzy stopped writing.

***

The interview was over and Abel stood with Izzy next to her black Acura. It was nearly three o'clock, and he was eager to get on the road back to Philadelphia. "Do you think he'd really do it?" Abel asked.

"I don't know," she said. "The guy is a bundle of nerves, isn't he?"

"Just the guy I want carrying a gun to school every day," Abel said.

She looked at Abel. "Would you feel safer at school if there were staff with guns?"

"In a way," he said. "But there's an unsafe feeling that comes with knowing you *need* guns to feel safe. Does that make sense?"

"I guess," Izzy said. "Do you ever feel in danger when you're teaching?"

Able thought for a moment. "It's always in the back of my mind but, no, I don't feel like I'm in any danger."

Izzy nodded, but he could tell she wasn't satisfied with his answer. There was nothing quotable in what he'd said. She looked back at Will's house. "I'm not sure what to do about this," she said.

"I don't think he'd do it, *at this stage of the game,*" Abel said.

Izzy shook her head as she dismissed the thought. She looked at her watch. "Train to Charleston leaves at 9:10," she said.

"*Tonight?*" Abel asked.

"Tonight," she said. "It's an overnight ride. We'll be there by 6 A.M. We sleep on the train. Do the interview tomorrow morning, hopefully, then spend the night in Charleston. Giving myself plenty of time. Back on the train Tuesday morning. We'll be back late that night."

Abel's mind was still processing. "You want me to get on a train with you tonight?"

She looked at him with eyes that were beginning to burn with impatience. "I told you this, Abel."

"I know. I know," he said. "It just didn't seem real until now. *On a train to Charleston tonight.*"

Izzy smiled wryly. "It didn't seem real?" she asked. "Do you think this is all a dream?"

Abel looked at her while she spoke. The lengthening shadows of late afternoon had begun to highlight her features. He looked around. "We need to get out of this man's front yard," he said. "Can we go get a drink somewhere?"

She shrugged. "I need to go get all this stuff written down," she said. "I also want to call this Greg Burton. I don't have time to sit down with him, but I would like to get some reaction to what Will said about him." She looked at Abel. "You need to go home and get yourself ready for the trip. The train leaves Wilmington at 9:10. You could just get a train from Philly and meet me at the station."

Abel nodded. "Okay, I'll be there," he said, still trying to sort out the details in his head.

"What is it?" she asked.

He looked at her. "How are you going to handle this?" he asked. "Are you worried Will could actually kill himself?"

"I don't know," she said. "He didn't say he was actually going to do it."

"But he said he might. Isn't that enough to be worried?"

161

"Just give him some time to calm down," Izzy said. "The story isn't about him. I'll call him later. I'll try to get him to understand that he's not the focus of the story. People won't blame him."

Abel smiled. "You gave it to him pretty good in there, you know that? When he started in on his concealed weapon stuff. No wonder he got freaked out. You are fearless, you know? Just like they said. Have you always been like that?"

"Always," she said.

***

Abel tried to avoid looking at himself in the mirror as he drove north on I-95. He had barely had time to process the new information he had learned today. Abel kept telling himself that none of what Will Janicki did or didn't do should matter anymore. But every time he did, that face in the mirror kept telling him it was vitally important. Abel knew he would torture himself over the possibilities of what never happened. He stepped on the gas.

He cruised north, through Christiana and Newport, with no intention of stopping. Northern Delaware is narrow to the point that an interested driver can catch a glimpse from I-95 of almost every town. Today, Abel was not interested in any of them, until he came to the first Wilmington exit. He decided he needed to stop.

He momentarily considered finding a bar to have a drink but figured that could wait. He slowly navigated his car through the streets of the west side of Wilmington, passing the car dealerships on Pennsylvania Avenue as he entered the city's tiny Little Italy neighborhood. He checked the clock. Half past three. He made the turn onto Chestnut Street and parallel parked. Before he got out, he checked the front and back seats. He grabbed the CDs on the seat and stuffed them into the glove box. He stuffed the small amount of visible spare change in his pocket. No reason to tempt any passersby. He exited the car and locked it.

Abel crossed the street and took the walkway toward the door of the small townhouse. He had not been to this place in a long time, but the memories were good. Safety. Privacy. Warmth. He extended his right hand to knock, but before he could the door opened. The old woman who opened it smiled. She had seen him coming. She opened her arms in celebration.

"Norman!" she shouted.

They embraced.

***

Izzy was disappointed to see that her mother wasn't home. That meant she would probably not be seeing her until she returned from Charleston. This wouldn't ordinarily have been a big deal, but a lot had happened since they had last seen each other, and she wanted to share.

She walked to the rear patio and lit a cigarette. Her mother wasn't home, so it was best to do it now while she could. No need to face a dirty look, a lecture, or both by waiting until later. However, if she heard her mother's distinctive footsteps approaching, she would have no recourse for covering it up. Her mother's sense of smell was beyond belief. It was about three o'clock and the train didn't leave until nine that night. She had time but felt she should be working on the story. The problem was she had only interviewed one subject of the five, and she had no idea where to start. The research was finished. The interviews and the writing were all that remained.

She looked across the patio at the swimming pool and thought a swim might feel good. She could also use a nap. *Forget it*, she thought. She took a seat at the table on the patio and unpacked her notebook and tape recorder. She needed to go over the interview. There was no time to waste.

***

The small house was exactly as Abel remembered it. The cluttered neatness of an aging woman's home was everywhere. Faded, framed photographs. Vases full of dusty artificial flowers. Candle holders. Shelves stuffed with VCR tapes, books, and outdated magazines. Eighty-nine years of life collected and stored in the two-bedroom

163

home where Abel had spent a good portion of his childhood, and some of his adulthood.

"Beer or whiskey?" his Aunt Sally asked, darting toward the kitchen.

"Just a soda, please," Abel said as he took his usual seat at the dining room table.

The woman stopped and turned around. "Did you stop drinking?"

"No."

"Then why don't you have a beer?"

"Because I'm going to have one later."

"So why not have one now, too?"

"I'm trying to cut back."

"I'm getting you a beer."

"Fine."

"I have some pierogi," the woman said. "I'll make it."

"Don't go to the trouble," Abel said, knowing his words were useless.

"Shut up," the woman said, placing a cold Dogfish Head on the table. "Still your favorite?"

Abel took a long drink, without answering. "You always take such good care of me," he said.

The woman began boiling a pot of water, poured herself a glass of white wine from an open bottle, and sat across from Abel. She reached out and took his hand. Abel squeezed. Her hand was warm and familiar. Weak but strong. She looked into his eyes and smiled. "Why have you been away so long?"

Abel shrugged. "I've been busy."

"It's been almost a year, Norman," she said waving at him dismissively. "I keep that beer in here just for you, but it gets old. I end up giving it to the neighbors. I was about to give that batch away."

"I'm glad you didn't," Abel said as he took another long drink.

"Well, relax and stay a while, okay? I want to see you."

"I have some time."

Sally stood to drop the pierogi into the pot. Then she dressed the table with forks and knives, butter, and sour cream.

She sat back down and looked at him. "You're still teaching," she said.

"Done for the summer."

She sighed pathetically, the way a dramatic old woman will. "You're too smart to be a teacher," she said.

"You sound like my dad."

"He was right about that," she said. "You could have really done something with your life. You still can."

"I like teaching," Abel said. "And a lot of people consider it to be a noble profession."

She waved at him again. "Please. June, July, and August. That's why you teach."

Abel couldn't argue with that.

"And a Catholic school, no less," she continued. "They're probably paying you with change out of the collection baskets."

"Pretty much."

"Let me give you some money."

Abel raised both hands in front of him. "No."

She looked at him and shook her head. "Are you still Catholic?"

"Sure," he said, smiling. "I go almost every Sunday."

"You were never Catholic a day in your life," she said. "Your poor grandmother would have a stroke if she knew you were going to Catholic services every week."

"Rituals are a good thing," Abel said. "Besides, I like going. It's quiet. Nice people."

"Those people just want to tell you how to live your life."

"They've never done that."

"They want your money," she said.

"They know I work there. I hardly ever put anything in the basket."

She leaned forward in her chair. "I don't think your parents ever even had you baptized," she said. "Your father was Episcopalian,

165

just like his parents, and me. But he stopped going long before you were born."

Abel nodded. "I know that," he said. "And I've been baptized. My friend did it. He's a priest."

"What?" she gasped.

"He's a priest at the church," Abel said.

Her eyes widened. "You mean you told them you weren't Catholic? Will they fire you?"

"No," Abel said. "I told him in confession. He has to keep it a secret."

She put her hand to her mouth. "What did you tell him?"

"Don't worry," he said. "I just told him I lied about my religion on the application. He didn't even care. He said I was a great teacher, and that's all he cared about."

She shook her head as she looked out the window. "What the hell kind of people are running that place?" she asked, posing the question to no one in particular.

Abel took a drink. "They're good people."

She stood to take the pierogi from the stove. Sally was the last member of Abel's family who continued to hold firmly to the Polish traditions that ran through her father's side of the family. She spoke the language when she had the chance, which was rare, but she still made the food, and lots of it. She placed the pierogi into a glass serving dish along with some sliced Polish sausage she took from the refrigerator. Abel filled his plate with the buttery noodles and covered them with sour cream. He devoured them quickly.

"You have something to tell me," she said.

Abel looked up from his plate. He had always been amazed by his aunt's sense of intuition. She could not read his mind, but she could always see through his thick curtain and detect when there was something there. This was a talent that Abel's mother never had, and if his father had possessed it, he had drowned it with alcohol.

Abel had known since he was twelve that his father had a serious drinking problem.

166

It would take his life fourteen years later. Abel had worried sometimes that he may have inherited the problem, but his Aunt Sally, who was actually his father's aunt, had made a career as an emergency room nurse, and she assured him that he was not an alcoholic like his father. She told him as long as he could get out of bed every day without having to think about his first drink, then he was not an alcoholic. Abel was pretty sure that this had never been a problem. Besides, she explained, his father had not been an alcoholic in the medical sense. He was not addicted; he simply used it to drown out the demons that tormented him. Abel sometimes wondered if he were doing the same.

Abel took a breath before he spoke. "I'm going to tell someone my story," Abel said. "I'm going to tell everything."

She stared at him with a concerned expression, not the surprise Abel had expected. He watched as her face became concerned, then happy. "You've met a girl!" she nearly shouted.

Abel was shocked. "What? No, I didn't."

She jabbed a finger at him playfully. "Yes, you did! You're in love, and now you think you need to tell her everything!"

Abel stammered. "No. That's not it. I mean, she is a girl, but it's not like that."

"I hope she's worth it," she said.

"She's a newspaper reporter," Abel said. "She's going to interview me. I'm going to tell her everything. I thought you should know, at least before it's published."

Aunt Sally raised her eyebrows thoughtfully and took a sip of her wine. "Your mother should know before you do something like that," she said.

"I know," Abel said. "I thought you could tell her."

"Why should I tell her?"

Abel stood from his seat and walked to the bookshelf that took up most of the wall. "You're better at this kind of thing," he said. "I know if I tell her, she'll get all weepy and I'll feel guilty."

"You're worried she'll talk you out of it," she said.

167

Abel shrugged and turned to look out the window into the backyard. Looking across the yard, he saw the narrow alleyway where he and his brother would play hide and seek. They would run the length of it, knowing the boundaries set rigidly by Aunt Sally, and always sure to use quiet voices until ten in the morning. Then he saw his reflection in the window. "I can't tell her," he said.

"Fine, I'll tell her," she said. "God knows, you've always had a problem with confrontations."

"I don't want to talk about that."

"It's probably why you could never ask a girl on a date."

Abel scoffed and took his seat. "Thanks for telling my mom," he said. "I'll call her in a couple days."

"When's the last time you spoke to her?"

"About a week ago."

Sally stood to collect Abel's plate and what remained of the food. "It's been twenty years," she said, assessing the news. "Nobody cares what happened twenty years ago."

"They'll care about this," Abel said. "Evan Long's execution is in a few days. The girl who's writing this story has uncovered some new details. It's going to be big news."

"How do you know all this?"

Abel shifted in his seat. "I'm helping her with the story. She's uncovered a lot that's never been made public. She seems to really care about getting the story right, and I want to help her. I'm taking the photos too."

Sally smiled devilishly. "She must be something."

"It's not like that," Abel said. "I want the story to be good."

"You've got a thing for this girl. I can tell."

Abel took a drink. "She's a reporter for a college newspaper," he said. "She's practically a teenager."

"It didn't stop you last time," she said.

Abel was quiet. Even though Sally had never been one to mince words or avoid an awkward subject, he was still surprised that Sally had brought this one up. Shortly after his father had died, Abel had briefly dated a student he had taught years earlier. He had been

168

twenty-six at the time, and it didn't last long. Physically, the relationship had not advanced past a prolonged kiss. They had stopped talking after the girl went to Virginia for college. He hadn't spoken to her since.

"I don't want to talk about that," he said. "This isn't like that, anyway. I'm just helping her with a story. She's a good writer and a really good interviewer." He looked at the table. "That other thing was just stupid. Dad had just died."

Sally reached across the table and took his hand again. "We all cope with loss in our own ways, God knows." She looked around the kitchen. "Your mother became a control freak. I cooked. You screwed a teenager."

"Aunt Sally!"

Sally broke into laughter. "I'm teasing you," she said, slapping the table. For the past ten years, Abel's aunt had increasingly begun to revel in the humor that came when old people made inappropriate comments. "It was getting too serious in here. Do you want any more food?"

"No, thanks. I can't stay that long."

"Why? What are you doing?"

"I'm catching a train," Abel said. "To South Carolina."

"Wow. What's in South Carolina?"

"One of the people this reporter wants to interview lives there now. She was a camp counselor at the time."

Sally's face lengthened with concern. "Are you going to be okay with this?"

"What do you mean?" he asked.

She stood and slowly walked next to him and put her left hand on his shoulder, and her right hand to his cheek. She looked deeply into his eyes. "All you have been through. Seeing Jacob go like that," she said. "Changing your life so many times. God knows you've been running around so much that I don't think you've ever had time to really deal with what happened."

169

Abel took her hands in his. "I'll be okay," he said softly. "This job I have has really helped. Working with kids. Going to church. It's been good for me. This will be good for me too."

She chuckled. "I'm glad you're enjoying it, but it's not who you are," she said. She jabbed a finger into his forehead. "You're no teacher."

"What am I then?"

"God only knows, Norman. You never say much, so it's hard to know, and I know you better than *anybody*."

"You do."

"But I shouldn't," she said. "A man your age needs a girl, not an old woman that he sees once a year. My mother used to say, 'Still waters run deep.' That's you, my dear. You need someone who has the energy to get into your head and bring out the best in you. I hope this thing you're getting into takes you to a good place." She paused and looked in the direction of the telephone. "And your poor mother. I hope the reporters don't come after her." She let go of him and tried to keep herself from crying.

"I'll talk to her in a couple days," he said. "The story won't come out until after the execution, so the madness should be over by then, if there even *is* an execution."

Sally frowned. "They're going to hang that boy?" she asked.

"That's the plan," Abel said.

"They should hang him, then pull his pants down and slice his pecker off."

Abel didn't laugh. "You want me to put that in the story?"

She shook her head. "Leave me out of it," she said. "Just be careful, Norman. I know how much you keep Jacob with you. I hope this thing you're doing is a good thing. For you, I mean. Digging up the past has a way of making things better, or worse."

"I'm counting on better," Abel said. "I've already met one poor guy so full of guilt that he actually made *me* feel better."

170

She looked at him for a long time, thinking. "Good," she finally said. "Let someone else torture himself. You did enough, God knows."

Abel nodded.

Sally smiled again. "And I hope you get the girl."

"I have to go."

***

Abel was on his hands and knees next to his bed. For a small apartment, he always had such a hard time remembering where he kept his travel bag. Finally recalling that he had stuffed it under his bed after his last trip to the Jersey Shore, he was hurrying to get it filled so he could get to the train station on time.

His aunt had convinced him to stay awhile longer so he could let the effects of the beer die off while they watched a few reruns of MASH, which had always been their favorite show to watch together. He didn't mind hanging out with her longer, but now it was seven o'clock, and he needed to be on a train to Wilmington by eight.

There was a knock at the door.

Abel ignored it, pretending he wasn't home, but it continued, becoming increasingly urgent. It wasn't loud enough to indicate panic, but it was annoying enough to let him know that he should answer, even if he was in a hurry.

He got to his feet and went to the door. Through the peephole he could see a small figure, a woman, bouncing from one foot to the other.

Opening the door, he recognized her immediately but could not remember her name. He didn't have to.

"Sheila Avery," she nearly shouted, thrusting her hand out for him to shake. He shook it. "I work for Governor Springer."

"I remember," Abel said.

"May I use your bathroom?" she asked sheepishly.

"Why are you here?" he asked.

Sheila looked like at him as if she had momentarily forgotten. "Oh, I need to talk to you about something. Something really

171

important," she said. "But I really need your bathroom first. Is it okay?"

Abel thought he should probably tell her to get lost, but he wasn't sure he was prepared for her reaction. Instead, he invited her inside and pointed her to the bathroom. "I'm in a hurry," he called after her as she darted down the hall. "So we'll need to keep it short, whatever it is."

"Of course. Of course," she called back.

Abel took a seat on his living room sofa and waited.

"I'm sorry about this," Sheila called as she washed her hands. "I've been drinking coffee and water all day, and I really needed a bathroom."

"It's okay," Abel called.

She emerged from the bathroom and asked Abel if she could sit. Abel told her she could, but was surprised when she took the seat next to him on the sofa. He watched as she settled in casually. She smiled at him.

"That's a pretty clean bathroom for a bachelor," she said.

Abel nodded. "I like things clean."

"How old are you?" she asked.

"Why?" Abel asked.

"I'm thirty-four," she said.

"I'm thirty," he said.

Sheila nodded as she looked around his small apartment. "Do you like it here?"

"Can I ask you what this is about?" Abel asked.

Sheila refocused on Abel. "Of course," she said. "I wanted to talk to you about this story your friend is writing. Izzy Buchanan?"

Abel sat up in his seat. "I just met her a couple days ago," he said.

Sheila smiled knowingly. "I'd be careful what you say to her."

"Okay."

Sheila looked puzzled, like she'd expected Abel to ask why he should be careful. "You know," she said, "she's not who she says she is."

172

Abel's eyebrows arched. "She isn't Izzy Buchanan?"

Sheila chuckled. "That's the name she writes under, but it's not her real name," she said. "Do you know anything about her?"

"Why don't you tell me?" Abel said.

Sheila shrugged. She looked around the apartment again before her eyes met Abel's. "Where did you go to school?" she asked.

Even though they were presently sitting on a sofa in Philadelphia, this was a question that was strictly between Delawareans. In fact, it was the most loaded of all Delaware questions. "Where did you go to school?" Anyone from Delaware knew that this meant, "Where did you go to *high* school?" It was asked often, and in a state the size of Delaware, the answer meant volumes.

There is a strangely wide variety of high school options for Delawareans, from urban public, to elite boarding schools, and where a Delawarean attended high school is often used as a gauge to measure that person's character and that of his family. It is a question asked as a friendly aside to potential business partners, romantic interests, or at family gatherings to the new man a young lady is dating. It is a question loaded with judgment, and it is easy for the answerer to see the wheels spinning inside the asker's head as he is quickly sized up based on the answer.

"I went to E.I.," Abel said, aware that Sheila almost certainly already knew where he had attended high school, and positive that she knew E.I. was short for E.I. DuPont High School. Even still, he watched the familiar reaction in her eyes. The reaction that said *public school, but one in North Wilmington, not too bad, I guess. A fairly affluent, well-funded community. It's not like you went to school in New Castle.*

"And you?" Abel asked.

"Iron Hill," she said.

Her tone was as harsh as they both knew it should be. Iron Hill had been considered to be an institution ranking just shy of a penitentiary by most people in Delaware, and certainly by the private schoolers.

For generations, those with the means had done all they could to avoid sending their children to public schools, especially after the

173

state had begun bussing children from the suburbs into the cities, and vice-versa. Any parents who could afford it began pulling their children in droves out of the public schools and signing them up at whichever schools they could afford - private or, at the very least, Catholic. Those who were unlucky enough to live in the areas of Wilmington and Newark that were serviced by Iron Hill High School either forked over the cash, moved, or bit the bullet and hoped their kids could somehow succeed despite the horrid environment of "The Hill." Apparently, Sheila Avery had. Not only had she succeeded, but she had even managed to become a close advisor to the state's governor, a man who was steadily rising as a national figure, and who could someday soon be running for president.

There was supposed to be an unspoken, mutual admiration between Abel and Sheila, as there almost always was between two successful Delawareans who had attended the public schools. Abel knew this, and he was impressed that Sheila would use this premise to start their conversation.

He offered the expected response. "You survived."

"Survived and thrived," Sheila said. "As did you."

Abel nodded. He appreciated her saying that. "So, what can I do for you?"

"Of course," Sheila said. "Izzy Buchanan, the *Highlands girl.*" This was to let Abel know that Izzy had certainly not survived public school, but she had attended Highlands Academy, a highly-regarded private school. It was just a half step away from St. Luke's, a boarding school that drew rich kids from all over the country.

"What about her?" he asked.

"Do you know why she is writing this story? Interviewing these people who have tried so hard to move on with their lives? Why is she bothering?"

"I don't know," Abel said.

"She hasn't told you?" Sheila said, implying that she knew the answer, and Abel didn't. "Don't let her convince you it's for some award."

174

Abel shrugged. "What can I do for you?" he asked again. "I really need to get out of here."

Sheila looked at her watch. "It's late," she said. "Where are you going?"

"Meeting a friend."

Sheila nodded. "I see," she said, getting to her feet. "I just thought I'd ask. I guess I'll get going."

Abel stood with her. "I'm sorry I can't give you more information," he said.

She smiled and glared from the corner of her eye. "That's okay, Abel. I understand." She started for the door but stopped when she got to it. "Oh," she said. "There is one more thing I wanted to tell you." She took a breath. "The Capitol police routinely run background checks for anyone who visits the governor. It's standard procedure."

"I'm sure," Abel said.

"And I thought you should know something." She sounded genuinely concerned now. "It seems they came across a young woman named Jessica Sheehan whom you had a secret fling with a few years ago."

Abel's eyes narrowed. "She was eighteen," he said. "And I didn't keep it a secret. I'm just a private person."

Sheila shrugged playfully. "I thought it was cute when they told me," she said. "The whole teacher-student thing." She looked at him for a response.

"Nothing illegal happened," he said. "There's no reason that would be on a background check."

"Oh, and one more little thing that came up," she said. "Mrs. Meghan Gayton." Again she waited for him to respond.

"What about her?"

"Your sister, right?" she asked.

"It sounds like you already know that."

"Yes, well, this is a little difficult." He watched as she turned the concern level up a notch. "The background check revealed she hasn't filed any income taxes for three years."

Abel bit his lip. "You ran a background check on me, and you found tax information on my sister?"

"The police ran the check, and it is quite thorough when dealing with the governor, who was also a member of Congress."

Abel felt his breath quickening. "My sister is unemployed," he said. "She's raising her two children while her husband works."

"I'm sure," Sheila said in mock reassurance. "The problem is that every other week she deposits checks for anywhere between two and six hundred dollars. I'm sure that if the IRS were to investigate, they would probably view that as income."

Abel started to sweat. He could feel the blood rushing through his head, behind his eyes. He said nothing.

"But I'm sure they would have no reason to look into it," she said dismissively. "I'm sure your sister will be fine." The two stared at each other for a long moment. Neither blinked. "But if somebody did ask them to look into it, Meghan could end up owing the IRS a lot of money. She could even be charged with tax evasion."

Abel said nothing.

Sheila smiled. "Crazy being from Delaware, isn't it?" she asked. "Everybody knows everybody. And if you don't, you know someone who went to school with them, right?"

Abel didn't smile back. He wasn't amused, though he knew she was right. Delaware was too small a state to be anonymous, which was why he was in Philadelphia.

Sheila reached out to pat him softly on the shoulder. "Thanks for letting me use your bathroom," she said in a whisper. "And have a safe trip to South Carolina, if you still decide to go."

She walked out, closing the door behind her.

***

After packing an overnight bag, Izzy dialed the familiar phone number of Professor Dennis Griffin of Brandywine University. Though it was a Sunday evening, she hadn't thought twice about making the call. He answered on the third ring. Though

176

he had been writing and teaching in Delaware for better than forty years, he maintained an accent that betrayed his deep Southern roots.

"What's going on, young lady?" he asked. It sounded as if he had been expecting the call and simply wanted an update. A month earlier, Izzy had told her trusted journalism professor about her story. They had just finished dinner at his North Wilmington home. Izzy and Mrs. Griffin sipped chardonnay while the professor sipped Jim Beam, which he loved more than anything except his wife and his job. Each semester, he would explain to his Journalism 101 class that he would go through sometimes an entire bottle of the stuff while he read and graded their first written assignments. The rambling, profane, and sometimes illegible comments he would add in red ink were proof of this. It was not uncommon for a wide-eyed freshman to read in smudged red ink that he would have been better off wiping his ass with printer paper and handing it in than in attempting to write a news story. Amazingly, neither the professor nor the university ever received any complaints about the abusive feedback. This was mostly due to the brilliant lectures the professor would deliver, which were a cross between stand-up comedy and Aristotle.

The professor had an incredible reputation for producing excellent writers by way of his Introduction to Journalism class. Unlike all of his colleagues, he insisted on teaching entry-level journalism year after year, despite the effects it had on his liver. As the semester progressed, and the writing of his students improved, the intake of bourbon, and the rambling comments came progressively under control. Professor Griffin relished in taking everything an eighteen-year-old had been taught about writing, forcing him to incinerate it in his mind, then starting with a blank slate.

Izzy had taken the professor's course two years earlier. Professor Griffin had recognized her potential early on and steered her away from the more mundane stories of bank robberies and stabbings toward the direction of investigative reporting. He had encouraged her to use her skills to "get to the bottom of things." She did. He was the one who had encouraged her to reopen the broken window story. "People need to know what really happened, and you're the one who needs to tell them," he had said.

During her research and writing of the story, she had become a frequent dinner guest at the Griffins' home. As the liquor flowed, the conversations became more and more lively among the three of them. They would debate heartily as to what should be left in the story or excluded. These conversations inevitably expanded to full-throated debates of journalistic principles and ethics. Disagreements arose often, and they usually ended with the good professor storming out of the room and passing out in bed, leaving Izzy and Mrs. Griffin to continue the conversation over cigarettes and countless bottles of white wine. Dr. Vivian Griffin was an esteemed journalist in her own right. She had retired from teaching decades earlier to focus her energy on writing full time, which she did to great results. Together, and separately, the Griffins had molded Izzy into a top-notch investigative reporter with an infinitely bright future. They were all disappointed when the story came in second place.

Never having had children of their own, they found that having a young person in their home on a regular basis was a pleasure they had not expected. Well into one late night, Mrs. Griffin confided in Izzy that the couple's love life had enhanced dramatically since she had shown up. Izzy took it as a compliment, and Mrs. Griffin assured her that she did not take it as an insult.

When the professor had heard Izzy's idea of revisiting the campground shooting, his white eyebrows had raised as he stroked his white goatee. After thinking for a long moment, he said, "If there's anybody who can get those people to talk, it's you. But going into death row?" He looked at her and knew that she would do it whether he approved or not. He sipped his bourbon and said, "I hope you'll call if there is anything we can do."

More than a month later, she was on the phone seeking his advice. He was listening. She explained in full detail how she had convinced Abel Ryan not only to be interviewed but to *cooperate*. "Good going," he said, remembering Abel as another promising

178

young journalist. "That boy has a great mind for journalism, if not the gumption. Takes good pictures too."

She went on to outline her unfortunate encounter with Governor Springer's staff. He scoffed at their treatment of her and Abel. "You don't need a nose to smell that story," he said.

This brought her to her present dilemma, which she outlined succinctly for the professor: a former maintenance man racked by guilt and driven by his love of the Second Amendment had announced possible intention to commit suicide once the story was published.

"Yikes," he said. "I guess you won't be able to use him for the *thirty*-year retrospective."

Izzy didn't laugh. "I was supposed to be getting on a train in an hour to interview the next witness. Should I keep going with this story?"

"Shit yes! This thing is your winner," he shouted. "Don't look back."

"What if the guy kills himself?"

"He won't," the professor said. "He's still gettin' over his wife dyin'. That won't last. If you're really worried about it, call the state police and let them know. They'll take it from there."

"What if they tell me not to publish?" she asked.

"They can't do that. You know that. Say, don't you have a contact in the State Police?"

The professor knew she had been in a relationship with a state trooper. It had lasted only a few months, and they hadn't spoken in weeks. "It's been a while, but we're on good terms," she said.

"There ya go," he said. "No rush. Don't get the police all riled up over this thing until you have to."

Izzy got the message: end of topic. The story prints, no matter what. "Everything else is okay," she said. "I just need to get the governor on board. Then Evan Long."

"If you get the first, you'll get the second, the way I see it. If he believes in the story, he'll get the warden to let him talk."

"That's my plan," she said.

"Good."

"You don't know the warden, do you?" she asked.

"Naw," he said. "I'd have already called him."

"You know the governor."

He sighed. "I do, but I'd rather you deal with him yourself. He's an old friend, of mine and the University's, and I don't want it coming across like a conflict of interest. But he'll talk. I think once he hears from you personally, he'll believe in the story."

"He did believe in it," Izzy said. "But his staff thought better of it."

"That's their job. You need to find a way around them."

"I'm working on it."

The professor paused. "How's your mom?"

"Thanks for asking. She's been great."

"You always say that, but I'm still glad to hear it."

"Thanks for your help," she said.

"Anything I can do. You know that."

"I do."

"Now quit talkin' to me and go give them hell. No compromises."

"Damn right," she said. "No compromises."

***

Abel had been staring into his bathroom mirror for more than twenty minutes when the phone rang. He decided to let it ring. After stopping for a second or two, it rang again. His mother, he thought. By now Aunt Sally had spoken to her, and his mother wanted to know all the sordid details and what she could expect to see when she read the story. She would want to talk him out of it. She would try to appeal to his sense of decency, and to their love of privacy, which he and his mother shared. He allowed the phone to keep ringing. He would not change his mind.

"I'm not changing my mind," he said out loud to the mirror. He said it again, this time listening to the sound of his own voice. Abel often wondered what Jacob's voice would sound like if he were alive today. As children, they had been told many times that their voices, like their personalities, were nothing alike. Would this still be the case? Would time, and perhaps distance, have reshaped their voices to reflect their different lives? Or would they have still been inseparable, like they had been before, causing their voices to inevitably take on a similar cadence and tone?

None of it mattered. Jacob Suddard had perished at the hands of Evan Long. Nine other children had been killed that day, but none in the way Jacob had. Rather than being the victim of a gunshot, he had died of rapid blood loss, brought on by a deep knife wound. Evan Long had slit his throat. The stabbing was swift and effective. Jacob had died quickly.

By the time Abel, who at the time had been known as Norman, stood over his lifeless body, Jacob was far gone and lying in a grassy, muddy pool of blood. He had not had the chance to speak any last words to anyone. He just died.

But before he had left the relative safety of that thin concrete wall where they had hidden, Jacob had spoken very clearly, and Abel could still hear his voice in those last words that he spoke to the future Governor Mike Springer. As Abel cowered in fear, while Springer looked frantically at both their faces, while Joe Conway charged Evan Long with nothing but a tennis racket, Jacob spoke urgently, without a trace of nerves in his ten-year-old body.

"Give me the bat," he had shouted. "Give it to me now!"

His mother answered the phone.

"Hello?"

"Hi, Mom."

"Hi, honey."

"Have you been trying to call me?" Abel asked.

"No," his mother said.

Surprised, Abel wasn't sure what to say. "What's going on?" he asked.

"I just got off the phone with Sally."

Abel was silent.

"You need to tell me something, Abel?"

"Did Aunt Sally tell you already?" he asked.

"She said you have a new girlfriend."

"Oh my God," Abel said.

His mother laughed.

"Did she tell you anything else?"

He heard his mother sigh. "It's your life," she said. "You think it's time to tell it, then do it. Just make sure you're doing it for the right reasons."

"I am," he said. "At least I think I am."

"That's good," she said.

"I wasn't going to tell you until it was over," he said.

"I know that," she said. "Why did you?"

"I thought if Jacob were here, he would want me to tell you now."

She paused. "Been looking in the mirror again?"

"Too much lately," he said.

"Stop doing that," she said. "You need to decide for yourself, not based on what...on what you think someone else would do."

"You don't think I should have told you?" he asked.

"I'm glad you told me," she said. "I just wish you ~~would have~~ done it because *you* wanted to."

"I guess I did, in a way."

"You're more like your brother than you know," she said.

"Jacob had balls, mom," Abel said. "I don't."

"That's your father talking."

"He was right about that."

Neither spoke.

"I hear you're taking a trip," she said.

"South Carolina. I'll be back Tuesday."

"Be careful, honey," she said.

"I'm always careful."

Friday, August 6, 1976

Shannon Maher steps carefully into the staff room of St. Maria Goretti's Campground. She is expecting to see Joe sitting at the table, sipping coffee and reading the newspaper, but the room is empty, and the only sound is the ticking of the time-clock. She has ten minutes before she is supposed to clock in and meet her group of four-year-olds at eight o'clock. She looks around the room, wondering why Joe is not there like he always is on Friday mornings. She steps to Joe's locker, takes a quick look around, and opens it. His tennis racket is not inside. He must be hitting balls on the tennis court. Then she remembers that her group has lessons early this morning. Her four-year-olds would normally be at the pool at that time, but yesterday's rain forced them to reschedule. She has a dilemma.

Shannon wants to talk to Joe before she sees him on the tennis court. She knows he will probably stop back in the staff room before he goes back, so she finds a pen and paper and writes a note that she knows will get his attention. "Game room closet. 9 am." *She signs it with a heart and no name. She folds it, tapes it to the inside of the locker, and closes the door. After a deep breath, she opens the locker again and reaches for the note. She stops when she sees the photos taped to the inside of the locker. One photo of Joe and his wife together, and another of Joe's wife by herself, this time visibly pregnant. After closing Joe's locker for the second time, she walks to the time clock and punches her card.*

She's made her decision, hoping it's for the best.

PART 3: GUNPOWDER

Sunday, June 16, 1996

"This way, Abel," was how Izzy greeted him as he stepped off the train in Wilmington. She was at the end of the platform, dressed in jeans and a white zip-up sweatshirt with a black tank top underneath. She had her bag slung over her left shoulder and was looking every bit the sophisticated traveler. Abel was suddenly a bit embarrassed to be carrying his sister's old duffel bag that read *Wilmington Softball* in huge letters on the side. He acknowledged Izzy's call with a nod and quickly made his way through the crowd to her, happier to see her than he had expected.

"Cool bag," she said, pointing. "Know someone who played for Wilmington?"

"My sister," he said.

She looked surprised. "You have a sister?"

"You didn't find her?" he asked.

"No," she said, looking disappointed.

"I'm glad there's something you don't know about me."

"I'll see about that," she said.

Abel looked around the station. "Can I ask you something?" he said.

"Of course."

"Why are we taking a train? It's cheaper and faster to fly. We won't be in Charleston until tomorrow morning."

"I know," she said. "But I hate flying. And being on the train for a long time will force me to work. I brought my laptop." She patted her bag.

"I see," Abel said. "Where do I get a ticket?"

"You don't," she said. "It's already paid for."

"Stop," Abel said.

"Already done. Don't worry. The paper will pay me back."

Abel laughed. "The Brandywine Review will pay you back? I doubt it."

"Once this story is out there for the world to see, they won't have any choice, believe me."

Abel rolled his eyes and stopped arguing. "Which way?"

After offering to carry her bag, and having her refuse in a way that denied further discussion, Abel followed Izzy across the station to their waiting train. Abel was surprised when Izzy continued walking past every open train door and toward the very end of the train where access was restricted by chain gates. She stopped and showed her boarding pass to the uniformed attendant at the gate.

"Second floor," he said extending his hand to the door. "First room on the left. I'll be up to check on you before we disembark." He looked at Abel. "Right this way, sir."

Not sure exactly what was going on, Abel continued following Izzy. They boarded the train and ascended the steps to the second floor. Abel watched as Izzy found the room they had been direct to and opened the door. They stepped inside. Abel's jaw dropped.

"What the hell is this?" he asked.

"This is our room," she said.

"I didn't know trains still had rooms."

"They do," she said, laughing. "And this is a long trip."

He looked around the space. What would be considered compact anywhere appeared as surreal spaciousness. In his mind, Abel had pictured cramming himself into a tiny seat, hoping the seat next to him would open up at some point so he could spread out a bit. Instead, he was looking at a room that contained a sofa, fold-out tables, and a fully-equipped bathroom. There was also a ladder that led to an upper berth where two beds formed an L-shape.

"This sofa folds out into a bigger bed, too," she said. "So we can draw straws to see who sleeps where."

"This has to cost a fortune," he said.

"It's not costing *you* anything."

"There is no way the paper is going to pay for this."

185

"We'll see," Izzy said, stuffing her bag into a closet and making herself at home.

Abel stood still, watching Izzy negotiate her way around the room with deft familiarity. When she realized he was watching her, she stopped and asked, "What?"

"Are you rich?"

"Why?" she asked.

"I didn't even know trains still had these things," Abel said. "This has to be a lot of money."

She looked confused.

"And that brand new Acura you were driving the other day."

"It's not brand new," she said.

"As old as your driver's license, I'll bet. And that's not that old."

She smiled and sat on the sofa, put her feet up, and opened one of the complimentary bottles of water. "Want one?" she asked,

"Are you rich?" he asked again.

"What does it matter?"

"It doesn't, I guess," he said. "It's just that I've never known a rich person before."

"Well, I'm pleased to meet you," she said, lifting her bottle. "Let's enjoy the ride."

***

"Charleston? You mean in South Carolina?" Bob Casarini wasn't understanding.

"Yes," Sheila answered, sounding as annoyed as ever. "They are both about to get on a train right now."

"How do you know?"

"I was in his bathroom a few minutes ago," she said. "He had it all written down. It was probably her handwriting, actually. *Wilmington to Charleston - 9:10 - Philadelphia.* I called a friend at

Amtrak. She confirmed. The train leaves Wilmington tonight at 9:10 and arrives in Charleston tomorrow morning at 8:25."

"Why the hell are they taking a train?"

"I don't know."

"What's in Charleston?" Bob asked.

"*I don't know.*"

"We need to find out," Bob said.

"Do you think *he* knows?" Sheila asked.

Bob thought for a moment, then said, "Beats me. I'll ask him tomorrow."

"Do you know anybody down there?"

"In Charleston? No," Bob said. "At least nobody who'd be willing to help us with something like this."

Sheila waited for him to speak. When he didn't, she said, "Should I go?"

Bob exhaled loudly. "Get down there. Jesus Christ."

"I'll be on the 7 A.M. flight," she said.

***

"Phone call for you, Long." It was the deep, familiar voice of Chris Aument, the corrections officer who had been assigned to death row for as long as Evan could remember, but only on the weekends. Evan had asked several times about the logic and circumstances behind the guard shifts on death row, but he never got a direct answer. Whether they were decided by seniority, merit, or luck of the draw remained a mystery to him. He looked up from his book. Having finished *The Great Gatsby*, he had moved on to *Childhood's End*, another one he'd neglected to read while he was in high school.

"Let's have your hands, Long," Aument said. Evan put the book down and placed his hands through the small opening in the steel door so the officer could cuff them. Aument then opened the cell door and asked Evan to turn around, placing one hand on his left shoulder while a younger officer, one Evan didn't recognize,

187

placed shackles on his feet and secured them to the handcuffs with another locking chain.

Evan felt Aument extend his neck to look into his cell while he held him. "Finished with *Gatsby?*" he asked.

"Yesterday," Evan said.

"You like it?"

"The stuff about the Twenties was good. I didn't like the end, though."

The officers turned him back around.

"Why not?" Aument asked.

"I don't like when the main character dies," Evan said.

Aument nodded. He glanced at the book Long had put down. "*Childhood's End*," he said. "It's been a while, but I remember it."

"It's not what I expected," Evan said.

"You want to talk about a crazy ending? That one is nuts."

Evan frowned.

"What?" Aument asked.

"I might not finish it."

The officer's eyes momentarily showed confusion until the reality of what Evan had said registered. "You want me to tell you how it ends?" he asked.

Evan thought for a moment. Chris Aument had been one of only a few guards who had ever engaged him in conversation over the years. He had come to look forward to the weekends when he would see the burly, boisterous guard outside his cell. They would occasionally chat about what Evan was reading at the time, but little else. The conversations were always brief, but Evan enjoyed them.

"Do you know why I'm here?" Evan asked him.

Aument nodded. "I do."

"Why do you talk to me? Nobody else does."

The officer shrugged. "I don't know. Moral separation, I guess?"

"What's that?" Evan asked.

188

Aument stepped forward to explain, speaking in a near whisper. "It means separating what a man did from who the man is, or was," he said. "I might have cheated on my wife a decade ago, but that doesn't make me a cheater. It makes me a man who once did a bad thing. Understand?"

Evan nodded. "Do they teach that at prison guard school?"

Aument smiled and shook his head. "I took a few philosophy courses when I was in college, but that's not where I learned it either."

"Then where?"

"The way I was raised," he said. "The Bible."

"The Bible scares me a little. 'An eye for an eye.'"

Aument shrugged. "It's a big book, Long. It says a lot of things."

"Which parts do you believe?"

Aument looked to his left and twisted his lips. "We don't have the time to get too theological here, but I like to look at it as if the old folks laid down the truth in the Old Testament, but then Jesus came along and set it straight it in the New. Like it needed to be clarified. You know, 'Go ahead and throw your stones, but let the one who's never committed a sin throw the *first* one.'"

"That's pretty good," Evan said.

"Yeah. Hate the sin, but love the sinner. I believe in that."

"You can do that with me?"

Aument shrugged again. "I try not to think about what you did, Long."

Evan looked at Aument and realized that since this was Sunday night, this was possibly the last time they would see each other. "Are you on the execution team?" Evan asked.

Aument shook his head. "I can't tell you that."

"I hope you are," Evan said.

Aument placed a hand on Evan's shoulder, a gesture that Evan initially thought was one of affection.

"Turn around, Long," he said. "We need to get moving here. Your lawyer's on the phone."

189

Abel slid the cabin door shut and turned to walk down the narrow hallway of the train, which had begun the trek south toward Charleston. He slowly made his way down the steps, holding the railing to stabilize himself while the train rocked gently back and forth.

A uniformed attendant at the bottom of the steps greeted him. "Can I help you, sir?" the man asked. He was old but energetic.

"Is there a place to eat something?" he asked.

The man pointed with his hand. "Walk through the next two cars," he said. "Dinner is over, but there's still food for sale in the lounge car. They'll heat something up for you."

Evan nodded gratefully. "Beer?" he asked.

The man smiled. "Whatever you like, sir. Have it there, or bring it back to your room."

Abel smiled. "Nice."

Izzy reclined in a corner of the dimly lit room within the train, pecking at her laptop computer. She wasn't writing yet, still organizing. Transferring notes from her pad to her computer raised them to an elevated state of importance, if only in her mind. *Doors chained to fences. Photographs still taped to a locker. A small child desperately grasping the leg of a maintenance man. The ominous words of an ancient priest.* These were the details of a story that she knew, now more than ever, would be the story of the year, if not the decade. She smiled to herself, knowing that her previous major story, one that blew the dust off a decades-old case and shed new light on a tragic accident, would be nothing more than a footnote in her career. This time she was uncovering unknown details about the worst mass murder in the state's history. A crime of unspeakable horror. In the wake of Evan Long's execution or pardoning, this story would take the state, and possibly the country, by storm. She already had enough for a story, and she was just getting started. She could feel an excitement

190

building inside her into something amazing. But there was no time to indulge in that now.

She closed the cover of her laptop and flipped back through her notepad. Finding what she was looking for, she placed the pad on the table and fumbled for her pen. *Abel Ryan* was scrawled across the top, with a long list of items under it, most of which had check marks next to them. Before reviewing the list, she added one item: *Sister??* This was intriguing. She had tediously researched just about every aspect of Abel's life, but somehow his sister had eluded her. Next to the word, Izzy wrote *softball* and *Wilmington*. That was all she knew at the moment. For now, this sister was a ghost, as Abel had once been. Izzy remembered the early days, months ago. Meticulously reconstructing the scene of the murders, drawing maps and diagrams, comparing the words of one eye witness to those of another. Recognizing when the accounts matched and when they conflicted. Determining who had it right, and whose memory had been warped by the horror of quickly unfolding events. Continuously coming back to a boy who was screaming for the maintenance man to save another boy who had been stabbed in the throat, from bleeding to death. A boy who gave up on the maintenance man then begged the future Governor, Mike Springer, who was busy pointing a pistol at Evan Long, who lay motionless on the grass, bleeding from his head.

After obtaining copies of camp attendance sheets of that day from public court records, Izzy was able to narrow down the identity of the boy to one of three children who had never spoken on the record themselves, or through their parents. After more research, she learned that two of those had not been at camp that day. One had signed up for that week but had never attended due to last-minute vacation plans. The other, a boy named Paul Celano, had feigned illness so he didn't have to go that week. Having never been thrilled with Maria G's, the overweight ten-year-old had been trying all summer to get out of having to go. His mother finally relented, allowing him to stay home by himself. He ended up spending his days watching television reruns, raiding the fridge, and fielding worried phone calls from his mother, who could not get out of work. Later in life, he would be racked by overwhelming feelings of guilt over the deaths of two of his best friends. When Izzy rang his doorbell on a rainy Saturday morning and asked him to share his thoughts, the man sobbed uncontrollably for over an hour. The interview had not given Izzy much in the way of useful material, except that the name of one of the boy's friends was Jacob Suddard. The man believed that Jacob had a brother named Norman who had survived the shooting, but he could not say for sure.

After eliminating all but one, Izzy had gone through every witness statement that had been made to the police and to the press. One name was left: Norman Suddard, whom most witnesses reported as being ten years old. Izzy checked every directory she could get her hands on. A thirty-year-old man with that name who had attended the camp did not exist, at least not one whom she could find. At that point, she decided to begin working under the assumption that Norman Suddard had changed his name, probably his parents' attempt to keep him out of the media. It had worked. *But why go so far as to change a child's name? As parents, couldn't they just keep reporters from talking to him?*

Making matters more confusing was the fact that the name Norman Suddard did not appear in any of the police reports either. The closest was the name Norman Jefferson, which appeared on the police report, but nowhere on the camp attendance list. Izzy assumed that this was either a mistake made by the officer writing the report or an intentional attempt to mislead someone. But who would have done this, and whom were they trying to mislead? A few witnesses, including Mr. Celano, had said that Norman and Jacob were brothers. Izzy hoped that Norman, now Abel, could corroborate this, and possibly even provide an explanation for the secrecy.

While in the thick of her research, Professor Griffin suggested to Izzy that she contact the Social Security Administration. She had already done that, of course, but he provided her with the name of a contact who could help her. She hit pay dirt. Norman

Suddard's name had been legally changed to Norman Jefferson two weeks after the shooting. The change was authorized by Norman's father, Dwight Suddard.

Mr. Suddard appeared to be covering tracks - changing his son's name and relocating. However, it seemed he hadn't wanted to leave Delaware entirely. The Suddards, along with Norman Jefferson, soon picked up and moved downstate, far below the C and D Canal, a landmark that many in Northern Delaware regarded as the end of civilization unless they were headed to the beach for the summer.

Norman Jefferson and his parents, Dwight and Cindy Suddard, and apparently a sister, spent the next several years in Leipsic, Delaware, from where Dwight continued to commute to Wilmington every day to work. Cindy eventually found work at a local office of the Bureau of Fish and Wildlife. Halfway through his ninth grade year, Norman disappeared again.

With more help from the professor's contact, Izzy found that Norman had reemerged, living on Wilmington's West Side, an area characterized by row homes and ethnic neighborhoods. It was also an area where, like most of Wilmington, one street could be populated with families and concerned citizens, and the next block could be one that people rarely walked down after dark.

Living on Chestnut Street with a woman named Sally Suddard, whom Izzy assumed was an Aunt, Norman was now known as Abel Ryan. He attended E.I. DuPont High School, where his aunt had made a career teaching English. Upon graduation, Abel enrolled at Brandywine University where he had majored in history and minored in journalism, making a name for himself as a writer and photographer before graduating and moving to Philadelphia. As had been his parents' plan, he had escaped every level of education without ever being associated with the shooting at St. Maria Goretti's.

He remained Abel Ryan when he took a job teaching in a Catholic middle school in Manayunk, where he was still employed. His keen eye for black and white photographs, along with his nose for journalism were shelved indefinitely as he took on the role of teaching eighth-grade social studies. Izzy wondered how he would have been able to land such a job, having no prior teaching experience and having taken no classes in education, at least none that she could see. Like many, Abel Ryan had a story to tell.

Izzy considered her progress and was happy. The interview with the governor had not worked out, but that was okay. The way in which it was handled would give her leverage. If she published the story and included the exchange, this would put him in a very bad light. His people had to know that. They just wanted to be able to coach him before finally caving to the interview. It was just politics. The interview with Will Janicki had gone better than expected, aside from the suicide threat. The chance meeting with Fr. Antonelli was an added bonus. As for speaking to Evan Long, Izzy was sure that once she got to speak to the governor, he would convince the warden to allow the interview. If not, Professor Griffin probably knew someone in the Department of Corrections who could help. At the very least, she had ~~several written correspondences~~ from Evan from which she could glean some good quotes for the story. She would much rather meet him in person, though. Pictures would be good. Now, she was on a train to interview, or at least *try* to interview, the only remaining witness whom she had not contacted. She was optimistic about her chances. Yes, things were progressing nicely.

And then there was Abel. *Norman.* The subject who seemed to hold so many secrets. The man whose parents had painstakingly kept him out of the public eye for decades, but who had agreed to step back into it. She wanted to hear his entire story and see him swell with emotion. She wanted him to know that he could reveal his past to her while knowing that what he told her would be considered sacred. Izzy wanted to hear it all and know it all. She wanted to know Abel the way that no one else ever had. In her heart, Izzy knew that he was the story she was looking for.

***

194

"Mr. Long," the squeaky voice said. "Thank you for taking my call."

Evan squinted. He had expected to hear his lawyer's voice on the phone, and this was not him.

"I hope I'm calling at a good time?"

"I'm on death row," Evan said sharply.

The voice laughed. "I understand. I guess you don't get many phone calls, do you?" This stranger's voice was trained and professional. It sounded like he made phone calls for a living.

"Who is this?" Evan asked. "They told me my lawyer was on the phone."

"Of course, Mr. Long," the voice said. "I apologize for not introducing myself. My name is Victor Gregory. I work for Raymond Woodson. I'm his assistant, and he asked me to call you so we could exchange some important information."

"Why didn't he call me himself?" Evan asked. "I don't know you."

"I understand," the voice said again. "He is currently out of town and unable to make calls to clients himself, so he has given me permission to contact some of his clients. Be assured that I am a paralegal, and as such, I am well aware of the importance of attorney-client privilege. Anything you say to me will be kept between us, and of course with Mr. Woodson. Do you understand, Mr. Long?"

Evan rubbed his forehead with his left hand. "Well, Mr...."

"Gregory. Please call me Victor."

"Victor, it's just that I have never discussed my case with anyone but Raymond, and I'm a little surprised that he's permitting this. He knows how I feel about this kind of thing."

"I understand, Mr. Long. He knows, and he has told me. That is why I am only calling to relay a few important things to you. Is this okay, Mr. Long?"

Evan squinted. His eyes were still adjusting to the much brighter light than what was in his cell. "I guess that depends on what information has to be relayed, *Victor,*" he said.

195

"I understand, and I will get right to it. First, your psychological evaluation is tomorrow morning at 9 A.M. Dr. Cras will conduct the examination. It is private, but you may choose to make the results public for the purpose of your hearing later in the week. Is this okay?"

"I guess," Evan said.

"Great. Secondly, Raymond would like for me to discuss with you the possibility of having

a priest or minister visit you over the next..."

"No."

"I understand. You have been asked that several times, and your feelings are well-known on the matter. Raymond wanted me to ask you anyway. He also asked me to let you know that this remains an option right up until the execution, if you were to change your mind. Raymond does not plan on an execution happening, but he does want you to know that this remains an option, again, if you were to change your mind."

"I won't."

"I understand. Third, I was asked to speak to you about a last meal request. The prison is willing to honor just about any request you make, within reason."

"Fried chicken is my favorite food."

"Fried chicken it is. With all the fixings, I'm sure. How about dessert, Mr. Long?"

"Well, I...look. I wanted to talk to Raymond about the doctor's visit tomorrow."

The man's voice stopped, thrown off its rhythm. "I see," he said. "What would you like to talk about?"

"I wanted to talk to Raymond about strategy."

"I understand," the voice said, falling back into cadence. "You just be yourself and answer all of the doctor's questions honestly."

"That's it?"

"That's it, Mr. Long."

Evan paused and looked around the cell. He peeked over his shoulder to see the stone-faced expression of the guard, one he did not know. "Look," he said. "This is my life on the line here. It could be my last chance. I need some advice."

"I understand, and don't worry. Raymond's opinion, at the moment, is that this examination will not make a world of difference either way. He's been reading a lot of precedents from around the country, and a psychological evaluation this late in the process won't hold much sway with the Board of Pardons."

Evan switched the phone to his other ear, a difficult movement, considering the chains. "What the hell does that mean?" he said, trying not to shout. "He's giving up?"

"Absolutely not, Mr. Long. Raymond has no intention of giving up. He has filed another emergency petition before the Delaware Supreme Court. They will be considering another appeal to your case."

"I don't know anything about this," Evan said.

"I know. Raymond has been doing a ridiculous amount of research over the last few weeks, and he's decided that this is the strongest course of action, coupled with a psychological evaluation in your favor."

"What's the appeal? What's the basis?"

The voice chuckled. "I'm not really even sure myself. He's been so busy. Something about the way the jury voted. He thinks he has a chance to get another delay. Then work from there."

Evan was suddenly hit with the familiar but almost forgotten, feeling of helplessness he had experienced so long ago. "I don't believe this," he said.

"You have an excellent lawyer, Mr. Long. He's working very hard."

"That's good to know."

"Great. Now, about your dessert."

Evan sighed. "Are you kidding? Something cold, I guess."

He hung up the phone and waited for the guard to take him back to his cell.

***

197

Abel was sober as a rock. He hadn't had a drink the entire day, and it was getting late into the evening. He had decided that he would remain that way until the interview was over. After finding the lounge car crowded with late-night revelers, he had decided to walk the length of the train. He'd found himself amazed by the self-contained city, complete with the upper and working class ends of town, rumbling toward South Carolina. He realized once again that there were so many layers of life with which he was utterly unfamiliar. It was a realization that had once driven him as a journalist to seek out the unusual and reveal it in poetic language to the public. Stepping carefully through the cars, around people who seemed as familiar with long train travel as one could be, his natural curiosity had gotten the best of him. He kept walking, taking in as much of the new experience as he could.

Abel had always possessed an insatiable desire to experience things foreign to him but common to others, to find and celebrate the beauty in the extraordinarily ordinary. In his second year at Brandywine U, he had written a feature story on pedestrian overpasses. He found and visited every walking bridge that spanned a road in all of New Castle County. Some crossed over the busy streets of small towns while other spanned major highways. He took beautiful photographs of, and from, each one. He spoke to people who walked them every day. Most of them had never really considered how awesome the notion of standing only feet above cars traveling eighty miles per hour really was. After a few suspicious, and sometimes concerned looks, Abel could usually get his subjects to admit that the idea was at least interesting. A few were kind enough to tell him they would take more notice from now on.

With none of his editors finding the story even remotely interesting, Abel submitted it to the Wilmington Journal, Delaware's largest daily newspaper. The editors there recognized his talent for writing and taking pictures, but were also not at all interested in printing it. However, there was one editor who had been taught at Brandywine University by a Professor Dennis Griffin, whom Abel

198

told him he knew. The editor called a friend at the *Delaware Sun*, the state's monthly news and feature magazine. The friend loved it and paid Abel $200 for the story and another $100 for the photos. It ran in the next month's issue and readers loved it. Letters poured in imploring the magazine to keep up the good work. Not wanting to let go of such a talent, the magazine offered Abel a part-time job on staff. He turned it down, stating that he needed to stay focused on his school work. The people at the magazine understood but told him to send them a story anytime. He never did again. Six months later, Abel was informed that the article was being considered for a major publishing award, one that would give him a leg up in the field of journalism. It would make him a big name in writing at the age of nineteen. After speaking to his parents about it, he asked that the article be withdrawn from the competition.

A life spent striving for anonymity had made for a short career as a journalist. Abel had been good at making the small things big: pedestrian bridges, massive abandoned textile mills that had become creative sanctuaries for teenaged artists, a 78-year-old farmer who had never left Delaware. His eye for stories was nothing like Izzy's. She found the big stories and blew them up. Her stories made things *change*. Abel's made people stop and look and see what they had missed all those years while they were trying at full speed to survive and thrive.

Abel began to make his way back through the several cars that led to the sleeping cabin. He was ready to talk.

Izzy would write the story, and he would change again.

"Is this the new U2 CD?" Abel asked as he slid the cabin door closed behind him. Izzy was reclined with her feet up. The rhythmic music was quietly pouring from her laptop computer next to her.

She nodded as she smiled. "It's not new anymore. It came out three years ago."

"It's new to me," he said as he settled into a seat across from her. "Anything after *Joshua Tree* is new to me."

"You don't like it?" she asked.

Abel paused and listened. The music was nothing like the sound of the band he had grown up listening to. Instead of Bono's heavy, dramatic vocals singing over The Edge's anthemic guitar riffs, he heard the brooding voice of the great guitar player, reciting poetry in monotone over what sounded like a machine-manufactured drum beat. Abel shook his head. He didn't like it.

"I like everything they do," Izzy said as she clicked the mouse to stop the music. "They could fart into a synthesizer and I'd buy it the first day it went on sale."

Abel looked at Izzy, then at the empty plastic cup that sat in the cup holder next to her. He leaned over to pick it up, but she playfully slapped his hand away. She smiled at him mischievously.

He smiled back. "You beat me to it tonight," he said. He reached for the cup again. This time she let him take it. Abel held the cup and its remaining ice cubes to his nose. Whiskey. It was mixed with what looked to be Sprite. "You're drinking seven and seven?" he asked.

She smiled again as her left hand slid into the space between her seat and the window. After a couple seconds, she produced a nearly full bottle of Seagram's Seven. She looked at him and bit her lower lip, trying not to laugh.

"Did you find that in my bag?" he asked.

She nodded.

"You went into my stuff?"

"You didn't hide it very well."

"I wasn't hiding it, and I don't mind sharing," he said. "Just ask."

"Okay," she said. "Now grab a cup. There's ice in the bucket."

"Later," he said. "I thought you were going to interview me. You can't do that if you're drunk."

"I'm not drunk," she said. "Not even close. I'm just relaxed."

"I didn't think you drank," Abel said.

Izzy looked out the window, smiling dreamily as the lights streamed by. "Something about being on the train," she said quietly. "Sipping whiskey or brandy while you slowly rumble toward your destination."

Abel laughed. "So you're a Romantic?"

"Just on the train."

He nodded. "Are we going to talk?"

"What's so funny?" she asked.

"Nothing," he said. "Let's get to it. I'll drink after that."

Izzy sat up in her seat and placed her miniature tape recorder on the folding table and produced her notepad and pen. Even though her head was a little light, she knew she was in fine shape to conduct an interview. She had been far worse in Professor Griffin's dining room on many occasions, and she considered many of those instances as among her best as a journalist. As she prepared to ask the first question, Abel beat her to it.

"Have you ever done it on a train before?"

"What?" she asked, eyes wide.

"Have you ever done an interview on a train before?"

Izzy exhaled. "No," she said. "I've never interviewed someone on a train before."

"I have," Abel said.

"When?"

"In high school," Abel said. "I interviewed kids who went to St. Alban's in Claymont."

"Why?"

"Because it was different," Abel said. "A lot of kids take the train there since it's right near the station. It's the only school in Delaware that's like that."

"So what did you do?"

She listened as Abel explained how he woke at the crack of dawn on a Tuesday morning during the winter of his senior year in high school and boarded the Claymont transit train toward Philadelphia. Once there, he switched to the southbound train headed back to Delaware. He looked for the small groups of kids in Catholic school uniforms that he had seen before. He introduced himself, sat with them, and asked them what it was like to travel to school by train every day.

"You thought this would be interesting?" Izzy asked.

"It *was* interesting," Abel said. "In some places, everybody goes to school by train but not in Delaware. It's got to be the only state where kids who live a block away from a school get on a bus to go to school in another town."

Izzy stared blankly at Abel.

"What?" he asked.

Realizing the awkwardness, she shook her head dismissively. "I just would have never thought of that as news," she said.

"It wasn't news," Abel said. "It was a feature story."

"In your high school newspaper?"

Abel shook his head. "They wouldn't print it."

"They didn't like it?"

"The editor loved it, but the advisor said that since I had skipped school to do the research, they couldn't print it. She wouldn't even read it."

"Did you try to publish it anywhere else?"

"No."

"I'd like to read it," Izzy said.

Abel smirked. "I'm sure you would."

"I would," Izzy said. "You have a perception that I don't have." She turned to look out the window. "You see the beauty in little things that I would never notice." She looked back at him. "Window washers. Pedestrian bridges. Kids riding trains to school."

"You read my bridges story?" he asked.

She nodded. "I thought it was brilliant."

This, of course, was a lie. Izzy had come across the story while researching Abel's journalism background. She had been impressed with the details but found no consequence in the content. She found it a waste of space for a topical magazine and thought the article would have been better placed in a travel guidebook. The photos were good, though.

"I already know you better than that," Abel responded. "You didn't like it, and you don't need to pretend you did. You write about the big things."

202

Izzy inhaled slowly. She was not used to having her wits matched, and the whiskey was making her a bad liar. She pressed "RECORD."

Izzy: In a couple of months, it will be 20 years since the day of the shooting. How often do you think about it?

Abel: All the time. Every day. Several times a day.

Izzy: Is there one aspect of what happened that you think about the most?

Abel: I think about my mother's face a lot.

Izzy: How do you mean? She wasn't there, was she?

Abel: No. But when she and my dad came to pick me up, the first thing I saw was her face. It's weird because my dad was walking in front of her. So I should have seen his face first, and I probably did. But my mom was right behind him, and our eyes met, and we both cried really hard.

Izzy: Did your dad cry?

Abel: No. He picked me up and squeezed me really tightly against his chest. And my mom put her hand on the back of my head. She squeezed, too. My dad felt hot and my mom felt cold.

Izzy: What happened after that?

Abel: One of the cops came over and asked my dad what my name was.

Izzy: They didn't know your name?

Abel: Well, it's complicated. My brother was killed. We were identical twins.

Izzy: I never knew that. Your brother?

Abel: Identical twins. Big reveal, right?

Izzy: It is. That would have been a big story. I kind of understand now.

Abel: Nobody could tell us apart except our families. When it happened, I was too upset to talk to anyone. So nobody could be sure which one of us was still alive. So the cops needed my mom or dad to confirm which one I was.

Izzy: I see. So who was Norman Jefferson?

Abel: Jefferson was my middle name. He didn't want to tell them my real name.

Izzy: Because you were identical twins?

Abel: I think he was worried about media attention. Headlines saying 'The surviving twin.' Stuff like that. So he gave the newspaper a phony name, though I'm sure he told the police my real name. He didn't want the media finding out.

203

Izzy: In the time that followed, your parents went to great lengths to hide your identity, didn't they?

Abel: (Laughs) You could say that. They were big believers in putting the past behind and moving forward. They wanted me to have as normal a childhood as possible, and, for them, that meant a whole new identity for me.

Izzy: But you were still the twin brother of a murder victim. That didn't change just because your name changed.

Abel: My parents would like to have thought it did. We never talked about Jacob after his funeral. Ever.

Izzy: Getting back to the day of the shooting, your parents had to have been devastated about your brother, but how glad were they to see you?

Abel: It's hard to say, and I've always had a hard time with that. I remember my dad saying to the cop, "This is Norman. Jacob is dead." Over the years, I've replayed that so many times in my head. I've tried to read the tone of my dad's voice. Was he glad it was me? Would he have rather it been me who died? Of course, he would never acknowledge it either way, but he had to feel something about it. Right?

Izzy: I guess.

Abel: I've spent the last twenty years trying to figure it out, but I don't think I ever will. My brother and I were very different personalities, so he had to have some kind of an opinion as to who he'd rather have survived. I'm convinced of it, and I wouldn't blame him for it.

Izzy: How were you different?

Abel: I was a thinker; Jacob was a doer. I overthought everything. I still do. Jacob would rather wrap his hands around something and take care of it.

Izzy: Can you give me an example?

Abel: There was a kid at school in second grade. Big fat kid. He'd bully me and another kid around at recess and lunch. Pick on us. Throw food at us. I would always think of ways to avoid him. Find ways to keep him from calling us names. Jacob was in a different class. When he heard that the kid was being a bully, he just went right after him.

Izzy: What did he do?

Abel: The next day at recess he went right up to the kid and punched him in the mouth.

Izzy: Wow!

Abel: Yeah. And the funny thing was that for a second the kid thought it was me who did it! He was on the ground, spitting out blood, saying, "I'm gonna' kill you, Norman!" And when I heard him say that, I wished it was me that had done it. But I would have never done anything like that.

Izzy: Did Jacob get in trouble?

Abel: Yeah. He got detention for three days. I went instead of him the last day. The principal never knew. And my parents wouldn't let him play outside for a week. But my dad was always glad he punched that kid. I still wish I had.

Izzy: Do you remember the boy's name?

Abel: Stanley Kowalski.

Izzy: The same one who was at camp?

Abel: Yes. He was killed by Evan Long three years later. I went to his funeral.

Izzy: He and your brother were friends.

Abel: Yes, they were. How did you know that?

Izzy: His mother spoke at one of the memorials. She mentioned Jacob's name.

Abel: Jesus. You remember everything. They did become friends after the fight.

Izzy: Boys are like that.

Abel: True.

Izzy: Where was Stanley when the shooting started?

Abel: I don't know. I've always assumed he was swimming. He was found near the pool, I think.

Izzy: He was wearing his swim trunks and goggles when they found him.

Abel (exhales deeply): Are you trying to get me to drink?

Izzy: Sorry. Where were you when it started?

Abel: Jacob and I were outside the pool fence playing wall ball.

Izzy: Anyone with you?

Abel: Another boy. Brian Moore. Ran like hell in the opposite direction when he heard it. Smart thing to do, actually.

Izzy: You didn't run?

Abel: No. I froze. Then Jacob grabbed me and pulled me to the ground behind the wall. After a minute he told me we had to run. I said we should stay *there. I've always thought that he would have eventually convinced me to run, though.*

Izzy: Why didn't you?

Abel: Because right then was when Joe Conway showed up. He knelt right next to us. He was breathing really heavy and sweating. He asked us if we were okay. Neither of us answered. Jacob asked if we should run the other way, like Brian did.

Izzy: What did he say?

Abel: He looked around, kind of frantically. Then he nodded and said, "Yeah. Run."

Izzy: But you didn't.

Abel: No. That's when I saw that he was holding a tennis racket and a baseball bat, one in each hand. Jacob asked what he was going to do with them. Joe didn't say anything. Then Mike Springer came running up and joined us behind the wall. He had come from the same direction, but wasn't as fast as Joe was. He was also sweating and breathing really hard. I could smell him, too. Like cigarette smoke and sweat.

Izzy: Did he say anything?

Abel: Yeah. He was a real mess. He kept asking Joe what the hell was happening, like Joe had any idea. Then Joe stood up and reached up to the top of the wall and pulled himself up so he could see over the top. Like he was doing a chin-up. He stayed up there a while, then dropped back down with the rest of us. Now there were four of us crouching behind that little wall.

Izzy: What were you thinking?

Abel: I was thinking I was going to die. I thought we'd all die. I remember hoping to hear police sirens.

Izzy: What happened then?

Abel: Then Joe told Springer what he saw when he was up there. He told him that the guy was walking outside the pool fence and making his way to the front, where we were. But he said the guy was facing the pool, shooting into the pool. He told Mike he thought he could sneak up behind him and knock him out. Mike just nodded. Didn't say anything. Then Joe said, "I'll go. I'll hit him in the head as hard as I can while he's looking the other way." Those weren't his exact words, but something like that. At that point, Mike said that someone had to have called the police by now, and that they should wait for them to get

206

there. But Joe just said he had to go. People were getting killed, and he had to do something about it. He was a real hero.

Izzy: That's what they say. Then what?

Abel: Then Mike told Joe that if he was going to try to bring the shooter down, then he was going with him. Joe said, "I'll go first. I'll knock him down. You come up behind me and jump on top of him. Then we'll get the gun from him."

Izzy: He had it all planned.

Abel: Yeah. Then he looked at Mike and said, "You want the racket or the bat?" Those were his exact words. I'll never forget that.

Izzy: Mike Springer took the bat.

Abel: Yes, he did. Joe kept the tennis racket. Then they just kind of stayed there for a second. They just looked at each other. Jacob and I looked at them. It was a weird feeling. Now, I would describe it as the look that maybe soldiers give each other as they're about to go over the top. I wouldn't really know. I was never in a war. Neither were they.

Izzy: Wow.

Abel: Then Joe said to Springer, "You ready?" Mike nodded. Then they waited for Long to pass us on the other side of the wall. It seemed like Joe knew right where he was the whole time.

Izzy: Why didn't you and your brother run away?

Abel: I don't really know. I guess it seemed safer with those two there. And remember, everything I just told you happened in about two minutes.

Izzy: I understand.

Abel: So then Joe stepped to the other end of the wall and peeked around the corner. He looked back at Mike and said, "Here he comes." Mike just nodded.

Izzy: Scary.

Abel: Very scary. Then, just before they went, Joe looked down at me and gave me the message.

Izzy: For his wife.

Abel: Yes. He put his hand on my shoulder, looked at Jacob and me. He said it so slowly: "Try to find a way to tell my wife I love her." He was so calm about it. I can still hear his voice. Then he got this look, as if he had just remembered something. Then he kind of took a breath, like he was trying to find the right way to say it.

Izzy: What did he say?

Abel: "Tell her to remember that picture of us in front of that ice cream stand. That's a really important picture."

Abel took a breath and sat back in his seat. He looked across to Izzy, who was holding her pen and paper, but barely taking any notes. He watched as her expression changed. She switched off the tape recorder.

"What?" she asked.

"I just realized it," Abel said. "I gave her that message twenty years ago at Joe's funeral. She nodded and hugged me, like she understood. Then she told me she still has that picture."

"So what?"

"So I think she was wrong," Abel said. "One of those pictures taped to his locker was Joe and his wife in front of an ice cream stand. I don't think she has the picture he was talking about."

Izzy put her pen down. "She has a copy of it. I saw it when I spoke to her."

"Are you sure?"

"Yes," Izzy said. "And he wrote on the back of it. *Our first trip to the beach together!*"

Abel thought about this. "That was his last message to his wife?"

"I guess," Izzy said. "You're disappointed?"

"It's none of my business," Abel said. "I just always thought it would have been something bigger than that."

"Abigail told me they loved going to the beach, and they would talk about bringing their children there someday. And that picture was taken in the spring. She was pregnant in the picture, so it was the only picture of the three of them at the beach."

Abel scratched his chin. "I guess that makes sense."

"Sure it does," Izzy said. "Can we continue the interview?"

Abel looked across the table at Izzy, watching as the fast shadows from outside the window danced across her face. He looked out the window to see the sleeping East Coast quickly moving by them. He saw the backs of townhomes with their porch lights on, and he

208

wondered if the sound of the train zooming by would wake the families inside, or if they had grown so used to the sound of the train rushing by that it would take something else to wake them from their comfortable slumber. A collision, perhaps. He looked back to Izzy. "I'm ready," he said. "What's your next question?"

Izzy picked up her notebook and scribbled the words *identical twin brother.* So far, that was the only thing that was new to her. She had known just about every detail of his story so far, aside from the personal perspectives, including the state cop asking his father to identify his son. Abel's parents had been so fiercely protective of Abel's privacy over the years that Izzy had never come across anything indicating that Abel and Jacob were even brothers, much less identical twins. She had deduced that they were brothers but had never been able to confirm it.

Looking at the man across from her, she realized she was now seeing the same face of the boy who was killed by Evan Long twenty years ago. His expression was stern, and his thoughts were somewhere else. He was suddenly suspicious of something, but Izzy couldn't tell what. Was he angry at her for finding his whiskey? Doubtful. He had seemed disappointed about the picture, and the message he had carried to Joe's widow. He had assumed there was a much deeper meaning behind it, not merely a memorable trip to the beach. But Izzy had seen the photo before, along with countless others. Abigail had explained Joe's endearing habit of writing his thoughts on the back of family photos, rather than just the date and place.

She pressed RECORD.

Izzy: Let's start with the three questions. You probably already have your answers ready.

Abel: Pretty much.

Izzy: What do you remember most about that day?

Abel: The smell. Gunpowder. It was summer. Just had 4th of July, and sometimes we'd sneak off and light firecrackers. Same smell. I was close enough to smell it, and I'll never forget it.

Izzy: Do you want Evan Long to be executed?

Abel: I did for a long time, but I really don't care now. He's been in since he was 19, and he'll be there 40 more years if he gets life. That might be worse than death.

Izzy: If you could have done something different that day, what would it be?

Abel: That's a tough one. I don't think I could have done anything differently.

Izzy: Why?

Abel: I was ten years old and frozen in fear. It's who I was. It's who I am.

Izzy: It's been twenty years since the shooting. You were there, and you've never spoken publicly about what happened. Why?

Abel: For most of my life, it's been about my parents and their wish for me to live as normal a life as possible. I guess they were extreme about it, but I've grown to understand why. It just became a part of life. Now it's a part of who I am.

Izzy: And you chose to continue hiding as an adult?

Abel: I don't call it hiding, but yes, I did continue living that way. I took up journalism in college, mostly photography and city news. But then I started writing features. Opinion pieces. My stuff was good, and sometimes controversial. I was getting a lot of attention from readers. Students, professors, even people who just happened to read my stuff. It was mostly complimentary, but it was that little bit of attention that made me realize how much I enjoyed my privacy. So I gave it up. Moved to Philly and went into teaching. Disappearing and reappearing is easier than most people think. You just have to know what to do, and what not to do.

Izzy: Was it hard finding a job as a teacher? Did you have any background in it?

Abel: No. Of course, when I applied, I embellished my experience and background.

Izzy: How?

Abel: I told the nun that hired me that I had a degree in education, and was waiting on my certification. She never asked to see paperwork.

Izzy: Wow.

Abel: I know. I have found that they are very trusting people in the church.

Izzy: Was it hard going into a classroom with no teaching experience or training?

Abel: The first year was tough, and I wondered if I would keep doing it. But I liked where I lived, and I'd made friends with one of the priests, so I decided to give it another year. It's gotten easier each year. I've since gotten my teaching certificate.

Izzy: Do you enjoy teaching?

Abel: Very much. But after this, I will be moving on. I'll need to disappear again.

Izzy: When?

Abel: After this is printed. It'll be out there, and I'll need to move on.

Abel watched as Izzy processed what he had just told her. Working against the alcohol, it took her longer than usual. He saw her realize something, and he knew what it was. She pressed the stop button on her tape recorder.

"What is it?" Abel asked.

"You can't do that," Izzy said.

Abel looked at her consolingly. "This is how it has to be, Izzy. It's not your problem," he said softly.

"This can't happen," she said, this time more to herself than to him.

"Good journalism has consequences," Abel said. "You knew this story would change things."

Izzy stood from her seat, stepped around Abel's feet, and began pacing the small room. "This isn't what I wanted," she said.

"It's not about what you want," Abel said. "I'm ready to leave my job. I'm ready to disappear again."

"I'm not using your real name," she said.

He shook his head. "Doesn't matter. Someone will figure out it's me, though."

Izzy stopped pacing and looked at Abel. She held her hands emphatically. "You can't do that! You're a good teacher, Abel."

211

"Izzy, your job is this story. Not my career or my life. This story is worth it, and I've already made my decision. It's not like I'm threatening suicide here."

"Stop it," she shouted. "You're a good teacher. Your students love you!"

"What are talking about?" he asked.

"It's true."

"How do you know?" Abel asked.

"I spoke to some of them," Izzy said.

"What?"

"Once I figured out who you were, I posed as a city reporter doing a story on Catholic school education."

"When was this?"

"Two weeks ago," she said as she returned to her seat. "I stood a block away from your school for two days holding a notepad, looking for the uniforms and grabbing them as they passed by." She looked at him. "*You* walked right by me, twice."

"That's creepy," he said.

"And this is terrible," she said, putting both hands over her face. "You should have heard what they said about you. They love you."

"Why did you interview them?" he asked.

"I thought it would be good for the story, especially if you decided not to cooperate. At least I'd have quotes from people who know you."

"I don't believe this. How long have you been following me?"

"It doesn't matter," she said.

The train came to a slow stop, and bright blue light began to bleed through the blinds. A soft voice crackled over the intercom. "*Ladies and gentlemen, we will be at this stop, Washington, D.C., for approximately fifteen minutes,*" it said. "*If you step off the train, please don't go far.*"

Izzy looked up. "I'm stepping outside for a minute," she said. "Can you come with me?"

"I don't smoke," he said.

"I know. Just keep me company. Might be weirdoes out there."

212

Abel shook his head. "Just be quick. Then let's finish this so I can have a drink."

***

Mike Springer stepped quietly through his rear screen door, quietly closing it behind him. It was nearly midnight, and he didn't want to be heard. His wife, Lilly, and two sons, Joseph and Anthony, like him, were light sleepers.

He lit a cigarette. A heavy smoker in college, and the decade after, he had spent the last fifteen years trying to kick the habit entirely. When his second son was born, he decided to stop messing around and be done with it. Until now, it had worked.

He pulled the cellular phone from his pocket and dialed Bob's number. He answered on the first ring. "She's on her way to Charleston, sir."

"Sheila or the reporter?" Mike asked.

"Both."

"What the hell is in Charleston?"

"Don't know," Bob said. "That's why Sheila's going. Catching an early flight. She'll get there before they do. Find them and figure out what they're up to."

"Christ, Bob. Is this legal?"

Bob paused. "She's acting independently, sir."

"Damn right she is. I don't want any part of this."

"I understand."

"I'm rethinking the whole thing, Bob," Mike said. "I should have just done the damn interview."

"I understand," Bob said again. "We just want to be sure of her intentions, considering her background. There is a lot at stake here. For you, I mean."

"For you too, Bob," Mike said. "And trust me. You don't know the half of it."

"I do trust you. That's why we're going to get this figured out before you talk to her."

213

"The kid doesn't even know what she's getting herself into," Springer said. "If she finds everything she's looking for, Sheila and you won't have to shut her up. She'll wish she never even opened this can of shit."

There was a long pause. Mike found a seat on an expensive piece of patio furniture. "Bob, this is where you're supposed to say, 'I understand,'" he said into the phone.

"I don't understand, actually," Bob said. "Can you explain, so I know what the hell we're dealing with here?"

"You'll find out sooner or later, probably from Sheila."

"Find out what?" Bob asked.

Mike extinguished his cigarette on the brick walkway. "I'm not getting into that, Bob," he said. "But let's just say there is a reason I've never embraced being called a hero."

"Okay," Bob said. "That's not a lot, but I'll take it."

Mike sighed. "Just tell Sheila not to get careless down there. And I better not see any travel receipts."

"Never. Everything is on her card. Or cash. I'll figure it out later. Sheila is damn good, sir. Relentless."

"I know she is. Keep me posted," Mike said. He closed his phone.

Mike stood to go back inside but was surprised to see Lilly standing at the screen door. She was smiling and shaking her head. She had caught her husband in the act, up to his old habit. "What's all this about?" she asked. Her voice was easy. She wasn't there to give him a hard time.

Mike smiled back, realizing he must look as anxious as he felt. As a career politician, he had learned there was one person who could spot one of his lies every time, and he was now married to her. "There's a reporter," he said. "She's digging up an old story. Not a pretty one."

Lilly opened the door and beckoned him to come in. "Is it going to make you look bad?" she asked. It was a question she had asked many times before.

Mike thought for a moment. "Bob and Sheila seem to think it will."

"They're pretty smart."

"I'm smart, too," he said, surprised.

"Then what do you think?"

"It won't make me look *good*," he said. "But it might make some other people look *really* bad. They're trying to keep it from getting out."

He watched as she stepped closer to him. She winced at the smell of the smoke, but put her arms around his waist and gently put her head in his chest. "Tell me about it?" she asked.

"No," he whispered.

"Anything you can do about it right now?"

"No."

"Then come back to bed."

"Okay," he said.

"After you brush your teeth."

"Yes, ma'am."

***

It took three calls for the professor to finally pick up the phone.

"Hello?" he said, his voice weak with sleep.

"Dr. Griffin. I need to talk to you," she said.

"Izzy? It's after midnight."

"I know. I'm sorry about that."

"You know I start drinking on Sundays during dinner, and I don't stop until I have passed out. You know this, don't you, Izzy?"

"Yes, but…"

"Then you know you are calling a man who has just recently passed out. The only reason I should be waking up right now is to piss."

"I'm sorry," she said.

"This better be important."

215

"It is," Izzy said.

"Get to it then."

Izzy quickly summarized for the professor her most recent predicament. The subject of her interview had told her that he would be leaving the teaching profession after her article went to print. She explained how he would be revealing that he had lied about his credentials to get the job in the first place. And now he was giving it all up.

"That sounds like a good story," the professor said. "Get a good quote."

"But he's a good teacher! I don't want him to quit. You should have heard what his students said about him!"

The professor groaned. "Izzy, do you know what you sound like?"

"What?"

"You sound like a groupie. Start sounding like a journalist."

"This is different."

"You're taking it personally. This is about the story. Plain and simple. One guy says he's going to kill himself; the next says he's going to change professions. Boo-hoo. That's not for you to worry about. Just finish your damn interview, and write your damn story. And don't drink next time you do an interview. It clouds your judgment."

"I didn't drink," she said.

"I can hear it in your voice," he said. "Now hang up the phone and go get the damn story!"

He hung up.

Izzy was trying to stay focused. Angry for letting herself lose control of the situation, something extremely rare for her, she decided the most important thing was to stay focused. The professor was right. The drinks had made her take her interview with Abel personally, something she would not allow to happen again. She recalled Professor Griffin berating a journalism student who said he was a Philadelphia Eagles fan. "There are no fans in journalism!" he

216

had howled as the kid's face turned red. "I'm the biggest liberal at this university," he shouted. "There are some politicians I support, and others I despise. But you start being a fan, you start getting in good with people. You start doing them favors, and they start doing you favors. Then you're not a journalist anymore; you're a P.R. person, something every journalist should hate. There are no fans in journalism."

Izzy reflected on the professor's words. *Was she becoming a fan of Abel's?* She was impressed with his insights into writing feature stories. And the students she had spoken to told her many stories of Abel's compassion and humor. He genuinely cared for them. His past had made him vulnerable and delicate, and she marveled at how he had overcome that to become someone beloved by so many. The professor was right. She was feeling something that she knew was only keeping her from her goal. She stepped on her cigarette and stomped back to the train. No more drinking. There was work to be done.

Thursday, July 22, 1976

Joe Conway holds his wife's hand as they walk through the medical building on their way to the prenatal medicine department. Abigail's baby is due in less than a month, and her doctor wants to see her once a week. He holds the door for her as he follows her into the spacious, crowded waiting room. He places a hand on the small of her back and says, "I'll check us in. Find a place to sit."

Abigail smiles and shrugs at the same time. It has been a pleasant pregnancy, but lately, her size and changing dimensions are taking their toll, especially in the hot July weather. Joe feels bad, but he knows there is little more he can do besides be the attentive husband.

Joe steps to the receptionist desk and begins to write his name on the clipboard when the receptionist's voice interrupts him. "Mr. Conway!" she exclaims. He looks up to see a familiar face. Fresh and bright, but no name comes to mind to match the face. Her expression turns to playful teasing. "You don't remember me, do you?"

He smiles. *"Of course I do,"* he lies. *"You used to come to Maria G's."*

"Good guess," she says.

Joe turns and motions to his wife, who has found a seat. "That's my wife, Abigail, back there," he says. "We're due in a few weeks."

The receptionist covers her mouth and gasps. "That's so wonderful!" she says.

"Thank you," Joe says, as he glances to his left. But emerging through the door that leads to the doctor's office, he sees another face, this one much more familiar, one that is just as fresh and bright as the receptionist's. However, this one is anxious. Nervous. He knows the face and is about to raise a hand. Shannon Maher. He wants to get her attention. He wants to help.

He raises his right hand as the woman's eyes meet his. For some reason, her expression turns to urgency. Her eyes are sending a message that tells him to hold his tongue. Don't say a word. He sees another figure move gracefully through the doorway, an older woman who puts a hand on the younger one's shoulder. Her mother? The older woman leads her out of the office.

Joe Conway takes a seat next to Abigail and waits for her to be called.

Sunday, June 16, 1996

Izzy pressed record.

Izzy: What do you remember about Joe Conway?

Abel: Interesting question. What he's become is much bigger than what he was.

Izzy: How so?

Abel: He was full of energy. The kids loved him because he'd tell a lot of jokes. Make fun of the camp counselors who worked for him. If he was around, everybody knew it. He was a nice guy. He'd never get mad at anybody. If somebody was getting picked on at lunch, or had any problem, he was the one you went to. He was always smiling, wanting to make sure everybody was having a good time. Then he smashed a killer's head with a tennis racket and got himself killed doing it.

Izzy: Sounds like a hero to me.

218

Abel: He was. But not like they're saying now. I read somewhere that they were going to make a statue of him. He would think that was crazy.

Izzy: Why?

Abel: I don't know. He just would.

Izzy: Abigail said the same thing when I interviewed her.

Abel: I'm not surprised.

Izzy: But he saved so many lives. He stopped a killer with a tennis racket. Why not make a statue?

Abel: It's hard to explain. When I was a kid, I saw him as larger than life, but kids see a lot of people that way. I look back and see him as a regular guy who did something very, very brave.

Izzy: So you think he's been idealized? Idolized?

Abel: Of course. But that's what people do with things like this. We build them up as heroes. Then we cringe when we hear they weren't perfect. Washington and Jefferson owned slaves, but they'll always be seen as heroes for the great things they did.

Izzy: What were Joe's faults?

Abel: None that I could see, as a kid. But that's your job, as a journalist. Find some faults to go along with the heroics. Give the story some balance. Some depth.

Izzy: I'm looking now. Can you tell me any?

Abel: No. But I don't have to, do I?

Izzy: I don't know what you mean.

Abel: You're smarter than that. The groundskeeper.

Izzy: What about him?

Abel: He told us that he caught Joe using that cot in the maintenance shed, more than once. They called it "the shack."

Izzy: So what? He didn't say he was with anyone when he caught him. He could have been just sleeping.

Abel: Are you kidding?

Izzy: He didn't say he was with anyone.

Abel: Because you didn't ask him.

Abel watched as Izzy stopped the tape recorder. Her cheeks were flush, and he knew he had struck something raw. She glared at him. "What is this about?" she asked.

Abel was silent.

Izzy glanced around the room, then returned her eyes to Abel. Unsure of what she was thinking, Abel was now quite clear on something: Izzy was movie star-hot when she was angry.

She finally spoke. "Do you think I'm naive?" she asked in a growl that Abel had not heard until now.

"No, I don't," he said.

"Then why are you suggesting I've missed something?"

"I don't think you've missed anything," Abel said. "I think you're choosing to ignore certain things. I'm not sure why."

"Why would I do that?" she asked.

"I said I didn't know why," he said. "And I've said it before, too. There's something you're not telling me."

"About what?"

"About this story," Abel said, pointing to her notepad. "You said you'd tell me everything if I told you everything. I haven't forgotten about getting kicked out of the capitol building. I remember what Springer's stooges said, too. You're not being straight with me. I'm not naive, either"

"What do you think I'm hiding?" she said, raising her voice.

"Whatever it is, you've got Springer's people scared of you," he said. "They kicked us out, and that woman came to my apartment."

Izzy's eyes widened. "What? Where?"

"At my apartment. She knew where I was going tonight, and she had already dug up dirt on me, and on my sister."

Izzy jumped to her feet and put both hands on her head. "Why didn't you tell me this before?"

"I'm telling you now, and I don't want it to get in the way of the story."

"I don't believe this," she said. "What did she say to you?"

"She knew that I had dated one of my students a few years ago."

Izzy looked at Abel. She wanted to know more.

220

"She was eighteen," he said. "And it was only for a few weeks."

"How would she know that?"

"She works for a governor who might run for president. She knows how to dig."

"Anything else?"

"She knew my sister was making money under the table babysitting kids in her home. She practically threatened to report her to the IRS."

"Oh my God! Why would she do that?"

"Because she wants to convince me not to talk to you, and to try to convince you not to write this story," Abel said.

Izzy opened a bottle of water and took a sip. "I don't understand this," she said. "I'm not trying to smear Mike Springer."

"It's not about that," Abel said. "Whatever I, or anyone else, knows about Mike Springer will come out eventually. She has to know that."

"What then?" she asked.

"You," Abel said. "Whatever it is you're hiding, she knows it."

Izzy fell onto her bed face-first and put both her hands on the back of her head. "I can't believe this," she said. "It was never supposed to be like this."

"Digging things up is dangerous," Abel said. "You didn't expect this to go smoothly did you?"

"I didn't expect this," she said.

"There are reasons people don't talk for twenty years."

Izzy sighed deeply. "Can we finish the interview tomorrow, or on the train ride back?" she asked.

"Yes," Abel said without hesitation. "I'm going to go get a drink in the bar car."

"Wait," Izzy said. Abel looked at her. She glanced around the small space, seemingly unsure of herself. "Why don't you stay here? Have a drink with me."

He watched as her eyes blinked and darted, waiting for his response.

"Not right now," he said. "I'll be back in a little while."

He stepped quickly into the hallway and shut the door behind him. He paused for a moment, exhaled, and walked down the hall.

***

After having been left alone in the suite, Izzy kept her face buried in the pillow on her bed. She shuddered with embarrassment. Even after her blunt talk with the professor, she had still asked Abel to have a drink with her. *Jesus.* She hastily tried to erase her feelings by thinking about the story.

She should spend the night writing, developing an outline, she thought. But the whiskey was taking its toll. It had run its course, first making her relaxed and thoughtful, then inquisitive, as she had hoped. Then it lowered her inhibitions. Now it was making her tired, and she needed sleep.

Deciding against breaking out her laptop, she decided instead to organize things in her head as best she could. She had now spoken to two of the five people she had set out to interview, and she had had a provocative encounter with a third. She considered the most important information she had obtained from each:

Abel Ryan: His twin brother was killed while he watched. He was the last person to speak to Joe Conway. He had witnessed Mike Springer do something that would damage his reputation, but he hadn't told her what. Not yet. Governor Mike Springer's staff had threatened to cause him trouble.

Will Janicki: He had a chance to stop Evan Long before the shooting. If he had opened the bag he'd found in the shack, he would have seen what was inside and called the police. He harbors enormous guilt over this. He carries a gun with him every day.

Mike Springer: He had agreed to talk, but his people had turned her away. Izzy wasn't finished with him. Abel believed they were afraid of what he knew, and who she was.

Still out there were Shannon Maher, who had been living in Charleston for the past twenty years, and Evan Long, who would probably be dead in a few days.

222

Izzy turned over in her bed, trying her best to drive away thoughts of Abel. She thought of Shannon Maher, and what she would ask her. She had all but memorized the list of questions she had prepared, but she knew that they were almost useless. Every reporter knew that a list of questions could be disregarded almost immediately, based on what the subject of an interview might say, but this was especially true in the case of Shannon Maher. Izzy had no idea what the camp counselor who had led sixteen children to the safety of the main road while chaos unfolded behind her would have to say. Maybe she would continue her silence, refusing to even say hello. Maybe she would have new information that would change everyone's perceptions of that day. That possibility excited Izzy. This excitement was what drove her to these stories in the first place, the anticipation of discovering the unknown. The feeling was a good one. This time, however, there was something else lurking behind that familiar rush. There was a foreboding feeling that Izzy had tried to avoid, but she knew she would have to face. She thought of the professor's admonishment not to make it personal. He'd said in class at least a thousand times. *Never make it personal.*

Sometimes, that's just not possible.

***

Abigail Conway ejected the cassette from the VCR and placed it back in its cardboard cover. She and Father Bill Johnston had just finished watching *Forest Gump*. It was her second time through and his fifth. His first three had been in the movie theater. She glanced at her watch. It was nearly midnight. She turned around and watched as the priest emerged from the kitchen with a freshly-cracked can of Miller Lite. She stared.

"What?" he asked.

Abby said nothing.

Bill pointed over his shoulder to the kitchen. "Did you want one?"

Abby shook her head slowly.

"Abby, what's wrong?" he asked.

"They're going to kill him in a few days."

Bill nodded. "Probably."

"How do you feel about that?"

Bill fell back into an easy chair and bit his lower lip. "I thought we were going to talk about Forrest and Jenny."

"How do you feel about it?" she asked again.

"How much wine have you had, Abby?"

"Dammit, just answer me."

"Fine," Bill said. He scratched his chin and thought before he spoke. "Technically, the death penalty is allowed under church law," he said. "But that's only if it's really keeping the rest of society safe. The way we incarcerate prisoners today...there's really no need for it. Society won't be any safer when he's dead. It's punitive instead of rehabilitative. Does that make sense?"

Abby stared at him.

Bill shifted uncomfortably. "Abby, you're freaking me out."

Her eyes narrowed. "I didn't ask for the pope's opinion. I want to know what *you* think. Evan Long, who killed my husband, your friend, and a bunch of innocent kids, is going to be executed. How do you feel about it?"

Bill took a drink of his beer. "Tell me what you think, Abby."

"Don't do that."

"What?"

"When you don't feel like answering a question, you turn it around and ask me. I want to know what *you* think."

"Okay," he said. "I don't like the death penalty," he said, choosing his words carefully. "I never have. Not because I'm a priest, but because I always thought we should be able to do better than that. I think we lower ourselves as a society when we resort to doing *to* the criminal whatever it was he did."

"Interesting," Abby said quietly.

"We don't rape a rapist, or take a car thief's car, right?"

Abby nodded slowly.

"So, what do you think?"

She walked back to the sofa and sat down. She curled her feet under herself and looked across the room at Bill. She knew she was making him uncomfortable, but she had always valued his opinion, both as a friend and as a man of God. She shrugged, a gesture that she hoped would lighten the mood. She could feel the priest's relief. "Here is what I think," she said. "Nineteen years ago, or even fifteen years ago, I would have said, 'Yes, kill him.' Twenty years later, I'm not really sure if killing him has anything to do with what he did. He's probably not even the same person that he was back then." She reached for her glass and took a sip. "If I ~~would have~~ had thought that killing him would keep one more psychopath from doing the same kind of thing, I'd be all for it. But now I think it's just one more person to bury. I'd honestly rather just see him rot in jail for another fifty years."

She watched as Bill processed her words.

He leaned forward. "So, if they ~~would have~~ had executed him closer to the time of the crime, you'd have been for it?"

"I *was* for it," she said. "But then came the appeals, the postponements. Two decades go by and the whole thing seems like a lifetime has passed. It's almost meaningless now."

He took a drink of his beer. "A lot of people disagree with that."

"I know," she said. "There's a part of me that does, too." She sipped her wine. "Here's a hypothetical for you, Father Johnston."

"I hate hypotheticals."

"You get a call from the prison tomorrow."

"Okay," he said.

"Evan Long wants you as his priest. He wants you to guide him through his final days, forgive his sins, and grant him absolution before dying. What do you do, Father?"

"Have I told you I hate hypotheticals?"

"What would you do?" she asked again.

"I'd tell him to go to hell."

She felt herself begin to laugh. "Appropriate in this situation, isn't it?"

225

"That's not what I meant."

"Do you think he's going to hell?"

Bill shook his head impatiently. "Is this why you invited me over here Abby? If I thought we'd be engaging in this kind of talk, I wouldn't have had three beers."

"Four."

"Whatever."

"Well, I needed to get you drunk. How else could I take advantage of you?"

"Shut up," he said, waving a hand.

"I know you love when I do that," she said with a grin.

"I really do. There just isn't enough temptation in the world."

"Sorry, Father," she said.

"I hate when you call me that. Let's talk about something else."

"Okay," Abby said, turning her head to face the blank television screen.

Neither spoke for a full minute. Abby was happy to let the awkwardness of the moment fill the space. Finally, she said, "All those poor parents. They've been waiting for justice. Hoping that when Evan Long is buried they can move on with their lives. *Fools*."

Bill scoffed. "How can you say that?"

"I've earned every right to say it," she said.

"I know a lot of them," Bill said. "I speak to some of them every week. They're suffering. And you'd be surprised. A lot of them don't even care whether he's executed, or he spends the rest of his life in jail."

"I'm suffering too," she said. "In my own way."

"I know you are. But you've been able to move on with your life. A lot of them haven't."

"I haven't moved on," she said.

"You've raised a child on your own, and made yourself a fortune while doing it," he said. "I'd say you've moved on better than most."

She shook her head. "Thanks," she said. "I have a daughter who never met her father. I never remarried. I never even *wanted* to."

"That's understandable," Bill said. "But you've done a lot."

"My husband died twenty years ago," she said. "I have been with three men since then. None of them lasted. I've had sex eleven times in twenty years. Do you think that's healthy?"

"It's more than I have."

"You're a bad example," she said. "Trust me. It's not healthy."

"I get it," he said.

She turned to look at him again. "I'm sorry. Am I making you uncomfortable?"

"Not at all," he said. "I took a vow of celibacy for this exact reason, so I could listen to beautiful women tell me they don't get enough sex."

Abby laughed. "Okay. We can talk about something else."

"Thanks."

"Did Joe ever confess to you?" she asked.

"What?"

"You heard me."

"Jesus, Abby. I don't think I can drink with you anymore."

"It's a simple question. Can you answer it, please?"

"No, I can't."

"Why not?" she asked.

"There are rules," he said.

She leaned forward and pointed at the table in front of her, as if it held the rulebook for priests. "You can't tell me what someone says *in confession*. But you can tell me if someone confessed to you."

She watched as Bill's eyes considered this, then searched for the right answer. She interrupted him before he could answer.

"Don't bother. It's obvious that he did," she said. "He always thought of himself as a good Catholic."

Bill said nothing.

"And don't worry. I won't ask you what he confessed. We both know those details, don't we?"

"He loved you," Bill said. "And he loved his daughter."

Abby smiled and shook her head. "He would have gotten a real kick out of her, wouldn't he?"

"Yes, he would."

She stopped smiling. "He made a fool out of me, didn't he?"

"No one has ever made a fool out of you."

She ignored him. "All those young girls running around that camp. Looking up to him. Running to him for advice. It was too easy for him, wasn't it?"

Bill finished his beer.

"Are you leaving me now?" she asked

"Do you want me to?" he asked.

She shook her head. "No, but you seem like you want to."

"You're not exactly making for easy conversation."

"I know," she said. "Everybody wants Evan Long dead. You can't tell me anything about my husband that I don't already know. This state and the whole damn country still hail him as a hero."

"He *is* a hero."

"I know," she said. "But he had his faults."

"We all do, and the whole world doesn't need to know ours, or his."

She sat back in her chair, smiled, and took the last sip of her wine. "But they will," she said.

"What do you mean?"

"You don't know?" she asked.

"Know what?"

"There's a reporter," she said. "She's working on an article. Wants to find and speak to every person who was at the shooting who has never spoken out about it. There are five that she has been able to locate."

"Pretty ambitious," Bill said.

"Especially since Evan Long is on her list," she said.

228

"Holy shit," he said. "How do you know that?"

"She told me when she interviewed me."

"Why would she interview you?" he asked. "You weren't there."

She nodded. "She said she was getting background information. I won't be in the story."

"Well, if she wants to interview the killer, she better hurry."

"She'll get him," she said. "She's very good."

Abby stood and picked up her wine glass. She looked at it, trying to decide if she wanted more wine.

"How do you know how good she is?" Bill asked.

"I've read her stuff. Trust me. She'll find everyone, and she'll talk to everyone."

She watched as the priest's dark eyebrows arched, revealing his concern.

She smiled knowingly. "It's all going to come out, Bill," she said. "All of it."

Monday, June 17, 1996

"Right this way, folks," the polite old man with the Russian accent said as he pointed to a table at the end of the car. "I'll be over in a minute with a couple menus."

Abel looked in the direction of the table the man had pointed to. "There are people at that table already," he said.

Before the attendant could answer, Izzy said, "That's what they do on trains."

The old man nodded politely and walked away. Izzy took Abel by the hand and led him through the narrow center of the dining car. "They always make you sit with other people," she said. "Space is limited."

"Makes sense, I guess. It's just weird," Abel said.

"Not really," she whispered, now within earshot of the people at the table, an elderly man and woman. "You'd be surprised how interesting people on trains can be. Funny things come out when you're forced to sit together."

Abel sat across from Izzy and next to the woman. The couple smiled and introduced themselves as Annie and Ian Harris.

Abel was surprised at how quickly what seemed like awkwardness transitioned into easy conversation. Izzy had been right. They were lovely people with an interesting story that they didn't mind sharing. They had met in the Army and had fallen in love soon after. Annie was an intelligence officer, and Ian worked under her command. This was a problem since officers dating enlisted personnel was strictly off limits. They kept the relationship a secret until Ian's enlistment was up, and they quickly got engaged. It had to be quick since their son was born eight months later. Abel liked the story. Scandalous and romantic.

As they made their way back to their room, Izzy said to Abel, "I told you, didn't I? You meet all kinds of interesting people."

"They never asked about us," Abel said.

"I know!" she said, sounding disappointed. "I had a story ready, too."

"Me sweeping you away from your disapproving parents to marry you in a state where the age of consent allows for it?"

She smiled as they entered their room. "Something like that."

As they packed their bags, the man on the loudspeaker politely informed them that the Charleston stop was thirty minutes away.

PART 4: EYES

Sheila Avery was already out of breath as she raced through the Charleston International Airport. She had caught a 7 A.M. flight, the first one available to Charleston, a city that she had never visited before. It was now 9:30, a full hour after the overnight train had arrived. With her only bag slung over her right shoulder, she frantically followed the signs that pointed the way to the car rentals. When she made her way to the desk, she was glad to find that Bob had already made the arrangements for the car, a 1993 Ford Taurus. Not bad. She signed the papers, took the keys, and stepped out the door to find the car waiting at the curb. She dropped her bag in the back seat, got behind the wheel, and started the car.

The car was in drive before she realized she had no idea where she was going.

***

The 20-minute drive from the Charleston train station in North Charleston to James Island would have been picturesque if either Izzy or Abel were able to take it in. They had rented a car and Izzy had insisted on driving. Suffering a familiar summer hangover that he would normally sleep through, Abel did not protest. Neither was at all familiar with the city, but the lady at the car rental was quite happy to provide them with a map, complete with a highlighted route to their destination. Nothing like Southern hospitality, Abel thought.

Abel could see that Izzy was in her journalistic zone. He stole glances at her, and observed her expression as she recycled the questions over and over in her head. He had many questions of his own, but dared not ask. Now wasn't the time. It was nearly nine in the morning, and the sun was already high in the South Carolina sky, having risen over the Cooper River to the East as they moved south toward James Island and the home of Shannon Maher.

"Why do you keep looking at me?" Izzy asked, sounding slightly annoyed.

"Sorry," Abel answered. "I like watching you work."

Izzy smirked, knowing he was reading her mind. "I just want to be prepared," she said.

"You haven't had *any* contact with her?"

"No," Izzy said. "Just an address and a phone number. And I didn't want to call. Too easy to hang up."

"Do you want me to wait in the car?" Abel asked.

"I don't know. What do you think?"

"I think we should both knock on the door, but I'll leave my camera in the car."

"Sounds good to me," she said.

"What makes you think she'll be home?" Abel asked.

"Nothing."

"What if she's at work?"

"Then we come back later," Izzy said.

"What if she's away on vacation?"

Izzy groaned in frustration. "Then we get on a plane and fly to Palm Springs!"

"What are you talking about?" Abel asked.

"Can you just shut up and let me think?"

"Sure," Abel said.

Izzy exhaled and looked at Abel. "I'm sorry. I just need you to trust me when I say I know what I'm doing."

Abel could hear the tension in her voice. He was interfering with her rhythm. It was time to shut up.

***

"Excuse me," the woman's voice called. "Is your name Shannon, by any chance?"

Startled, Shannon Maher turned her head, careful not to move her fishing rod. "Yes," she said. "Can I help you?"

232

Watching the woman step carefully across the sandy stretch of beach, Shannon was sure of two things: she had never seen the slender brunette woman before in her life, and the woman was not from anywhere in the South.

"I think you can," the woman answered. "My name is Sheila Avery. Can I speak to you for a few minutes?"

Shannon turned her attention back to the bay, where she had been fishing since seven that morning. "I don't know you, Sheila Avery," she said, as kindly as she could. "And I'm working here."

"Oh," Sheila said, gesturing to the fishing rod. "I didn't realize you were working."

"That's my work," Shannon answered. "I catch fish; then I test them. Make sure the water is fit."

"I see," Sheila said. "Can't you just test the water?"

"You're right," Shannon said. "This is a waste of time." She reeled in her line and began to pack up the small testing kit she had brought with her. "No bites today anyway," she said.

"I didn't mean to disturb you," Sheila said.

Shannon turned to look the strange woman in the eyes. "I think that's exactly what you meant to do," she said. "You came all the way from Delaware to disturb me at ten in the morning."

Shannon watched as the woman shuddered in surprise. "Delaware?"

"When I hear the word 'wooder' instead of 'water,' it's pretty easy. You a reporter or something?" Shannon asked.

Sheila scoffed. "*Not* a reporter," she said.

"Well, Ms. Avery, you need to know that I enjoy my privacy, and I do not appreciate it when people from Delaware step into my life."

"I understand. But if you do value your privacy, I think you will want to hear what I have to tell you."

"I doubt it."

The two women stared at each other for a long moment. Finally, Sheila said, "But the clock is ticking here. We should talk."

Shannon looked the woman over. She wore a navy blue suit, one that would have been worn to a business meeting. No notepad. This woman was not a reporter.

"Okay," Shannon said. "But I do have work to do. Make it quick."

Sheila looked around the area. It was an open park. People could park there and fish, or walk or swim. But there was nobody there this morning except for Shannon Maher. Sheila wondered if it was risky to remain in the open air, or if she should ask Shannon if they could walk back to her house, which was only a few hundred feet from where they stood. Shannon looked very much like she had in the old newspaper photographs, only older, but she had aged well.

Sheila was mad at herself for her pronunciation of *water*. If her boss was ever elected President, she would certainly have to get rid of that. Saying she was proud to be from Delaware was one thing. *Sounding* like a Delawarean was another.

"Is it safe to talk here?" she asked Shannon. "I mean, is it private?"

Shannon looked around, amused. "Who would be listening?"

Sheila nodded. "Okay. I won't take much of your time, and I won't even ask you any questions, except one."

"What's that?"

"Have any reporters contacted you about the campground shooting?"

She watched as the blood ran from Shannon Maher's face. Otherwise, the woman did not react, not even to blink.

"No," Shannon said.

Sheila watched as Shannon fumbled into her handbag for her cigarettes. She lit one with trembling hands and offered one to Sheila.

"No, thanks."

"How on earth did you find me?" Sheila noticed the woman had acquired a Southern accent. It was faint, but definitely there.

234

"I didn't want to disturb you," Sheila said. "This is my job."

"And what is your job, Ms. Avery? You're clearly not a reporter."

"I work for a politician who was present at the shooting."

"Mike Springer," Shannon said.

"That's right," Sheila said. "And there is a reporter who is trying to write a story about the shooting. She wants to interview five people who were there but have never spoken about it."

"And I'm one of them," Shannon said.

"Yes."

Shannon sighed. "Some people have a lot of nerve," she said, glaring at Sheila as if she were the one writing the story.

"It's okay," Sheila said, satisfied that she might just get the woman to cooperate. "The governor knows that there are certain delicate issues surrounding your departure from Delaware."

She looked at Shannon for a long moment.

"And?" Shannon asked.

"Joe Conway was a good friend of his."

"I know that," Shannon said, and Sheila detected just a hint of bitterness in the woman's voice.

"There are many issues that the governor wants to be at the forefront of his coming campaigns. The hero status of Joe Conway is not one of them."

"I don't follow," Shannon said.

"It's like this," Sheila said. "Mike Springer has spent the last twenty years of his life making a hero out of Joe Conway."

Shannon's eyes widened. "Actually, Ms. Avery, Joe Conway made a hero out of himself when he took down an armed man with a goddamned tennis racket."

"Of course he did," Sheila said. "That is his legacy, and the governor would like to keep it that way, without dragging you, *or anyone else*, into the spotlight."

And Shannon understood. It was the way the woman had said those three words: *or anyone else*. But how could she have known?

235

Shannon looked out across the water, taking in the fact that she had suddenly been plunged into a new set of circumstances. It was one she had known would eventually emerge, but not like this. Not with women in suits. Not with presidential campaigns. She shook her head.

"I don't have any interest in talking to any reporters," she said.

Sheila breathed a sigh of relief. "I'm glad to hear that," Sheila said. She kept looking at Shannon.

"What?" Shannon asked.

Sheila smiled. "It's just that this reporter can be very persistent," she said. "She'll try everything she can to..."

"I'm not going to talk to her," Shannon said as she stepped on what was left of her cigarette. "I have nothing to say to anybody about this, including you."

Sheila was convinced. "I appreciate that," she said. "And so does the governor."

"I'm sure he does," Shannon said.

"I mean it," Sheila said. "He knows a lot of people. So do I. If you ever need anything..." She extended her hand, which held a small business card."

Shannon looked down at the card. "I just have one question," she said.

"Go ahead," Sheila said.

"Why did he send you all the way down here? He could have just called me."

Sheila pulled the card away and held it in front of her. "That's a little complicated," she said, choosing her words carefully. "There are a lot of things going on here that the governor would rather not deal with directly, and he sent me because he knew I could find you."

Shannon's eyes narrowed. "So, in other words, if I didn't want to cooperate, you would have threatened me with something, and *the governor* can't get his hands dirty."

Sheila shook her head, not in denial, but at a loss for words. "It's not like that," she said. "There are a lot of moving parts here…"

"Save it," Shannon said. "Just do me a favor and tell Mike something for me. The last time I saw Joe Conway, he was charging down a hill ready to take down a killer. And the last time I saw Mike, he was a clumsy kid, obsessing over which female counselor he could get up the courage to ask on a date, and he always went after the ugly ones. They were the only ones who paid him any attention. He was afraid to talk to me then, and he's afraid to talk to me now."

"Well, a lot has changed since then."

"Not as much as you think," Shannon said. "Tell Mike not to worry. I won't say anything. Now get the hell out of my life." She turned and quickly walked away.

***

"Leave your camera in the car," Izzy said as she checked her looks in the rearview mirror. Abel thought about reminding her that leaving the camera was his idea, but he figured she was just nervous. He was too

They climbed out of the car and Abel followed Izzy as they walked toward the door of the small house. When they reached the door, Abel heard Izzy take a deep breath before she knocked. He did the same. Both of them had noticed the Honda Civic in the driveway and the Mercury Comet parked on the street, making them believe someone was home. No one answered.

"Do you think she's sleeping?" Abel asked.

"I don't know," Izzy said.

"Is she married?" Abel asked.

Izzy shook her head. "I didn't find anything that said she was married."

"Two cars," Abel said.

"Could be a neighbor's," Izzy said. She knocked again. Nothing. "We'll come back at lunchtime."

"You think she comes home for lunch?" Abel asked.

237

"She works for the South Carolina Department of Natural Resources," Izzy said. "There is a lab here on James Island and a state park nearby. She probably walks to work when the weather is nice. So she might."

Abel thought about this, but before he could offer an opinion, the door opened. Izzy jumped as she turned to face the door.

A young, shirtless man, no older than twenty, stood holding the door. He looked confused and in need of sleep. "Can I help ya'll?" he asked.

Izzy looked at her notebook, then at the man. "I uh..I..."

"We're looking for a lady named Shannon Maher," Abel said. "Does she live here?"

"She does," the man said. "But she's at work."

"I see," Abel said.

"Do you want to leave your name or anything?" the man asked, looking the two over.

"No thanks," Abel said, feeling Izzy's glare. "We'll try back later if that's okay."

"That's fine, sir," the man said. "She usually stops in around noon for lunch."

"I had a feeling," Abel said. "We'll try back then."

"May I ask ya'll what this is about?"

"We're reporters," Izzy said.

The man's eyes narrowed a little. "This about those red drums?" he asked.

"I'm sorry?"

"The red drum fish," the man said. "She's workin' hard on making them repopulate. It's kind of a big thing."

"I see," Izzy said. "I'd love to talk to her about those red drums. We'll try again later."

"Ya'll sound like you came a long way to ask about some fish."

Izzy looked at him, puzzled.

The man smiled. "Y'all don't sound like locals," he explained.

Izzy smiled and nodded. "We're from up North. It's a big story," she said.

"Okay, then," the man said politely. "I'll let her know ya'll came by."

He closed the door and Izzy and Abel walked back toward the rental.

As they climbed into the car, Abel said, "That went well."

"Shut up," Izzy said.

***

Evan Long extended his chained right hand toward Dr. Cras, who had just completed the much-anticipated psychological evaluation. The doctor looked at Evan's hand, nodded and said, "All my best, Mr. Long." He then stepped through the door and exited the private visit cell. Evan watched, his hand still extended, as the doctor walked toward his lawyer, Raymond Woodson.

"You will have the results of my evaluation by the end of the day," the doctor said to Raymond.

"Thank you for your time, doctor," Raymond said.

Raymond stepped into the cell as the doctor walked away.

"He can't shake my hand?" Evan said. "His mind is already made up."

"He's doing this for free, Evan," Raymond said. "And his results will favor our side."

"How do you know?"

"It's what he does," Raymond said. "He's against the death penalty."

"So he can't shake my hand?" Evan said. "They're about to execute me."

Raymond shook his head. "Not if I can help it. And Dr. Cras is against capital punishment as a matter of principle. He lost a son seventeen years ago. The killer was executed ten years ago. He's been against it ever since. He hates murderers, but he hates the death penalty even more."

"So he'd rather see me 'rot in jail'?" Evan asked, making finger quotation marks.

239

"He's on our side, Evan. And his report will reflect your state of mind when the crime was committed, and how you're different now. You're not the same person. He might also mention that you don't quite understand all that's happening to you."

"What?"

Raymond raised his hand in a calming gesture. "It will help us. Trust me," he said.

They took seats at opposite sides of the small metal table. Evan looked across to Raymond. His lawyer looked older than he usually looked. Heavier and tired.

"Who was that guy that called me yesterday?" Evan asked.

"My paralegal. He told me you weren't too happy about his calling instead of me."

"It's just that I've only ever dealt with you. It was a surprise."

Raymond leaned forward, removed his glasses, and massaged the space between his eyes. "I've been working at this, Evan," he said. "We may be able to avoid the death penalty on an appeal to the State Supreme Court."

Evan thought about this. He was used to Raymond delivering this kind of development slowly, carefully choosing his words so as not to arouse any emotions. Evan knew they were past that. "Your guy told me," he said. "This is something new?"

Raymond nodded. "It might be our best shot. It's an argument about the way in which you were sentenced. I've seen it argued in other states very effectively."

"So, what do you need me to do?"

"Nothing," Raymond said. "Just try to keep calm. I'm sure it's difficult."

"I'm fine," Evan said. "I appreciate your help."

"There is one more thing," Raymond said.

"What is it?" Evan asked.

"No interviews."

Evan sighed. "I want to do it."

"And as your lawyer, I am strongly advising you *against* it, again."

Evan slapped the table with both hands. "Why?"

240

"Too many variables," Raymond said. "We've been over this. I need to be in control of everything you do and say."

"I'm doing it," Evan said, his breath starting to quicken with frustration.

Evan watched as his lawyer glared at him, then slowly said, "Evan, in twenty years, you have never ignored my advice. Listen to me now, please."

"But I really want to," he said again.

"This is where I would typically tell a client that he needs to find someone else to represent him," Raymond said loudly. It was the first time Evan had ever seen his attorney angry.

"You can't do that."

Raymond inhaled deeply and gritted his teeth. "I can, but I won't," he said. "I need to see this through, and you haven't got time to find a new lawyer."

"Thank you," Evan said.

"But just know that I have worked my rear-end off for two decades to save your life. First getting paid next to nothing, and now working for free, all because I don't want to see the state kill you. And now you're threatening to throw it all away because you suddenly have the urge to tell your story. It's reckless. And I don't do reckless." He stood abruptly and stepped toward the door.

"Where are you going?" Evan asked.

"Dover," Raymond hissed. "To fight for your life." He pointed his finger at Evan and shouted, "No fucking interviews!"

It was the first time Evan had ever heard his attorney curse. He sat silently for a moment, considering the situation.

"Let's go, Long," the guard said before Evan could think about it too much. "Back to your cell."

***

Abel took the hotel room key from Izzy.

"I'm going to freshen up," she said. "I'll knock on your door at 11:15."

241

"Okay," Abel said. Izzy had reserved two rooms at the Hilton in Charleston. They would be spending the night and leaving in the morning.

"What are you going to do?" she asked.

"I'm not sure," he lied, glancing toward the bar, which had just opened.

"It's ten in the morning," she said.

"Why don't you join me?" Abel asked. "I'm sure you can smoke in there."

"I have an interview to prepare for."

"You've been prepared for weeks," Abel said.

Izzy shrugged. He was right. "That guy at the door was a surprise, wasn't he?"

"I guess," Abel said. "It's been twenty years, though. We don't know anything about her life."

"I know a few things," Izzy said.

"You know where she works, and that she probably has never married, right?"

"And that she owns that house she's living in."

"That's not much," Abel said.

"You think he was a boyfriend?" she asked.

"He was young. He couldn't have been older than twenty-five," Abel said. "How old is she?"

"She'd be forty now," Izzy said. "He's young."

"Maybe he's just a guy that lives there. A college student or something," Abel offered. "There are lots of colleges around here."

Izzy thought about this and shook her head. "I'm going up," she said. "I'll be at your door at 11:15."

"Don't bother," Abel said. "I'll be at the bar."

Izzy glared at him.

"It's a couple drinks," he said. "You're the one doing the interview."

"You're my photographer. If she smells liquor on you, she might say forget it."

Abel sighed. "Fine. 11:15. I'll take a shower."

They walked together to the elevator, rode it to the seventeenth floor, and parted ways at the elevator door. Abel found his room and soon realized how tired he was, having slept very little on the train. He collapsed into the bed and began drifting in and out sleep.

He thought of many people and how this story would affect them, if it ever was completed. His father showed up in his thoughts. Abel had always harbored the torturous feeling that his father would have preferred he had died instead of his brother. As he grew older, he began to understand that this was probably not the case, but he could always remember that look in his father's eyes when he would tell him at the dinner table about how he'd been cut from the baseball team, or how he'd let a loudmouth at school walk on him, rather than stand up and give it back. His father would glance at his mother, then at the table. Abel had always known what his father was thinking: *Your brother would have kicked the kid's ass.* He was right. Abel wondered if he would have the courage to tell that to Izzy. His mother would hate him for saying it, probably even make excuses for his father. His mother might hate him for even being in the story, but she would get over it.

Abel thought about Izzy as well. If she did manage to complete this story and interview everyone on her list, it would probably make her famous, at least in Delaware. Would she really interview Evan Long? Would he join her for *that* interview? Abel doubted he would be able to sit across from the man who had killed his brother. He marveled at Izzy's courage. She was relentless and unflinching, not like him. He had many thoughts about Izzy, and he was hating himself for turning down her offer on the train to have a drink with her. He could hear his brother laughing at him, as he had many times before. Abel avoided every kind of confrontation, good and bad. He'd been on the run his entire life, and now he was sneaking off to bars to drink by himself.

Izzy would be learning a lot about him in the days to come. His cowardice, and his brother's bravery. But what he feared most was that she would see him shudder with fear when it was time to interview Evan Long.

He heard footsteps outside his hotel room door, followed by a strong knock. It was time to go.

***

Shannon Maher sat staring at the door, waiting for the knock. She was actually looking forward to saying the words. "I'm sorry you came all this way, but I had nothing to say twenty years ago, and I have nothing to say now. Goodbye." Door closed. Conversation over. If they knock again, call the police. It would be fun. She had already decided to take the rest of the day off. She would go into Charleston and do some shopping. Maybe have her hair done. The ugliness of these unwelcome visitors would be behind her, hopefully forever.

She heard the sound of a car parking in front of her house, followed by two car doors closing. She waited for the knock.

"Bring your camera," Izzy said. "She knows we're journalists." She placed her pen neatly in the holder of her reporter's notebook. She checked her hair, and removed her sunglasses - let the subject see your eyes. *Trust.* She was ready to speak Shannon Maher.

Walking with purpose, she approached the door as Abel followed behind.

She knocked.

The woman answered immediately. Izzy smiled. The woman didn't smile, but instead inhaled deeply and drew back, perhaps swallowing words.

"Hi, Ms. Maher," Izzy said softly. "I'm…"

The woman raised her right hand to stop her. Izzy stopped talking. The two women looked at each other for a moment.

"I know who you are, dear," the woman said. "Come inside so we can talk."

Sheila called Bob Casarini from the airport. He answered right away. "Done?" he asked.

"Done," Sheila said. "She's not talking."

"You're sure?"

"Positive." She summarized her exchange with Shannon Maher. It had gone better than had expected.

Bob exhaled. "Good. Good."

"What's she hiding?" Sheila asked.

"It doesn't matter," Bob said. "You told her *exactly* what I told you to tell her?"

"Word for word," Sheila said. "You're not going to tell me?"

"Maybe at some point, but not now. Was she mad?" he asked.

"Furious," Sheila answered. "She had some very harsh words for Mike too."

"Write them down," Bob said. "But don't tell him."
    "I would never."

"Good," Bob said again. "Good work, Sheila. Come on home."

Izzy took a seat at the picnic table across from where Shannon Maher would sit, next to Abel, who still had not said a word since they arrived.

Shannon was busy in the kitchen preparing a pitcher of iced tea. Izzy thought the woman looked younger than she had imagined. Her skin, though showing the effects of a lifetime of sun exposure, looked soft and healthy. Her hair was dirty-blonde and pulled into a ponytail. This was a woman who worked outside and with her hands. She had a lean and strong look, like a gymnast. She was an attractive woman, and Izzy could imagine she would have been quite a sight twenty years ago. Exiting the house, Shannon asked, "Would ya'll like anything else besides tea?"

"Nothing for me, thanks," Izzy said.

"I hope ya'll don't mind sitting outside," Shannon said as she took her seat at the table. "Charleston gets so hot in the summer. We should take advantage of a day like this."

"Not at all," Izzy said. "I should probably introduce myself."

She watched as Shannon smiled and looked away. "Go ahead, dear," she said.

Shannon had taken on the casual demeanor of the Southerners Izzy had seen in movies, and she spoke like she had lived there her whole life. But there was something else in her voice, a quality Izzy could not place, as if she were playing along at a game that only she understood. Not sure what to make of the woman's strangely casual mannerisms, Izzy started with Abel. "This is Abel Ryan," she said. "He's a photographer who is helping me with this story."

"I'm pleased to meet you, Abel," Shannon said, reaching across the table to shake hands.

"You as well," Abel said, not mentioning that the two had met many years ago.

"And my name is Izzy Buchanan," she said. "I'm a journalist with the Brandywine University newspaper."

"I see," Shannon said, still smiling. "All the way from Brandywine U to interview little old me?"

Izzy and Abel exchanged amused glances, unsure if the woman was sincerely flattered, or making fun of herself, or them.

"Would you like to hear what my story is about?" Izzy asked. "We told the gentleman we met earlier that it was about the red drum fish, but it's not. I'm sorry if that's going to be a problem."

"I know what your story is about," Shannon said. "And I think it is a fantastic idea. Joe would be so proud."

Izzy drew back from the table and stared at Shannon, who still wore her all-knowing smile. Izzy turned to look at Abel, who appeared just as confused.

"How could you know?" Izzy asked.

Shannon shook her head dismissively. "We'll get to that. Just go ahead and ask me your questions. Do you mind if I smoke?"

Izzy shook her head slowly. She just watched as the woman lit her cigarette and exhaled, never losing the smile. *What the hell was going on here?*

"No, I don't mind," Abel said, filling the silence. "I'll have a beer if you have any."

This brought Izzy back. "He's joking," she said. "No, I don't mind if you smoke."

Shannon laughed. "Join me?"

Izzy shook her head. "Not now, thanks."

"Good," Shannon said. "I can see you're a little out of sorts right now, so why don't I start?"

"Fine," Izzy said.

"Do you want to use that pen?" Shannon asked pointing her nose in the direction of Izzy's pen and notepad.

Izzy refocused again. She picked up the pen and opened her notebook.

"My name is Shannon Maher," she said. "I know you already know that, but I want to be thorough. I am thirty-nine years old, and I was born in Wilmington, Delaware. I went to Talley High School, then did two years at Brandywine U. I left there in 1976, then finished at Clemson. I went to Clemson for grad school also. I have degrees in biology and environmental toxicology.

"And, very importantly, I was working at Maria G's Campground when Evan Long decided to kill eleven people. I was nineteen at the time. I was with Joe Conway on the tennis courts when he decided to charge after that killer with a tennis racket. I was the one who ran to the road with sixteen four-year-old children while my friends stayed behind to experience hell on earth. I heard the gunshots and the screams while I had those children lie down in a muddy ditch by the side of the road. I sang songs to them while they covered their heads with their little hands. When I ran out of songs, I prayed out loud. First the Lord's Prayer, then the Hail Mary, over and over again. I tried not to cry when I heard the shooting stop. But I knew then that Joe Conway was dead. It was strange, but somehow I knew.

"When a man pulled over with his pickup truck, he kindly offered to have them pile in the back so he could drive them to safety. I lined them up and quickly got them on board. I sat with them while he drove us to a church parking lot. I still remember my hands shaking when I used a pay phone at that church to call the police. They asked me for the names of all the children I had with me. I knew them all. I still know them all. Funny, but I can't remember the name of the man who picked us up."

"Tom Wayock," Izzy said, amazed at how the information was pouring from the woman's mouth. "A retired high school teacher."

"Very good," Shannon said. "And, yes, I was one of the few who refused to even give a statement to the police, then decided not to speak to anyone about that day ever again. I even took the extra step of moving out of state. As you know, everyone in Delaware knows everyone else, and true privacy is near impossible. I left for South Carolina that fall. A few years later, I finished college, went to grad school, got a job at Natural Resources in Charleston, and I bought this house five years ago. It's small, but it suits me just fine. And that was pretty much it until you knocked on my door."

"Why South Carolina?" Izzy asked.

"I have family here," Shannon said. "My aunt and uncle live in Pendleton. It was an easy transition to make, all things considered. My parents were sad to see me go, but they understood. They moved down here a couple years later."

"Why didn't you want to talk to anyone?" Izzy asked.

Shannon scoffed at the question. "That's difficult to explain," she said.

"I have time, Ms. Maher."

"Call me Shannon, dear," she said. "And I'll get to all that soon. In the meantime, can you ask me something else?"

"Okay," Izzy said. "Why are you talking to me now?"

Shannon laughed loudly.

"What's so funny?" Izzy asked.

"I'm sorry, dear," Shannon said. "It's just that, you see, I can't begin to know where to start."

"Why not at the beginning? When you arrived for work that day," Izzy suggested.

Shannon looked into the distance, her face becoming serious for a moment, like she was trying to remember something. Seeming to find the answer she was searching for, she laughed again. "That's a bad place to start, actually," she said. "I'll start with here and now, then work backward. That would be easier. Okay?"

"However you want to do it," Izzy said. "Do you mind if I use my tape recorder?"

"Not at all," Shannon said. "Here's how my day started. I was out at the state park fishing, which is part of my job, believe it or not. Out of nowhere comes this serious young woman who informs me that a reporter would be paying me a little visit."

Izzy felt her eyes beginning to burn with anger as Shannon Maher relayed the whole story of Sheila Avery's attempted interception earlier that day. Izzy was so angry she felt she might pick something up and throw it. She kept looking at Abel to see if he shared her anger. Instead, his expression was more of intrigue. He'd be interested in *that* story, Izzy thought. An assistant to a state governor tries to intimidate a woman into not giving an interview.

"So, then I come home for lunch and Conny tells me that these two reporters had already stopped by," she continued. "By then, I was fuming mad, just waiting for you two to come knocking. I was ready to chase ya'll clear out of town." She looked at both of them, still smiling.

Izzy's next question was so obvious that she hardly wanted to ask it.

"Then why are you talking to us?" she asked, now growing slightly concerned about what the answer would be.

Shannon laughed again. "That is the question, isn't it, dear? And here is the answer that you might already know." She leaned forward on the picnic table and looked directly at Izzy. "It's your eyes, dear."

Izzy shook her head. "I don't understand."

Shannon laughed again, but this time it was a bitter laugh, one that said she didn't appreciate being toyed with. "Those eyes, my dear, are

249

the same ones that looked into mine all those years ago. Those eyes could talk me into just about anything. They're the same ones I used to dream about when I fell asleep at night, hoping he'd leave that pretty wife of his. I *still* dream of them. They're the same ones that told me I had to run away just before he took that tennis racket and went charging down that hill. I couldn't say no to those eyes then, and I can't say no to them now."

Izzy looked at the smiling woman for a long time. Shannon had known all along.

"When did you figure it out?" Izzy asked.

"As soon as I opened the door," Shannon said. "I could never forget those eyes."

A realization was slowly coming over Abel as he watched the two women stare at each other. He now knew what Izzy had been keeping from him, and it was something that placed her right in the middle of the story. It was something that would spark the interest of a politician who was running for president.

"You look surprised, Mr. Abel," Shannon said. "She didn't tell you?"

Abel shook his head, never taking his eyes off of Izzy.

"He was your father," Abel said softly. "Joe Conway was your dad. And Abigail Conway is your mother."

Izzy turned her head to look at him. She nodded slowly, still not speaking.

Shannon stopped smiling. The secret was out. "Honey," she said. "Your father was a great, great man."

"I know he was," Izzy said.

"But there a lot of things that I will bet you don't know. Difficult things."

"I'm sensing that," Izzy said.

"I know you are," Shannon said. "There are things very few people know. Big things. And if you put them in your story, everybody will know them. It might turn into something very messy. Are you ready for that?"

250

"I'm ready for the truth," Izzy answered. "Whatever it is."

"But there is more than you could know," Shannon said in a voice dripping with implications. "If you want it all, you'll get it all. And you need to decide now is if you're a journalist or a daughter."

"I'm a journalist."

"You're twenty years old," Shannon said.

"I will be in September."

Shannon smiled as if she remembered. "Of course," she said. "That mother of yours, gorgeous even when she was eight months pregnant. She is to this day."

"So what?" Izzy asked.

"So you're nineteen, and you're writing a story that's going to wake the dead. You'll be dragging history out of the shadows. You're going to make people *uncomfortable,* to say the least. People will be embarrassed. You might end up on talk shows, discussing the secret life of the Hero of St. Maria Goretti's."

"Can I quote you on these things?" Izzy asked.

Shannon's eyes turned to daggers. "You're not taking me seriously, dear?"

"I want to know the truth."

No one said a word. Abel looked down at his camera. He shifted uncomfortably on the picnic bench while the two women stared at each other.

Shannon smiled again. "How about that cigarette now, dear?" she asked.

"Thanks, I will," Izzy said.

Abel stood. "I'm getting a beer. I'll help myself."

***

Evan Long shuffled to the visiting room. Just days until his execution, he was starting to enjoy the extra attention. After years of the nearly continuous monotony of solitary confinement that was death row, there was suddenly a relative flurry of activity. Visits from the warden, requests for interviews, extra calls to and from his lawyer's office. He was enjoying it, though it would all be over soon, one way or another.

Warden Wood entered the room. Abel slowly got to his feet. "I got to hand it to you, Long," he said. "If nothing else, you are polite."

"I'm polite to people who are polite to me."

The warden ignored the compliment. "I'm here for two reasons, Long."

"Okay."

The warden pointed to the bench on Evan's side. They both sat. Wood looked directly at Evan when he spoke, as he did with everyone he spoke to. "First, in regard to the interview request. That is denied."

Evan was surprised. "Why, Warden?"

"It's too close to the day, Long. And you still have legal matters pending. It would be irresponsible of me to allow you to talk to the media when your execution date is so close."

"Shouldn't that be up to me?" Evan asked. "I can decide what risks to take, can't I?"

"You lost that right when you were convicted," the Warden said. "It's now my job to look out for your best interests in this matter. If you really have something you want to say to the public, you may do so through a statement by your lawyer, or any other person willing to publish it after your execution, if that happens. You can write it and mail it, or I can see that it gets to whomever you wish."

"I want to do the interview, Warden," Evan said. "Please reconsider."

"My decision is final," the warden said. "Now, if and when you are executed, you will be given the opportunity to make a final statement in the presence of members of the media. You can say whatever you want."

Evan lowered his head and frowned. He had been looking forward to the interview.

"I'm sorry, Long," Wood said. "I can see you're disappointed. I think this is for the best."

"I know," Evan said, feeling himself start to cry. "I just think I should be able to talk if I want to."

The warden allowed the news to sink in, and for Evan to regain his composure.

"There is another reason I am here," he said.

"What?"

"You have a visitor."

Evan's eyes brightened. "Who?"

"A priest," Wood said.

Evan would usually have erupted angrily at this, but today he just felt more disappointed. "Tell him to go away, Warden," he said, filling up again. "I've told you over and over I don't want a priest."

The warden leaned forward and spoke in a near whisper. "I know you have, Long," he said. "You've told me a thousand times."

"Tell him to go away!"

"Listen to me, Long," he said. He then reached across the table and placed a hand gently on Evan's left shoulder. It was the first time in years that Evan had been touched in kindness. Even his lawyer had never touched him. He spoke to Evan in a whisper. "I know you read your Bible. I do too. And I know that every person is better than the worst things he's ever done. Now, you say you want this man to go away, and all I ask is that you tell him yourself. Can you do that, Evan?"

Evan gasped. The warden had called him by his first name. No prison employee had done that in his entire time in confinement.

"The guard will stand outside the door," he said. "Nobody is listening. Tell this man whatever you want, okay? Tell him to get lost. Just knock on the door and the officer will see that he leaves immediately. Can you do that?"

Evan nodded his head. "I might tell him to fuck off, though," he said through tears.

Wood smiled. "I'm sure he can take it. I'll send him in."

The warden lifted his huge presence from the table and left the room. Evan did not stand, as he usually did. He sat staring at the

253

table. After a few minutes, he heard the door open, and he felt the man dressed in black stand beside him in the small space."

"Visitor for you, Long," the officer said. "Take your time."

Evan kept looking at the table as the priest closed the door behind him and took his seat across from him, his large black shape filling Evan's peripheral view. After a minute or so, Evan finally raised his eyes to look at his visitor.

They made eye contact. Neither man smiled.

Evan filled with anger. "*You?*" he said. "What in the hell do *you* want?"

***

Shannon Maher had carefully placed photographs all over her picnic table. There were over a hundred. Most of them were of children at camp in various stages of summer bliss. Abel recognized some of them, but did not see himself in any. Izzy's tape recorder was running continuously as Shannon spoke, and she only wrote in her notepad occasionally. Talking slowly and easily, Shannon spoke fondly of her three summers working at the camp. Abel sat, mostly listening, but contributing occasionally to what was turning more into a conversation rather than an interview. Izzy, no longer hindered by having to hide her identity, came across as much more open and engaging than Abel was used to.

For Abel, it had been a surprise to learn the truth of Izzy's Identity, but not a shock. He had known all along that she had been keeping something from him, and from everyone else involved in the story. This explained why they had been chased away from the governor's office. If his staff had found out that a reporter was not who she said she was, of course they would see it as a problem. Why put a man who may soon run for president at risk in that way?

What was troubling Abel more than being turned away by the governor's staff was being harassed by them. Why would Springer go to such lengths? Was he worried that the truth about his actions that day would hurt him politically? Springer and his staff had to know that refusing to do this interview would not help in that regard. Those details would come out eventually, anyway. This was probably why Springer had agreed to meet with Izzy privately, in the first place: Get all the details out there early enough for them to be kicked around by the public. Be open and honest as soon as she asked. *"Regardless of what I did that day, Joe Conway was a hero and I honor his memory."* There couldn't be much political cost to that. Springer would have an easy time explaining his actions.

But once his staff found out that Joe's daughter was writing the story, everything changed. Did she have an agenda beyond what she was claiming? Whatever it was would carry a lot more weight than the work of just any college reporter. The daughter of a hero could not simply be dismissed as a crackpot journalist, so they had to be careful. To Abel, however, their actions so far seemed extreme. Intimidating at least two people so far just to stop a story that would come out eventually anyway? Was he hiding something else?

Izzy inwardly took note of every move Shannon Maher made as the tape recorder documented her words. The woman's actions were a seemingly rehearsed form of graceful. Every photograph she pointed to was an elaborate presentation. She would tell the story of the picture, allowing the words to roll off her tongue as if she had been waiting years to proclaim them. Every voice inflection seemed practiced; every chuckle seemed perfectly timed. Izzy wondered with whom she had been sharing these stories all these years. In the pictures, children were paddling in kayaks, smiling through ice cream-covered faces, throwing water-soaked sponges, playing tennis, and splashing in the pool.

"Who took all these photos?" Abel asked. Izzy assumed he was trying to sound like an interested photographer. Of course, he was halfway through his second beer, so maybe he was just making conversation. The next time Shannon stood to go back into the house, Izzy would be sure to cut him off.

255

"I took most of these," Shannon said. "Except the ones I'm in, of course. Those were taken by other counselors, or Joe. I never let the kids use my camera."

Izzy carefully picked up one picture. It was of Joe Conway, her father. He was in the pool with a group of children. He was throwing one child while others eagerly awaited their turn. The child was screaming with Joy. She turned the photograph over. She saw the writing. *-7/14/75 - In the pool, throwing Jeff B-*

"Is this Joe's handwriting?" she asked.

"That's your father's writing," Shannon said. "And look at this."

Izzy watched as Shannon slowly began turning over every picture. Each one of them had her father's handwriting on the back. Each was labeled with the date and the people in the photograph. Her father had meticulously labeled every one of them.

Izzy watched, not sure what to make of this. "He wrote on all of these?"

"He did," Shannon said. "He insisted on labeling and dating pictures. He was always worried that people would never know who was in the pictures, or when they were taken."

Izzy didn't say anything, choosing instead to read her father's writing, something she had seen very little of until now. Thinking about it now, she could remember seeing the backs of some of the pictures in her home, and noting that they were all labeled with dates, people, and places. She had never realized it was an obsessive habit of her father's.

"Is this all of them?" Izzy asked.

Shannon drew back on the bench where she sat. Izzy watched as Shannon thought carefully about her words. "There are more," she said. "I keep them in a separate box." Shannon slowly lifted a small, pink tin box that had been next to her on the bench and placed it on the table in front of her. She placed a hand on the box. "If you'd like, I could open this and show you the rest," she said, her voice dropping to almost a whisper. "Would you like to see them?"

Shannon looked at Izzy, and they both understood. The realization was coming over Izzy like a slow, cold flood. She had noted the insinuations by Will Janicki, had ignored the pressings of Abel, and had decided that her story would not turn into one for the tabloids. But here she sat, across from a woman who had deliberately avoided any contact with journalists for two decades and was finally telling her story. She was telling it to a reporter who had decided to revisit a story, dragging all of the beauty and ugliness into the open so that the public could devour the truth. The reckless, ignorant, curious public would need to be educated. Shannon Maher was a resource. Izzy was the teacher. This would have to be shared.

And then the ugliness would start. The local newspapers would decide to investigate further. There would be opinion pieces. It might even go national. Maybe there would be a movie. Izzy Buchanan, the journalist, would have to include every sordid detail that she came across in her investigation. It was her sacred responsibility to report what she had learned. She would have to bring the light of truth to a waiting public. *To her mother.*

Unless the box remained closed.

It was Izzy's choice. She could allow the woman across from her to tell her story. To present each picture and its narrative. Izzy could likewise ask her to keep it closed. She already had plenty of information for the story. She could simply report what the woman said and cross her off the list. She would move on to the governor and the killer, and she would have her award-winning story. That would be it.

She watched as the woman read her thoughts. Izzy knew that Shannon could see her working the dilemma through the complex logic of a daughter and a journalist. Shannon's eyes turned from sympathetic to urgent. Her eyes began to fill, not with sadness or sympathy, but with anger. The two women had communicated volumes without saying a word.

Izzy's eyes narrowed. "How long have you been waiting to show someone what's in that box?"

Shannon inhaled through her nose, trying to keep her rage from expelling out of her nostrils. "We were supposed to be together," she said through clenched teeth.

257

Izzy had made up her mind. "Open the box," she said.

"He had to be a hero," Shannon said, her voice shaking with urgency. "He was going to leave her. We were going to be together."

Izzy reached across the table for the box, but Shannon's hand caught hers. Both their hands rested firmly on the lid of the small container. They looked at each other.

Shannon spoke. Her voice was harsh. "If you see what's in here, I want it all in your article. Everything," she said.

Izzy sneered. "I decide what goes in this story. You want a soap opera, you can call someone else."

"This *is* the story," Shannon said.

"I will decide that," Izzy growled.

Shannon squeezed Izzy's hand. "There is more than you think."

"Open the box!" Izzy shouted.

***

"Leave," Evan said.

"Why?" the priest barked through his Italian accent.

"I've already made my peace with God," he said. "I don't need a priest, especially not *you*."

Father Francesco Antonelli noticed that Evan had spoken the last word with a special type of disdain, one that he had rarely heard in his many years as a priest. He had heard countless people speak harshly of his Mother Church, and of men of the cloth in general, but very rarely had anyone spoken so harshly of him personally. Most of those times had come when he had crossed paths with a family tragedy. The parents of an unfortunate eleven-year-old boy who had survived childhood leukemia, only to be killed a year later by a drunk driver came to mind. They had blamed and hated him for failing to adequately explain the complicated workings of God. This was understandable. He knew that even this was not personal. However, what he heard today was different. Evan Long was sitting across from him with hatred in his heart, and in his eyes.

258

The priest could see that Evan Long was full of a raging, *personal* hatred.

"I have only to come to offer you peace," the priest said, "and reconciliation with God's church."

"I don't want either," Evan said. "I have made my peace with God, and it has nothing to do with you or your church."

"You've read the Holy Scriptures, then?" the priest asked hopefully.

"It's none of your business," Evan said. "I'm going to tell the guard that I don't want you here."

Father Antonelli waved in the guard's direction. He was standing with his back to the door and could be seen through the small window in the door. "I know this man. He used to work for me. I told him to give me five minutes, then I would leave if you wanted me to."

Evan's eyes filled with even more rage. "You can't *do* that!" he said.

The priest smiled. "He is a very religious man," he said. "He wants your soul to be saved. He sees the good in you. He wants me to help you."

"I'll tell the warden," Evan said desperately. "You can't just come in here and do this. I have rights."

"You may be dead soon, my son. It is my job to offer you the chance of redemption."

"I don't need you!"

The priest leaned forward and spoke in a hushed, urgent voice. "Evan, I have known men like you who sit for hours every day, reading the Scriptures," he said. "But this can be very dangerous. You can make all kinds of interpretations that are false. A man in your desperate position could make all kinds of incorrect conclusions. I can help you with this!"

"I have been in this *desperate position* for years," Evan said. "And I probably know the Bible better than you do by now."

"This is impossible," the priest said. "You've had no formal education."

259

"God has forgiven me!" Evan shouted.

"God has the power to forgive you, yes!" the priest shouted back. "But you need to be forgiven by his Church. I can do this!"

"What do I need that for? God loves me."

The priest opened his hands and gestured to the ceiling. "After Reconciliation, you can receive the holy sacraments," he said. "This will bring you into physical contact with Christ. You will feel this love more intensely than you can imagine. This must happen before you die."

Father Antonelli watched as the man's angry expression turned to confusion. He had clearly never heard anything of this sort before. He hoped he had made a connection. He wanted to offer Evan the chance to confess his sins, then receive the body and blood of Christ in the accidents of bread and wine. He wanted to anoint the man with the sacred chrism before his imminent death.

"The Scriptures are not enough, my son," he continued. "There is the sacred tradition of the Holy Church. It is God's instrument on earth. You must see this."

Evan's eyes darkened again. "The only thing I see is a pathetic old man trying to sell me a lie. I've done what I need to do on this earth, and I am prepared for the next. Now leave me alone."

Father Antonelli placed his right hand on his own head and rubbed it slowly. "Is there something personal you hold against me, my son?"

"What?" Evan asked.

"Do you hate me, Mr. Long, personally?"

Evan didn't say anything.

The priest continued, his Italian accent flaring. "One hot summer day, you walked onto my campground, bringing evil with you. You kill so many innocent people. You try to kill more. You ruin the lives of so many families. You come here, and they say you must die for what you did. They tell me you have seen the error of your ways." He pointed to the guard outside the door. "They tell me Evan Long is nice to everyone in the prison. I believe this. But I come here to grant you absolution, and you don't say, 'No, thank

260

you, Father.' You are full of hatred, my son. Is it me or is it the Church I represent? I must know this."

Father Antonelli watched as the storm clouds formed in Evan Long's eyes. His chest began to expand and contract as his breath quickened. His eyes filled with rage and tears that he was trying desperately to hold inside.

"Leave now," Evan said. "Don't ever come back here."

After a long moment, the priest stood and walked to the door. Before knocking to be let out of the room, he turned and said, "I will pray for you, my son. Your journey may end this week or in many years. But as long as I am alive, I will pray for you."

The priest lingered behind Evan for a moment. Evan considered his options. He could tell the guard that he wanted to speak to the warden. He would then inform the warden that he no longer wanted to meet with any priests. But this meeting had been too short. The guard would be suspicious, possibly noting the tears in Evan's eyes. He didn't want this. The guard might leak it to the media. Tell them how Evan Long tearfully demanded a priest leave. He would look *weak*.

He heard the door begin to open. "Wait, Father," Evan said. "Come back inside."

The door closed and the priest stood next to Evan, who sat with his eyes fixed on the table, where his chained hands rested clenched together.

"Yes, my son?"

"I want to talk to a priest," Evan said. "But not you."

Father Antonelli sighed with relief. "I will ask the prison chaplain to send a priest immediately. This won't be a problem."

"No," Evan said. "I want that fat priest that's always on T.V."

Father Antonelli thought for a moment. "I don't know this man on T.V."

"Yes, you do. Father Johnston," Evan said. "I want that priest who always speaks at those memorial services to come here. I'll talk to him."

"Why will you talk to this man, Evan?" the priest asked.

"It's him or no one," Evan said. "I'll make my confession to him."

"I can speak to him, but I don't know if he will come," Father Antonelli said. "He is a very emotional man. You took his friend, and he has become very close to many of the victims and their families."

"He'll come," Evan said. "Just tell him Evan Long wants to make his final confession. I'll see him this evening."

"I will try," he said.

"Thanks, Father," Evan said as he turned to look at the priest. "You can leave now."

The priest turned to walk through the door. Evan heard him knock to alert the guard that he was ready to leave. When he heard the door open, Evan said, "Thank you for coming, Father. I will pray for *you*."

***

The box was open, and three five-by-seven color photographs lay on the picnic table between Izzy and Shannon. That was all of them. Abel had briefly studied the contents of each photo, but he was more focused on the reaction of Izzy. Looking at the photographs, Izzy showed almost no immediate reaction, save for a few deep breaths.

"This was in the pool," Shannon said, pointing to a picture of a younger version of herself, her left arm wrapped around Joe Conway, holding him close. Shannon was looking at the camera while Joe seemed to be laughing at something off to his left. They were in the deep water of the pool, immersed up to their shoulders. She pointed to another picture. "Here we are in the staff room, just the two of us." This picture showed Shannon and Joe sitting at the

262

table in the room where Izzy and Abel had met Father Antonelli. It was off center and appeared to have been taken by Shannon, probably by extending her arm while holding the camera. Joe appeared to be surprised by the picture. Shannon's head leaned in to touch his, and Joe's mouth was open. The third picture was similar, except they looked to be sitting in a car. Both wore sunglasses and had their heads rested against the worn tan leather of a front car seat. "We had both taken the day off," Shannon said as she carefully tapped the photo. "A getaway to the beach, just the two of us."

"Which beach?" Izzy asked.

"Avalon," Shannon answered. "At the Jersey Shore."

"I know where it is," Izzy said. "He took you to my family's beach house?"

Shannon smiled. "Yes, he did."

Izzy placed a finger on the first photograph. "Who took this one?"

"Why do you ask?"

Abel shifted uncomfortably, worried that a confrontation was about to ensue. The beer was helping.

Izzy glared at Shannon. "It's obvious that *you* took the other two," she said. "I want to know who took this one."

"Because?" Shannon asked.

"Because I want to know who else knew about you," Izzy said.

"You mean about *us*," Shannon said.

Izzy laughed dismissively. "These pictures say a lot about your relationship," she said.

"How is that?" Shannon asked.

Abel watched Izzy, once again finding himself amazed at her ability to adapt to a difficult situation. He had never seen anyone handle herself in interviews the way she did.

"He obviously doesn't even know his picture is being taken in this one," Izzy said, pointing to the one in the pool. "And in these other two, he looks surprised to see his picture being taken. I'd bet he made you promise never to show those to anyone, didn't he?"

"I'm right, aren't I?" Izzy asked.

"More than you know, my dear," Shannon said. "He had me tear up both of those pictures in front of him. I promised him there were no doubles. I lied." She pointed to the one in the pool again. "He never even knew about this one."

"So in the time you spent together…"

"Two summers," Shannon said.

"In two summer together, you had only three pictures taken?"

"That's right. He would not allow it. Too worried his wife, your mother, would find out."

"So, it sounds like you were his summer project, two years in a row."

Shannon's eyes welled up. "It was more than that."

"Did he have any others?" Izzy asked.

Shannon drew her lips inward. "If there were others, they meant nothing to him," she said.

Izzy shook her head. "I see," she said. "So you were the only fling that *meant* something to him."

"I did mean something," Shannon said, her voice raising. "And for a reporter, you're starting to sound like an angry daughter."

Abel knew Shannon was right about this, which is why he had been lightly tapping Izzy's right foot under the table for the last few minutes. She was going too far, but Abel could hardly blame her.

Izzy half-nodded, appearing to acknowledge what Shannon had said. She turned her attention back to the pool photo. "So who took this?" she asked again.

The woman said nothing, just glared at the photographs as if she were looking directly at the past.

"Can you tell me?" Izzy asked.

Abel finally spoke. "She doesn't have to tell you," he said. "It's obvious who took it."

He watched as the two women simultaneously turn their gazes toward him.

"Is it?" Shannon asked. "You think you know who took this?"

264

Abel downed the last of his second beer and plopped the can on the picnic table. "It had to have been the one public figure who has never spoken about the shooting. The one guy who's spent the last twenty years rallying the public to worship at the altar of the Great Joe Conway. The last thing he'd want is for the public to know that St. Joe Conway was having an affair with a counselor, and that he had known about it all along, even helped him keep it a secret."

Nobody spoke. Shannon lit a cigarette. Izzy wrote in her notepad, and Abel alternated looks at the two of them.

Finally, Shannon said, "Good old Mike," she said. "He could never get a girl like me, but he was happy to run interference for his buddy. Joe used to say Mike was living through him. Of course, Joe was just using him. He'd pretend to like anybody if it served his purpose."

"That includes you, I guess," Izzy said. Abel kicked her again.

"He did like me," Shannon said.

"I'm sure he liked *something*," Izzy said.

Izzy felt Abel kick her right shin as he loudly said "Okay," before Shannon could respond. "Would it be okay if I took these photos with me?" Abel asked, sounding all business. "I'll mail them back to you."

Realizing that she had indeed crossed too many lines, Izzy quickly composed herself. "I'm sorry," she said to Shannon. "That was out of line."

"I understand, dear," Shannon said, waving her hand dismissively. "He was your father, and you've heard your whole life what a hero he was. This must be devastating."

Izzy shook her head, determined not to give Shannon the satisfaction. "Not really," she said. "Men are men." She glanced at Abel. "Sorry," she said.

Abel smiled. "There aren't too many saints in this world."

"No, there aren't," Shannon said. "But Joe Conway was a hero. He saved many lives. And you are right to think of him that way. He was a great man, but nobody is perfect."

"Thank you," Izzy said. Inside, her rage at the woman across from her had dwindled to a slow burn. She knew she would need to keep her emotions together until the interview was over. After that, she could vent, probably joining Abel in drinks. She prepared her next question, trying to sound as collected as ever."

"Aside from these photos and their stories, what can you tell me about that day?" Izzy asked.

Shannon's eyes narrowed. "But these pictures, they will be in your story, right?" she asked.

"Probably," Izzy said. "Unless I decide that your history with Joe is not important to this story." Izzy realized she was still in character, calling her father "Joe."

Shannon gasped. "It's important," she said. "You have no idea   how   important."

"Then tell me," Izzy said.

Shannon finished her cigarette and put it out. She looked at the three photos in front of her. Izzy watched as she carefully picked them up and placed them back inside the pink box. She looked at Izzy. "Let's go inside," she said.

Izzy followed Shannon Maher into her kitchen. Shannon gestured toward the table. Izzy and Abel sat while Shannon made a pot of coffee.

"How much time do y'all have?" Shannon asked.

"Our train leaves tomorrow morning," Izzy said.

Shannon nodded as she scooped coffee into the maker. "Then we have plenty," she said. "I have more to tell you."

Izzy felt it was time to set some ground rules. "That's fine," she said. "But I need you to know a few things first."

Shannon turned to face her. "What's that, dear?" she asked.

"This story is about what happened at the campground that day," she said. "It's not about Joe Conway, and it's not about you. Yes,

266

you'll both be important parts of the story, but I am writing it because I want the public to hear the voices of the people who were there and who've never spoken."

"I understand," Shannon said.

"Good," Izzy said. "So, you were in love with Joe?"

Shannon frowned. "I was," she said.

"And you think he was in love with you."

"Yes, I do. I *know* he was," she said. "I was only nineteen at the time, but I wasn't stupid."

"I get it," Izzy said. "And I can put that in the story. You're right. It is important. But there are more important things."

"Like what?" Shannon asked.

"I plan to interview Governor Mike Springer," she said.

"I know."

"And Evan Long."

"Oh my heavens," Shannon said as she turned around to finish making the coffee.

"And I've already learned a few things about that day that nobody knows."

"Am I one of them, dear?"

"Yes," Izzy said. "And the groundskeeper. He's told us things that have never been made public."

"So what is your point?" Shannon asked.

"It's this," Izzy said. "I want you to tell me everything you can. Forget that he was my father, and forget about my mother. Stop trying to get me to react by telling me about you and my dad. Just give me the facts and let me do the rest."

Izzy watched as her words sank in. Shannon nodded slowly. "I can do that," she said. "And you're right. I've not been very nice to you, dear. But once I'm done telling my story, I think you'll understand me a little better."

"That's a deal," Izzy said. She turned to look at Abel. "You're going to conduct this interview," she said.

Abel's eyebrows jumped. "Why?"

267

"To keep it from getting personal," she said. "I'll chime in when I need to."

Abel thought for a moment, then nodded. "Okay," he said.

Izzy placed her tape recorder on the table and hit the record button.

Abel tried to gather his thoughts. It had been ages since he had conducted a proper interview.

"I thought you were a photographer," Shannon said.

Abel looked at Izzy and smirked. "I am," he said. "But I used to be a reporter."

"He's a good reporter," Izzy said.

Abel looked curiously at Izzy and wondered if she really thought that. He shrugged, took a deep breath, and began.

"I'm going to start by asking you three questions. They are questions that we intend to ask everyone we interview who was there that day, and I'll ask you to keep the answers short and to the point."

"Okay," Shannon said. "Go ahead."

"First, what do you remember most about that day?"

Shannon frowned. "That's easy. The look in Joe's eyes when he told me I had to run away. There were things we desperately wanted to tell each other, but we couldn't."

"Second, do you want Evan Long to be executed?"

Her eyes narrowed in hatred. "Yes, I do, and I hope it hurts."

"Okay," Abel said. "The third question: If you could do anything different that day, what would it be?"

Shannon had to find her words. "Earlier that day, I had left Joe a note. I wanted to meet with him, to tell him something very important. I wish I hadn't done that," she said.

Abel was confused. "Why?"

She shook her head. "It created uncertainty," she said. "I could see it in his eyes, even before any of the shooting started. I hated seeing him like that. He knew I had something important to tell him, but he didn't know what. Then he died never knowing what I was planning on telling him."

268

Abel looked at Izzy. She nodded. The three questions were out of the way.

"Thanks," Abel said to Shannon. "I'd like to ask a few more questions."

"Okay," Shannon said.

"First, just to review, you said you were with Joe Conway and sixteen children on the tennis courts when it started, right?"

"Right."

"Okay," Abel said. "All of the children there were very young, so there has never been a reliable witness to speak of the events that unfolded on the tennis court when it all started. Can you tell us in detail what you remember?"

Shannon took a breath and glanced to her left. "I sure can. Joe was about to start a tennis lesson. It was really hot that morning, and he was taking the lesson slowly, eating up time with talking about tennis rules. He wanted to spend as little time as possible having them run around," she explained. "It was so hot. So we were all sitting in a big circle in the one shaded area of the courts. Joe was across from me. I had a little boy named Nathan in my lap. He was a rammy little guy, so I had to keep him with me all the time."

Izzy interrupted. "Nathan McLean," she said, her pen still going. "He's at Penn now. Wharton School of Business."

Shannon looked at her. "How do you know that?" she asked.

"She knows everyone who was there that day," Abel said, "and their life stories."

Shannon shook her head in amazement.

Abel continued. "So you're in a circle waiting for the lesson to start. What happens next?"

Shannon inhaled. "It started," she said. "Joe heard it first. Loud bangs. Sounded like firecrackers. We all looked around. I looked at Joe. He stood and walked to the fence and looked out over the campground. I followed him, and some of the children crept after us. There's a perfect view of the pool from there. Funny that I had never even noticed that until then."

"When did you realize it was gunshots?" Abel asked.

269

"We saw the people in the pool trying to get out of the far gate. It was locked and they were screaming. Then the guy came into view. He was walking from the left side. Firing his gun. A pistol. We knew what was happening." Her tone of voice became hushed, almost distant in the way she told of the events, not at all like the rehearsed, precise approach she had taken when revealing her relationship with Joe Conway. She continued. "The week before that one, we had actually discussed it."

Abel stopped her. "How is that?"

Shannon's eyes found Abel's. "What?" she asked.

"How could you have discussed it the week before?"

Realizing what she had said, Shannon gasped and shook her head. "I'm sorry," she said. "I'm being foolish. It was the tenth anniversary of that shooting at that college in Texas. And then earlier that year, there was another shooting at a school. This stuff was in the papers, and we were talking about it."

Abel glanced at Izzy, who had stopped writing and looked back. They knew they had something interesting. "What did Joe think about those things?" Abel asked.

"He hated them," Shannon said, her voice intensifying. "He just couldn't stand the thought of innocent people dying for no reason."

"He talked about that a lot?" Abel asked.

"Yes, he did. And he said it, a bunch of times, that if he was ever in the situation where he had to risk his life to save innocent people, he would."

"Wow," Abel said. "I'll bet a lot of people would say that." He looked at Izzy. "But he actually *did* it."

"Heroic," Shannon said quietly.

Izzy looked at Shannon. "I don't understand," she said.

"Don't understand what, dear?" Shannon asked.

"He had a wife. A child coming. Didn't he think of them?" she asked.

Shannon shrugged. "Knowing Joe, he probably expected to get out of that situation alive. But he would have done it anyway."

"I don't understand," Izzy said again.

Shannon tapped the side of her head with her index finger. "He had a lot going on in his mind, dear. He was holding a lot of guilt."

"Over what?" Abel asked. "You?"

Shannon shook her head. "Not over me," she said. "Vietnam had just ended."

"He felt guilty about the Vietnam War?" Abel asked.

Shannon nodded. "He had many friends who went there. Philadelphia was a very generous city when it came to that awful war. But Joe was never drafted, and he never volunteered. His parents saw to that."

"How?" Abel asked.

"As you may know," she said to Izzy, "his parents were part of the high society of Philadelphia, and their boy wasn't going to run off and die alongside all those poor boys. They had a doctor friend who would raise a boy's blood pressure just enough for him not to pass a physical. Unfortunately, Joe's condition was chronic. It lasted the duration of the war. The affluent always have their ways of avoiding those messy things the rest of us must face, don't they?"

"I get it," Abel said. He looked at Izzy. The uneasiness shone on her face.

"Did Joe want to go fight in the war?" Izzy asked.

"He told me he did," Shannon said. "Not because he necessarily believed in that war. I don't know if he did or didn't. He just hated that so many of his friends were going, some by choice, some not, while his parents were insisting he stay behind. He felt like less of a man because of it. He felt he was neglecting a duty to his country, to his friends."

"I didn't realize Joe's family was so wealthy," Abel said.

"They surely were," Shannon said. "His father was a prominent Philadelphia businessman. Joe was a child of wealth, and he enjoyed it. When his parents insisted he have a job, he gave tennis lessons." She laughed. "Then they had the nerve to insist he put his business degree to use, and he told them that giving tennis lessons *was* a business. They grew tired of the game, so his daddy made a large donation to the Holy Church in Wilmington, and their boy was

271

suddenly taken care of. That Italian priest saw to it. Out of their hair and out of Philadelphia. Joe moved to Delaware and got into the business of running a campground. He was a free spirit, and it was a leisurely existence. He surely didn't need the money. He did it for fun, and for other things." She flashed a devilish smile, and Abel could feel Izzy seething next to him.

"So Joe Conway was a rich kid who got out of having to go to Vietnam, and he was feeling guilty about it," Abel said.

Shannon shook her head. "It *tortured* him," Shannon said with conviction. "His parents put so much pressure on him, and he just could not stand up to them. They saw to it that he carry on the family name at Penn, so he did it. They told him it was time to settle down and get married, so he did, at least the *married* part." She turned to look out her kitchen window. She stared blankly, as if seeing something that only she could perceive. "I think the only decision he ever made for himself was to take that tennis racket and smash that killer over the head with it." She sighed deeply and lowered her head. She stared at the kitchen table. No one spoke.

"And he could never tell that pretty wife," Shannon said. "I mean about how he avoided the war."

"Why not?" Izzy asked.

Shannon looked at Izzy. "Because of Doctor Daniel Heller, dear."

"My grandfather," Izzy said.

"Yes, your grandfather. He was the doctor who helped your father avoid going to Vietnam. It would have crushed your mother to know her father was helping her future husband commit a federal crime," Shannon said. "That Abigail. Such a stickler for the rules." She looked at Izzy. "Did you know Joe and Abby's parents had been friends since childhood?"

"Yes," Izzy said blankly. "They've barely spoken since my father was killed."

Shannon smirked. "No surprise, is it? All they cared about was their boy. Once he was gone..."

Abel looked at Izzy, who seemed to wince every time Shannon mentioned her mother. She was visibly trying her best to keep herself together in light of these revelations.

"Please continue," Abel said. "Joe was feeling guilty."

"Yes, he was," Shannon said. "And one evening, we were lying in bed, and we heard on the radio about the tenth anniversary of that shooting at that college in Texas. And there had recently been another shooting at a school somewhere. I can't remember where exactly. That's when Joe told me all this."

"What did he say?" Abel asked.

Shannon twisted her mouth in thought. Abel watched as a tear began to trickle down her left cheek. Without wiping it, she said, "He told me if that ever happened at the campground, if somebody ever tried to hurt one of the children or one of the counselors, he would do everything he could to stop it." She gasped for air as she tried to finish. "He said he sometimes even hoped for something to happen, so he could prove he was no coward, even if it meant losing his own life. He said he'd do it." She looked at Izzy, who had been trying to keep from crying. Shannon was now sobbing. "And he did it, didn't he?" she gasped. "He didn't die fighting in Vietnam, but he died right there at Maria G's Campground. He just up and left so much behind. Sometimes I really hate him for it." She covered her eyes as she wept.

"He saved many lives," Abel said. "There are dozens of people, many of whom have married and have had children of their own. They wouldn't be here today if he hadn't done what he did."

"But he was safe with us!" Shannon shouted. "He could have run away with me and the other children on that tennis court. I wanted so badly to tell him that. He should have thought of me, of himself. He should have thought of his *own* children!"

Abel took it all in. It was his first interview in years, but he knew he had done it well. He felt for the woman who sat across from him, but he relished in that almost-forgotten rush he had felt during his days as a reporter when he knew he had gotten what he wanted.

Shannon Maher had become a sobbing mess, but she was the story today. Abel and Izzy had exactly what they needed.

He glanced at Izzy, who had stopped scribbling. He watched as she placed her pen carefully on the table and looked at Shannon.

"What do you mean *'children'*"? Izzy asked.

Shannon stopped crying when she heard the question. She lifted her head to see the young woman across from her, staring back. Her expression was stone cold, but there had been something in the manner in which she had asked the question. Shannon had long prided herself in being able to read the tone in people's voices better than most, a talent she attributed to having mastered Mid Atlantic and Southern dialects. She had always been fascinated with the way a person's voice raised and dropped, betraying the speaker's emotions. There was an urgent curiosity in Izzy's question.

Shannon took a breath. She knew she had done it. In her flurry of emotion, she had said it. She had planned to tell her soon anyway, but not like that.

"Your father was a courageous man," she said. "Do you think you have his courage?"

"I beg your pardon?" Izzy asked.

"Courage," Shannon said. "You chase down these people to interview them, and you ask them challenging questions. Do you think that takes courage?"

"I don't really know," Izzy said.

"No, you don't know, dear," Shannon said. "It's been twenty years since that day, and do you know what the most courageous thing anybody can do will be, once this story is written?"

"Tell me," Izzy said.

"A mother will pick up that story and read it," she said. "A mother who hasn't held her child in twenty years will find herself reliving the horrors of the greatest tragedy of her life. Will you be proud of yourself when she does that? A mother remembers what the top of her baby's head smelled like when she fed him. A mother remembers the sound of her baby laughing when she tickled his tummy before bedtime. She can still feel the coldness of tears on her cheeks when she hugged him. She will keep reading your little story because she will feel like she has to. And while she does, you will be basking in the publicity your story has garnered."

"Why would she feel like she has to read it?" Izzy asked.

"Because a mother needs to know what happened to her baby. It's her job to know. You uncover all your new facts and intriguing storylines, but remember the human beings, the *mothers*, who still cry themselves to sleep at night because they remember what they were wearing when they heard the news that their baby wasn't among the survivors. Because they remember taking down the decorations in their baby's room after they finally accepted that he wasn't coming back. That mother will read your story because she will think her child deserves for her to know all the facts. You're revisiting this will cause nightmares you can't imagine."

"Why are you telling me this?" Izzy asked. "Do you think I shouldn't write this story?"

"Oh no, dear. Don't misunderstand. You *need* to write this because you feel a duty as a daughter, and as a journalist. And after what you've learned you *really* need to write it. You'd be compromising your integrity if you didn't. But you also need to know the pain, dear. You didn't lose anyone that day. You've lived without a father because of it, but you didn't *lose* him. If you want this story to be what it needs to be, you need to have wisdom beyond your very few years, and I am not certain that you do." She reached across the table and took Izzy's hand. "I am sure you will write with passion and emotion, just like you always do, but you need to remember who the courageous ones are. And you need to write it in such a way that you are able to live with the nightmares you have caused by writing it."

"The mothers," Izzy said. "The fathers, too."

Shannon nodded. "Have you ever spoken to any of them?"

"No."

"A pity," Shannon said. "You will talk to their killer, but you won't talk to them."

"They aren't a part of this story," Izzy said.

"Then remember them when you write it."

"The parents," Izzy said. "You're a mother, aren't you?"

"I am," Shannon said. "And it's hard being one. Can I tell you about it?"

"Yes," Izzy said.

"Look around you," Shannon said quietly. "Use your eyes."

"My eyes," Izzy said back to her. It was acknowledgment. She knew.

"They were his eyes."

"My father's," Izzy said.

"And I can still see them. I've looked into them for the last twenty years."

"I've already met him," Izzy said.

"Now open those eyes, dear." Shannon smiled and gazed around the room. "Look around you," she whispered.

And Izzy allowed her eyes to wander. They wandered away from the tear-filled eyes of Shannon Maher and fell temporarily on Abel's confused face. She saw his expression change, though. She saw him begin to understand. Izzy looked around the room. There were framed pictures in every part of it. The boy's face was everywhere. From a newly-born child to the young man she had met a few hours before, some with Shannon, and some without. In some of them, he was with older people, whom Izzy assumed were the boy's grandparents. In others, he was with friends. He was on a boat, in a bathtub playing with toys, in front of a statue, at a dinner table. And those eyes were in every one of them. They were the eyes she had seen in the photos of her father, and they were the eyes that Izzy saw in the mirror every day.

"Does he know?" Izzy asked quietly.

Shannon shook her head.

"Are you going to tell him?"

"I suppose I'll have to," Shannon said.

"Does my mother know?"

276

"Goodness no," Shannon said. "I have never spoken to your mother."

Izzy stayed focused, aware that the realization of what she had just been told had not completely sunk in yet. She had a brother. He was her age.

"Did my father know about him?"

Shannon frowned and put her head down. Her right hand massaged her forehead. "I think so," she said, wiping a tear.

"You don't know?" Izzy asked.

"You see, he saw me earlier that week. He was at the doctor with your mother. She was about to pop, and I had just found out I was pregnant. We saw each other but pretended not to even know each other, of course. But I'm sure he was suspicious. And we hadn't been very careful that summer. *I* hadn't been very careful."

Izzy thought she heard guilt in the woman's voice. "Were you trying to get pregnant on purpose?" she asked.

Shannon scoffed. "I don't think I ever thought of it that way," she said. "It's just that I loved him so much, and a young, dumb girl will do stupid things when she's in love."

"But he was married," Izzy said. "He had a family."

"He told me he loved me, dear," Shannon said, her voice shaking again. "And I believed him. Whether I was stupid to believe him, I don't know. It was so long ago. But I did believe him." Her trembling hands fumbled for a cigarette, which Abel helped her light. She thanked him and said, "I was going to tell him that day. I had left him that note that said we needed to talk. I think he got it, but I could never be sure. But on that tennis court, after the shooting started, when he told me I had to go with the children..." She stopped and looked at a recent picture of her son that was stuck to the refrigerator door. "You can say so much with a look, can't you? I looked at him that day, and I told him I was carrying his child. He knew. I think he did."

"Odds are, he suspected it when he saw you at the doctor, right?" Abel asked.

Izzy looked at Abel. "Sorry," he said. "I'm just trying to get the story straight." Izzy saw his curious expression turn worried. "Sorry," he said again. "I know it's an emotional moment. I'll shut up."

Izzy smiled. "It's okay. Now you're the unfazed reporter, I guess."

"I'm sure he suspected it," Shannon said. "By coincidence, I just happened to go to the same obstetrician as Abigail. Otherwise, he may have never known."

"And you're sure he's Joe's?" Abel asked.

"Jesus, Abel. Of course, she's sure," Izzy said, surprised to hear herself come to Shannon's defense.

Abel showed his palms. "I don't know," he said. "It was the 70's. I've heard a lot of things."

"Yes, I know he's Joe's son," Shannon said. "I know I was sleeping with a married man, but he was the only man I was sleeping with." She was not offended.

Izzy and Shannon locked eyes again. Neither said anything.

"Should I go for a walk or something?" Abel asked.

"What's his name?" Izzy asked.

Shannon smiled. Izzy recognized it as a mother's smile, the kind that only a woman who has reared a child can form. "I wanted to name him Joe," she said. "But your father was the only Joe for me. So I named him Conway. I call him Conny."

"Is that what everyone calls him?" Izzy asked.

"His friends call him Con," Shannon said, rolling her eyes. "I hope he never turns into one."

"Really?" Abel asked.

Shannon smirked. "He's a good boy," she said. "But he is nineteen. He has his moments."

"We all do," Abel said.

Shannon looked at Izzy. "I've never told him that he has a sister, and I'd like you to be there when I do. Will you meet us for dinner tonight?"

"Absolutely," Izzy said.

Abel closed his car door and waited for Izzy to start the car. "Nothing new from her, huh?"

"Shut up," she said.

"Okay. Can you tell me what you're thinking?"

"Not right now," she said, pulling her cigarettes from her purse.

"Come on," Abel said. "You're not supposed to smoke in here."

"Shut up," Izzy said again as she opened the window. "I just found out I have a brother."

Abel conceded with a nod. "Are you going to tell your mom?" he asked. "Or let her find out with the rest of the world?"

Izzy shook her head as she pulled away. "Let's go back to the hotel," she said. "I need to make a phone call."

"Your mother?" Abel asked.

"No."

***

"I need to know what's going on, sir." Bob hoped that being blunt would get the point across to his boss. So far, he had had very little success.

Mike Springer winced. "It's just the two of us here, Bob. Call me Mike."

"Sorry," Bob said. "Habit."

"Spending too much time with Sheila?" Mike asked.

Bob rolled his eyes. "She's something, isn't she?"

"I'm glad she's on our side."

Bob nodded. He was glad too. The woman was relentless. She was built for politics - a working-class girl with an excellent education and incredible instincts. She was a true find, and Bob knew that if he hadn't been so impressed he'd be more worried for his own job.

"So where is she now?" Mike asked.

Bob raised his eyebrows as he nodded at Mike. It was a familiar, subtle gesture between the two. It was a gesture that asked the

279

question, *do you really want to know?* Mike responded by nodding, almost imperceptibly. He wanted to know.

Bob glanced at his watch. "Landing any minute now. She's on a plane back from Charleston."

Mike nodded again. "Everything go okay?" he asked.

"She says it went fine, sir."

Mike Springer leaned forward in his chair and placed his hands on the conference table in front of him. Bob could see that he was trying to find the words. He knew the governor had a question but was afraid to ask it. They had walked this delicate line many times in the past. Bob was technically Mike's lawyer, so anything they discussed was protected by attorney-client privilege. However, anything that was revealed to the governor in these meetings meant that he may someday have to deny knowing it, which meant he would have to lie. And that meant he may find himself caught in a lie, which was never good, even in politics.

"Would you like me to tell you what she was doing in Charleston?" Bob asked. "Nothing illegal, sir."

"Then tell me," Mike said. "And stop the 'sir' shit, would you?"

"Shannon Maher," Bob said. He saw the governor's eyes register the name. "You know the name?" he asked.

"I do," Mike said. "I could never deny that. She was a counselor back then. Little blonde..." He stopped himself. "Attractive young lady."

"Got it," Bob said.

"Wow. If that reporter found her... she really *does* know what she's doing. And just a kid."

"She's *Joe Conway's* kid," Bob said.

Mike nodded. Sheila had told them that important news only a few minutes before the interview was supposed to happen. Mike would have never known until he saw her in person, having met her a few times, but not knowing that Elizabeth Conway was writing under a pen name, Izzy Buchanan. Sheila had saved him from something that could have gone very badly.

280

Bob continued. "So, like I said, I need to know what's going on, so we know how to proceed here."

Mike leaned back and scratched his chin. "Okay, Bob," he said slowly. "You can't share this with anybody."

"I know that," Bob said.

"So what do you want to know?"

"Mostly, I want to know what we are trying to keep from coming out."

"Why?" Mike asked.

"So I can keep it from coming out," Bob said, feeling a little frustrated. It was not typical for Mike Springer to play games with him.

"Sorry, Bob. Am I pissing you off?"

"Yes."

Mike stood abruptly. Bob knew to stay still and give Mike space. He didn't look at the governor, just felt him pacing the floor of his office. Bob could feel his boss debating with himself as to what his next step should be. This was the time to shut up and listen.

"There a few things going on here, Bob," the governor said. "First, this Shannon Maher in Charleston. She's a problem."

"Because…"

"Because she's going to turn our hero, Joe Conway, into a tabloid star."

Bob thought about this. "What did she do, sleep with him?"

Mike leaned against the window and faced Bob. He nodded. "Very little sleep."

Bob nodded. "This happened while Joe was married?"

"Right. And she wasn't the only one," Mike said. "But none of the others have ever mentioned it. Over the years, I've spoken to most of them about it. We were all friends, see? And they all agreed to keep it quiet, out of respect for Abigail, and for the kid. But if Shannon Maher starts running her mouth and getting attention, you never know what the others will do. And there were probably others besides them."

"Got it," said Bob. "But you've never had this conversation with Shannon Maher."

"She disappeared after it happened. Moved away. I tried to track her down a few times and gave up. I guess I'm not as good as Sheila is."

"And you think she'll tell all?" Bob asked.

Mike winced as he thought. "She was different. Not like the others. They were all pretty much in it for a good time, but Shannon was really deep, you see? Artsy. Earthy. Very emotional. She got attached to people. It's hard to explain. Beautiful girl, but she was a head case."

"She actually viewed Joe's willingness to have sex with her as some kind of a commitment," Bob said. "How naive."

Since Bob's voice barely changed when he used sarcasm, it took Mike a second to pick up on it. "We were kids, Bob. And it was summertime."

"He was a married man."

"I know," Mike said.

"You think she might talk if she gets the chance," Bob said.

Mike nodded. "But Sheila says she won't, right?"

"She says she told Shannon Maher about the reporter, and she blew up. Said she'd never talk to anybody about that day. And…"

"And what?" Mike asked.

Bob sighed. "Apparently, she had some choice words for you as well."

Mike looked surprised. "I never did anything to her. What's her problem with me?"

"I don't know," Bob said. "That's just what Sheila told me."

Mike shrugged. "Well, I can't imagine what that's all about."

"What else is there, Mike?" Bob asked.

Springer sighed. "Abel Ryan."

"You mean the guy she was with when she came to interview you?"

"He was there also. At the shooting. He's never talked about it either," Mike said.

"Was he sleeping with Joe too?" Bob asked, again with no change in his voice.

"Jesus, Bob. You have a sick sense of humor."

Mike was right, but Bob took great satisfaction from watching his boss try to suppress his laughter.

"You probably shouldn't be joking about this," Mike said.

"Sorry. What is Abel Ryan hiding?"

Mike turned to look out the window. "That's hard to say," he said.

"Why?" Bob asked.

"Well, I don't know why he's never talked about what happened. He was right there with me and Joe, and his brother. He saw the whole thing."

"So what are we worried about?" Bob asked.

Mike sighed. Again, he seemed to be searching for the right words. "Here's the thing," he finally said. "Shannon Maher can be a problem because she was so in love with Joe. She might be angry over the hero we've turned him into, while nobody knows anything about her."

"He is a hero," Bob said. "And she could have come out and spoken up anytime she wanted to."

Mike nodded. "I know that," he said. "What I mean is she could be carrying a lot of anger. She wanted him to leave his wife. She told me that. She was expecting a life together with him. She thought she might be pregnant."

"Was she?" Bob asked.

Mike shook his head. "Beats me. She disappeared. But maybe she's waiting for the right time to come out with it." He looked at Bob. "Like the twentieth anniversary, or when I'm running for president. I'm telling you, if she's anything like she was then. She really *loved* him."

"What did he think of her?" Bob asked.

Mike shook his head. "He liked her, but he *loved* his wife," he said. "Just couldn't help himself."

Bob could see where the governor was going with all of this, and he agreed. Joe had been built up as a saint for the past twenty years, so having a woman start telling tales of Joe screwing around on his wife, a wife who was regarded as a living saint, could prove politically difficult, especially to the candidate who'd been devoted to raising Joe up for the past twenty years. He could hear the media now: *Governor, did you know Joe Conway was screwing around on his wife?*

"It's inconvenient," Bob said summarizing the situation. "But it's not horrible. It'll be a week or so of touchy press conferences. It's not like *you* were cheating on your wife. Besides, the guy still did give his life to save all those kids, my kid included."

Mike nodded. He had already made that calculation.

"So what about the guy, Abel?" Bob asked.

Mike ran a hand through his hair. "I'm much more worried about him," he said.

Bob paused. He had heard the governor use a tone of voice that he typically saved only for the most sensitive of conversations between the two of them. Bob pulled his chair closer to the table.

"There is a good chance that the boy is angry at me," Mike said in the same hushed voice. "His brother died, right in front of us. He thinks his brother would still be alive if it weren't for me."

Bob leaned back in his chair. He was confused. "He was just a kid, right?" he asked.

Mike nodded.

"So of course he blamed you. That's what kids do in situations like that," Bob said. "Hell, that's what everybody does."

Mike walked to the chair behind his desk and dropped into it. "This is different," he said quietly.

"Why?" Bob asked.

Mike swiveled his chair to look at the photo of himself with Joe Conway that hung on the wall behind his desk. He stared blankly at it for a few moments.

284

"Because it's true," he finally said. He looked at Bob. "We'll never stop this story from getting out. I need you and Sheila to help me contain it."

"Okay," Bob said.

"There are two problems here. First, the story about Joe sleeping around on his wife hits the tabloids and starts spreading all of over the webs or whatever the hell it is. Then once the story gets out there, the details about these two kids, Abel and Jacob, start to get talked about."

Bob was impressed watching his client do his job for him. "So if we stop the first, we stop the second."

Mike shook his head. "We can't really stop any of it. It's all going to come out. It's the timing I'm worried about."

"So maybe sooner is better," Bob offered. "She's timing it to coincide with Long's execution. So it goes out this weekend."

"Right," Mike said. "And by now that Abel kid has told her everything. We need to do two things here. First, we get the story delayed until the fall, preferably after the election, but anytime in the fall will do. She's going to print it in that college newspaper, so that's not a problem. I know plenty of people over there, and they'll be willing to help. Second, we schedule a television interview. Somebody national. It has to be soon so it coincides with the execution. I'll tell them all about that day. What I did and how I've spent my entire career as a public servant trying to redeem myself. Pushing for background checks and psychiatric screenings for gun owners. All the usual."

Bob smiled. "It sounds like you've got the speech prepared."

Mike nodded. "That's how to do it," he said. "Tell the public on our terms. I can sit down with a friendly interviewer on national T.V., and talk about the whole thing while violins play in the background. Maybe Barbara Walters. That way the kid's story doesn't pack so much of a punch. By the time hers hits the stands, it's old news."

Bob thought about the governor's plan for a moment. "Stop it, sir."

285

"Stop what?"

"Stop doing my job. I need the work."

"I need to make a phone call," Mike said.

"Who?"

The governor shook his head. "I got this," he said. "And whatever scandals Sheila's cooked up for these two, tell her to call it off."

Bob decided that at this point it was best to feign confusion. "Sir?" he said, though his boss saw right through it.

"Knock it off, Bob," Mike said dismissively. "Tell Sheila to leave it alone. She talked to Shannon. That's enough. The more we try to stop this girl, the angrier she'll get. You saw that, didn't you? At the Capitol?"

Bob had seen it. The girl was intense, quick, and smart. "She scared the hell out of me," he said.

Mike smiled. "Me too. That's her mother. Anyway, tell Sheila not to bother trying to scare her into not publishing. It'll all come out, but we'll do it on our terms."

Bob sighed deeply, sitting perfectly still. This was his signal that even though his boss had ended the meeting, he was not finished.

"What?" Mike said.

"Sir, you hired me because politics is a cutthroat business," Bob said. "And I hired Sheila because she knows how to cut throats."

"So?"

"So, you make your phone call, but let us do our job. You don't need to know a thing about it."

"Come on, Bob," the governor said. It sounded almost like a plea for mercy.

Bob looked at his boss. "We can use this to our advantage, sir. We cannot have some college reporter setting our agenda, especially when we'll be going national. We need to send a message. Let us do it. It's what you pay us to do. We will get out ahead of this thing and make examples of those two. You stay the hero."

"Bob!" Mike said angrily.

But Bob shook his head and kept talking. "I know you've never said a word about it, sir. And I know *why* you've never said a word. But you were glad to let other witnesses do the talking. Everybody knows you were pointing that boy's gun at him when the police came. You never said anything, but you *let* others tell the story. You let people *assume* you were a hero, and it got your name out there. It eventually got you elected. It wasn't dirty, but it was *underhanded*, sir. It's not fair, but that's how you win in politics. That's why you are going to let Sheila and me handle this. Let *us* handle it."

Governor Mike Springer swiveled his chair again. This time, he fixed his gaze directly out his office window. "Okay," he said quietly. "You do what you need to do."

***

Professor Griffin's Monday afternoon office hours were usually devoted entirely to grading papers, but today had turned into a series of phone calls. His desk sat covered in ungraded papers. Stacks of essays and pretend newspaper stories that had been organized by class were now mixed together into an insurmountable pile of crap, causing the professor at least to consider grading them simply for completion. Usually relying on Jim Beam to help him through such a mess, he realized now that there probably wasn't enough bourbon in the state of Delaware to help him today. As he had gotten older, procrastination had grown from an amusing habit he would use as an excuse to his understanding students, to an art form.

He had decided to spend the entire afternoon grading, but he was constantly being interrupted by phone calls, including one very unusual one. He had a feeling that the next one would be rather unpleasant.

He answered on the first ring. It was Izzy. Her voice was breathless. *Was she crying?*

"Izzy, it's awfully nice to hear from you. I was hoping you'd call. How's that story coming along?"

He listened while his student explained the new revelations about Joe Conway and his mistress, or perhaps *mistresses*. He listened with fascination as she told him all about the discovery of Joe Conway's illegitimate son.

"Did you know about any of this?" he asked.

"No way," she said. "The groundskeeper had made some references, but I had no idea that I had...that Shannon Maher had a child."

"That's got to be in the story," he said.

"I think it does," she said. "It wouldn't feel right not to."

The professor held the phone, thinking of how to say what he had to tell her.

"Professor, are you there?" she asked.

"I'm sorry," he said. "You just caught me thinking. I'm still here. Quite a story you have."

"I know," she said. "It's a bit overwhelming, but I still think I can get it out by the end of the week. I have a plan to get to Mike Springer and Evan Long. Once I interview them, this thing is going to pour right out of me."

"That's great," the professor said. "Look, Izzy, I've been meaning to talk to you about the release of this story."

There was silence on the phone. "You have?" Izzy said.

"Yeah," he said. "It's just that the news is going to be so busy with all this, especially if they go ahead and execute Long... I'm thinking that now might not be the right time."

Izzy could hear the nervousness in Professor Griffin's voice, and she hadn't a clue what to make of it. She was sitting at the desk in her hotel room. She had called the professor because she wanted to run the latest revelations by him. She thought he could provide some guidance on how to keep this story, which was becoming increasingly more personal, from becoming *too* personal. Professor Griffin and his wife were the only two people at the University whom she had told about her true identity. She trusted them like family.

"What do you mean it might not be the right time?" she asked him. "We talked about this, and we agreed the timing would be perfect. To coincide with the execution. Take away the attention from Long. Don't give him the satisfaction of being the big story." It was true. These were all the points the professor had made when they had discussed, at length, the timing of the story. It would appear in the school year's last edition of The Brandywine Review. The story would have to go to print for the Saturday edition or be put off until the fall.

She heard him try to laugh. "I know we talked about all that," he said. "I'm just starting to think of the victims. Maybe having the execution, then this story all come out in the same week would be too much for them."

Izzy couldn't believe what she was hearing. "This goes Saturday," she said. "Why are you saying this?"

"Izzy, listen to me," he barked. "I am head of the journalism department at Brandywine U. If I say this story doesn't run in the Saturday issue, then it doesn't."

Izzy was stunned. She felt herself losing her breath. "You never involve yourself in the paper," she said. "Have you ever even done anything like this before?"

"That doesn't matter," he said. "The story will publish in the fall, and that's that. It'll be a hell of a story, and you'll still get your award."

Izzy could feel every muscle in her body tighten as she tried to speak. "Professor, I don't understand..."

"It's just not the right time," he said. "Now finish your interviews and get back here. Then you can take your time and make this thing really great. I'll help you."

Izzy felt her grip tighten on the receiver, allowing the pain to sharpen her senses. "I don't need any help, Professor." She hung up the phone.

***

289

Will Janicki knocked softly on the solid wooden door of the office. The sound echoed through the empty church. He listened as the person inside the small room made his way toward the door. The door opened.

"William, what do you need?" Father Francesco asked abruptly. "Is everything all right?"

Suddenly realizing that the priest must have assumed something was wrong at the campground, he nodded reassuringly. "Everything is fine, Father. I'm here for confession. Am I too late?"

The priest's eyes brightened. "It's never too late, William," he said, his accent filling the space. "You have never seen me for confession before."

"I know, Father," Will said. "I haven't been to confession for many, many years."

"The Holy Spirit will grant you a good confession, my son," Father Francesco said, motioning to a chair in the small office. "All of your sins will be forgiven. God is here."

"Thank you, Father," Will said, taking his seat. "I kind of forget the routine."

The priest placed a folding chair in front of Will's and sat in it. "How long has it been, my son?"

Will sighed. He could not even remember the last time he had confessed sins to a priest. "I don't think I've been since my first confession," he said.

The priest stared blankly into Will's eyes for a moment, then erupted in laughter that filled the small room and probably echoed through the church. Will thought that if anyone was walking outside the church, he probably would have heard it.

"We will be here a long time!" the priest said, barely able to contain himself.

Will shifted nervously in his seat. He tried to laugh along with the priest. "I didn't go to Catholic school," he said. "My parents never really made it a priority."

Father Francesco waved his hand dismissively. "Not to worry!" he shouted. "Let's do this. Rather than trying to tell *everything* that you have done since you were a child, why don't you just tell me the one or two things that have brought you here? Surely, something is on your mind, yes?"

"Yes, something is."

The priest leaned forward and closed his eyes. He made the Sign of the Cross in front of Will. Remembering, Will blessed himself in the same way. "Tell me, and God will grant you peace," the priest said in a quiet voice.

Will stared at the floor. "It's hard to say, Father."

"Then just say it, William. God will forgive you."

"Will you?"

The priest opened his eyes and sat back in his chair. "Will *I*? What have you done to me?" he asked.

Will swallowed and felt the dryness of his mouth. "Father," he began. "There is going to be a story in a newspaper."

"That girl who visited us on Sunday?"

"Yes, that's the one. The article is going to say something that I never told anyone."

"I see," the priest said. "And what is it?"

"That morning, Father. That terrible morning." Will felt himself losing control of his emotions. Feeling his breath quicken, he began to weep. He felt Father Antonelli's hand gently rest on the back of his head as he wiped the tears from his eyes.

"I could have stopped him, Father. I could have saved every child's life that day."

Will felt the priest's hand tighten on the back of his head. "How can this be?" he asked, the friendly tone having left his voice.

"I found his bag that morning," Will said through tears. "He'd left it in the maintenance shed. I didn't look inside or even pick it up. I just left the shed and went looking for whoever left it there. I figured it was one of the counselors. I'd catch them in there sometimes. But then I saw him. He was right in front of me. I *spoke* to him. I let him go get his bag! I told him to leave. I'll never forgive myself, Father! All those kids!" He sobbed.

291

Father Francesco felt his hands begin to shake. He had relived that day so many times in the last twenty years. He'd imagined so many scenarios of how he could have prevented what had happened. He had walked every inch of the campground, imagining that he could have intercepted Evan Long at some point before he began shooting. He imagined talking to him, convincing him to hand over his weapons. Embracing him and telling him there were other ways to deal with his anger. He had imagined taking Evan Long's gun into his hands, the only one the priest would ever hold in his life, and telling him that it would be okay.

"My son..." he started to say.

"I'm sorry, Father," he heard the man say.

"What did the boy say to you, William? That morning."

"I don't remember, Father. He just seemed like an ordinary kid. I figured he'd found a place to spend the night there after his parents kicked him out of the house. Something like that. I never imagined he would..." Will started to cry again. "Do you forgive me?" he asked desperately.

Father Francesco's mind was racing. He had to force himself to focus on the man in front of him, asking God for forgiveness.

"God forgives you," he said breathlessly.

"Do *you* forgive me?" Will asked again.

The priest nodded. "Of course. Of course, Will," he said. "You could have never known what this boy was going to do. You did nothing wrong."

"I should have called the police."

"No William," he said, fumbling for words. "You made a mistake, yes? We make little mistakes and forget about them. We make big mistakes and they consume us with guilt. That guilt we feel is not because we did something wrong, but because God wants us to use that guilt to help us to do better. And you did, William. You don't need this guilt anymore."

"Thank you," Will said.

"Do you know an Act of Contrition?" the priest asked, managing to refocus his thoughts.

"I don't remember it."

"This is a short one, then," Father Francesco said. "Repeat after me: Jesus, Son of God, Have mercy on me, a sinner."

He listened as Will repeated the words. When he was finished, he asked, "Are you sorry for all of your sins?"

"Yes, I am," Will said.

"Will you go forth, and try to sin no more?"

He listened as Will took a deep, uneven breath. "Yes, I will, Father," he said.

"Good then." Father Francesco raised his trembling right hand, extended it over William Janicki's bowed head, and prayed the sacred words of Absolution.

Will Janicki knelt before the Tabernacle that held the sacred body of and blood of Jesus Christ. As instructed by Father Francesco, he prayed the Hail Mary, followed by the Our Father. His penance was not complete, however. His next step, according to his confessor, was to thank God for forgiving him of his sins, and then to ask God how he could forgive himself. He listened for God's instructions. He saw the faces of nine children, a young camp counselor, and Joe Conway. He imagined the twenty-two faces of grieving parents. He thought of his encounter with Evan Long. He let his mind wander to the maintenance shed, to the tennis courts. To the pool.

He silently thanked God again. He knew what he had to do.

Will stood to leave. He quietly made his way past the baptismal font, placed his hand into the cool holy water and made the Sign of the Cross. Then he made his way toward the exit door. As he left the church, he heard something in the back of the church.

It sounded like the smashing of wood against wood. Perhaps something dropped. Maybe something had been thrown in anger or emotion. For an instant, he decided to investigate and make sure all was okay. Then he stopped and closed his eyes tightly for a moment and walked out of the church.

***

"The Blind Tiger," the happy taxi driver announced as he slowed the car to a stop. Izzy looked out the window to see her destination. Her stomach rumbled with anxiety. "Ever been there?" the man asked.

"It's my first time in Charleston," Izzy said.

The man's eyes widened in the rearview mirror. "Well then! You're in for a treat," he said, his voice dripping with Southern hospitality. "This area here is the Historic District. Broad Street is full of history. Blind Tiger used to be a speakeasy."

"That's cool," Izzy said as she considered which role she was playing this evening, a reporter seeking information for a story, or a teenager about to meet a long-lost brother. Maybe both, she decided.

"That's what they say," the man continued. Then he jabbed an index finger as he pointed out his window. "One block up is the Old Slave Mart," he said somberly. "Lots of bad memories there. It's a museum now."

Izzy's stomach churned again. "Holy shit," she said feeling both sad and awe-struck, taking note that the driver was African American.

The man smiled. "Those days are over," he said. "But people should go see it. Folks need to see just how evil people can be. I think it makes them better, somehow." The man paused and seemed to be thinking out loud. "People can be really bad, or really good, when they put their minds to it."

"I *will* go see it," she said.

"Okay then. Now go enjoy yourself at the Blind Tiger. No sense in dwelling on the past when there's good times to be had."

Izzy paid him and climbed out of the car. As the taxi sped away, she took in her surroundings. It was 5:30 and she was early. Broad Street was busy with foot and car traffic. It was hot and humid, with only an occasional light breeze.

She looked at the entrance to the restaurant and pondered. *How much of what was about to happen would be in her story?*

Entering the pub, she immediately heard her name being called. She looked to see Shannon Maher waving a hand, then beckoning her over to the end of the bar. Izzy walked in her direction. Shannon had her face made up and was wearing a light blue dress that complemented her nicely. She was very beautiful.

"You look amazing, Izzy," Shannon said, her voice shaking with nerves.

"So do you," Izzy said.

"And you're early," Shannon said.

"So are you."

Shannon laughed. "I know I am. I'm always early. And I wanted to get here before Conny."

"I'm very nervous," Izzy said.

"So am I, dear," Shannon said as she took Izzy's arm. Izzy could smell that Shannon had already had a drink. "Can we be friends, Izzy? I know we started off on the wrong foot, but I want to be friends with Conny's sister. I want to be friends with _you_."

Izzy wasn't sure what to say. How would her mother feel if she were friends with her husband's mistress? Shannon let her off the hook before she could answer.

"Don't tell me now, dear. Just tell me that we are not enemies, okay?

"Of course," Izzy said.

Shannon embraced Izzy and held her tightly. "You have handled yourself so well, darling. Your father would be so proud of you. I hope you know that."

"I think I do," Izzy said.

"Great," Shannon said. "Now let's go out on the patio and have a cigarette. They have a beautiful patio."

"Okay," Izzy said, glancing at her watch. It was still twenty minutes before her brother was supposed to meet them. She was eager to talk to Shannon about exactly how she would be introduced. She turned to begin walking outside when she felt Shannon's moist hand grab hers.

"Wait!" Shannon said urgently.

"What?" Izzy asked.

"He's here!"

295

Izzy looked toward the entrance and saw the man she had met at Shannon's house walking through the door. She watched his familiar eyes scan the bar until he found his mother. Then he started walking toward them.

"Does he know I'm here?" Izzy asked Shannon.

"No," Shannon said squeezing Izzy's hand. "I just told him I wanted to meet him for dinner. I didn't give him a reason."

As he approached, Izzy could see her brother's expression more clearly. She saw his confusion when he recognized Izzy as the reporter he had met earlier that day. She saw his eyes dart from hers to Shannon's. Then he stopped, seeming to consider something before continuing. Izzy's brother stood about ten feet from his mother and his sister, looking from one face to the other as if comparing them. Izzy watched the way his face changed. He wasn't confused anymore. Then he stepped to Izzy and stood in front of her.

"Hi," Izzy said, not sure what else to say. She heard Shannon's voice next to her.

"Conny, dear, this is..."

Before Shannon could finish, the man wrapped his arms around Izzy and held her tightly. Izzy lost her breath in the strong embrace. She felt a warm kiss on her left cheek. Her brother held her tightly. Izzy squeezed him around the waist, and she felt a tear trickle down her right cheek.

"How did you know?" she asked into his ear.

She felt him kiss her again. "I'm just like you," he said, still holding her tightly. "I'm a nosey *bastard*."

***

It felt good to be nearly drunk while the sun was still up. Abel was finishing his second bourbon at the hotel bar and he had no plans of slowing down. However, he would soon switch to beer; he didn't want to be passed out before ten. This was the way he had

296

planned on spending his summer days. Wake up late; start drinking after lunch; fall asleep by midnight.

After downing the last of his whiskey and ordering a beer, he began to examine the possibility that he was having feelings for Izzy Buchanan. She was far too young for him, he thought, and probably far too rich. Girls like her ended up with lawyers and bankers. Probably *older* lawyers and bankers, but not teachers. Not even journalists.

Her behavior was astonishing to him. With just a few words, she had managed to put a governor's senior staff on their heels. She had made *them* afraid. She had manhandled them like she manhandled the priest, one of the most respected clergymen in Delaware. He railed mercilessly against politicians in newspapers and in crowded town meetings, facing them down with steely-eyed determination. But he turned almost to putty in the presence of Izzy Buchanan, a nineteen-year-old college news reporter.

Abel wondered if her courage was a product of her lack of life experience, or of the life she had lived being raised by an equally brave widowed mother. *Abigail Conway.* What kind of a woman was she, really? How would she react to these developments? Had she known of Joe's infidelities? Had she been damaged by them?

He took a long drink of a cold IPA that tasted even more refreshing after the bourbon. He thought about the interview he had still yet to finish, probably on the long train ride home. He would reveal everything, for Izzy and the world, regardless of the consequences. His brother's memory was too important to be compromising with a governor who threatens his family. *Fuck him.*

He looked at his watch. It was about dinner time. He ordered a bowl of seafood gumbo and a club sandwich. He wasn't going anywhere.

***

"I'll leave y'all alone to catch up" were Shannon Maher's parting words before she disappeared from their small table on the patio of the Blind Tiger and floated noiselessly away, leaving Izzy sitting across from the closest likeness to her father she would ever know. He was tall and lean with sandy brown hair, blue eyes, and rugged cheeks that were used to being outside. He was handsome, with the confident chin of a football team captain, though his sport of choice was soccer.

"How did you get that name, anyway?" he asked. "Izzy Buchanan."

Izzy sipped her light beer. Neither she nor her brother had been asked to produce proof of age before ordering drinks. "Short for Elizabeth," she said. "I've always been called that, and Buchanan is my mother's maiden name. I've published all of my stories under that name. Conway is too big a name in Delaware, and I got tired of people asking if I was related to Joe."

"Like that's a bad thing?"

"It's not," Izzy said. "Unless you're trying to make a name for yourself."

The boy nodded thoughtfully. "Conway," he said in a trance. "I never knew my first name held so much weight."

Izzy tapped her empty glass on the table. "It's a great name," she said.

"Let's have another."

"Okay, Conny," Izzy said, amused at using the name.

"Call me 'Con.'"

"Are you a con?" Izzy asked playfully.

"I'm a good kid," he answered.

"Not too good to be at a bar drinking underage," she said.

Conny smiled. "I know a lot of people in this town." A waitress came and he ordered another round. "I do a lot of gardening. Businesses. Restaurants. All over town. I get to talking to people."

"Gardening?"

"This is Charleston. People take their gardens very seriously. I grew up doing it," he said.

"That's called landscaping in Delaware," Izzy said.

"Whatever. I know a lot of people. Restaurant owners."

"So you're a charmer," Izzy said. "I hear that runs in the family."

Conny nodded. "I guess so," he said.

"Is that all you do?" she asked.

He shook his head. Izzy noticed that her brother was not shy, but was in no hurry to answer any questions. Every mannerism he displayed was drawn out and deliberate. She hadn't noticed this in Shannon, and she wondered if her father had been the same way.

"I go to *C of C* - College of Charleston," he said. "Just finished my first year."

"Have a major?" she asked.

He shook his head slowly. "Are you interviewing me?"

"No," Izzy said. "I just want to know you."

"I don't have a major yet. Not sure what I want to do."

"Do you like it there?" she asked.

"Nope," he said. "I don't like Charleston very much."

"It's a pretty city," Izzy said.

"I know it is," he said. "But I been here my whole life. Ready for something else."

Izzy nodded. "So where then?"

Conny took a long pull from his beer and looked around, seeming to ignore her question. "Right now, I want to go to a different bar," he said pointing to his glass. "Let's finish this crap and get out of here."

"You're a beer drinker?" Izzy asked.

"Stop with the questions," Conny said. "Let's just hang out and get to know each other. Okay?"

"Fine," Izzy said as she began gulping down her drink.

"There's a place around the corner with real beer."

***

Shannon Maher strolled contentedly into her small home, thinking only of her son and his sister. They were both so beautiful.

Having witnessed their glorious meeting, one she had looked forward to for so many years, she felt a sense of completion that she had not experienced for many years. She felt that warm fullness she had once felt while she lay in the arms of the only man she would ever love. It was a love she would never feel again.

They had all eaten, drunk, and laughed together. Funny stories had been told, tearful memories shared. It was everything she had hoped it would be, even after Conway had surprised them. *He had known all along!* She had always known that her son held many secrets, normal for a boy without a father, but she had never suspected that Conway knew the story of his father, and she never would have guessed that he would recognize his sister with enough confidence to embrace her so joyously. It was the perfect meeting, and she decided to leave them alone to be young siblings for the first time.

The day she had anticipated for so many years had come and gone so very quickly. She had revealed everything to Izzy Buchanan, and everything would soon be revealed to the world. There was only one more communication left to make. She walked into the kitchen, sat at her table, and picked up her cordless phone. She reached into her purse and found the small business card that the assertive young lady had given her that morning, a morning that now seemed like ages ago.

She relished the thought of Sheila's pretty face as she informed Mike Springer of the worst: that Shannon Maher had told the college reporter everything, and that Joe Conway, would be exposed as a two-timer, and the saintly widow Abigail Conway would be ridiculed for her naiveté.

The world would soon know with whom the great Joe Conway was really in love all along. Shannon's work would be finished.

***

The Southend Brewery did have good beer, and Izzy hated it. It reminded her of the high quality, horrid stuff she drank a few days ago in Philadelphia while she was trying to get Abel's attention. "Could I just have some water?" she asked.

"No way!" her brother shot back. "We're brother and sister, and we just met. We're getting drunk."

"I already am drunk."

Conny ignored her and flagged down a waiter, apparently a friend of his, and ordered Izzy a glass of Pinot Grigio. Izzy wasn't crazy about wine either, but it would be better than the beer.

"What do you think of my mom?" Conny asked.

"You mean the homewrecker?"

Conny laughed. "I wonder if it would have ever come to that."

"I doubt it," Izzy said.

Conny finished his beer and started on the one she had passed up on. "You don't understand," he said. "My mom *loved* your dad, in an almost crazy way."

"So did my mom," Izzy said.

He shook his head. "Not like this. Trust me. *Crazy*."

"How do you know that?" she asked.

"I've read her diaries," he said. "She's kept one since she was twelve. I've read all of them. She was crazy in love. Still is."

"She let you read her diary?" Izzy asked.

"No."

"You sneak!"

"I am," he said. "You know, she's never been with anybody else?"

Izzy looked at him with disbelief. "She's nearly 40," she said. "You're telling me she hasn't been with anyone since she was 19?"

Conny closed his eyes and nodded his head severely. He was still smiling, but the mood had changed.

"She's a beautiful woman," Izzy said.

"She's committed to one person," Conny said.

Izzy shook her head. "He was never hers in the first place."

"Try telling her that." He took a drink of beer. "There has not been a single day that she has not thought about him. I'm sure looking at me every day doesn't help."

"You look like him," Izzy said.

Conny nodded again. "I'm her daily reminder that she lost the love of her life. Sometimes I think she's waiting for me to do something heroic."

"I hope you never have to," Izzy said.

"We all have to some time, don't we?" he asked.

"Have you ever done anything heroic?" Izzy asked.

"You're interviewing me again," he said, jabbing a finger at her. "Let's do a shot. If we get drunk enough, we're sure to tell each other our life stories."

Izzy exhaled. "Okay," she said.

***

Bob Casarini answered the phone. "Yes, Sheila," he said.

"She talked."

"Who?" he asked.

"The bimbo in South Carolina."

"How do you know?" Bob asked.

"She just called and told me," Sheila said.

"What did she say?"

"Everything," Sheila said. "She was most adamant about Joe being truly in love with her, not with his wife."

Bob processed the information for a moment, then said, "Beautiful."

"So what now?" Sheila asked. "I told you we should have gotten ahead of this."

"I know you did," Bob said. "And Springer agreed. In fact, he thought of it himself."

"So now what?"

Bob considered this. This would have political ramifications, but he wasn't sure to what extent. Joe Conway had been a shining

302

example of the need for more gun legislation, Mike Springer's defining issue as a politician. The fact that he had been unfaithful to his wife twenty years ago would not necessarily reflect badly on Springer. On the other hand, it would always be mentioned, even in hushed voices, every time Joe Conway's name came up. It would be a distraction more than anything.

"I've already spoken to Mike about all this. We're going to set up a national interview. It should be easy since it's the twentieth anniversary. Let the governor get all this out there before she does," Bob said.

"Why do I feel out of the loop on this?" she asked.

"You're not," Bob said. "You were in Charleston, doing the work. I was going to call and get you caught up, but I figured you'd be exhausted."

"Let me worry about how tired I am, okay?" she said. "And there's one more thing."

"I can't wait," Bob said.

"She had Joe Conway's child."

"What!"

"He's nineteen. Conway Maher. Handsome kid."

Bob sighed into the phone. "It's Monday night," he said somberly. "The girl's story won't be published until the fall. We can set something up for the Sunday talk shows. That gives us all week to prep him."

"She's not running the story until the fall?" Sheila asked.

Bob explained how Springer, always an advocate for state and federal funding of Brandywine University, had made an arrangement with the head of the Journalism Department. By coincidence, there would also be a Joe Conway Scholarship starting in the fall semester as well.

"Brilliant," Sheila said.

"His   idea."

"We've taught him well," Sheila said. "He'll be ready for Sunday."

Abel was drunk, wandering the streets of a city that was foreign to him. He wasn't looking for anything, or anyone, just allowing the familiar blissful haze to take him where it may. Even in his state, he knew he had never seen anything like the majestic beauty of Charleston. Philadelphia had charm and character, but Charleston was a lady of grace and elegance.

He had walked east from his hotel until he came to a park situated along the water of the Cooper River. The view was magnificent, and it blended perfectly with the light and sounds coming from the city behind him.

He plopped himself onto one of the benches that lined the river and leaned back. Hoping not to fall asleep, he closed his eyes and thought about his brother. What would Jacob think of this? It was not an easy question, but one he always had to ask himself when something new came along. Would the thirty-year-old Jacob urge his brother to strip off his shirt and plunge into the river? Would he be annoyed, insisting they find another place to keep drinking? Abel wished he knew, and he longed for the years of love and rivalry that came from being brothers. They were taken from him. *Wasted.*

He wondered, also, what Jacob would think of his traveling companion. Jacob would point out that she was far too much for him, and that she could do much better than a Catholic school teacher. A girl like her is probably better off on her own anyway, Abel thought.

Hearing the sound of easy laughter, he looked to his right. In the distance, he saw a young couple stumbling toward the river in each other's arms. Through the night air, he could hear their laughter and excitement as they approached the water, unaware of Abel's eyes. Now the woman pulled away from the man and stepped toward the railing by herself. She stood gazing out into the river while the man stood behind her. After a moment, she turned and embraced him fiercely. They laughed again as they held each other.

"Want to jump in?" Conny asked.

Izzy shrieked. "Are you serious?"

"Hell yes."

"Then hell yes!" she said.

Conny kicked off his shoes and pulled off his shirt. Izzy removed her sandals and stepped out of her dress. She had never done anything remotely this impulsive, but it felt good. She watched her brother carefully shimmy his way over the handrail before she did the same. She took his hand and together they plunged into the river.

The water was colder than she had expected. Refreshing and beautiful. Her head emerged first, and she watched as he came to the surface. They looked at each other, laughing desperately. She embraced her brother, both out of love and a need for warmth.

"Let's get out of here!" he said.

Conny pulled himself out of the river then helped her. They quickly pulled their clothes back on and began laughing uncontrollably together.

"I'm never drinking again!" Izzy shouted. They laughed while she looked around. "Do you think anyone saw us?"

***

Abel recognized her voice, though in the brief time he had known her, he had not heard it sound so happy. He had watched, amused while they quickly undressed, held hands, and plunged into the water. From their cries, he'd assumed it was a cold awakening. Now, he watched as they awkwardly pulled their clothes over their soaking wet bodies and ran arm-in-arm back toward the city. He was glad for them, seeing two people so happy, filling long-empty holes in their lives.

He envied them. A brother and sister uniting around the memory of their father, whom neither of them had met. Abel thought often

305

of his own father, but tried not to when he was drinking. He'd been a loving husband and father before he gave in and allowed himself to be destroyed. It was a selfish surrender, one that had left what remained of his family vulnerable and alone. Abel hated his father for it, and he hoped that his brother would feel the same way. Maybe Jacob would have stood up to him in those darkest times, the ones that preceded his father's death. But Abel knew that had Jacob still been alive, his father would have never become dependent on alcohol. Abel had never stood up to the man, even when he was putting his wife through hell. *Screams and accusations. Broken doors and windows. Worse.* Abel had silently let it all happen, usually holding his hands over his ears.

Watching Izzy and Conway disappear into Charleston, Abel longed more deeply for his brother than he ever had before.

***

Father Bill Johnston sat uncomfortably and watched as the two uniformed guards awkwardly but efficiently guided Evan Long, shackles and all, into the small cell that served as a meeting room and sat him at the metal bench across from him.

"Can you remove those shackles?" Bill asked.

The larger of the two guards shook his head. "No, sir," he said as he locked Evan to the floor of the cell. "Take your time, Father. We'll be right outside." Bill got the sense that the guard was trying to sound reassuring. He had told them it was his first time visiting a prisoner on death row, though he had said it more out of interest than anything. Did the guard think he was afraid?

"Don't worry about me, Officer. I won't hurt him."

The guard half-smiled and stepped out of the room.

For the first time, Bill looked into the eyes of Evan Long. They were clear and bright, though he squinted in the light of the room he had been moved to.

"How can I help you?" Bill asked.

"What took you so long?"

Bill was surprised at the question. "I live in Hockessin," he said. "I didn't hear you were asking for me until just a couple hours ago."

"I asked for you before dinner time. It's almost eleven now."

"There are many qualified priests in this area, including the one who is on call. He would have been here in under an hour," Bill said.

"I wanted you," Evan said.

"And here I am," Bill said, opening his hands to present himself. "Why don't we get started? You want to make a confession?"

"I have some things to say to you first."

Bill shook his head. "If these *things* you have to say aren't related to you making a confession, I'm not interested in hearing them."

"I want to know why you never say my name when I see you on TV,"

Bill stuck his chin out at Evan. "What do you care?" he asked.

Evan's eyes widened in surprise. "I just want to know," he said.

"I didn't come here to explain myself to you, Mr. Long, but if you must know, I don't use your name when I'm speaking in public because I want those events to be about the victims, not about you."

Evan nodded. "Did it ever occur to you that I was a victim that day too?" he asked.

Bill decided to ignore the question. "I'll hear your confession now."

"I'm not ready," Evan said.

"Then call me when you are," Bill said as he stood. "The warden has my number."

"Wait," Evan said.

"For what?"

"I thought priests were supposed to be nice."

"Give it a rest will you?" Bill said. "It's late, and I didn't come here to make you feel good about yourself. If you're not going to receive a sacrament, I'm no good to you."

"Fine," Evan said. "I don't need your sacraments."

"Good for you," Bill said as he knocked on the door to alert the guard.

"I'm sorry for my sins," Evan continued, "and God has forgiven me."

Bill felt something in the pit of his stomach. Earlier in the evening, he had received a call from the old priest, his unmistakable voice booming over the telephone with a very odd request. Bill had explained to Fr. Antonelli that he had no interest in visiting the mass murderer tonight or any other night. When the old priest mentioned he may have to call the bishop, Bill relented, got in his car, and began driving south. Antonelli's friendship with the bishop was well known, and there was no saying no to the boss, at least not in Bill's line of work. On the long drive to the state prison, Bill had decided he would not allow Evan Long any access to his mind. He had brushed off the attempt at conversation and the adolescent provocations. But this one, *God has forgiven me*, would be harder to ignore.

Bill held a finger to the guard. He needed a little more time.

He walked back to the table, his heavy footsteps echoing through the cell, and took his seat. Evan Long's expression was defiant, like so many he had seen in his years of teaching high school theology. This student had thrown down a challenge. The mass murderer had challenged the legitimacy of the sacraments that he was here to administer. Perhaps, Bill thought, it was time for a short lesson in forgiveness.

"What do you think you know about God and forgiveness?"

Evan cleared his throat. "For God so loved..."

"Are you really just going to quote the Gospel of John?" Bill asked, raising his voice a touch. "I've already read it. Don't bother. Tell me what you think it means."

"It means that if I believe in Jesus, he will forgive me. I won't suffer because of what I did."

"Are you sorry for what you did?"

"Of course I am. Jesus knows that."

"I'm sure he does," Bill said.

"And think of Jesus dying on the cross," Evan continued. "He tells the guy next to him that he'll be with him in paradise. All he had to do was believe."

"So you're a true believer?"

"Yes, I am," Evan said.

Father Bill thought about this. He took a quick look around the room before settling his eyes back to Long's. They were forward-facing, confident eyes. *Righteous.*

"Let me tell you a story, Mr. Long. A hypothetical," Bill said.

"Okay." Evan sounded amused.

Bill spoke slowly and deliberately, painting a picture for his student. "A priest has a meeting in a jail cell with a convicted killer. The priest used to play football – a tackle for West Chester. And the killer is a puny little guy who probably doesn't even bother to do pushups in his cell. The priest knows he could squash the little punk like a bug if he really wanted to, especially considering the guy killed his good friend twenty years ago.

"But the priest manages to hold it together throughout the meeting, and when it's over he walks out of the cell. But when he does, he decides to take out his frustration on the guard outside the cell. He tells him he smells of body odor, or that he should get a real job, or some other damn thing, just to unleash some of his frustration. You with me?"

Evan nodded.

Bill continued. "So the guard doesn't say anything back to the priest, out of respect and surprise, but what the priest said really bothers him. It bothers him so much so that he thinks about it the whole drive back to his house. So he stops at a bar to get a drink, even though he promised his wife he'd be home early. He has a few, and he gets even angrier. He curses at the bartender for making his drink too weak, then he leaves in a huff.

"He gets home and his wife is understandably upset. Her husband, who was supposed to be home early smells of booze and he wants to go right to sleep. So at that point, the wife looks at the dinner she worked hard preparing, gets upset and yells at the kids for not doing enough around the house. At the same time, that poor bartender is taking out his frustrations on the guy that does the dishes. The kids don't sleep because they've been yelled at, so they're miserable at school the next day. One of them starts a fight. You still with me?"

"I think so," Evan said.

"Now here's the thing about forgiveness," Bill said as he leaned closer to Evan. "The next day the priest realizes he was out of line, so he calls up the guard and apologizes to him for what he said. The guard is still pissed, but he forgives the priest for what he did. Being a priest, Bill also knows that God will forgive him, too." Bill smiled dryly, then looked at Evan Long. "Now tell me, is everything okay?"

Evan didn't answer; instead, he stared blankly at the priest.

"You're right," Bill said. "Everything is definitely *not* okay. Because that priest's one bad action - one *sin* - has caused damage beyond what he can even perceive, much less repair. There is no way he can track down the bartender, the wife, the dishwasher, the kids, and the poor kid who got his ass kicked at school and apologize to all of them. He can't do this, even though the guard forgave him."

Evan's eyes narrowed. "So what's that all mean?"

"You're not stupid," Bill said. "Yes, God can forgive you, and he probably does if you're really sorry. God's good like that. But you still need to answer for all the damage you've done." Now Bill glared at Evan Long, looking the killer directly in the eyes. "The priest in my story told a cop he has body odor. You killed eleven people. Just imagine trying to make up for that. Trust me, spending twenty years in this place isn't enough. You will be suffering for a long time. In this life and the next."

Bill saw the understanding creep into Evan Long's eyes, like he had seen so many times in the young faces of his students. But this time it was mixed with real fear. He enjoyed seeing the fear in the man's eyes.

"What kind of a priest are you?" Long asked.

"I try to be the honest kind."

"Aren't you supposed to make me feel better?" Evan asked.

Bill smiled. "I love dispelling the myth that all fat men are jolly."

"So what can I do?" Evan asked. "If that's all true, what can *confession* even do for me?"

Bill stood again and walked to the door. "It's a first step," he said. "It'll get you back into communion with the Church. The rest is in God's hands. If you want to confess your sins, have the warden get the priest on call. I'm not coming back here anymore. You'll be forgiven. But you've done too much damage to think you've earned yourself a ticket to heaven just because you believe Jesus died for your sins."

Bill tapped the glass and waited for the guard to open the door. As the door opened, he turned back to Evan Long and said, "I'd recommend praying. A lot. I imagine it's all you have left."

***

Izzy could still make out her brother's round eyes in the dark. They lay across from each other in her hotel room bed, holding hands and whispering. They were both intoxicated, and the initial bliss of their reunion had waned into a numb awareness of their shared story. Izzy wanted to know her brother more deeply than she could know anyone. She wanted to somehow fill the gap of nineteen years so she could see him completely, and let him see her.

"What is your future?" she asked.

"I am never leaving South Carolina," he said.

"But you didn't like it here."

"My mother," he said. "I worry about her. I can't leave."

"That isn't fair," Izzy said.

"She's had a hard life. I'm worried if I leave, she'll have a nervous breakdown or something."

Izzy closed her eyes and thought hard about this. She could never imagine deciding to stay put for her entire life. "My mother has been through a lot too," she said. "But I would never stick around just for her."

"Has she ever gotten drunk and cried for hours, waiting for you to come home from a movie?"

"No."

"Has she ever hugged you so hard you thought you'd suffocate and beg you never to leave her alone?"

"Jesus."

"My mom is fucked up," Conny said. "I can't begin to tell you ~~half~~ even half of it. She quit drinking five years ago because she could see what it was doing to me. It helped, but I kept reading her diaries. I still do." Conny turned from looking at Izzy and looked at the ceiling. "She's crazy. Crazier than she seems."

"Why do you say that?" Izzy asked.

"She writes it all. Not just stuff that happened, but stuff that she *wishes* would have happened. *Today, Joe and I met with Conny's math teacher. She's so nice, and it's a shame that Conny has such a hard time with math.* She never met with any math teacher of mine."

"Holy shit," Izzy said. "She *is* crazy."

"And that day still kills her," he said. "She calls it *wasted love* in her journals."

"Wasted love," Izzy repeated.

"This life she could have lived with Joe. The lives of all those kids and their parents. She goes on for pages about how when we would go back to school shopping, she couldn't stop thinking about the moms who'd already done their kids back to school shopping only for them that summer at the camp. Wasted. She imagines family vacations that could have happened and never did. It's awful."

"That is awful," Izzy agreed. "I wish I could help her."

Conny sighed. "I'll never leave her," he said. "She's young and healthy, but she's a total basket case."

"That's really sad," Izzy said. "She seems like one who could really make something of herself, too. She's so pretty. She could fall in love."

Conny scoffed. "You have to go on dates. You have to sleep with people. She doesn't do either. I have to say, though, tonight she looked happier than she has in a long time. Maybe our meeting

312

and being friends will help. Maybe she'll *want* to meet new people now."

"My mom's like that. She hasn't been with anybody in a long time."

"Does she want to be?" Conny asked.

"Yes, but she still feels guilty about it."

"She talks to you about this stuff?"

"Yes," Izzy said. "I don't need to read her journals."

"When's the last time she's been in bed with a man?" Conny asked.

"About a year, I think," Izzy said. "It was one of my teachers at my high school."

She saw her brother's expression change. "Really? What was that all about?"

Izzy laughed. "I had a crush on him, myself," she said. "She knew it. That's why she did it. We have a strange relationship like that."

Conny put his hand on his forehead. "Sweet Jesus! That's pretty weird."

"I could write a book," Izzy said. "I probably will, actually. We are very close. Like sisters sometimes."

Conny laughed loudly, and Izzy did the same. The alcohol was still doing its work.

"And what about you?" he asked. "You a virgin, sis?"

Izzy broke into laughter, not because the question was a funny one, but rather the way it was asked. "I'm not!" she said, as she punched his chest.

"So when was your last time?"

"About a month."

"Who?" Conny asked.

"You don't know him."

"Of course I don't. Tell me about him."

"He's a cop," Izzy said. "Older than me, obviously. His wife doesn't mind though."

"Holy shit, girl! Are you crazy?" Conny shouted.

313

Izzy laughed again. "That was a joke. He's not married. He wants to be though."

"I got it," Conny said. "Do you love him?"

Izzy thought about it. "I thought I did, but now I think I just loved that I was with him. A police officer. State trooper."

"How old?"

"Twenty-nine," Izzy said through clenched teeth.

"Hot stuff," Conny said.

"He was, actually." She looked at her brother, his eyes beginning to grow heavy. "What about you?" she asked.

He waved his hand at her. "I'm friends with a lot of women, but I've never been in a serious relationship."

"Why not?"

He turned his body back toward her. "I always wondered that," he said. "My mom always says it's because I never had my dad around. She says I never learned how a man should talk to a woman."

"Is that what you think?"

"I think it's because I don't want any girls to meet my crazy mother," he said. They both laughed again.

"Do you ever think she could be holding you back?" Izzy asked.

Conny nodded. "I know she is."

"That's a problem," Izzy said.

"Okay, but you've got your share, too."

"What are mine?" she asked.

"It ever occur to you that you were sleeping with a thirty-year-old state cop, a guy who risks his life for people, and you have a dad that was thirty when he gave his life to save people?"

Izzy fell back to her side of the bed and lay on her back. "Great," she said. "I guess I have daddy issues. Are you a psychiatrist or something?"

Conny laughed. When he stopped, he said, "My mother needs one. Seriously. I've heard her talking in her sleep. I worry about her."

"I know you do," Izzy said. "We're both children of single mothers. That's a challenge in itself."

"And we both have a dad who's a hero," Conny said.

"He was a hero who had many faults," Izzy said.

"You're going to write about all that?" he asked.

"I have to," she said.

"Why?"

"It's the truth," she said. "Besides, a hero with demons is the best kind of hero."

He turned toward her again. "But aren't you a little worried about the consequences? My mother has been waiting my whole life to tell this story to the right person. And now she has. She thinks the whole world will know that she and Joe were just as happy as can be. I don't know what she'll do next. I don't know what she expects to happen. I think she believes People Magazine will be knocking down her door the day after it publishes."

"They might," she said.

"But are you worried about the consequences?" he asked again. "What is it you're hoping will become of this?"

Izzy let her mind drift for a moment while she thought about the question. "A year ago, I wrote a story that was up for a national award for college journalism. I should have won, but I came in second. So at first I just wanted to do this thing to win the award. But now it's bigger. I want people to know the truth. I want the people to know *why* some witnesses have never spoken before now. I want people to know that their heroes don't have to be perfect. And, yes, I do care about the consequences. I almost decided not to write this thing a couple days ago when one guy told me he was going to blow his brains out."

"Oh my," Conny said.

"It made me feel shallow," she said. "A man's life for an award."

"Why would he do that?"

"He thinks he could have stopped it," Izzy said. "He came face-to-face with him earlier that morning, and he let him go. All he had to do was look in the guy's bag and that would have been it. He could have prevented so much catastrophe for so many people."

Conny looked at her for a long moment. Finally, she realized he was waiting for her to see the irony.

"I'm writing the story," she said. "It's going to be great. It's going to change people's lives, and I am going to win that damned award."

"Good for you," Conny said. "And what about your boyfriend?"

"He's my photographer."

"Stop it."

"He's not my boyfriend. He's helping me with the story," she said.

"There's more to it than that. I know it."

"It's not what you think," Izzy said. "He was at the shooting. He was the last person to speak to Joe Conway before he went after the shooter."

"And he's never spoken to anyone about it?"

"Not publicly. That's my story: the five people who were there and never spoke about it."

"But there were six," Conny said.

Izzy sat up. "Who?" she asked.

He smiled. "You're talking to him now."

Izzy laughed. "Can I interview you?" she asked. "You can tell the world how crazy your mother is."

"I'll pass," Conny said. Neither spoke for a time, then he said, "This is weird."

"What?"

"This morning I woke up thinking about whether I'd ask this cute little thing I work with if she'd like to go out with me tonight. I think she'd say yes. Instead, here I am in bed with my sister, who didn't even know I existed until today."

Izzy smiled. "There's no place I'd rather be."

Conny laughed. "That's even more weird."

They both lay with their eyes closed for a long time, then Conny said, "Why don't you go climb into bed with your photographer. Make his year."

"I don't think so," she said.

"He's old enough for you."

"Shut up," Izzy said, punching him again.

"Do you like him?" he asked.

Izzy thought about it. "He's very smart. He sees a lot, things I wouldn't see. But he's very insecure."

"He's seen some awful things," Conny said. "He might be stronger than you think."

"He lost his brother in the shooting," she said. "He's been telling me about it."

"Well, then you have that in common," he said.

"You mean we both lost family in the shooting?"

"Yeah," Conny said. "Wasted love."

Izzy nodded, though she knew her brother's eyes were closed. "Wasted love," she said.

***

Abel closed his eyes and leaned back against the wall of the elevator. Hearing the door open, he opened his eyes and stepped into the hallway. It was almost two in the morning. He turned left and began making his way to his room. As he approached his door, he heard the sound of uneven footsteps. He looked to his left to see Izzy coming around the corner toward him.

"Abel!" She said excitedly. "Where were you?"

He smiled at her. It was funny to see her so drunk. "Just exploring the town," he said.

"Me too!"

"How did your meeting go?" he asked.

She inhaled deeply and her eyes became intense. "It was wonderful. It is so amazing to know I have a brother!"

"I'm glad for you," he said. Then he watched as her expression changed from joy to sorrow. She lunged forward and embraced him, holding him tightly.

"I'm sorry I said that, Abel!" she cried.

317

"It's okay," he said.

"I can't imagine losing my brother, Abel. I just met him, and I love him so much!" She wiped her eyes and looked at Abel. "I'm sorry," she said. "I'm really drunk."

"It's okay," he said. "Why don't you go back to your room and go to sleep? The train is early tomorrow."

Izzy nodded and started to walk away.

"Izzy?" Abel said before she got too far. "Why were you out of your room?"

"What do you mean?" she asked.

"What were you doing walking around the hallway this time of night? Are you looking for the vending machine or something?"

Her expression changed again. It was serious now. "I came to say goodnight to you," she said.

"Oh," Abel said.

Very suddenly he felt her grab his face in both of her hands and pull him toward her to kiss him. She kissed him hard on the lips then pulled away, still holding his face in her hands. She looked at him.

"What is it?" Abel asked, the alcohol still dulling his senses.

"I could fall in love with you, Abel," she said.

Abel stared at her.

"But not tonight," she said.

"Okay," he said.

"Can you be strong?" she asked in a whisper.

He didn't answer.

"I'm strong," she said.

"I know you are," he said.

"But I'm not strong enough for both of us."

Abel stared blankly at her, not at all sure of what to say.

"I'm sorry," Izzy said. "Am I freaking you out?"

He tried not to laugh. *You have no* idea, he thought. "It's okay," he said. "I'm going back to my room to abuse myself."

She smiled and kissed him again and turned and walked back to her room. Abel went into his room and lay in bed. After a very long time, he fell asleep.

Tuesday, June 18, 1996

Will Janicki steered his truck up the winding narrow road that led to the Joseph Conway Memorial Tennis Courts. It was just after five in the morning, and he was alone on the campground. He smiled as he drove past the maintenance shed, once known as "the shack," and he laughed to himself at the thought of discovering the young lovers who used to make use of the cot inside. That was a different time, he thought. Nothing like that happened anymore. Today, things were predictable and regimented. Everybody had a morality complex. No fun.

He parked when he arrived at the tennis courts, which were barely in view due to the lingering darkness and pouring rain. He pulled the hood of his poncho over his head, picked up the heavy bolt cutters that sat next to him, and climbed out of his truck.

Through the soaking rain, he marched toward the front gate. Without hesitation, he used the bolt cutters to chop through the heavy chains that secured it. The chain clumsily slipped through the metal of the gate and fell like a dead snake to the ground. Will loved the sound, and he knew Joe would appreciate it too.

Next, he made his way to the other side of the courts and did the same to the chains on the rear gate. No more locks. No more fear. He walked back to his truck and threw the severed locks and chains into the back of his pickup. He looked down the hill toward the pool. *The Pool of Eternal Childhood.* An appropriate name, but one he had always hated. He was about to climb into his truck to make the short drive to the pool when he had a change of heart. He would *walk* down the hill to the pool and remove the chains and locks on those gates as well. Had he been younger, he would have run it. *No more locks*, he thought. Starting the long walk through the pouring rain, he decided to take the shortest possible route, the one that crossed the baseball field. He reached back and removed his hood to let the pouring rain soak his head. It was a great day, the first in a long time.

***

"So when do you think about him the most?" was the question that Izzy chose to start the rest of her interview. Abel's head continued to pound even after downing three glasses of orange juice and two cups of coffee in the dining car.

"I'm dehydrated," he said, rubbing the space between his eyes.

"So am I," Izzy answered. "Do you want to do this later?"

"No," Abel answered. "Just give me a minute to think."

The train had left Charleston an hour earlier, bound for Wilmington, Delaware. Abel had been woken first by a wakeup call that Izzy had set for him at six A.M., then by her loud knocking a half-hour later. He had pulled himself out of bed, dressed in a fog, packed his bag and shuffled down to the lobby where Izzy looked surprisingly awake and refreshed.

Neither spoke of Izzy's strange proposal a few hours earlier.

"You recover well," he had said, and she answered only with a smile.

Then Izzy drove them to the train station, returned the rental car, and they found their train. Once again, Izzy had reserved a sleeper cabin, though this was a morning to night ride. Abel was glad that he could lie down in relative privacy. If he decided to have a drink, it would not be until well after lunch.

Now, he sat in a reclining seat across from Izzy. The blinds were drawn to keep the room dark. Izzy was not taking notes, choosing to let the tape recorder capture everything. *Smart,* Abel thought. Make it as conversational as possible.

"I think about my brother every day," Abel said. "Birthdays are still the worst, for everybody."

"How do you mean?"

"Growing up, every birthday was like a celebration and a funeral," he said. "One kid is here growing a year older, while the other is in

320

the ground, and we know exactly what he would look like if he were still here."

"He was your identical twin?"

Abel nodded. "And I could always see it in my parents' faces, especially my mom's. That look of happiness, followed by the flash of sadness, then that...distant look."

"What do you mean?"

"My mom," he said. "She would get this look, like she was looking *through* me, to someone else. She never said it, of course, but I always knew what she was thinking."

"What was she thinking?" Izzy asked.

"That she could be looking into the eyes of her other son," he said. "Imagining who he would be then, what he would have become. Even in the months after we lost Jacob, sometimes in the middle of the night, I'd climb into bed with my parents, like I did when I was really little. I'd started wetting the bed again. And sometimes I'd hear my mom ask if I was Jacob or Norman. And see the disappointment in her face when she squinted to see who I was."

"That's so sad," Izzy said.

"I still see it today whenever we're together. She hugs me, kisses me on the cheek, then she looks at me, then she looks at Jacob. Or she looks *for* him. I don't know. She gives me that distant look."

"Wow."

"It's not much fun," he said. "It's a life sentence, for her and for me."

"For you too?"

"I hate looking in mirrors," he said. "For most people who lose a child or a sibling, they wonder years later what they would like as an adult, or as an old man. I don't. My mother doesn't. You'd think that's a good thing, but it's not." He turned toward the window and gently pulled the blind aside, letting the sunlight cover his face. "I am always hoping I am living up to his standards," he said.

"His standards?" Izzy asked.

Abel nodded. "He was brave. Strong. He never backed down from anybody, it didn't matter how big the other kid was. He was

321

tough. I never was. So I always feel like he's watching to see how I'll handle a situation, a confrontation or something, the way he would. The next time I walk by a mirror, I feel him looking at me. Judging me."

"That's a lot of pressure," Izzy said.

"I know. And sometimes it's the stupidest stuff too," he said. "If there's a woman I want to ask out, but I can't get up the nerve, I feel him watching me, wondering what my problem is. If I get into an argument with my sister and I don't have the guts to tell her like it is, he's laughing at me."

"Do you ever think he'd be happy with you?"

"Sometimes."

"When?"

"I'm a good teacher," he said. "I used to have kind of a power trip attitude about it. I was overly strict. I enjoyed being in charge and using my authority. I don't think he would have liked that. I'm much better now. I know how to be fair, and respectful. I know how to make them *think*. I feel like he would appreciate that."

"You're a good person," Izzy said. "You shouldn't let all that get to you. You've got a lot of students who respect and love you. Your brother would love that."

He chuckled. "It's easy to get an eighth grader to respect and love you," he said. "But two nights ago I had a beautiful woman ask me to join her for a drink. I turned around and left. I went and drank. I could actually hear my brother calling me a wuss."

Izzy blushed. "That girl had had too much to drink," she said.

Abel smiled. "Maybe." He leaned back in his seat and cracked the blind again. He saw the backs of businesses, homes, industrial parks - the dirty side of things he never saw from the road.

"Anyway, I try to avoid mirrors," he said. "Unless I am feeling absolutely fabulous about myself."

"Can you tell me anything about your father?" Izzy asked.

Abel closed the blind and looked at her. "Why?" he asked.

"You've told me about your mother," Izzy said. "What about him?"

322

"He was a good man, but he drank himself to death," Abel said. "He couldn't deal with the loss. He couldn't deal with the way my mother dealt with the loss. I've always hated him for it."

"Does your mother hate him?"

Abel thought for a second and said, "No."

"Do you think Jacob would have hated him?" she asked.

Abel nodded. "I like to think he would," Abel said. "Maybe he's happy that I haven't ever forgiven him."

"Or maybe he would have had the strength to forgive him," Izzy said.

Abel sighed and said, "Let's talk about something else?"

"Okay. Can you tell me the rest of what happened that day?" Izzy asked.

Abel let the blind close. "Can you tell me what you're hoping to accomplish with this story first?"

She shrugged impatiently. "Jesus, how many times do we need to go over this? I want that damn award."

"Really?" Abel said, allowing his disbelief to register. "A man threatens suicide. I'm threatened by a governor's staff. A woman reveals an illicit affair that she's convinced was meaningful and, by the way, she had the hero's love child, a hero that happens to be the writer's father. And God knows what else you're going to find out. Are you really just after an award?"

"I'm after the truth," Izzy said.

"The whole truth? No matter what? You're going to smear your father's name," Abel asked.

"He's a hero for taking down a killer, not for being a good husband," she said. "If I decide to include all that stuff, my mother, and the rest of the world will have to deal with it. It's the truth."

"*If* you decide to include it?" he asked. "Why wouldn't you?"

"I'm not sure it's important enough to the story to ruin a man's reputation," she said.

Abel scoffed. "I can tell you're still in journalism school," he said. "And there's more to come, believe me."

"Tell me," she said.

"That governor, and his two lackeys. They figured out pretty quickly who you were, so they sent you away. No interview."

"I'll get the interview," she said.

"You probably will. But then they figured out who I was. The last person to talk to Joe before he died."

"So what do you know?" Izzy asked.

Abel thought about his words. "Okay," he said. "Here is what Governor Mike Springer does not want the world to know. Ready?"

"Yes, I am."

"He chickened out," Abel said.

"Can you explain?" she asked.

"Remember I said the four of us were crouching behind that wall with Joe and Mike?" he asked.

"Yes."

"When Joe saw that the killer had walked past the wall and had his back to us, he turned to Mike. He asked him, 'Which one do you want?' I can *still* hear his voice. He was holding his tennis racket, and Mike was holding the bat. He was offering to trade with him."

"I take it Mike chose the bat?" Izzy asked.

"That's right," Abel said. "He said he'd take the bat. So Joe told Jacob and me to stay put, then he told Mike his plan. He was going to go first and smash the shooter over the head with his tennis racket. Then Mike would follow behind with the bat and hit him again while Joe disarmed him."

"What happened next?" Izzy asked.

Abel continued. "Joe peeked around the side of the wall again then turned back and said, 'He's reloading his gun. Let's go.' He was still so calm, and I remember looking at his hand on the tennis racket. He wasn't trembling or anything. That's when he looked at me and rattled off that message that I gave to your mother. Then he was gone."

"Holy shit," Izzy said. "Then?"

"Mike didn't move," Abel said. "He just stayed with us, behind the wall while your father went after Evan Long."

"My God."

324

"He stayed on one knee, peeking around the side of the wall. He was on the ball of his foot, like he was about to go. But he never did. I could hear Joe's footsteps, running up to him. Then we heard the sound of Joe's racket smashing into the guy's head. We heard him scream in pain. Mike heard it too, but he stayed right there. Then Jacob shouted at him, 'Go! He's waiting for you!'" Abel took a deep breath. "Then I heard my brother yell, 'Give me that bat!'"

"Your brother took the bat," Izzy said.

"My head was down now. I just couldn't look," Abel said. "I thought we were all going to die. But when I looked up..."

Abel lowered his head and began to cry. Izzy fumbled through her seat pocket for a tissue. Abel took it and wiped his face, trying to regain his composure. He looked at Izzy. "I've never told that to anyone before."

"It's okay," she said. "What did you see when you looked up?"

"I saw my brother, who was ten years old, carrying a baseball bat charging after a man who had a gun."

"Jesus," Izzy whispered.

Abel nodded and wiped his tears again. "If Springer wouldn't do it, my brother was going to. He took that bat that he could barely carry and went off to help your father stop a killer."

"They did stop him," Izzy said.

Abel nodded. "Joe probably knocked the guy down when he hit him with the racket. Probably managed to wrestle the gun out of his hands. I always figured he didn't try to pick it up because he would have thought Mike was right behind him. He could get it."

"Makes sense," Izzy said.

"But Mike never came, so that gave Long time to get that knife out and stab Joe in the belly. That's probably when my brother showed up. Probably tried to hit him with the bat. But all I heard was Jacob's footsteps running after him, then the bat hitting the ground."

"Nobody knows about this," Izzy said. "No witness ever reported seeing any of that."

"It's all true," Abel said. "He jammed that knife right into the side of Jacob's neck. I have never seen so much blood. Pure fucking evil."

Izzy rested her head in both of her hands as she listened. "Your brother was a hero," she whispered.

"That's when Joe got him a second time with that racket," Abel said. "The guy was probably too busy watching my brother die to see your father coming for him again. So Joe hit him twice and Long was down for good. By then Springer had finally come out from behind the wall. He ran over and picked up the gun and pointed it at Evan Long, but he was pretty much unconscious by then anyway. And Jacob and Joe were bleeding to death."

"Then you came out?" Izzy asked.

Abel nodded. "I saw my brother bleeding, so I started screaming for somebody to help him. It seemed like forever before anybody else got there. The two maintenance men came running over and one tried to help Jacob and Joe while the other jumped on top of Long. Will Janicki was one of them. It was too late though. Then the police came. And ambulances. Too late."

"You were still there for all of that?" Izzy asked. "Why didn't a counselor take you away?"

"I wouldn't leave him," Abel said. "I screamed when they tried to take me away."

"Did you see them arrest Long?"

"Yeah. The police sirens woke him up, but by then both the maintenance guys were on top of him. They had him face down on the grass. One was kneeling on his neck. The other had his hands pinned behind his back. It seemed like they knew what they were doing.

"And he started screaming when he realized he was being arrested, saying he was supposed to die. He'd wanted to kill himself." He paused and shook his head. "I never get that," he said. "These assholes kill people then kill themselves so they don't have to face the consequences. What could be more cowardly than that?"

"I don't know," Izzy said.

"But your dad didn't let him, did he?"

"Neither did your brother," she said.

He nodded. Abel appreciated her saying that. He had never really thought of it that way.

"Do you want him to be executed next week?" she asked.

Abel thought about the question for a long time before he answered. He had gathered himself and was no longer in tears. "I started going to church a couple years ago," he said. "I started believing in God for the first time in my life. I even got myself baptized." He smiled and shook his head. "There's a lot in the Bible about the death penalty. *An eye for an eye. Turn the other cheek. Let he who's without sin cast the first stone.*"

"Which do you believe?" she asked.

"I don't know," he said. "I asked my priest how the Catholic Church feels about the death penalty."

"What did he say?"

"He said they're pretty much against it, but it's not out of the question. Like if a murderer in jail still somehow posed a threat to innocent people, or even to other prisoners, it might be justifiable to use the death penalty."

"Do you think Evan Long falls into that category?"

"No," Abel said. "I'm sure he's harmless in there."

"Has your faith helped you cope with the loss of your brother?"

Abel thought about it. "In a way," he said. "It's been a blessing and a curse."

"How so?"

"It's a blessing in that I've learned a lot about the ways God works. We all have free will, so we can do really good things, or incredibly bad things. God lets it all happen and tells us it's all part of his plan, even when it doesn't seem like it.

"On the other hand, I now have this belief that I'm going to see my brother again someday and that freaks me out like you wouldn't believe."

"Why?"

"It's like I said before," he said. "I'm always wondering what he would think of me and how I've lived my life. And I believe I'll see him again. It's like I'll be handed my report card when I die. He'll tell me everything I did wrong and everything I did right."

"Maybe he'll just be happy to see you," Izzy offered.

Abel laughed to himself, then looked out the window again. "I guess I'll find out someday. It's always amazed me that that is the one thing every person on earth - you, me, Evan Long, Mike Springer - that we all have in common."

"What's that?" she asked.

"We're all going to die," he said. "We're all going to meet our maker. And I wonder all the time what Jacob will look like when I finally do see him again. Will he be the same as he was when I last saw him? Will he look how I look?" He shook his head. "My faith in God has changed my life. It really has. But sometimes it scares the living hell out of me."

Abel had grown fond of the Holy Sacrament of Reconciliation. He had begun making monthly visits to his friend, Father Thomas Patel, two years earlier. Occasionally they would be more frequent, prompting the priest to kindly warn him that if he continued to confess the same sins, he was really asking more for permission to sin rather than for God to forgive him. He usually heeded the advice, but vices are hard to give up completely. As he sat across from the woman who would write and publish the story that would change so many lives, he could not help but think of that sacrament. Would this bring reconciliation? Would the state, the world, forgive Will Janicki for failing to act? Would it forgive Mike Springer for his failure? Would the world forgive Abel for being the weak brother who watched the stronger one charge off to die?

Izzy leaned forward in the small cabin, and Abel could smell her. It was the subtle but unavoidable smell that only a woman can bring to a room. Soap. Lotion. Shampoo. Perfume. Clean things.

She spoke softly, barely loud enough for him to hear. "Thank you for telling me your story, Abel. Thank you for your help," she said.

Abel nodded, unsure what to say to the one who had spun his life so drastically over the last two days, but had filled him with such a feeling of calm, despite the storms inside of him. He was glad to help her, but he was unsure how far he could go.

"Just leave that part about my wetting the bed out of it, okay?" he asked.

She smiled. "Can you face Evan Long when I interview him?" she asked.

Abel thought of Evan Long. Locked in solitary confinement, softening from lack of activity, his eyes squinting in a dark cell. Surrounded by guards who may soon watch him eat his last meal then walk him to his death.

"I don't know," Abel said. "I think I can, but only because my brother would want me to. I don't know if I can actually talk to him, but I want to see what he looks like now. Pathetic, I hope."

"He's been in a solitary cell for twenty years," Izzy said. "He's in his cell pretty much all day."

Abel nodded. "Reading the Bible from what I hear," he said.

"It's true," Izzy said. "He reads it a lot. A lot of other books too."

"How do you know that?" Abel asked.

"I wrote him a letter, asking if I could interview him," she said. "He wrote me back, saying he wanted to talk. 'Break the long silence' was how he put it. "

"Poetic," Abel said.

"He said he wants to tell me what he's learned from reading the Bible, among other things."

Abel smirked and shook his head. "Asshole. Don't let him start talking about the Bible if you get to interview him. He thinks he's going to be remembered as a martyr. Last man to hang."

"I *will* interview him," Izzy said. Abel looked from the window to see that Izzy was waiting for him to make eye contact. "And I want my photographer there," she said.

He could feel his palms starting to moisten. "He killed my brother, Izzy. I watched him die."

329

"I know," she said. "I want you there with me."

"Let me think about that, okay?"

"Sure," she said. "I have one more question I want to ask before the interview is over."

"Go ahead."

"Do you blame Governor Mike Springer for your brother's death?"

Abel shook his head. "First of all, he wasn't a governor back then; he was just a dopey camp counselor who liked to talk about law school, especially when lady counselors were around. Secondly, I blame Evan Long for my brother's death. Nobody else."

"Do you think your brother would be alive today if Springer had acted differently?" she asked.

Abel bit his lower lip. She wasn't letting up on him. She wanted a quote for her story, and he didn't want to give it to her. He considered his words carefully, then said, "If everyone was as brave as my brother, or your father, a lot of people would still be alive today. I wasn't that brave, and Mike Springer wasn't that brave."

"You were a child," she said. "Springer was a grown man."

"My brother was a child," he said back to her. "All things are equal when there's a man shooting a gun. Men, women, children. It all comes down to who's brave and who isn't."

***

Lunch was less crowded than breakfast had been, and Abel and Izzy were able to sit alone at a table in the dining car. Izzy's stomach was still feeling sour from the night before, so she ordered fruit and toast. Abel had advised "something greasy" to soak up the hangover. She disagreed and kept it light. He had asked her to promise to try it next time she was suffering a morning after. "A western omelet and bacon does wonders. Trust me, I'm an expert," he'd said. She responded that there was no need to make that promise since she would never get that drunk again in her life. He said he doubted that.

"Are you worried about that woman that works for the governor?" she asked.

"Sheila Avery?"

"Yes, her," she said. Izzy didn't like saying or hearing her name.

"A little bit," Abel said. "A week ago, I would have been terrified. I'd have never even talked to you. But now..."

"What?" she asked.

"You woke up the journalist in me," he said. "It's starting to feel good again."

"So you're not worried?" she asked.

"I'll talk to my sister," he said. "She'll understand. It's a dirty, asshole thing to do to a person. Politicians are so slimy. But the truth has to come out."

"Good," Izzy said. She sipped her coffee while Abel guzzled his orange juice. The food arrived and they both began to eat in silence, enjoying the rhythmic din of the train against the tracks.

"So what's the plan when we get back?" he asked.

"Springer," she said. "I have to talk to him."

"They won't let you near him," he said.

"Let me worry about that," she said. "I have a plan."

"I'm not part of it, am I?" he asked.

Izzy was surprised. "I need you to be part of it, yes."

Abel coughed on his orange juice.

"Why do you need me?" he asked.

He could see the confusion in Izzy's face. "I've got it all figured out. I just need you to make an appointment to speak to Sheila Avery," she said. "Ask to meet her in her office."

"A diversion?" he asked.

"Yes. Just keep her busy for thirty minutes," she said.

Abel put down his fork and drew back from the table. "I'm not very good at those kinds of things."

"What kinds of things?"

331

"Confrontations. Acting," he said. "I don't do well with them."

"Just have a conversation with her," Izzy said. "She didn't have any problem coming to your apartment. She poked her nose into your life."

"That's her job," Abel said. "I'm a teacher."

"I need you to do this."

"I'm not sure I can," he said, feeling his palms start to sweat.

Izzy exhaled sharply. "Look. Not every story is about kids riding trains and walking across bridges. Sometimes you have to stick a tape recorder in someone's face and get the story." She looked angry now.

He lowered his head and squeezed the space between his eyes. "That's not fair," he said. "This story is too personal. We *are* the story. You and me."

"We don't have to be," she said. "I'm writing under a pen name. Your photos will be under an assumed name. Nobody needs to know who were are. You're going to be fine, Abel."

"It'll come out soon enough," he said. "People figure things out."

"So what? What are you so afraid of? By then we'll have published a huge story. People will be lining up to interview us."

"And you'll have your award," he said.

"I hope so," she said.

Abel stood from the table. "I don't think I need to be a part of this anymore, Izzy. You can take the camera. The pictures are yours."

"What are you talking about?" she said, drawing the glances of the other diners.

"You want the fame," he said. "The spotlight. I don't. I've been running from it my whole life. Use my interview and the pictures I've already taken. Good luck."

Izzy calmly wiped her mouth and placed her napkin on the table between them. "We can talk about these things later," she said. "I need to make a few calls at the next stop. Then I'm going to work on my laptop for the rest of the ride back." She looked at him. "What are you going to do?"

"I'm going to try to sleep," he said.

"I'll work in the lounge," she said. "The room is all yours."

"Thanks," he said, then stomped out of the dining cart.

Izzy seethed as she watched Abel exit the dining car, but she didn't have time for his fear. Abel Ryan, or whatever his name really was, wasn't up for a confrontation, especially one with Sheila Avery, a woman who hadn't impressed Izzy in the slightest.

As she finished her coffee, Izzy considered all of the men she'd dealt with over the past few days: a man too afraid to help her outmaneuver a governor's staff, her brother afraid to leave his mother's side; a professor afraid of offending some people with a piece of journalism; a maintenance man afraid of facing a world who couldn't forgive his mistake; a future governor who froze rather than follow his friend, her father, as he faced a killer.

Was her father the last heroic man she would ever know? But she didn't know him at all. Did anyone?

Feeling the train come to a stop, she found the exit and walked onto the platform to look for a payphone. She found one and dialed. She was calling someone she had hoped never to speak to again.

"This is Duncan," said the voice on the other end.

It was good to hear his voice. Izzy could feel his strength in the sound of it. It had been months since she had heard his voice, and now she realized now how much she'd missed hearing it.

There were many things she had missed about Nate Duncan besides his voice. She missed the way he would take her in his arms and squeeze. The way he would *look* at her, especially when he undressed her. Like he had won the lottery. They had always had to make love in the daytime because he worked nights. She loved seeing his face when they did. His always powerful features melting under her power, if only for a short time. She was sad when it ended, but she knew it had to. He was older, ready to start a family. She wasn't even close, and they both knew.

"Officer Duncan," Izzy said when he answered.

333

There was a long pause. "Izzy," he finally said. His voice was pleasant. "It's been a long time. How have you been?"

"I need your help," she said.

"I doubt that," he said.

She smiled. "I do."

She heard him exhale. "It must be big," he said. "Do I even want to know?"

"I need to get into the capitol building," she said. "Can you get me in there?"

"That's easy," he said. "What do you plan on doing once you're in?"

"I need to interview Mike Springer, away from his assistants," she said. "They can't know I'm there."

"That's a tough one, Izzy," he said. "But it can be done."

"I need to do it tomorrow," she said.

"I'm not even sure he'll be *in* the capitol tomorrow, Izzy."

"Can you find out where he is then? I really need to talk to him tomorrow. I got to him once, but his minions called it off."

"You trying to get me fired?" he asked, but she could tell he was joking.

She laughed. "I really need to talk to him," she said. "I'm writing a story about Evan Long, and I want to get Springer on the record before he's executed."

"Where are you now?" he asked. That was a promising question, Izzy thought.

"I'm in North Carolina," she said. "Getting on a train in a minute."

"You and your trains," he said. "I'm off duty at ten tonight. Call me when you're back in town. We'll talk."

Izzy smiled. "Thanks, Nate. It's nice to talk to you again."

"Call me when you get back in town."

***

334

The air in Abel's apartment was hot and stale, but it felt good to be there, all the same. He was home. He switched on the air conditioner and heard it spring to life. He had been away two hot June days, and it would take some time to cool down.

Abel opened his refrigerator and grabbed a bottle of beer. He reached for an opener but changed his mind and put both back in their places. He wasn't in the mood to drink, and he felt good about this.

Abel had never considered himself an alcoholic. He was sure he didn't have a drinking problem. He was never drunk at an inappropriate time; he never even took a drink to relieve anxiety. At least he didn't *think* he did. Drinking was only an activity he did when he was in good spirits, or at least in a neutral mood. But despite all of that, he thought often of his father and wondered if it had started the same way for him.

It had taken a long time for him to liberate himself from the guilt he had felt over being the brother who'd survived. He had not been brought up in any faith. His parents had never taken him to a church or introduced him to God in any meaningful way. When the Almighty or anything having to do with him was mentioned in conversation or on TV, he had always regarded it as something important that others believed, but not him. He had friends who complained of Sunday school and CCD. Abel would sometimes ask his friends what went on at these strange meetings. When they responded with "boring," and "stupid," he was glad that his parents had not forced him and his siblings to participate. He had asked his parents once why they didn't go to church and their response was evasive. "We don't have one to go to," his father told him from the driver's seat.

When Abel pointed out to his father that they routinely drove by at least five churches in a day, his mother interjected. "We've never gone to church, Abel," she said. "Unless there's a wedding or a funeral. We don't belong to one." She'd said it with a tone that implied finality. The topic was closed for discussion, which of course prompted Jacob to pursue the matter forcefully.

"Do we believe in God?" Jacob asked immediately after that. It was a challenge, and he asked it only because of his mother's tone. Jacob didn't like backing off a challenge, especially one he thought he could win.

Their father took it. "It's up to you," he said. "I believe in God, but I never went to church. My parents never took me."

"Then why do you believe in God?" Jacob asked.

Their father thought for a moment. Their mother shifted uncomfortably in her seat and scoffed as she turned to look out the window.

"Mostly because of love," he answered. "I'm a scientist, and I think science can explain just about everything, except love. The way I feel about you two and your sister. The way I feel about your mother. The way you two love each other. I don't think anyone could ever explain that to me, except to say that someone, or *something*, is in charge of it all. *Creating* it all. I don't have to go to church to know that."

Abel and Jacob had been eight years old when they heard their father discuss his thoughts on God for the first and only time. This was before the shooting. Before his father had turned to intoxication to drown the horror of losing a son. Many years later, after accepting a job at a Catholic school, under the false pretense that he was a practicing Catholic (whatever that meant), Abel began to wonder if his father had been right. Was there really a God, and was he responsible for all the love in the world? Surrounded by statues, rituals, and lit candles, he started listening to everything with new ears. He started looking at the world differently, wondering if there were signs of God where he had never seen them before.

It turned out there were. The ancient rituals of the church did not impress him, but the Scriptures did, as did much of the sacred teaching, things he had never heard or considered, but made a lot of sense once he began trying to live them. A year after he started teaching at the school, a new priest, Tom Patel, arrived at the parish. He was right out of the seminary, and only a few years off the boat from India - young, brilliant, and problematically introverted. The middle school teacher in Abel recognized the priest's anxiety and made an effort to befriend him. It worked, and in the months and years to come, they spent many long hours discussing their mutual vocations between gulps of high-quality beer, something the rectory was never short of. To Abel, the polarity of church teaching began to make sense - rigid, unbending rules on one end, compassion and forgiveness on the other. A few months after their first meeting, Abel asked his friend to baptize him.

After that, Abel was a semi-regular at Saturday evening mass, never one for waking early on Sunday mornings. Finding religion had enlightened and liberated him, but his family looked on his new faith with suspicion and confusion. *You're not going to become a priest, are you? Is this priest friend of yours gay? Is this just a way to meet girls?* Eventually realizing Abel had not outwardly changed into an evangelist preacher, they grudgingly accepted it.

However, for Abel, even after accepting God's church and all of her rituals, he still could not find a place for the death of his twin brother, or the others who died that day. The gift of free will and the human capacity to carry out evil simply did not suffice. "Free will is a gift," his friend Tom had said many times. "The way humans use free will is up to us. But God has a hand on everything."

Bullshit, Abel thought, as he considered his ten-year-old brother bleeding to death in the grass. But the solace Abel finally found was that he would see his brother again. He would meet him in the next life and have many things to talk about. Jacob, who had been baptized in his own blood, would greet him with open arms and want to discuss the life of Abel Ryan - of Norman Suddard. Abel's knowing he would need to answer not to God, but to his twin brother, brought him an otherworldly sense of relief. He could live almost happily as long as he thought his brother would appreciate the way he lived. He was living for two people, and his faith made this very clear to him. It was a blessing. And a curse.

He lifted the receiver of his phone and dialed the number to learn that he had twelve unheard messages. *Wow.* There were rarely more than two, even after he had been away a few days. He hoped one of them would be from Izzy, though he doubted she would have called. They had not parted on good terms. An icy goodbye - no handshake. He hadn't even wished her well on the article. He would not be reaching out to her. Part of him felt cowardly about it, but he was sure that they had very different expectations. She was ready to face down a governor and his staff, interview a mass murderer, and enjoy the spotlight that came with it. This was not what he had in mind when he had agreed to help her.

He listened to the first message and was surprised to hear the familiar voice of Jessica Sheehan, the girl he had had a brief relationship with a few years earlier.

"Hi, Abel. It's Jessica. I don't know what's going on, but I just had a reporter calling me asking me how I knew you. Can you call me back?"

He put his beer down and listened to the next message. It was Jessica again, asking why he hadn't called her back. He felt his stomach beginning to turn. The next message was her again. Had she left twelve of these?

No. The next was from his sister. Her voice was straining with anxiety.

"Abel, can you call me back?" There were two more like that from her. The next two were from his mother. She sounded out of sorts, but she always sounded like that. She wanted a call back from him also. Abel squeezed the space between his eyes. He knew what was happening, and it wasn't good.

His blood boiling, he turned to see his reflection in the hallway mirror. He had always hated its placement in the hallway. He had not put it there. It had been left over by prior tenants. Abel had asked the landlord if it could be removed. "You're free to remove it yourself," his aging and lazy landlord had said. "Just put it back when you move." Abel could never bring himself to take it down. He picked up the phone and called Izzy. She didn't answer.

***

Izzy was waiting in her car when Corporal Nathan Duncan of the Delaware State Police arrived at his house in New Castle. He was in his cruiser. It wasn't a bad neighborhood, but it was a tough one, and the peace-loving neighbors always appreciated the sight of a state police car parked on the block. Izzy watched him from across the street as he climbed out of his car. It was nearly nine p.m., and she had come directly from the train station. Though she had managed a shower on the train, she desperately needed to freshen up in her own bathroom and change her clothes. She wished she had had time to clean up before this meeting, but she knew he wouldn't care. There was no time, anyway. She opened her door and stepped out of the car.

Nate's face lit up when he saw her. "How are you, Iz?" he said, stepping forward to hug her.

"At the moment, I'm smelly," she said. "How are you?"

"Just finished a twelve-hour shift, so I'm smelly too," he said. "But it's always good to see you. Come on inside, and we'll talk."

She followed him up the walkway and into his two-bedroom rancher. It did feel good to see him again. To smell him again. She had always loved his smell, even after a long shift.

"You're working days now?" she asked.

"Moving up in the world," he said as he removed his holster. "My shifts are almost human now."

It felt odd seeing him at night. She had been accustomed to letting herself in before seven in the morning, waiting for him to get home from an all-night shift. When he did arrive, he would remove his holster in the same way. Then they would jump right into bed and make love until she had to go to class. He would be asleep when she quietly left the house.

They had met at the scene of a robbery. Izzy, who had been sitting in the newsroom late one night in her freshman year, heard the police scanner report that a nearby convenience store had been held up. She had grabbed her keys and rushed out, hoping to be there as the police arrived. When she got there, it was only Nate and one other officer. She spoke to the clerk first, who did not seem at all frightened, just angry. Then she moved on to Nate, who politely answered all of her questions, then invited her to join him for coffee at the end of his shift. When she did, the conversation was easy. They both enjoyed getting right to the point of the matter, and they could discuss just about anything, except politics, which neither of them was really interested in. They both liked movies about crime and historical documentaries. He liked watching romantic comedies and she liked watching boxing.

She liked his easy way of asking difficult questions, ones her mother had never bothered asking. *Why don't you have any friends your own age? What was the hardest part of growing up without a father?* She didn't have good answers, but the ensuing discussion helped her learn a lot about herself. However, the toughest question came on a rare Saturday evening together as they sipped coffee in a diner after watching an early movie. *Why haven't you told your mother about me?* She couldn't answer. He had told his parents about his young girlfriend with whom he thought he was falling in love. *Do you think you will fall in love with me?* The relationship, which had progressed quickly, came to a rapid end after that. It turned out that Izzy loved being with Nate, but she wasn't in love with him, and she didn't need him the way he was beginning to need her. He was a twenty-eight-year-old state police officer. She was an eighteen-year-old freshman in college, and it had only taken a brief discussion of the future for them to realize that they were worlds apart when it came to their intentions. He ended it.

"Come on inside the living room," he said as he poured her a glass of wine and opened himself a beer. "Let's figure this out."

Izzy had shared the idea for her story with Nate before she started researching the principles. She had told him everything, including that she was the daughter of Joe Conway, something she shared with very few people. Nate had listened intently, his blue eyes lighting up every time she relayed a new idea she had come up with. *You're going to interview Evan Long?* His body would shake in laughter when she told him how she planned to confront the mass murderer. As was common in Delaware, he had known most of the people involved.

He knew Will Janicki from his frequent visits to his school. He had met the governor on many occasions.

Tonight, as she reclined on his sofa, and he sat in the chair across from her, she unfolded for him how things had progressed over the last few days. The light was low and the white wine was tasty. She was feeling sleepy, but she knew she had to fight it. There was work to do.

"You going to include that stuff about your dad?" he asked.

"Most likely," she said.

"Why wouldn't you?"

Izzy shook her head. "I just need to think about it some more," she said.

"It always comes out, Iz. Whether you publish it or not."

"I know."

"So you need me to get you in the capitol to sabotage the next president with an interview?" he asked.

She nodded. "You can do that, right?"

"Sure I can," he said. "But after I do, you never heard of me. I don't care if you get arrested, I had nothing to do with it. Got it?"

She nodded. "Thanks," she said. She took a sip of wine. "There is something else," she said.

"What?"

"The groundskeeper, Will Janicki?"

He nodded. "What about him?"

"He was very upset at the end of the interview. He said he thought about killing himself after the story was published."

Nate straightened his back. "Did he say how?" he asked.

Izzy nodded. "Handgun."

She watched his eyes widen. "He show it to you?" he asked.

"Yes," she said.

Nate stood up and walked toward the door. "Let's go," he said.

"Where?" she asked.

"Will Janicki's house," he said as he adjusted his holster. "You should come with me."

She remained in the chair, staring blankly at Nate as he picked up his blue-brimmed hat. She looked at her watch. She wanted to stay and make herself comfortable before jumping back into the story in the morning. She thought about asking him to go by himself while she waited.

"This will be an informal visit," he said. "I just need to make sure Will's no danger to himself. Come along. You might get some good stuff." He winked at her.

"I'll get my notebook," she said.

***

Will Janicki was about to plop himself down in his favorite chair to watch the Phillies play the Mets when he saw the State Police cruiser pull up and park in front of his house. *What the hell could this be about?* A break in at the campground? Maybe he shouldn't have cut those chains, after all. He walked to the front door and waited for them to come up the walk. It was nearly dark, but he could see that there were two of them, approaching somewhat faster than the usual official-looking march the troopers usually demonstrated.

"Will Janicki," the larger one said amicably as they came into view. "Remember me?"

Will did. "Nate Duncan," he called back. "Am I in trouble?"

"Not at all," Nate said. "I think you know Izzy Buchanan." He pointed to the familiar face next to him.

"Nice to see you again, Ms. Buchanan," he said. She looked much more tired since the last time he had seen her.

"Can we come in, Will?" Nate asked. "I'd like to ask you a few questions about what you told Izzy the other day."

Will looked from one face to the other, feeling the pit of his stomach tighten up. Suddenly realizing the reason for their visit, he relaxed. He knew why they were there, and there was nothing to worry about. "Sure thing," he said. "I'll get you a beer."

"Sounds great," Nate said.

Abel couldn't drink. He could barely even think. He was raging with anger and fear. He stared into the mirror, wondering what his brother would think, or what he *was* thinking. He hoped Jacob wasn't wasting his time in the afterlife staring into any mirrors. He wanted to shout into the mirror. *What can I do, Jacob?* But he wasn't that crazy, yet. All of the years in disguise. All those years formulating conclusions about what had happened that day. His journey toward faith, the death of his father, and his relationship with his family. It all seemed to be coming to a head with the looming execution of Evan Long and, more importantly, the publishing of Izzy Buchanan's article. *His and* Izzy's article. Would his name be on it too?

It might be time to disappear again.

***

The three sat on Will Janicki's screened-in back deck for more than an hour. Izzy felt immensely relieved when Will explained to Nate that he had been feeling very emotional at the end of her interview and that he had absolutely no intention of harming himself. On the contrary, he had found a way to make peace with himself. When he said that, he smiled at Izzy and said, "But I'm keeping that to myself."

Izzy was okay with that. She was just glad to hear that her story was not going to cause yet another death. However, she did want to finish what she had started a few days earlier. "Mr. Janicki, is it okay if I ask you again about that day, just two things?"

He smiled. "I'm in much better shape to answer. Go ahead."

"When we spoke a couple days ago, you mentioned that you'd like Evan Long to be executed because he wasn't repentant."

"Right," Will said.

"How would you know something like that?"

Will took a drink of his beer and seemed to be thinking. "Did you ever call Greg Burton at the prison?"

Izzy remembered Will mentioning the name during her last interview. "No," she said.

"Well, you should," he said. "Especially if you're planning to talk to Evan Long. That's about all I can say."

Nate interrupted. "Who's Greg Burton?"

"He was Will's assistant at St. Maria's," Izzy said. "Now a corrections officer."

Nate seemed to make the connection. He looked at Will. "Really? He told you that Evan Long is not repentant?"

Will shook his head and rubbed the back of his neck. He was now visibly uncomfortable. "Not in those words," he said. "Look, I don't want to speak for Greg, but from what I hear, that boy has himself convinced that he's a victim and that everyone will view him that way when he's gone. At this stage of the game, he goes on and on to anyone who will listen about how horrible his life was, but whenever anybody even mentions what he did, he just calls for one of the guards to come to his rescue. He's got a real ego. Wants to be a martyr."

"I'm going to interview him," Izzy said.

Will looked at her. "I know you want to, but you know you need permission…"

"I know all about it," she said. "I'm working on it, and I'm very close."

Will thought about this then nodded. "Good," he said. "At least you'll be able to say you confronted him. For your story, I mean. He'll only want to tell you his side of things. No way will he take any responsibility."

"I'm hoping to bring Abel, the photographer, with me. He was there when it happened. His twin brother was killed."

Will's eyes narrowed. "Hot damn. That's pretty good, young lady," he said, almost in a whisper. He turned his head to stare into the distance. "Call Greg, okay? He can help you. He can also give you the other side of the gun debate. He hates guns, even as a cop."

"I'll call him tomorrow," Izzy said. "Can I ask you one more thing?"

344

"Shoot," Will said, then he looked at Nate. "Sorry." Nate laughed.

"When we last spoke, I asked you if there was anything you would have done differently that day, if you could. You then told me about what happened earlier that morning when you met Evan Long. However, you never quite answered the question."

Will nodded. "You mean I went nuts. Ask me again."

Izzy smiled. "Okay. If you could, would you have done anything differently that day?"

Will sat back in his chair and considered the question. This reporter was practically a child. He thought about children and monsters and broken chains. He thought of baseball bats and tennis rackets. Pools and walls and duffel bags. Hot sun and rain. He thought of his wife and crying into her shoulder. Cleaning up her vomit after chemotherapy. He thought of death. People die when they are seven or seventy or one hundred and seven. He thought of compassion and offering a thirsty man some water. He sipped his beer.

"No," he said. "I wouldn't do anything different."

***

Nate was taking his time driving home, and Izzy was enjoying the ride. Even though it was a police car, the smell and the atmosphere reminded her of their brief but fulfilling time together.

"So you have a plan, huh?" he asked. He sounded amused. He knew her well.

"I do," she said. Both knew she wasn't sharing.

"You're going to offer the warden your body, aren't you?" Nate asked. "He won't be able to say no."

"You never could."

He sighed. "No, I couldn't."

They drove in silence for a time. Then he said, "Iz, we were just in different places."

345

"I know," she said. She reached her left hand to touch his. "It's okay."

He smiled. "I know you understand," he said. After a moment, he said, "Do you want to stay over tonight?"

She smiled. "I'll think about it," she said.

Sheila Avery quickly turned off her headlights and parked her car at the end of the block, hoping that no one in the car she'd been following had seen her. She'd been following the reporter, against the directive of her boss, in the hopes of finding something that could be used to discredit her, or at least one of her sources. Tonight, she had followed Izzy Buchanan to the home of a state cop, with whom Sheila learned Izzy had had a relationship, then to the home of Will Janicki, who had been present at the campground shooting, then back to the trooper's home. Now, Sheila was waiting with her long-distance camera at the ready, hoping to catch Izzy in a passionate embrace, or entering his home hand-in-hand. The photos could be leaked to the press if need be. They might call into question at least one the reporter's sources. *Was she trading sex for information?* Of course, there would be no link whatsoever between what Sheila was doing and the governor's office. Sheila loved the seedy side of politics.

As she focused her camera to catch the car's occupants, she was disappointed to see them simply shake hands and part ways. *Shit.*

She was about to start the car to leave when she saw that Izzy's car was making a dramatic U-turn and was now headed directly at her. She dropped the camera and tried to duck for cover. However, the seatbelt locked and she was unable to. She tried instead to cover her face with her hands.

The car was speeding directly at her with its high beams on. *What the hell was this?*

***

346

The night was cool and quiet. The city of Philadelphia had been treated to a late-night thunderstorm, a nice way to end a hectic day. The storm had passed and Abel lay in bed, trying to get his thoughts in order. He needed to speak to some people before the story was published.

His sister might be audited by the IRS. The girl he had dated years earlier might get swept up in a gossip story. His mother would break into hives at the thought of having to speak to a reporter about anything.

He glanced at the glowing numbers on his clock radio. It was two minutes after midnight. He had just turned thirty years old. It was his and Jacob's birthday. They had only celebrated ten together. However, for as long as he could remember, Abel would spend some time on each birthday, usually just before bed, staring into a mirror, wondering if his brother would look any different than he did.

He would have to visit his mother in the morning.

***

It should have been easy for her to fall asleep after the schedule she had put herself through the last few days, but Izzy was not sleeping. The night had been a productive one, but it had also taken an unexpected turn when she and Nate had arrived back at his house after their visit to Will Janicki. Nate had offered for her spend the night with him, and she had planned to accept. Inwardly, she had ruled out anything physical beyond actually sleeping in the same bed; she didn't want anyone, including Nate and herself, confusing what she was willing to do for a journalistic favor. She had looked forward to falling asleep in his arms until he would release her and turn to face the opposite direction, which had been his habit. However, it was as they parked in front of his house that Izzy noticed that they had been followed. The car that was parking a block behind them had been trailing them for most of the drive from Will's house. She had asked Nate if he had noticed. He hadn't, but he also admitted that his mind was on other things. As sorry as she was to disappoint him, Izzy had to tell him it was time to call it a night.

After exiting the car, Izzy shook hands with Nate, tried to ignore his bewildered expression, and walked back to her own car. She had considered whispering to him that she would explain later, but decided not to. She didn't have to explain her choices to anyone, especially to the man who'd dumped her a few months prior.

As she maneuvered out of her spot, she decided to make a quick U-turn. Confirming the identity of the one following her could only help the story. As her car approached the one in question, she angled her car directly at it and turned on her high beams. There sat the surprised, squinting face of Sheila Avery, frantically trying to cover her face and eyes. Izzy sped off, but not before lowering her window and extending her middle finger.

Now lying in her own bed, she tried to gather her thoughts, hoping that putting them in some sort of order would help her sleep.

Will Janicki was no longer a threat to himself, as far as she or Nate could see. And Nate took these things very seriously, she knew. Will had been an absolute bundle of nerves when they last met, but this evening he was relaxed and content.

Professor Griffin was also on her mind. He'd had the nerve to suggest the story be delayed. *Delayed.* After all those nights pouring over the possibilities at his dining room table and in his office. What was he thinking? Izzy realized that this was such a betrayal that she had hardly even processed its ramifications. This story had to be printed the weekend of Evan Long's execution. It would never have the impact she wanted unless it was. She would have to deal with that very soon.

She heard the distant rumble of thunder. She had always loved the sound of an approaching thunderstorm after a hot day. She wanted to open a window to feel the cool air the storm would bring, but the air conditioner was running at full force. Her mother insisted on a very cold house.

She thought of her mother. She hadn't called or spoken to her since the morning of the ceremony, four days earlier, and she hadn't been in the house when Izzy arrived home. She thought of her mother's beautiful eyes, and how they would fill when she learned the many truths her daughter had discovered.

She would have to talk to her tomorrow.

***

Evan Long was more restless than usual. He had not heard from his lawyer in almost three days, and he was only three days from execution. What was going on? He had begun to see the looks in the guards' faces. They were looking at a dead man, and they all knew it. There were faces he recognized, and new guards were starting to be rotated in. He was constantly being watched. The new ones would look at him with curiosity. The old ones would look at him with pity. He was already dying.

In the darkness of his cell, he placed his hand on his neck. He hoped it would be over quickly. The warden had explained that the rope was not going to strangle him, but rather break his neck. He would be dead quickly, and he would not suffer. But accidents could happen. Mistakes could be made. It had been decades since the last hanging. He could sense them practicing outside the prison, and he had seen the pictures of the newly-constructed gallows on his small television.

There hadn't been as much media attention as he had expected, at least so far. Sure, the evening news devoted a few minutes each night to the story, always mentioning Joe Conway and Mike Springer, and usually throwing in a few parents who'd lost their kids, but Evan had expected a frenzy. Maybe that was still to come. Maybe the people of the state of Delaware had simply moved on.

He turned over in his bunk and closed his eyes, knowing not a soul in the world really understood him. He hoped he would be able to talk to that reporter.

***

Shannon Maher was sleeping peacefully for the first time in years, dreaming of being wrapped in the arms of Joe Conway.

PART 5: SWEAT

Wednesday, June 19, 1996

"Greg Burton," was how the deep-voiced man answered the phone. He was not sitting comfortably at a desk. Izzy could hear it in his voice. He was standing, prepared to address a question in short order, then return to duty.

"Sergeant Burton, my name is Izzy Buchanan," she said. "Thanks for taking my call."

"Yeah, what can I do for you?"

"I'm a newspaper reporter. Will Janicki suggested I contact you. Is this a good time to talk?"

There was silence on the other end. Izzy was used to hearing this at this point in the conversation. The person on the other end was still trying to figure out why a reporter would be calling him, much less whether or not it was a good time to talk.

"Uhh. Well…"

"I can call back if it's a bad time," Izzy said.

"Let me call *you* back. Is that okay?" he asked.

"Of course," Izzy said. She gave him her number.

"May I ask what this is all about, Ms…?"

"Izzy," she said. "Izzy Buchanan. I am writing a retrospective on the shooting at St. Maria Goretti's. I interviewed Will Janicki. He told me you and he used to work together, and that I should speak to you."

"We did work together, though I'm not sure why he wanted you to talk to me," he said. "I've said pretty, much all I have to say about what happened."

"I know you have, but Mr. Janicki said you often disagreed on things like gun control," she said.

"We sure did. I'm sure we still do."

"I see," she said. "I would like to talk to you some more about this, if you don't mind."

There was a long pause. "I'll call you back," he said.

Izzy strolled onto the wooden deck outside her bedroom, notebook in hand, scribbling questions and follow-ups. She hated phone interviews, but sometimes, of course, they were necessary. She wanted to hear Greg Burton's take on Will Janicki. His account of the shooting had already been documented in newspapers and magazine articles. He had not been shy about telling journalists what he had seen that day.

"You don't even say hello to your mother anymore?"

Izzy gasped and turned around to see her mother. She was in a bathrobe, holding two cups of coffee. She stepped onto the deck toward Izzy, handed her a cup, and embraced her with her free arm. "You already smell like smoke," she said. "When did you get back?"

"Early this morning," Izzy said. "I didn't know you were home. I've been working on the story."

Abigail smiled. "I know you're busy."

"I'm fine," Izzy said. "Just in the thick of it."

"And how was Charleston?"

Izzy looked at her mother, and her eyes filled with tears. She wasn't at all ready to talk about the things she'd learned on her trip.

Izzy felt her mother's warm hand as it reached out to caress her cheek. Abigail had seen the hurt in her daughter's eyes. "Tell me," her mother said.

"Mom," Izzy struggled to say. "There are things we need to talk about, but I don't think I can do it now." She gasped for air as she felt the tears running down her cheeks.

"About your father?" Abigail said.

Izzy looked into her mother's eyes. They were as steady and strong as she had ever seen them. *Had she known all along?* Izzy couldn't speak.

"I loved him, Elizabeth," Abigail said. "He loved me. He loved you too, even though he never got to see you. He saved many lives

352

that day, and he sacrificed his own. He died a hero, regardless of how he lived. Nothing he did can take away from any of those things."

Izzy nodded and tried to sip her coffee. Abigail extended her hand to wipe her tears.

"You've got a job to do, Elizabeth," she said. "*Nothing* is going to stop you from doing it. Do you understand?" Her mother's words were as soothing as they had always been. As direct and provocative as they had always been. Abigail Conway had always taught her daughter to take action. *"Dwelling on things will get you nowhere."* Izzy had been hearing her mother say those words since before she knew what they meant.

Izzy nodded her head affirmatively. "Everybody is trying to stop me, Mom."

"I'm sorry you had to find out about your father this way," Abigail said. "I couldn't have brought myself to tell you. When you first told me you were going to write this story, part of me hoped you would never find that woman. God knows I didn't know where she was." She touched Izzy's chin with her left hand. Izzy looked at her. Abigail smiled. "The little tramp told you everything?"

Izzy nodded again. She had indeed been told everything. She had heard tales of her father, a man whom she had never known but had grown to love, to idolize, lying in bed with his young mistress and sharing his deepest feelings. They had taken day trips to their family house at the Jersey Shore, the house her mother still adored. They had made love in the same bed where Abigail slept. *Had she been conceived in the same bed as her brother?*

"Well, I'm sure there are things I don't know then," her mother said. "You're going to write it all?"

"Yes," Izzy said, having trouble getting the word out. "And there are other things. A lot of things you probably don't know."

Her mother nodded slowly. "It will be difficult for me. For you too. But we will get through it." She took Izzy's hand and squeezed it. "It will make us stronger."

"Okay," Izzy whispered. "There's something else."

"What?"

"The picture of you and him at the shore. The one the boy told you about at the funeral."

Shannon sighed and said, "Norman."

"Yes, I'd like to talk to you about it some more. Get some quotes for the story. That's all."

Abigail smiled again. "Of course. You know where to find me."

Izzy's phone rang and Abigail went back inside.

"Izzy?" It was Abel.

"Yes, it's me," she said, still wiping tears.

"They've gone after them, Izzy," he said, his voice angry.

"What?"

"Sheila Avery," he said. "I've got messages on my phone to call my sister, my mother, and that girl I dated."

"Jessica?" she said.

"How do you know her name?" he asked.

"It doesn't matter," she said. "Have you called them?"

"No," he said. "But Jessica said a reporter called her. What the hell? Do you think she told the press about me?"

Izzy sighed. "I don't know. I don't know."

"I thought she was screwing with me," Abel said. "I didn't think she'd really *do* anything."

"I'm sorry," Izzy said. "Do you want me to..?"

"No," Abel said. "Don't change anything."

Neither spoke. Finally, Izzy said, "Abel, I'm waiting for a callback. Can we talk later?"

***

Will Janicki answered the phone and smiled when he heard the familiar voice on the other end. "Greg," he said. "How the hell are you?"

"I'm fine, Will. You?"

354

"Doing great," he said. "I thought you'd be calling."

"Izzy Buchanan," Greg said. "She wants to talk to me about gun control?"

Will laughed. "You can tell her all your liberal crap," he said. "But that's not why I wanted her to call you."

Greg chuckled. "Okay, what then?"

Will searched for the right words. "You can *help* her," he said.

***

"Let me start by asking *you* a question, Ms. Buchanan," Sergeant Burton said to Izzy. "What is your opinion on gun control legislation?"

"That doesn't matter," Izzy said into the phone.

"Sure as hell does," Burton responded.

Izzy stood firm. "I'm writing this as an objective journalist," she said. "I intend to leave my opinions out of it."

She heard him scoff. "And do you have an opinion on whether or not eleven innocent people should have died that day?"

"Of course I do," she said. "Any decent human being would."

"My point exactly," he shot back. "If you don't think innocent people should continue to die at the hands of armed maniacs, then you should have an opinion on gun control. Do you follow what I'm saying?"

"Sergeant, I have opinions on many things, but I choose to keep those opinions to myself when I am writing stories and conducting interviews. Will Janicki, whom I am sure you've spoken to, has strong feelings on this. I gather that *you* have strong feelings on this. I would like to hear them. If you would rather not share, I will move on."

"Look, if you're going to put Janicki's nonsense in your story, then I'd like to say a few things."

"That's what I'm hoping for," she said. "Can I ask you some questions now?"

Izzy listened for a moment, hearing nothing but the man breathing. This was followed by a very low chuckle. "Okay, I guess I came on a little strong. I apologize."

"No need, Sargent."

"It's Greg."

"Okay, Greg," Izzy said. "Do you carry a gun at work?"

"Okay, good question," he said. "I'm a corrections officer. We don't carry guns inside the jail. It would be too dangerous if an inmate were to get hold of one. We do carry batons and pepper spray, though. Now, *outside* the prison - patrolling the perimeter, watchtower. They carry guns. But every officer who carries a firearm is certified and licensed to carry that weapon. Highly trained. You follow what I'm saying?"

"Do you think citizens have a duty to protect themselves?" Izzy asked.

"Yes, every citizen should protect himself. His family," he answered. "But that does not mean that every citizen should be carrying a gun."

"Who shouldn't be allowed to carry a gun?"

"Convicted criminals, for starters," he said. "Possibly the mentally ill. People with conditions that cause dementia, such as Alzheimer's disease."

"What changes would you like to see in gun legislation?" Izzy asked.

"I think automatic weapons have to be completely off the table," he answered. "And some semi-automatic weapons too. Any psychopath who gets a hold of one can do so much damage. Kill so many people. Stop selling them. Stop buying them. Stop *making* them for anyone other than the military and police. You follow what I'm saying?"

"Do you wish you had been carrying a gun the day of the shooting?"

"Hell no," he said without hesitation. "I wish *Evan Long* had not been carrying a gun that day. And if there had been some basic laws in place, he wouldn't have."

356

"What law would have prevented his having that gun?"

"Well, by all accounts, the guy just walked into a gun store two days before the shooting and bought that thing. No background check. Nothing."

"Would a background check have prevented him from purchasing it?" Izzy asked.

"No," he conceded. "But it shouldn't stop there. If you want to own a gun, you should have to be licensed. You should have to take a safety course. That way, instructors can throw up some red flags, and maybe catch the crazies before they become even more dangerous. You follow what I'm saying?"

Izzy scribbled furiously. "What are your thoughts on the Second Amendment?"

She heard him sigh. "Off the record, Ms. Buchanan, I think its time is long past. Too bad there are too many people in my line of work who would make my life miserable if they knew I felt that way. However, I will say this, on the record. When the Bill of Rights was written, it was just such another ballgame back then. The weapons weren't nearly as dangerous or easy to use. There was a real threat that the British could be returning to fight another war, and they would need a *militia* ready. And the amendment does specify that it should be a militia. A lot of these gun enthusiasts like to leave that part out of it. So back then, you needed ordinary people with weapons at the ready. Today, we have police to protect the citizens and a military to protect the country. The spirit behind that law is simply outdated. You follow what I'm saying?"

There was a pause while Izzy scribbled in her notepad. Then she asked, "What about protection from tyranny?"

"Give me a break."

"What would you say to a person who pointed out that good governments can and often do become tyrannical, sometimes very quickly? Wouldn't an armed citizenry be essential to preserving our freedom if that were to happen?"

"Do you believe this stuff?" he asked incredulously.

"I'm interested in *your* thoughts, Sergeant."

357

He chuckled again. "Well, I will say this. You are right. There are a lot of places all over the world where governments can become very dangerous. Even here, to some extent. But the limits we have written into our Constitution simply would not allow for that kind of thing to happen here. When people say that the U.S.A. is a special place, that's what they mean. Our laws don't let the government get out of control the way it could in other places. And I would seriously laugh at anyone who really believes that kind of thing."

"Thank you, Sergeant," Izzy said. "I'm almost finished. I'd like to ask you about Evan Long."

"Okay," he said. "I can give you background, but I cannot speak on the record about him."

"I understand," Izzy said. However, she did not understand. She quickly found herself confused about why Will Janicki wanted her to reach out to him. *Did he really want her to listen to anti-gun talking points?* She could have heard them anywhere. Not sure what to make of things, she decided to press ahead, even though they were now off the record.

"Do you think he should be executed for what he did twenty years ago?"

"Of course I do," he said.

"But you've said in the past that you think his life should be spared," she said.

"I know I have. I was pretty adamant on that," he said. "Look, you can't quote me on any of what I'm about to tell you, okay?"

"We're off the record."

"I used to be totally against the death penalty. I thought anybody could be rehabilitated, even if they spent the rest of their lives in jail. I still think most people can. But in this case, I don't think it's possible. There's really no getting to him. It's hard to explain, but it's like he's created a world for himself where what he did was *okay*, so he never has to truly be sorry. In his mind, he had no choice but to do what he did, so it's almost like it's someone else's fault, and he's just taking the blame for other people like him. You follow what I'm saying?"

358

Izzy looked down at her notes. She had circled the last part of the conversation so she would remember it was off the record. She wondered if she could somehow quote him anonymously. She thought about Will Janicki, then said, "It sounds like you're in direct contact with him." It wasn't a question, but she wanted to hear his reaction.

"I can't speak to that," he said slowly. "Security around death row is very tight, especially when an execution is imminent. But I can tell you, off the record, that part of my duty is scheduling which officers guard the men on death row and when. You follow what I'm saying?"

Izzy paused. There was something in the way he had said his last few sentences. Things were beginning to clear up. "Sargent," she said, "could we meet in person to discuss this?"

There was another pause. "I'll tell you what," he said. "It's probably better if you and I actually never meet in person."

***

Abel used his key to unlock the door and walked into his mother's home for the first time in six months. It was almost nine in the morning, and he could hear his mother shuffling around upstairs. She had to have heard him come in, but she didn't say anything. Abel went into the kitchen and helped himself to coffee, which was already brewed. There were pastries on the kitchen table and unopened orange juice in the refrigerator. She'd been expecting him.

He fixed himself a cup and slowly walked around the split-level, taking in the family pictures and the familiar knick-knacks. The house was clean and orderly, free of the stale smoke he had grown up waking up to every morning. He took a seat at the kitchen table and perused the newspaper.

His mother was smiling when she came downstairs. He stood and embraced her, and she softly kissed his cheek. "Thirty years old," she whispered. They held each other silently. A mother and son who had lost so much together. A son, a brother, a husband, and a

359

father. Both were victims of Evan Long. One stabbed, and one tortured for years in the form of nightmares suppressed only temporarily by vodka and rum and whatever else was available. It wasn't the alcohol that had killed his father; it was his brother's murderer.

Abel sat back down and helped himself to a scone. His mother poured herself a coffee and joined him. Having breakfast with his mother on his birthday had been the routine since he was twelve years old. With his father safely passed out upstairs, the two could chat quietly and enjoy each other's company until his father woke. At that point, Abel would have to give his father his full attention, trying to do everything his dad had planned - a Phillies game, fishing, a movie, whatever. Just don't get him upset. His mother would join them unless his dad insisted she stay home. In those cases, she would follow behind in her own car, knowing how the day would ultimately turn out. Sometimes within minutes, and sometimes after hours, the awareness of Jacob's unnatural absence would become too much, and his father would disappear for twenty minutes or so, reappearing with glassy eyes and the smell of breath mints. This marked the end of any pretending to have a good time. After that, it was walking on eggshells, knowing one false move, or even the wrong look would set him off. Eventually, his father would fly into a rage, and storm off in search of more alcohol. His mother would drive Abel home. The night would not end well. The next day, or the day after that, the apologies would come. His father would weepily beg forgiveness for a whole host of things, but never the *right* things.

Even after his father's death, the two continued meeting for breakfast on his and his brother's birthday. The two were apt to argue from time to time, but never during this annual meal of pastries, eggs, and bacon. This was always peaceful. Always quiet.

"Have you heard from Meghan?" Abel asked.

His mother nodded. "She'll be here later," she said. "She's bringing the kids for dinner. You're coming?"

"What time?" Abel asked.

"Dinner is at five, but come whenever you want. Aunt Sally is coming too."

Abel nodded. This meant he was obligated. "I'll be running around a bit today," he said. "But I should be back."

"I told Meghan about this story that you're working on," she said. There was an emptiness to it. A silent implication. Clearly, his sister had told her about the threatening calls from the IRS, or someone claiming to be from the IRS. They had put the pieces together. The story was causing trouble. However, rather than break the sacred rules of the birthday breakfast, his mother simply smiled and said, "We can discuss it later."

Abel nodded in agreement. He had returned his sister's calls before going to bed the night before. She was not happy, but he explained the situation. His sister had always been reasonable. She barely ever raised her voice, and she was often the only calm person in a household that had been torn apart by murder and addiction. Eight years older than the twins, she was often viewed by Abel, and previously by his brother, as a third parent, another figure of authority. In the wake of their brother's murder, she and Abel had grown especially close as she recognized the damage that had been inflicted on their parents. She had acknowledged long before her mother and brother had that her father was turning into a drunk, and her mother was becoming an emotional wreck who saw her dead son every time she laid eyes on her living one. When Meghan started college, she opted to live at home. Abel had always thought this was for the sole purpose of being near him, and every time she sensed her household beginning to erupt into flames, she would hurry her brother into her Honda Civic and speed away to Burger King for a milkshake. This was a merciful arrangement for Abel, but it was only possible until his father had picked up on the relationship and made it his mission to interfere.

When he was drunk, he harassed Meghan mercilessly, accusing her of ruining his relationship with his only surviving son, and even destroying his marriage. The abuse became so bad that she had been forced to move out. Unable to take Abel with her, she promised to

361

return as often as possible. Abel's home became an unlivable hell. It wasn't long until his mother decided he needed to go and live with Aunt Sally. After days of convincing him that she would be okay being alone with his father, Abel agreed. It was the kind of supreme sacrifice that only a mother can make.

When Abel explained to his sister why she was being investigated by the IRS, Meghan's reaction was measured. "So Springer thinks that harassing me is going to keep this story from coming out? *Prick.*"

"I don't think he even knows about it," Abel had said. "It's his assistants. They know it will get out eventually. They just don't want it coming from me."

They talked at length about all the possible repercussions of the story before they finally agreed that it would be better to move ahead with it. If the IRS was planning to audit her, she couldn't stop that. However, there were several ways that she could go public with what had happened to her. Whether anyone would believe what she said was an entirely different story.

He looked across the table at his mother. She had aged quickly after his brother's murder and his father's death. She had stopped drinking when she'd accepted her husband's affliction, but her smoking picked up and didn't stop until only a few years ago. During the hardest years, she barely ate. Her body and mind had been through a lot, and it showed.

However, today, she seemed slightly more filled with life than usual. She was made up, her hair colored and done; she was wearing a flower-print dress, and she looked like she was on her way to Sunday brunch. "You look nice, Mom," Abel said.

She took his hand and smiled. "You're full of shit," she said.

He laughed. "I mean it! You look great."

She stood and walked to the stove. "Enough of that. How do you want your eggs?" she asked. His mother was never one for sentimentality.

"Scrambled," he said as he stood. "I need the bathroom." He took the stairs to the second floor and walked past the bathroom to his old bedroom, which was now a guest room, where his mother's infrequent visitors would spend the night. He entered the room and, as he always did, walked right to the Mickey Mouse lamp that sat on the dresser. There was nothing else in the room that remained from the time he and Jacob had shared it. Immediately after his brother's death, friends of the family had come to remove all of Jacob's things. Under his sister's supervision, his neighbors had removed Jacob's dresser and pulled all of his clothes from the closet. Meghan identified items that he shared with his brother. They were kept. However, anything that was strictly Jacob's was taken away. To this day, Abel had no idea where they went. He had never asked.

The only trace of his brother that remained, and it survived to this day, was the Mickey Mouse Lamp. Abel had a Goofy lamp, and Jacob had Mickey. They had been Christmas gifts. Meghan came to Abel after the purge was complete and explained that the Mickey lamp would stay. It was a reminder of Jacob, and something of his should remain. Abel agreed, though inwardly he knew the only reminder he would ever need was in the mirror. Over the years, Abel's childhood belongings, including the Goofy lamp, cycled out, but Mickey Mouse remained. After Abel moved out, and all the furniture was replaced, the one item left in the room was the lamp that Abel now gently touched with his right hand. His mother had cleaned and dusted it, along with every other piece of furniture in the room. She treasured the lamp, and every guest who came to stay knew why it was there. But Abel had never once heard his mother speak of it. She was never one for sentimentality.

He used the bathroom and made his way back downstairs where breakfast was just about ready. They ate together, neither saying much. She asked about his job.

"I'm enjoying it," he said. "I think I'll stick to it, even after the story comes out."

She raised her eyebrows. "You mean you're going to let everyone know who you are?"

He nodded as he swallowed. "I think so," he said. "It's been enough time."

"You'll get a lot of attention," she warned.

"Only for a little while," he said.

"We worked hard for your privacy," she said sadly. "Even after your father got sick. He could still protect you." That was how she had always referred to his father's alcoholism. *Getting sick.* The years had severely damaged her perception of reality. Abel could remember times when she would refuse to acknowledge that he had been drinking, even in the face of irrational behavior and obvious odors. Abel knew how much she hurt over it, and he would never have a drink or appear even slightly intoxicated in her presence. This was part of the reason he visited so infrequently, especially during the summer.

"I know you both did everything you could to protect me, and I appreciate it," he said. "But I can handle it now. I know I can."

She looked across at him and raised her left hand to caress his cheek, a rare gesture of affection. "You were always so afraid," she said in a hushed voice. "Did we make you that way?"

He huffed. "I don't know, Mom."

"You've nothing to be afraid of, you know. We didn't hide you because we thought you couldn't handle it. It was because we wanted you to have a normal childhood."

He laughed. "Nice job," he said.

"Be nice," she said, tapping a finger on the table. "We did our best. Your father was ill."

He smiled. "I know," he said. Then he looked around the kitchen, his eyes finally landing on his mother's. "I don't know why I'm so afraid," he said quietly. "I stand at the front of a classroom and I rule the world. Nothing gets to me. I step outside of that and I avoid every confrontation."

His mother looked at him for a moment, then said, "It's because of what you've been through. Of course, it's affected you. The things you saw that day. The way you've had to live with it since then. It would affect anyone."

He nodded, wondering if it was, in fact, Evan Long who had made him the weakling he was today. He had memories of his brother

364

always being the stronger one, but were they true? Maybe he had overstated Jacob's toughness, even in his own mind. Maybe it was really just his imagination staring back at him through all those mirrors. Maybe he was judging himself, comparing himself to a hero that only half existed, but he doubted it.

"When does the story come out?" his mother asked, trying to rescue him from his thoughts.

"It's supposed to be this week, right before or after the execution."

"If there is an execution," his mother said. "They always find a reason to keep him alive."

"I think it's happening this time," he said.

She closed her eyes. "We'll see."

"Do you want him to be executed, Mom?" he asked. He had never asked her.

She nodded. "He murdered my baby," she said. "Took my husband from me too. He deserves to die. Now, I won't be terribly disappointed if he rots in jail forever, but I do hope they actually do it this time." She exhaled heavily. "There is one thing I really want, though," she said.

"What?"

She turned her face toward the sunlit window over the sink and took a breath before she spoke. "Whether he dies now, or fifty years from now, I want him to be afraid," she said. Her tone was thoughtful, not angry the way Abel imagined it should be. "I think so much what it must have been like for my baby to be bleeding to death. Knowing he was dying. Afraid." She stopped and looked at Abel. "You were there to see that," she said, frowning and taking his hand. "I want Evan Long to feel that same fear. Whenever it is that he leaves this world, I want him to be *afraid*."

***

"I have an appointment with Sheila Avery," Izzy told the uniformed capitol police officer. The man raised his eyebrows

365

suspiciously, and Izzy responded with a polite smile. She had called a half an hour prior to arrange the meeting, one that she promised would clear the air. Nate had informed her that morning that the governor was in the building today, as was his staff.

"There is no way I can get you to see him without going through his staff," Nate had told her. "They're sticklers these days, especially since none of them know me, including Springer. But I can tell you for sure that he will be in the building most of the day tomorrow."

Knowing the governor was in the building was really all she needed. She had a plan for the rest.

Abel, who had flatly refused to participate in the plan, was waiting at a hotel two blocks away. She had decided not to be upset with him. The man had been through a lot, and confrontations were clearly not his thing. "Have a couple drinks at the hotel bar," she'd told him, and she could see the relief register in his face. He was happy to take her up on that, having just had breakfast with his mother.

"I got quotes from my sister and my old girlfriend," he told her. "We might be able to use them if we have to." Izzy appreciated Abel's efforts, but she was pretty sure it wouldn't come to that.

She watched as the officer dialed the security phone and explained to whoever was on the other end that there was a young lady there who said she had an appointment to speak with Ms. Avery. Getting the answer he was waiting for, he hung up and smiled. "Walk through the metal detector, please," he said kindly. Izzy placed her purse on the small tray next to the machine, along with her car keys and stepped through. After not setting off the alarm, she was directed to take her purse and proceed to the elevator. Ms. Avery's office was on the third floor.

When Izzy arrived at the third floor, the elevator doors opened to reveal Sheila Avery standing with her hands folded, smiling the same artificially genuine smile that Izzy had been trying to erase from her mind. Sheila extended her right hand in greeting and said, "So nice to see you, Ms. Buchanan. Everything I say today will be off the record." Her smile was as bright as ever.

"Thank you for seeing me, Ms. Avery," Izzy said.

"It's Shelia."

"Thanks, Sheila. I know this meeting was short notice."

Sheila directed Izzy to follow her to an open seating area where they could sit on comfortable chairs. Izzy reflexively reached into her purse for her pen and notepad. A pointed cough by Sheila told her that she was not even to take any notes. *Fine,* Izzy thought. *I don't plan on quoting you anyway.*

Sheila carefully took her seat and said, "I don't mind short notice. I just don't like surprises."

Izzy looked across at her. She was on a mission and needed to focus. "I understand," she said. "I just wanted to let you know that I do appreciate the work you do, and that I do intend to interview the governor. He is a public figure, and I am a reporter."

Sheila smiled again. "You will get your interview," she said. "His office will be in touch when he is ready to chat."

"My story is going out this weekend," Izzy said. "The Saturday edition, probably. I will need to speak with him before that, especially if he plans on addressing anything that has been said about him in the story."

Sheila didn't flinch. "If you put those items in writing for me, I will be sure to take them up with the governor, and he will get back to you when he is able."

Izzy shook her head. "It's not going to work like that," she said. "And this story is running, with or without the governor's comments, and no matter how much you try to intimidate any of the witnesses."

Even Sheila's scoff was artificial. "This office would *never* engage in such activities."

"It would, and it has," Izzy said. "You implied to Abel Ryan, formally Norman Suddard, that his sister would soon come under investigation by the I.R.S. She has since received a phone call, probably from you indicating that she may soon be investigated."

Sheila rolled her eyes dismissively. "Anything else?"

Izzy continued. "A former acquaintance of Abel's, a woman he once dated, has also been contacted, again probably by you, and told that she was going to soon be in all of the newspapers as part of a scandal."

Sheila shook her head and stared down her nose at Izzy. "I don't appreciate these little accusations you are making about me. I've never heard of any of these things. Now, if you have anything of substance to say to me, please do it now. I don't have a lot of time."

"Do I even need to mention that you were spying on me last night?" Izzy asked.

"Nonsense," Sheila said, still smiling. "Anything else?"

"Yes, there is one more thing," Izzy said. "Shannon Maher."

Sheila just looked across at Izzy with a confused expression.

"You know her," Izzy said. "You gave her your card."

"I give my card to a lot of people."

"But do you ask many people not to cooperate with the press? That's what you asked her to do," Izzy said.

"I would never do that."

Izzy nodded. She was not sure at all if she was getting closer to her objective, farther away, or just going in circles. The woman was impossible to read. Izzy was impressed, actually.

"My concern is this," Izzy said. "I am going to print this story, and it is going out on Saturday. I plan on including how you and your colleague, Mr. Casarini, interfered with the governor's attempt to address the story. I will also have to include the pattern of harassment that I have observed as I have tried to gather information for this story."

Sheila's face flushed, but only slightly. "Really, the governor and his staff do not have time to go interfering with *college news reporters*," she said, emphasizing her detest for the last three words.

Izzy was unfazed. "I have two witnesses who've said that Springer was a coward. One says he was afraid of women, and the other says he failed to help his friend by allowing Joe Conway to face Evan Long on his own. He doesn't want to answer for that?"

As she asked the last question, Izzy looked closely at the woman's face, hoping that she could see the slightest trace of concern. She sensed the woman was breathing a little bit quicker than she had been. *Almost there.* Izzy waited for her to respond.

Sheila's words were measured. Her smile was fierce. "The governor will be addressing those, and other accusations, at a time in the near future, but not with you."

"I see," Izzy said. "Will it be before Saturday? That's when this story is running."

Sheila smirked. "I wouldn't bet on that. There are people much bigger than you calling the shots here."

She was bitter now, Izzy thought. *Go for it.*

Izzy looked around. "Are you embarrassed about the size of your office?" Izzy asked.

Sheila looked surprised. "Why would you ask that?"

"Because we're talking in a hallway. Your office is on this floor. Why don't we go to it? Are you afraid I'll put that in the story?"

Sheila's face reddened. "This meeting is over," she said. The smile was gone. She stood to leave. Izzy stayed put.

"I'm sorry," Izzy said. "I didn't mean to embarrass you. I'm sure your office is very cute."

Sheila scoffed. "Goodbye, Ms. Conway," she said. "I hope you don't mind if I use your *real* name. And if you're planning to print things that aren't true, the governor has no comment, except to say that you will hear from his lawyers." She was breathing heavily now, trying to contain herself. Izzy stayed silent, hoping Sheila would continue. She did. "You really come here and accuse this office of harassment? You're in way over your head!" Izzy could see the angry woman's teeth as she continued. "In fact, I *dare* you to print your lies," she said, jabbing a finger at Izzy. "You, that sister, Shannon Maher, the Sheehan girl. The governor will not lower himself to answer to wild accusations. *You* of all people should appreciate what this Governor wants to do."

369

"Why should I be so appreciative?" Izzy asked.

Sheila's eyes narrowed as she stepped toward Izzy. She spoke in a deep, scornful tone. "Because he wants to take guns out of the hands of criminals. He wants to fight for victims of gun violence. He wants to stand up for people like your father."

Izzy smiled pleasantly before saying, "It's interesting that you know the name of the girl Abel dated. *Sheehan*."

Sheila's eyes widened a touch, and Izzy knew she had her. *Score.* Izzy kept smiling as she stood to leave. "And I think it's great that Mike Springer is fighting for people like my father," she said. "But I would expect you to know that Joe Conway wasn't the victim of gun violence. My father was stabbed to death." Izzy smiled as broadly as she could and added, "You arrogant bitch."

Izzy walked back to the elevator, smiling the whole way.

***

Abel sipped his Dogfish Head. It was about 11 A.M., the earliest drink he'd had since the last day of school. He had committed to Izzy that he would see the story through to the very end, and he intended to. However, today was Izzy's. She had a plan, and she'd been nice enough to excuse him from participating. Tomorrow would be a different story.

Izzy had checked them into a hotel in Dover, one that was equally close to the capitol building and the prison where Evan Long awaited execution. She reserved two rooms, and had planned for them to spend the next two, or possibly three, nights there. Abel was fine with that, though he still had doubts about her ability to secure an interview with Governor Mike Springer, much less the killer, Evan Long. She shared only a few details of her plan and hurried off to the capitol. So Abel, who had made the forty-five-minute drive to Dover after breakfast with his mother, decided to wait, and drink, silently celebrating his birthday in solitude, occasionally staring across the bar at his brother's face. *Cheers*. His plan was to drink, sleep it off, then drive back to his mother's for dinner.

Izzy was hoping that tomorrow would be the day the two of them would pass through the extensive security of Delaware State Prison's death row and sit down with Evan Long for an interview. According to her, Long was receptive to the interview, having been convinced by her series of letters that pretended to sympathize with him. Of course, she had not revealed her true identity to the condemned killer. All that stood in the way was permission from the warden, which she was still somehow confident she would secure.

If the interview did happen tomorrow or the next day, he would simply take pictures, allowing Izzy to do the talking. A woman with no fear, as far as Abel could tell, she would execute an outstanding interview. He knew she would give her subject no leeway, and have no reservations about challenging her father's killer.

He thought of his mother's reaction that morning when he told her that, if all went as planned, he would come face to face with his brother's killer. Her eyes went dark and she drew back in her chair. *"You could never do that, Abel."* She emphasized the word *you* when she said it. But he assured her he would.

He'd gone on to tell her his plan to continue his teaching career indefinitely, an activity she and his father had long considered a waste of time. "I'm comfortable in the classroom, Mom," he told her. "It's the only place I feel truly confident." She shook her head in disappointment, knowing he was capable of much better things.

Abel finished his beer and ordered another. Whatever was going to happen, he believed he would be a small part of something great; Izzy would get her award, the story would come and go, and he would eventually fall back into his private, if no longer anonymous, life.

***

Mike Springer needed to smoke. He had just hung up the phone with Bob Casarini, who had informed him that he was going to appear nationally on NBC on Sunday morning. On that show, a friendly interviewer would ask him about his experience on the day

371

of the campground shooting. The only agreement Bob had made with the network was that their marketing department wouldn't promote the story in the days leading up to it, save to say that he would be a guest. They had all agreed that this story was too important to sensationalize.

Mike didn't *want* to talk about it, but people were coming forward. *Talking.* The truth would come out, but it would be on his terms. Rather than be revealed as a frightened young man who let a ten-year-old boy take a baseball bat from him and get himself killed, he would portray himself as a frightened, scared young man who froze when he was confronted with the unthinkable. Anyone might do the same. *Anyone except Joe Conway.*

His team had done their job and done it well. They had gotten ahead of the story. With this interview, he could even turn the whole thing into his advantage. Good publicity. That professor had been cooperative, agreeing to push the college newspaper story off until the fall and to perform the final edit himself before it was published. The professor knew how to compromise, especially when it helped the college. A Joe Conway Memorial Scholarship had done the trick. That and the promise of some federal dollars spent on the program to put it in the top tier of journalism schools in the country. Things could be done, as long as there was cooperation on all ends.

But Mike had to do his part too. He had to sit across from a national news anchor and recount the sudden panic he'd felt as his friend charged off to confront a killer. The interviewer would be instructed, of course, not to bring up his lack of service in Vietnam. His failure to act would be accepted by the general public as the unfortunate consequences of chaos and fear - what soldiers often called the *fog of war.* This was no different, really. Nobody could have ever predicted any of the events that had transpired that day.

The interview would include a lengthy monologue about the importance of gun legislation. His name and face would become even more associated with that noble cause. The experience and exposure would set him up perfectly for the 2000 election. From there, there was no limit. But first, the interview.

He walked out to the private courtyard and lit a cigarette. It was an old habit that he knew he would have to do away with before long, but this was private time that he cherished. Bob always did him the courtesy of allowing him his privacy. Sheila could not stand the smell of smoke, so she never accompanied him. He was glad to be alone.

But he wasn't. He heard footsteps behind him, followed by a vaguely familiar female voice.

"Do you have a light, Governor?" she asked.

***

Sheila Avery stormed into Bob Casarini's office without knocking. Surprised not to see him behind his desk, she turned her angry attention to her left, where he sat at a small conference table. His office was far more spacious than hers. *Not for long,* she had often thought.

"What?" the confused man asked, looking up from the *New York Times.*

Sheila was enraged. "That bitch!" she shouted at him.

"Who?" Bob asked. "What are you talking about?"

"Elizabeth Conway, or whatever the hell her name is," she said.

She knew Bob was completely confused, but she didn't care. "I did her the courtesy of speaking with her, and you wouldn't believe the way she spoke to me."

"Why would she want to talk to you?" Bob asked. "I don't get it. When did all this happen?"

"A half-hour ago!" Sheila shouted, now failing to understand why Bob wasn't sharing her anger at the reporter. "I just spent the last twenty minutes throwing things around my office."

Bob stood, an urgent look in his eyes. "Sheila, listen to me," he said, trying to remain calm. "You spoke to her on the phone, or in person?"

"She came here!" she said. "She called me and said she wanted to meet to clear the air."

Bob stepped toward Sheila. "Where is she now?"

She looked at Bob, whose face was now growing concerned. "She left," she said.

Bob's eyebrows raised. "You saw her leave?"

Sheila didn't answer. Her mind raced. *Had she seen her leave? No. She stormed off and had no idea where the girl had gone after that.*

"Jesus Christ, Sheila," Bob said. "You're smarter than that."

Sheila felt her stomach tighten. She grabbed the phone on Bob's desk and dialed Springer's office. "No answer," she said.

"Forget it," he said as he grabbed the phone.

"Who are you calling?"

Bob didn't answer.

***

Officer Nate Duncan happened to be in the security office of the state capital that morning. He was a familiar face among the staff, as were many state police officers who worked in and around the capitol. There were often state and capitol police coming and going for various tasks and meetings, so his presence wasn't at all out of the ordinary, and nobody asked any questions beyond the usual: *How ya doin, Nate? Enjoying the day shift?*

At the moment, he was rifling through his notebook, as if trying to get his facts in order before a meeting with a state prosecutor, or perhaps even a lawmaker. However, what he was really doing was listening intently for the phone to ring. Each time it did, he was all ears. It was a slow morning as far as calls to the desk went, so he hoped this would make things easier.

When he heard the desk sergeant say "This is Campbell," he knew this could be it - an interoffice call. Nate peered up from his notebook to see the sergeant's eyes lower with confusion, then fill with amusement. "Have I seen a tall blonde?" he asked incredulously. "No, sir. You have one for me?" *Bingo*, Nate thought. He smiled, playing along. He watched the man's face get serious again. "No, sir, I haven't seen one leave, but I can ask."

374

Nate took the cue. He quietly signaled the officer on the phone. "I passed one coming in," he said. "She was on her way out."

The officer covered the receiver. "You sure?" he asked Nate. "I got Springer's office on the phone here. They want to be sure she left the building."

Nate scratched his chin in thought. "It has to be the same one," he said. "She had on jeans and a purple top. Long blonde hair. In great shape." He listened as the sergeant relayed the description, leaving out the last part. The man waited for the person on the other end to confirm that it was the same person.

"Yes sir," he said into the phone. "If I see her again, I will let you know. I'll try to get her number first." He hung up the phone.

"What was that all about?" Nate asked.

The sergeant scribbled in his call log as he spoke. "One of Springer's people," he said. "They're worried about some reporter in the building who wants to talk to him. You sure she left?"

"Pretty sure," Nate said with confidence. "I don't think I'd forget her."

"Okay," the man said. "I'll let the crew up front know not to let her back in if she tries."

Nate folded his notebook and stepped toward the door. "I'll keep my eyes open," he said.

The sergeant smirked. "Yeah, me too."

***

Raymond Woodson was walking slowly down the long hallway toward the exit of the building that housed the Delaware Supreme Court. It was the first time he had walked slowly in days. It was late Tuesday morning, and Evan Long's execution was scheduled for Friday just after midnight. His hearing before the Pardon's Board was tomorrow, but Raymond knew his client had no chance with them. No stay. No overturning of the death sentence. Left to them, he would be executed by hanging, unless Raymond could convince him to take the needle, an option the warden had mercifully left open until the very last minute.

Raymond considered the scene that would unfold on Friday. Two methods of execution ready to go. Two sets of executioners. A gallows, a rope, a needle, sedatives, and poisons. He shuddered as he opened the door and stepped into the sunlight.

If there was hope for Evan Long, it was in the appeals brief he had just filed before the Court. Now, all he could do was wait, and hope to be called back to make an oral argument. He went over the case in his head, as he had a thousand times over the last two weeks. His client had a case, and he could win. Raymond knew it. He also knew that if he won, he would be saving the life of the worst criminal he had ever represented. The worst murderer in the state's history. Evan Long was pure evil, and Raymond had stopped trying to convince himself otherwise. But murder was murder, and as a man of principle, he could live with saving the life of a killer. As a man of the law, he could live with failing to win a case. What he could *not* live with was watching his client die, knowing he had not done everything in his power to save him. He got into his BMW and drove back to the hotel.

***

Springer recognized the woman immediately as Elizabeth Conway, though he could not recall the name she was operating under. *Isabelle?* He didn't care really, though the politician in him was disappointed that he had lost a name.

"How'd you get in here?" he asked.

"I found a way," she said. She motioned with her eyes toward her cigarette, which he lit for her, hoping she would not interpret the gesture as an approval of this unexpected visit. He glanced around to see if anyone was looking, but the courtyard was still empty, and nobody seemed to be peering out their office windows. He was wondering how far this would go before he left and called security.

376

The woman smiled and thanked him, and he was struck by her eyes, not because of their allure, but rather because they were the eyes of his friend Joe. He remembered them well.

"They even make *you* come outside?" she asked.

"Everybody," he said. "It's probably going to be a law soon, but I need to quit anyway. *Again.*"

"The more laws, the better, right?"

He smiled at her. "You're a Republican like your mother, I guess?"

She shook her head. "I'm not interested in politics."

He laughed. "You're still young enough to believe that, I guess. You'll learn."

"Maybe," she said. "Can I talk to you?"

He looked toward the door that led back inside. "I think you have a few minutes," he said carefully. "Pretty soon, my staff will start wondering where I am, come out here, and chase you away, *again.*

"I'm not afraid of them," she said. "Are you?"

"No, but I pay them to chase people like you away."

"Here's the thing, Governor," Izzy said. "I already have my story. I know what happened, and I know why you don't want to talk to me."

"Then we should probably leave it at that," he said, though he made no indication that he was going to leave.

He knew he should be walking back to his office. He knew he should politely alert the police that she was in the building. But he didn't. He just kept looking into her eyes, waiting for her to say something else.

"Can I just ask you three questions, Governor?" she asked.

He smiled. "God, you look like your dad," he said. "I could never say no to him either. You're a lot prettier, though. But he was pretty good looking."

"I've heard," she said.

"Make it quick," he said. "I might choose not to answer though, and I don't want you putting that in the story. Deal?"

"Deal," she said, and for some reason, Mike trusted her.

Izzy heard the words leave her mouth, but inwardly she was still trying to process the fact that she was finally asking them to Mike Springer, the governor of Delaware. "What do you remember most about that day?" was what she heard herself say, but all she could feel was the rush of emotion that came from securing the interview she had tried so hard to get. She couldn't enjoy it for long, though; there was work to do. She listened and scribbled as he spoke.

The governor looked toward the sky and closed his eyes in concentration. "Okay. I remember most the *feel* of that gun in my hands," he said, glancing around the courtyard. "It was still warm. It had blood on it, probably Joe's, or Jacob Suddard's, or both. That's the only time I've ever even held a gun. It was used to kill nine people, just a few seconds before. Then I was holding it. I can still feel it."

"Do you want Evan Long to be executed?" She asked the question then watched his eyes as they contorted between politics and honesty. She had expected this. There was an answer he wanted to give, but he knew she wouldn't accept it.

"I want justice for the victims and their families," he said.

She just looked at him. She didn't have to tell him that was no answer at all. The governor had been nearly silent on the death penalty his entire political career. The public knew that his liberal leanings pulled him away from it, but that his personal experiences, combined with popular opinion, made it very difficult for him to make a definitive statement on the issue. He had once said that the death penalty should be an option, but one only reserved for the worst kind of murderers. Izzy was about to remind him of this when she heard him sigh and begin to try to answer again.

"Evan Long has never shown any remorse for what he did. He killed eleven people, including my good friend. I've had two kids since then. They're teenagers now, and both of them would tell me that his life should be spared. I'm proud of them for that." He looked around again, then back at her. "But it just wouldn't seem right if Long was shown mercy - if his life were spared - and so many innocent people's weren't," he said. "I wouldn't lose any more sleep either way. Is that good enough?"

"Good enough," Izzy said. "One more question."

He nodded.

"If you could have done anything differently that day, what would it be?"

The governor finished his cigarette, dropping it on the ground deliberately and stepping on it with his right foot. "Well, I guess what I should say is that I wish I had followed Joe when he went after Evan Long," he began. His pace and tone were easier now, at peace with his words. "I should have been there to back him up after he hit Long in the head with the side of his tennis racket. If I had been there to finish him off, your dad would still be alive, and so would Jacob Suddard. But the truth is, that's not what I would have done differently. In fact - and I don't really know how to say this - part of me feels like what I did, or didn't do, doesn't even count. I was completely frozen with fear and panic." He struggled to find the words he was looking for. "What I mean is, most people in the world will never know what it feels like to be under attack like that. People getting shot and killed. Your own life in danger. For years, I hated myself for not following Joe and letting that little kid take that baseball bat and go after him. But the truth is I barely even remember doing it. I was so scared, and there was so much going on. I used to blame myself, but I've come to realize that there are certain people in this world who act one way in a life or death situation and certain people who act another. I could never have known that Jacob was going to do what he did. I didn't even know at the time *what* he was doing. So I don't blame myself, and I don't think I *could* have acted differently, even if I wanted to. Does that make any sense?"

"Yes," she said. "So what would you have done differently?" she asked again.

Springer smiled. "I'll go back to earlier that morning. We were in a bit of a rush that morning," he said. "There were things I wanted to tell Joe before camp started. I wanted him to sit and listen to me.

I had important things to say to him." He looked into her eyes. "You know, don't you?"

She was confused. "I know what?" she asked.

"You went to Charleston to visit Shannon," he said.

She stopped taking notes. "You knew about her?"

He closed his eyes and nodded.

She shook her head, trying to understand. "You know my mother, don't you?"

"Of course I do," he said. "Old friends."

"You never told her?" Izzy asked.

He closed his eyes again and slowly shook his head. "It wasn't mine to tell," he said. "Shannon moved away. I couldn't tell your mom anything. Hell, I was never even sure she had the baby."

"She did," Izzy said.

"I heard that yesterday." He scratched his head. "Your mother knew about your father, though," he said gently. "She knew he hadn't been faithful."

Izzy felt numb. Could her mother, who possessed all the strength and courage that Izzy had sought to gain, have sat by while her husband committed adultery? It didn't sound like the Abigail Conway she knew.

Springer could see it in the girl's face. She was hurt by what he had just shared with her. She had never known about her father's behavior. Her mother had never wanted her to know. Heroes are good to have, and it's a terrible realization to find out they're immoral, or worse, human.

"Are you okay?" he asked. He reached out and gently put his hand under her chin, raising it to see her teary eyes. "You don't cry much, do you?"

She wiped her eyes and shook her head. "No," she said.

"Just like your mother," he said. "One of the strongest people I know."

Izzy nodded.

380

"Do you realize the shit storm you're about to start?" he asked with genuine concern. "Are you ready for it?"

Izzy nodded again. "I think so," she said. "But can I ask you for something else?"

"That depends," he said.

"Those two assistants," she said. "Call them off, please."

He scoffed playfully. "I never know what those two are up to."

"Do you want me to tell you?"

"No," he said seriously. This was an avenue he did not want to go down.

"If you want, I could play you a tape I made of my conversation with Sheila a few minutes ago," Izzy said. "She all but admits to harassing witnesses, and she otherwise exposes herself as being a real bitch."

Springer sighed. "Look, I don't know all of what they're doing, but this is the big game of politics. You need to…"

"Trust me," Izzy said. "You don't want this tape going out, especially if you're planning to run for president."

Springer smiled and shook his head. "It wouldn't be as bad as you think, believe me. There are ways of brushing that stuff off."

"It wouldn't help," Izzy said.

He nodded. "Okay, I'll tell them whatever they're up to has to stop. But, for the record, I don't know anything about any of it."

"Fine," she said.

Springer looked at Izzy's face. Her tears had dried and she was fully composed once again. She was very special, and he knew it. He had always been a good judge of people. He had known Shannon Maher wanted to be a home wrecker. He knew Abby Conway was a model of quiet dignity. He was not surprised when Joe Conway took down a gun-wielding lunatic with a tennis racket. He knew he would have never done the same.

"I owe my life to your father," he said. "Please don't print this, but I failed him that day, and every day I wish I could somehow pay him back for it. You might not believe this, but that's why I've spent my whole life in politics. It's why I've tried so hard on gun laws. I don't know what Joe thinks of me now, but I did it all for him. I want you to know that."

"Thank you," she said. "And nobody knows what they would do in that situation, like you said. I think my dad would understand that." Mike exhaled deeply as he looked into his old friend's eyes. He had wanted so badly to repay Joe for saving his life. He didn't know what opinion Joe would have had on gun control. He probably wouldn't have had much of an opinion; Joe had hated politics. But here was his daughter thanking him for his efforts. It meant a lot.

"I owe your dad a lot," Mike said. He reached into his pocket and pulled out a business card. "Listen to me carefully," he said. "In a couple years, there's going to be a big announcement from my office. I might decide to run, or not to run, for president. If you're still a reporter, you're going to get the story first."

Her eyes widened. "What?" she said.

"I need you to write down a good number to call you on," he said, pointing to the card. "My old buddy's daughter is going to get the exclusive announcement. You can call into the radio, T.V., whatever. You'll be the one who broke the story. My office will confirm it after you go public."

He watched her hand tremble as she scribbled her phone number. "Thank you," she said absently. Mike knew it was a poker face. He had dropped a gold mine on her.

"Don't thank me," he said. "I'm returning a favor, and I'm glad I get the chance to do it. Is there anything else you need?" He watched the woman's expression change again.

"Yes, there is something else, actually," she said. "I have one more interview I need to do."

***

Warden Wood slammed the phone back on the hook. *Unbelievable*, he thought. He stood from his desk, maneuvered his massive frame with incredible quickness, and stormed toward his

382

office door, where he stood glaring. "Burton!" he shouted toward the desks and cubicles that occupied the space outside his office.

Greg Burton stood. "Sir?" he said.

"A moment, please," the warden commanded. He was always polite.

Greg Burton glanced around the room, and walked to the warden's office, stepped inside, and closed the door behind him. The warden pointed to a chair. Greg took it. The warden stood.

Warden Wood wanted to make himself very clear, using as few words as possible. It was a technique he had adapted from years of working with difficult prisoners. No need to bring emotion into things. Black and white. Here's what has to happen.

"Issue," he said to the man who sat in front of him.

"How can I help?" Greg asked.

"The governor just called me," the warden said. "He asks that I grant the request of a reporter, a woman, to interview Evan Long. Ultimately, the decision is mine to make, and I didn't want this thing to happen. However, I cannot ignore the fact that the governor, our boss, has made a special request, for reasons that elude me."

Greg's expression was surprised. "I understand, sir," he said.

"I hate it. Too damn close to his execution." He looked at Greg, asking for help. "Assuming I agree to this, do you think we can make this happen without jeopardizing anyone's security?"

"Yes, sir," Greg said. "I know we can."

"Good," the warden said. "Then it's going to be tomorrow. I know it's your scheduled day off, but I want you there for it."

"Yes, sir," Greg said. "I've scheduled myself to be on all week, considering all that's going on."

The warden nodded appreciatively. "I should have known that, Greg," he said. "You think of everything."

"I just want everything to go smoothly," Greg said.

"The interview will be in the conference room outside the cell," the warden said. "One reporter with a notepad. One photographer with a camera. You will stand outside the door and watch. I cannot be there. Depending on what he says, it would not be good for me to be a part of it. Do you understand?"

"Yes, sir," Greg said.

"In and out," the warden said firmly. "You see anything you don't like, you get them out of there and get him back to his cell. We're too close to zero hour for anything unusual."

"I understand, sir."

The warden eased his posture. "I know you do, Greg," he said. He stepped around his desk and fell heavily into his seat. "I appreciate this. I'm lucky to have you here. *These prisoners* are lucky to have you here."

Greg didn't react to the praise. "Anything else, sir?"

Wood smiled. He had known that was how it would go. Burton never could accept a compliment. "You're dismissed," he said.

***

Izzy hurried into the hotel lobby and started toward the elevator. She wanted to talk to her mother. She pressed the up arrow and waited, but before the elevator could arrive, she changed her mind. That conversation would take too long and now was not the time.

She went to the hotel bar ordered a glass of wine. The bartender didn't ask to see identification; they hardly ever did, especially the men. She glanced around half expecting to see Abel, but remembered he was going to his mother's house for dinner. The bar was empty except for the bartender and one patron who sat at the corner of the bar. He sat reading a newspaper, a cell phone placed in front of him as if waiting for it to ring. Izzy took her glass to a high-top table and took out her notebook.

She sighed loudly as she opened her notebook. Apparently, this got the attention of the man at the bar. "That kind of day already?" he asked kindly. "It's barely lunchtime."

Izzy looked up and offered a kind, but not overly friendly, smile. She had done it a thousand times. "I'm fine," she said.

"Me too," the man answered, seeming to not get the message. He was dressed in a business suit, bowtie, graying hair. Expensive glasses. Izzy guessed him to be in his late fifties. She directed her attention back to her notepad. Conversation over.

However, the man wasn't finished. "I can see you're busy so I will stop bothering you," he said. "But just so you know, I am not trying to pick you up. You're very beautiful, but not beautiful enough to make me straight."

Izzy couldn't help but laugh. "I'm sorry," she said. "I didn't mean to be rude."

The man waved his hand. "Stop," he said. "I'm a strange old man in a bar by himself. The last thing you want to see, I'm sure."

"A strange old *gay* man in a bar," Izzy said. "I don't mind that at all."

The man smiled and tried to laugh. It was then that Izzy noticed how tired he looked. "Join me for a drink?" the man asked.

Izzy took her glass back to the bar and shook hands with the man. His name was Raymond, and he was expecting an important phone call, hence the cell phone on the bar. "I'm actually a little nervous. That's why I'm making small talk," he explained. "Keeps my mind off work."

"So it's a work call?" Izzy asked.

"Yup, I'm a lawyer," he said.

"Are you waiting for a verdict?" Izzy asked.

"In a way," he said. "I just filed an appeal in the state Supreme Court. There is a chance that they may want me to come back to make an oral argument before they rule. I'll get a call either way."

Izzy glanced at his glass. He saw this and explained that it was club soda. He would have a real drink later.

"Are you on business here?" he asked.

"Yes," Izzy said, amused at the question. "I'm a reporter."

The man's face grew curious. "I see," he said. "You're not here to cover an execution by any chance, are you?"

385

His phone rang before she could answer. It was a loud, piercing ring that drew the attention of the bartender, who had retreated into a corner to read.

"Sorry," he said to both of them.

He excused himself and quickly walked back to the hotel lobby.

"What do you mean he's being interviewed tomorrow?" Raymond asked angrily as he walked away from the bar.

The man on the other end of the line, Warden Andrew Wood, explained that this had all been decided this morning. The governor himself had intervened. The interview was going to happen.

"I want to talk to my client, now," Raymond said.

"I can set up a call…"

"Now, Warden," Raymond demanded.

He heard the warden sigh. "Hold on, Raymond," he said. "I'll set it up."

Raymond walked into the lobby, glancing around to be sure he was out of anyone's earshot. He was upset, but he knew he had to contain himself. Evan Long was like a teenager. If he sensed that his lawyer was upset, he would probably become defiant.

"Hello?" he heard a voice say. It was Evan's.

"What the hell are you doing, Evan?" he shouted. "I haven't slept in days because I'm trying to save your life, and now you're giving an interview, even though I told you, in no uncertain terms, what a colossally bad idea that was?"

"Where have you been, Raymond?" Evan asked. "I haven't heard from you in a week. My hearing is tomorrow."

Raymond sighed. "I have been writing a brief that I just filed on your behalf. An appeal to the Delaware Supreme Court," he said.

"I didn't know anything about that," Evan said. "I thought we were preparing for the Pardon's Board."

"Evan, things are happening here," Raymond said. "I haven't had a lot of time to stop and explain, and for that, I apologize, but I have faithfully represented you for twenty years now, and you need to trust me."

"Well, what's the appeal?" Evan asked. "I thought we were done with appeals."

"Yes, we were," Raymond explained. "But the Supreme Court, the *U.S.* Supreme Court, just ruled on a separate capital murder case. It may have implications on yours."

"How?" Evan asked. Part of Raymond was impressed. Evan Long had never paid him a penny for any of his work, but he knew that, as his client, he was entitled to his lawyer's time right now. He could ask as many questions about his own case as he wanted.

"Okay," Raymond said patiently. "It's complicated, but it has to do with the way in which your sentence was decided. Your jury voted eleven to one for death, but the U.S. Constitution may require a unanimous decision. That's what I am arguing." Correcting himself, he said, "That's what *we* are arguing."

There was a pause as Evan seemed to think about this, but Raymond knew there wasn't much time. "Look, Evan," he said. "I have to keep the phone free in case they call me to come back. But I promise I will explain all of this to you in detail, okay?"

"Yeah, okay," Evan said.

"Now, back to this interview," Raymond said. "Here is why it is such a bad idea. We will be arguing before the Pardon's Board tomorrow, the same day as the interview. They can take into account anything you say during that time."

"The story won't be published until this weekend," Evan said. "I might not even be alive by then."

"Don't say that," Raymond said. "And you don't know what this reporter will do after he interviews you. The prosecutor could even subpoena his notes."

"*Her* notes," Evan said.

"What?"

"The reporter is a woman," Evan said. Raymond glanced back to toward the bar. The woman he'd been talking to had gone. "And I won't say anything that could get me into trouble," Evan continued. "It's only twenty minutes."

"You can say a lot to hurt you in twenty minutes," Raymond said. "I've worked too hard here. Please don't do this."

There was another long pause on the phone before Evan said, "It's my last chance to tell my side, Raymond. I'm doing the interview." He hung up.

Raymond immediately called his paralegal, who answered on the first ring. Raymond kept it short. "Find out why the hell the governor of Delaware would intervene to allow my client to be interviewed." He hung up and walked back to the bar.

***

Mike Springer could see and feel the glare of Bob Casarini from across his office. He wore an expression that Mike was sure he had never seen before in the decade that he had known him. He was pissed off and was doing very little to hide it. The room was hot with tension.

"Do you respect me?" Bob asked in a voice Mike barely recognized.

"Of course I do," Mike answered. "Why would you ask me that?"

Bob ignored the question. "I did the work on this," he said through clenched teeth. "I handled it. I got out ahead of it, the way I was supposed to. I secured an interview on a national stage. I promised an exclusive in exchange for a friendly interview. It was a lot of work. Long hours. Sleepless nights. Ass-kissing. I did all that."

"I know, Bob," Mike said. "Nothing has changed."

"Everything has changed, sir," Bob said, his voice raised a touch. "It's the national media. You screw these people over once, they don't forget it."

"What are you talking about?" Mike asked.

Bob's breath quickened, and sweat appeared on his forehead and temples. He was building into a rage. "You're not letting me do my job," he said.

"You're making too much of this, Bob. It'll all be fine. The girl is a good reporter."

"That's not the point, sir," Bob said, squeezing his right hand in his left. "I know this business. I know how to handle these things. It's dirty and it's underhanded, and you need to match fire with fire to win. You let yourself get ambushed. And on a smoke break. That's amateur shit."

Bob glared at the governor, who glared back. He had never spoken that way to his boss before. The two men stared in silence until Bob finally spoke again.

"I'm out," he said.

"What?" Mike asked. He couldn't believe his ears. "You're part of my team, Bob."

Bob shook his head as he stepped toward the door. "Not after today."

***

"Yes, sir," Professor Griffin said quietly into the phone.

"I appreciate your cooperation on this, Dennis," the man on the other end replied. "It's an important cause."

"I understand, Governor," the professor said. It was the second conversation he'd had with the governor this week.

"Please call me Mike," the governor said.

The professor sighed. "Okay, Mike," he said. He didn't like it.

"I'm glad this all worked out. My donors will be in touch soon," Mike said. "We'll make it happen."

Professor Griffin hung up the phone and looked at his watch. His first summer session course was commencing in just under thirty minutes. Students brand new to journalism. Fresh faces. Open minds.

He lowered his head and put his right hand over his eyes. Deep in his thoughts, he wondered to himself if there was any way he could salvage what was left of his journalistic principles.

389

It was nearly three P.M. and Izzy's stomach was growling. She hadn't eaten since the morning when she shared an English muffin with her mother. Since then, she had ambushed the governor of Delaware for an interview, secured an interview with a mass murderer for early the next morning and, best of all, stuck it to Sheila Avery. She wasn't positive, but she might have also had a run-in with Evan Long's attorney at her hotel bar.

She dialed a number on her hotel room phone.

"Layout," came the familiar voice on the other end.

"How's it going, Sweet Lou?" Izzy said. It was the office-wide nickname for Louis Sweetman, the layout editor at the Brandywine Review.

"Hi, Izzy," he said. "It's pretty slow around here, actually. How about dinner?" Sweet Lou had never been shy.

"No chance," she said. "Hey, I was wondering how much space you were giving me on Saturday."

There was silence on the other end, before Lou said, "Umm. Izzy. I was told you didn't have a story this week."

Izzy had been expecting to hear this. "Who told you that?" she asked, not sounding at all outraged.

"Miller," he said, indicating that he had gotten the order from the Editor-in-Chief, Michael Miller. "He said the order came right from admin."

"Unbelievable," Izzy said. "Anything else?" she asked.

"No," Lou said. "Except that it made me wonder what the hell you were up to. Miller said it was a monster."

"It's a monster, but he doesn't have a clue what it's about. You'll know soon enough," she said.

"What do you mean?" he asked. He was intrigued.

"Just keep your eyes open, Sweetie," she said.

"I love when you call me sweetie," he said.

She hung up.

Conway Maher parked in front of his mother's house and climbed out of the car. It was a hot day in Charleston, and work had been hard. He walked toward the garage door, as was his habit when he was covered in sweat and dirt. He was in need of a shower and hungry for dinner. As he approached, he was struck by the sound of a woman singing. *Was it his mother?*

He walked around to the back yard and there, sitting at the picnic table, pouring over one of her photo albums was his mother. She was wearing a dress and makeup. Her hair was done up, and she looked like she was headed out for the evening. She was softly singing one of the verses of "American Pie" as she slowly turned the pages.

"Mom?" The woman turned around. Her smile was radiant. Her eyes were full of life.

"Well, hello my darling!" she said. "How was your day?"

"How was *yours*?" he asked.

She looked at him, puzzled.

"Are you drunk?" he asked.

"How rude!" she said, in mock outrage. "Why would you ask such a thing?"

"Because I have never heard you sing before," he said. "Because you look like you're ready for a night on the town."

She laughed. "I'm just happy," she said. "I haven't been this happy in so long."

"What happened?" he asked. "Those reporters?"

She nodded. "I'm relieved," she said. "My family is intact," she said. "After all these years, you met your sister." She looked at the photo book like it was a sacred text. "And I told my story. Everything is settled now. I should have done it years ago, but I was so afraid. But I never expected her to come to me. And she's beautiful, your sister, isn't she?"

"She is," Conny said, but wasn't sure what to say next. "I'm happy for you, Mom. I really am."

He went inside to take a shower.

***

Abel knocked on Izzy's hotel room door. He heard her shuffle around the room for a bit before she opened it.

"Get some late dinner?" he asked.

She nodded and invited him inside. He was surprised to see her looking sad. He stepped into her room. The air was thick with cigarette smoke. Her laptop computer was open on the table. "Looks like you're busy," he said.

"I've been working on the story," she said. "And smoking way too much. Sorry. I'm quitting once this story is printed."

"I wouldn't write too much yet," he said. "Tomorrow could change everything. You never know what you're going to get from Long."

"I'm not going to spend much ink on him," she said, waving a hand as she took her seat behind her laptop. "The last thing I want is to give him a platform. He's a monster."

Abel nodded. He agreed with that. She would make him think he was preaching his word for all the world to hear, but when the story came out, it would be torn down to only a few statements. It was a good idea.

"I hate to make the comparison, but I did pretty much the same thing with Springer," she said. "If I wanted, I could have let him go on and on about gun control, but that's not what the story is about."

"Did he try?" Abel asked.

She shook her head. "No, but if his two lackeys had been there, they would have seen to it that he did." She looked at her watch. "Order room service?" she asked.

He waved his hand as if clearing smoke, then gave an exaggerated cough. "Why don't we go down to the restaurant?" he said.

She nodded, then she stopped and looked at him. "Didn't you have dinner at your mother's?"

"I didn't eat much," he said. "A little tense there."

"I'll grab my purse."

They took a booth in the non-smoking section and ordered sandwiches. Abel could tell that Izzy's mind was occupied. She said very little about the successes today had brought. When Abel ordered a beer and a shot of bourbon to go with it, she offered no comment.

"What's with you?" he asked.

"My mother," she said. "There's so much I have to talk to her about."

Abel nodded.

"Springer told me things," she said.

"Like what?"

Izzy summarized for Abel how Springer had revealed that her mother was aware of Joe's infidelities.

"Does your mother know about Shannon's son?" Abel asked.

Izzy sighed. "Not yet, but I'll have to tell her before the story prints."

Abel nodded.

"It's amazing," Izzy said. "All those years. My mom never brought any men home. I don't think she ever had a real relationship after my dad. Even after he died. Why not?"

"Maybe he was the only one for her," Abel said.

Izzy looked at him. "Really?"

"I'm a hopeless romantic," Abel said.

"That *is* hopeless," Izzy said. "She was a widow before she was thirty!"

Abel raised his hands in surrender. "Sorry," he said. "I have no idea what your mom's intentions are."

"Me neither," she said absently.

"You're going to talk to her before the story goes out?" Abel asked.

"I'll have to," she said.

The food arrived and they ate, mostly in silence. Abel inquired as to whether there was anything he could do to prepare for tomorrow's interview with Evan Long. Izzy told him to just be ready to take the picture. They would only have twenty minutes, but she thought that would be more than enough time.

"Got it," Abel said. He watched her eyes change. They focused on him for the first time in the conversation.

"Are you going to be okay tomorrow?" she asked.

"I'll be ready," he said. "I'll be nursing a hangover, but I'll be fine."

She nodded. Again, no comment.

"Am I allowed to bring the camera?" he asked. He knew he was, but he was trying to make conversation.

She nodded again. "We'll be in a room with him, with a door open and a guard standing right outside. Long will be shackled throughout the interview."

"You spoke to the warden?"

"He wasn't happy about it," she said. "But he's going to do everything he can to make it go smoothly."

"Good. Will he be there?"

She shook her head as she swallowed. "He'll be in the building, but he said he won't see us."

Abel understood. There were politics involved. The governor might run for president. The first hanging in decades. An election year. The warden didn't want to be there if there was any discussion of these things.

"But the good thing is that Will Janicki's friend, the maintenance guy who's now a corrections officer?"

Abel nodded.

"He's going to pull some strings and get us more time if we need it. If Long starts spouting off on the death penalty or Jesus, or anything, we can have more time."

"That's good," Abel said.

"I know," Izzy said. "He doesn't want Long to come across as a martyr."

394

Izzy put down her sandwich and wiped her hands. She reached across the table and gently touched his hand. She looked him in the eyes.

"What?" he asked.

"What if your brother comes up?" she asked.

"I'm ready for it," he said, though he wasn't sure that was the truth.

"And what if he recognizes you?" she asked.

Abel scoffed. "I was ten years old," he said.

Izzy withdrew her hand. "I know," she said. "I'm just worried about you."

"Don't be," he said.

She smiled at him. "You'll be sober, right?"

"Until shortly after the interview," he said.

Abel was glad to hear her laugh. "It's going to be a great story," he said. "You're going to get your award."

Abel watched as she frowned. Her eyes drifted around the restaurant. She sighed and said, "That's not in the cards anymore, actually."

"What are you talking about?" he asked.

She shook her head. "I'll explain later. Right now, my focus is the story. It's going to be a killer story."

"Poor choice of words," Abel said.

"Shut up."

They finished dinner and she went back to her room. Abel went to the bar.

***

Mike Springer was enjoying a meal alone with his wife, which seemed to be a rarity. They were in their home, and their two daughters were out with friends. He had planned to dine with Bob Casarini to discuss strategy for his upcoming interview, but those plans fell through after Bob's abrupt resignation.

395

The big question now was whether he should promote Sheila Avery to Bob's position, or hire another long-time political insider to take his place. He would probably have to do the latter, even though he was pretty sure Sheila could do the job if she put her mind to it. He'd be running for president, or possibly vice president, so he would need someone who knew the national scene. Sheila was relentless and smart, but she was still young and inexperienced. Her temper got her into trouble sometimes, too. Mike would need someone else.

"Are you with me?" his wife asked.

"Sorry," he said. "A lot going on."

"Always," she said. "But we don't get to do this very often."

"You're right," he said, touching her hand. "Everything can wait till tomorrow."

She smiled and they kept eating until the phone rang.

"I got it," he said. "Probably for me anyway."

"And I'm sure you just *have to answer*," she said.

He rolled his eyes and walked to the phone.

"*Are you up to something?*" asked the voice on the other end. It was Abby Conway.

"Abby," Mike said, pretending to be glad to hear from her. "I'm afraid I don't know what you mean."

"I just got a message from my daughter saying she interviewed you."

"That's right," he said pleasantly. "She did a very nice job."

"She said you were very cooperative." It sounded more like an accusation than a compliment.

"I tried to be," he said.

"So then what the hell are you up to?"

He sighed. "Here's what I'm up to, Abby," he said. "I owed an old friend a favor, so I did the interview. I even promised her an exclusive if I make any big decisions in the near future."

There was a pause. "That was nice of you," Abby finally said, the edge still in her voice.

"I thought so," he said.

396

"Can you explain this to me?" she asked. "You go twenty years without ever uttering a word about it, now you give an interview three days before the execution that you have the power to stop? That sounds to me like you're up to something. Remember, you told me what happened that day. Did you tell her?"

"I did," he said. "I told her everything. And the story isn't going to run until the fall. There will be no politics at play here."

"What are you talking about?" Abby said. "The story is running this Saturday."

"It's not," Mike said. "The journalism department at BU has agreed that the right thing to do would be to push it back. That's between you and me, Abby. Understand?"

"You son of a bitch," Abby said.

"It was their decision, Abby. Not mine. Your daughter knows about it."

"You son of a bitch," she said again.

"Look, you don't get to call me at my home and talk like that," he said. "You've been donating to my opponents for years, and I never take it personally. I have to do what I have to do. Don't *you* take it personally, Abby."

"She's my daughter," Abby said. "And you're screwing her over."

"I'm helping her," Mike said loudly enough that his wife took notice. He smiled at her, hoping she wouldn't get upset.

"You're helping yourself," Abigail said bitterly. "It's what you do best. It's what your whole career has been about. Taking advantage of people to get exactly what you want. *St. Mike: Hero of St. Maria Goretti's.*"

"I have never said I was a hero!" Mike said.

"Yeah, right. But all the times you heard someone say you disarmed the shooter, you never jumped up and said, 'Wait, just so we're clear here, I was hiding behind a wall while a ten-year-old was taking on an armed killer. And the only reason I got his gun is because by then, Joe had knocked the guy unconscious, even though he was bleeding to death.' You could have said that at least once."

397

"You could have said that anytime you wanted to," Mike shot back. "I never asked you or anyone else to keep it quiet. I've never spoken about that day out of respect for …"

"Don't say it!" Abby shouted. "You've never spoken about it because it would devastate your political career, and now you're saying it because you have to. Someone besides me finally knows the truth. So you're dealing with it *politically*. You're getting her story pushed back so you can spin the story your way first. What are you planning, Mike? Oprah? Barbara Walters? You can't just face it head on, can you? You never could."

Mike suddenly felt short of breath. "Jesus, Abby," he said. "That's not fair."

"Don't tell *me* what's not fair," she said. "My husband is dead. My daughter is getting screwed over. And you're thinking of nothing but your political career."

"I'm trying to help, Abby," Mike stammered.

"I've heard it all, Mike," Abby said. "Make the country safer by getting rid of guns, so only assholes like Evan Long can get them. Turn the whole damn country into a killing zone for lunatics. Good luck with that."

"Jesus, Abby," Mike said again. He bit his lip. "I've heard enough. Your daughter will get her by line, and she will still get her exclusive. But I need to do this thing the right way."

"Fine, Mike," Abby said. "Just remember that there are people who *know* you. Not the way you were, but the way you are. You'll always be that terrified boy who was afraid of girls, who let a ten-year-old with a baseball bat do what you had said you would do. I know it. That tramp in South Carolina knows it. Sleep well."

She hung up. Mike stood in his kitchen. Half in shock, half enraged. He turned to look at his wife, who was still sitting at the table waiting for him. His eyes were wide and he still held the phone to his ear.

"Everything okay?" she asked.

Mike smiled and hung up the phone. "Everything is fine," he said.

Thursday, June 20, 1996

"Wake up, Long," Chris Aument called. "Big day today."

Evan blinked until his eyes could focus. *Was today the day?* he thought. He looked around his cell and saw his breakfast being passed through the small opening in his cell door. Cheerios and creamed chipped beef.

"Good morning, Chris," Evan mumbled. It was good to hear Aument's voice. Evan had worried he would never hear it again.

"It's six o'clock, Long," Aument said. "You have a press interview in an hour. Your lawyer is coming at 9. Pardon's Board at 4. Big day."

Evan breathed a sigh of relief as the officer's words sunk in. His dreams, which he had already forgotten, had taken his mind in a thousand directions, all of them bad. Today was coming back to him now. The warden had allowed the interview. He would finally meet with the reporter. The one who'd sent all those letters. He had always imagined her as beautiful, and her face, which he had never seen, had fueled thousands of fantasies. He couldn't wait to see her and tell her his story.

"I expect your lawyer will want to spend quite a bit of time with you today," Aument said.

Evan nodded. This was good to hear. His lawyer wasn't his favorite person in the world, but Evan trusted Raymond. Spending hours discussing strategy wasn't exactly a picnic, but at least it was a break in the torturous routine of death row. Completely separated from every other prisoner in the facility, Raymond Woodson was the closest thing Evan had to a friend.

Today would be a good day.

***

Abel groggily rose from the bed and stumbled into the unfamiliar hotel bathroom. He frantically felt for the light switch but was not able to find it. He positioned himself above the toilet and vomited explosively. When he was finished, he sat on the bathroom floor and leaned back on the cabinet. He reached his right hand above his head and turned on the cold water, which he splashed on his head. He then took a handful and put it in his mouth.

He had drowned himself in bourbon the night before. He knew he would not have been able to sleep otherwise. His head and stomach twisted in pain as he tried to breathe deeply. A hangover was nothing new, but this morning's was especially rough. He stood and found the light. He switched it on and found himself looking at his reflection in the mirror. He was breathing heavily, eyes bloodshot. He had put himself through hell. His reflection glared at him. *Pussy*, he thought. *You couldn't even sleep the night before meeting Evan Long in a prison. I charged after him when I was ten years old. You should be looking forward to this, you asshole.*

He looked down from the mirror and splashed more water on his face. This was going to be a bad day.

***

Izzy was awake by five and had already consumed three cups of coffee when the phone in her hotel room rang. She answered and heard the groggy voice of Abel.

"I'm throwing up like crazy. I'm going to have to give you my camera, okay?" he said.

"You're kidding," she said.

"Izzy, I'm sick," he said.

"You're hungover," she said angrily. She had no time for this. "If you don't want to face Evan Long, I understand. But it won't be because you decided to get drunk last night. Now eat some eggs and bacon, drink some orange juice, and meet me in the lobby in one hour. Otherwise, come to my room, look me in the eye, and tell me you can't do this interview. I'll understand."

400

She hung up and poured more coffee. No time for nonsense. She checked her bag again. Two pens, tape recorder with a backup battery, notebook with plenty of space. The interview would be short, but the biggest one of her life. So far, at least. It was already a great day.

Friday, August 6, 1976

Norman Suddard watches in awe as his brother, Jacob, deftly tosses the worn tennis ball from a prone position in the grass. The ball sails smartly past him and the two other boys, including the one who is running desperately toward the wall. The ball smacks the wall with a sound far too loud to make any logical sense. The ball falls to the ground and the loud sound is heard again. Now there are screams. Shouts of terror.

Norman looks to his brother, who has risen from the grass. The boys look at each other for a moment before Jacob charges toward his brother, grabbing him and tackling him at the base of the wall. "There's a man with a gun," he says breathlessly. "I saw him."

Norman looks to see the two other boys sprinting toward the baseball field. "Let's run," he says. At that moment, one of the boys falls in a heap to the ground. The other keeps running.

"No, stay here," Jacob says. "He doesn't see us." Norman can feel the tight grip of his brother's hand on his forearm, the boy's nails digging into his skin.

They cower behind the wall, listening to the children screaming and the young adults shouting. They wait. Now they are joined by Joe Conway and Mike Springer. They are sweating and gasping for breath, but at least they are here with them. There is a flurry of activity that Norman doesn't understand. Norman's head is down, and he is crying. He feels the strong hand of Joe Conway on the back of his head as he speaks to Mike Springer.

"Do you want the racket or the bat?" he hears Joe ask Mike. Norman doesn't hear an answer, but he hears Joe say, "Follow me. Back me up. I'll knock him down. You knock him out. Hit his head." Again, he hears no answer.

401

Next, he can sense Joe's face right next to his. He smells his sweat. "Norm," Joe says calmly. "If I don't see you after this, you need to give my wife a message. Can you do that?"

Norman doesn't answer. There is still shooting. The screaming is louder.

Joe says, "Tell her I said the ice cream shop in Avalon. The picture. Can you tell her that? And tell her I'm sorry."

Norman is too terrified to look up, but he nods. He will never forget.

The shooting stops. "He's reloading. Now!" Joe says. Norman hears him hurry off, his footsteps sounding heavier as they get farther away.

Then he hears the voice of his brother, who has been crouching next to him, still holding his arm. "What are you doing? You have to help him!" he shouts. Norman hears a thud and a groan. There are men struggling, but he doesn't know who.

"Give me that bat!" he hears Jacob yell. Norman looks up and grabs his brother's forearm. Jacob is holding the bat.

The boys' faces are inches from each other. Norman's eyes are pleading for him to stay. Jacob's eyes are angry. "I'm going!" he says, squeezing Norman's arm one last time. His grip is stronger than Norman's, like it always has been.

Norman cries as Jacob follows Joe Conway. He and Mike Springer stay behind the wall and wait. He can hear his brother's footsteps trudging through the grass as he hurtles toward his target.

Until they stop.

PART 6: BLOOD

Thursday, June 20, 1996

"Press interview, Long," an unfamiliar guard announced. Evan examined the man's uniform. His stripes indicated rank, a sergeant maybe? He was thick and clean shaven from his scalp to his collar. His round head sitting on top of a huge neck. "Give me your hands," the man said as he unlocked the cell door. Evan noticed that the guard was not nearly as routine as the others. He skipped several steps that the other guards *always* took when moving him from his cell. They would have him turn around with his arms raised. They would tell him where he was going and how long. This one did none of that.

"I haven't met you before," Evan said.

"No, you haven't," the guard answered as he placed Evan's wrists in shackles, tighter than usual.

"Are you new, or a supervisor, or something?" Evan asked.

"I'm not new," the guard said, starting the walk to the small meeting room. "Come with me."

"How long is this interview?" Evan asked.

"I don't know," the guard said. "Up to the interviewer, I guess."

The guard led him into the small room and shackled him to the table, which was bolted to the floor. "They'll be here in a few minutes," he said.

"What's your name?" Evan asked as the guard took his post in the doorway.

The guard glared at him before he answered. Evan felt his stomach flutter.

"Burton," the man said. "*Sergeant* Burton."

The friendly young corrections officer escorted Izzy and Abel down the long corridor. Their shoes squeaked on the spotless floor. Izzy turned to Abel and said, "Cleaner than I thought."

403

"Inmates clean this place twice a day, top to bottom," the guard said. "Keeps 'em busy. Not the death row guys, of course, but the ones who are allowed to work."

"Mopping floors is a privilege?" Izzy asked. She was only making conversation to avoid nervousness. She had researched prison life extensively.

"Anything that isn't routine is a privilege," the guard explained. "And they can earn some money to make purchases in the commissary. Magazines, snacks, cigarettes."

"I see," Izzy said.

"And here is death row," the guard said as he pointed to the heavy metal door. An alarm sounded and she heard a heavy *click*. The guard pulled the door open and she and Abel followed him inside.

The guard stopped and turned to face Abel and Izzy. "I know the assistant warden went over everything with you already," he said. He motioned to the large prison guard standing between them and another locked cell. "This is Sergeant Burton," he said. "He and I will be outside this door the whole time. Only a few feet away. The door will be open. If you're feeling like you need to leave, just say 'I'm ready,' and we'll come inside. Do you understand?"

"Yes, we do," Izzy said. "Thank you." She nodded to the older guard and thanked him.

"Good," the guard said. "Long is right inside there. He's shackled. You have twenty minutes."

"Billy," the other guard said, interrupting the young man's rhythm.

"Sarge?" the younger man asked.

"I got this," he said. "Why don't you take thirty?"

The guard looked confused. He looked at Izzy, then at Abel. Then back to the older guard. "Sarge, I thought…"

"I got this," he said again. "You're relieved."

The guard stared silently at the cell where Evan Long waited to be interviewed, looking disappointed and confused. He looked back at his visitors. "Okay," he finally said. He nodded at the older man. "Sarge."

The older guard nodded back, and the younger one shuffled away. "I'm Sergeant Greg Burton," he said. "I'll be right here while you're inside." He opened the door to the small cell and gestured for them to enter. Then, he smiled and said, "Take all the time you need."

Abel was experiencing a feeling that he was not at all familiar with. He was anxious and could feel himself starting to sweat, but he was not afraid. He was not angry. He could feel his chest pumping oxygen as he stood almost perfectly still, and he could feel the quickening pulse in his temples.

His eyes focused only on the now open door that he would follow Izzy through. He sensed her turning to look at him, perhaps to offer words or an expression of encouragement. But he didn't look at her, only keeping his eyes directly in front of him. She turned back and walked through the door. Abel followed.

As they entered, all that was visible was a bench that was part of a larger table set, all bolted to the floor. Stepping through the door, Abel caught his first glimpse of the man who sat on the other end of the table, to their right. Abel still had his eyes focused in front of him. He still had not looked at Evan Long.

He carefully took a seat next to Izzy and began checking his camera. His brother's killer was less than three feet away.

Izzy made eye contact with Evan Long immediately as she entered the room and sat down. Knowing the killer's hands would be shackled, she did not offer her hand. Evan Long smiled and nodded politely as they entered and took their seats on the bench across from him. After they were seated, Izzy noticed that Evan thanked the guard, who ignored him completely, leaving him with a slightly unsatisfied expression. He looked back to Izzy. His hair was closely cropped reddish-brown, but going gray. He wore a mustache the same color. His eyes looked tired. He was thinner than he looked in the pictures Izzy had seen in the newspapers, even the most recent photos from a year ago. He wore a blue jumpsuit and glasses that she assumed were prison issue.

"Thank you for agreeing to this interview," Izzy said, as she pressed the button on her tape recorder.

"You're welcome," Evan said. "You're Izzy?"

"Yes," she said. "And this is Abel Ryan. He will be taking photos, if you don't mind."

Evan's eyebrows raised as he gave Abel a once-over. "No problem," he said. "But I thought you would be alone."

"I'm sorry if I didn't mention it, but it's important that we document our meeting with pictures. I'm not a photographer."

Evan just nodded. Izzy waited for Abel to say something, but he didn't. He just kept his eyes and hands on his camera, preparing it for the soft lighting inside Death Row.

Izzy decided to stick to her plan: Get right to it. "I don't have too many questions," Izzy said. "I'll start with this: It has been twenty years since the shootings at St. Maria Goretti's. Since then, every person who was present that day has spoken publicly about it except you. Now, you are willing to give an interview just two days before your scheduled execution. Why are you talking to me now?"

Izzy watched as Evan Long processed the question. He looked a little surprised to hear Izzy start this way. He leaned back an inch or so, which was all that was possible with his hands shackled between his legs. "I'm talking now for two reasons. First, because I want people to know why I did what I did, and second, because I want people to know the power of God's forgiveness."

"Why did you do it?" Izzy asked.

Evan shook his head dismissively. "I'll start with the second part, actually," he said.

"Okay," Izzy said.

"About a year after I came here, a man handed me a book and told me to start reading it. He was a chaplain. I was about to be sentenced, so I didn't bother with it. It sat on my shelf for another year or so. Then I finally opened it. I started at the beginning. Genesis, Creation, all that..."

Izzy interrupted him. "Mr. Long, we have a limited amount of time here. I do want to hear your answer, but can I ask you to sum it up? If you take us through every part of the Bible, we will run out of time quickly."

Evan Long stopped talking and looked with amazement at Izzy. He glanced at Abel, who had already snapped a couple pictures. "What is this?" Evan asked. "I thought you wanted to hear my story."

"I do," Izzy said. "Just try to keep it brief, okay? We don't have a lot of time."

Obviously disappointed, Evan gave in and said, "Fine. The point I was getting to was that I was brought up Catholic, and one thing I found that Catholics don't do much of is read the Bible. They get their little excerpts every week at Mass, then listen to the priest tell you what he thinks. It was all very empty to me. *Reading* the Bible is very different. You ever do it?"

"No," Izzy said, scribbling in her notebook.

"Well, you should," he said. "It changed my life. Jesus was executed alongside two criminals. He told the one not to worry; he'd be with him paradise. All it took was *believing*. Isn't that beautiful? No standing in line for bread and wine. No Rosaries. Just *believing*."

"And you believe?" Izzy asked.

"Of course I do," Evan said.

Izzy made a point to look at her notepad while she wrote this down, not because she found it particularly important, but rather because she hoped Long would see her write it and be willing to move on. She looked back to him. "Okay, can you tell me why you did it now?"

Evan sighed deeply, seeming a bit exasperated, but he relented. "Okay," he said. "I guess that's what everybody wants to hear. But you will write that I believe, won't you?"

"I will," Izzy said.

"Okay," Evan said, sounding somewhat satisfied. "So why did I do it? Well..."

"Let me stop you again," Izzy said. "I'm sorry, but before you get to that, can I ask you something else?"

Again, Evan looked at her with confusion. "I guess," he muttered.

Izzy knew exactly what she was doing. In her short journalism career, she had found that the worst interviews were the ones that were rehearsed. Ones that had the subject reciting lines he had prepared and rehearsed a thousand times. *Who had more time to prepare than Evan Long?* She had found that frequently changing the subject had a way of eliciting more honest answers.

"There are four other people I have interviewed for this story," she said. "And there are three questions I have asked them all. The first is this: What do you remember most about that day?"

Evan awkwardly leaned back again as his eyes drifted to the ceiling. He closed them and thought. "Okay," he said. "I guess the taste of my own blood is what I remember most. I'd never tasted blood before, and I can still remember it. Conway nailed me a couple of times with his tennis racket, and I went black for a little bit. When I came to, blood from my head had dripped into my mouth. Disgusting taste. I'll never forget it."

"Thank you," Izzy said. "Next, do you want Evan Long to be executed?" Izzy asked.

Evan looked at her and smiled. "Seriously?" he asked.

"It's the second question. I've asked everyone," Izzy explained.

"I'd love to hear what the others have said," Evan said.

Izzy didn't say anything.

"Okay, do I want Evan long, *who is me*, to be executed? Well, there was a time when I would have said yes. Everybody knows my plan that day was to kill myself after I was done killing everybody else. I was in a very bad state of mind. Joe Conway prevented me from doing that. He saved *my* life along with all those others. Now, my lawyer is trying to do the same thing, and I am grateful. I have a lot I can do for people if they'll let me. I can teach the Bible. I know it practically by heart. Let me put it this way: I am expecting to hang from the gallows very soon, and I'm ready for it, but if my sentence is commuted or overturned, I'll be happy about that. I'm not ready to die."

"Okay," Izzy said. "The last of my three questions is this: If you could have done something differently that day, what would it be?"

This time, Evan lowered his head, placing his chin in his chest. He closed his eyes again. "That's a hard one," he said, pausing to think for a moment. "I had just learned something the day before. Something that had me really in shock. I was really shook up. Y'know what I mean?"

"What did you learn?" Izzy asked.

Evan Long took a deep breath and let it out slowly. "I learned something really important about myself. I'll have to leave it at that, okay?" he said. He was starting to look agitated.

"If you don't tell me now, then when can you?" Izzy asked. "Don't you want people to know?"

Evan Long looked directly at her and coldly said, "No."

Izzy looked down and scribbled in her notepad. She was really just waiting, hoping that if she gave him time, he would say what it was he didn't want to tell her.

After a long pause, Evan calmly said, "So here is what I would have done different. Like I said, I was really shook, but when you're like that, there's only two ways you can go: good or bad. I went bad, obviously, and I hurt a lot of people. I could have gone good. I didn't. That's what I would have done different."

"Can you be more specific?" Izzy asked.

Evan shook his head quickly. "No, I can't," he said. "What I'm saying is that I would have done something *constructive* with the information I got."

"Like what?" Izzy pressed.

Evan groaned in exasperation and rolled his eyes. "Look, I know you want specific answers, but that's all I'm giving you," he said. "I agreed to this interview with you because in your letters you seemed like a reasonable person, like me. And I know you did your research about me. But all I'm going to tell you about that is that I could have handled things a lot different. I could have just tried to find what I was I was looking for. I didn't need to do what I did."

"What were you looking for?" Izzy asked.

409

"Stop!" Evan shouted.

"Steady, Long," the guard behind Izzy said. The guard's voice startled her more than Evan's outburst, which she had been expecting.

Evan closed his eyes and lowered his head, placing his forehead on the hard metal table.

When he raised his head, Izzy said, "Why did you do it, Evan?"

His eyes narrowed and his forehead, now red from resting on the table, wrinkled in thought. "I was a mess," he said. "You know my childhood - group homes, foster homes. I got made fun of my whole life. Beaten up. Abused. That day I just *snapped*."

"You were abused by whom?" Izzy asked.

Evan chuckled and shook his head. He looked distantly across the table in Abel's direction. "You name it," he said as Abel snapped a picture of him.

"Can *you* name them?" Izzy asked.

Evan shook his head absently. "It doesn't matter now, does it? I name people now and I hang in two days, so they, *if they're still alive*, have that to live with for the rest of their lives? They don't need that. Y'know what I mean?"

"Maybe they do need it," Izzy said.

He shook his head again. "Say, aren't you going to ask me about why I'm choosing to be hanged? Isn't that important?"

"Okay," Izzy said. "Why didn't you choose lethal injection, as was your right?"

Evan's expression changed again, and Izzy knew she was about to hear a well-rehearsed speech. This was fine, though. She could let the tape recorder run while she got caught up on her notes. She was wishing she could find out what this big news was that Evan was keeping to himself, but she was pretty sure now that he wasn't going to tell her. She let him ramble as she scribbled, and nodded.

"...so if they're going to kill me, it should be violent. People need to know that killing someone is an act of violence, whether I do it, or they do it. You can clean it up and call it 'lethal injection' all you want..."

She looked at Abel, who had stood to take a photo at a different angle. He had gotten some of Evan looking in just about every direction, including directly at the camera.

"I got to thinking about it when they gave me the choice," Evan continued. "I will probably be the last man in America hanged for a crime. Isn't that something? And what better way to make a statement against death, against *murder* by forcing Americans to see the brutality of the death penalty. A man hangs by the throat." Evan was smiling now, enjoying himself. "I never got to be a hero," he continued. "They wouldn't let me go fight in Vietnam. I tried to enlist when I was seventeen. They said they didn't want me. But maybe this is my chance to do something good." He turned to look to his right. "Of course, that's if it comes to that. My lawyer's still fighting. *I'm* still fighting."

Izzy continued to let him talk, knowing she pretty much already had what she needed, but she also knew that the best quotes often came at the end of interviews, when the subject's guard was down, thinking the formal interview was over.

"...so I'm going to go out strong," he continued. "I'm not afraid to face death. Like you two. You came in to talk to me and you weren't afraid." He looked at both of them and smiled. He was very friendly now. "I respect that. A lot of people would be afraid of me..."

Izzy watched as Abel sat back down next to her and looked around the room as if he had just noticed most of the details with his own eyes, rather than with the camera's. He turned his head away from Evan and seemed to be looking out the glass wall into the hallway. He had barely looked at Evan Long with his naked eyes. She wondered what he was thinking.

Abel stared into the glass and saw his own face - the face of his brother. He was listening intently to the man who had stabbed his brother to death. He could feel something rising inside him. He looked deeply into the eyes of the man in the glass who stared back at him. "I'm going," he said quietly to his reflection.

Izzy heard Abel mutter something under his breath. The camera was on the table and his head was still turned toward the glass.

"I appreciate you both coming in here and listening to me," Evan said kindly. "And I appreciate that you weren't afraid of me. I'm just a human being, like everyone else."

At that moment, Abel turned his head toward Evan Long and looked at him. In a cold voice that Izzy had not heard until now, he said, "Why would either of us be afraid of you?"

Izzy turned to Evan and saw that he was surprised. "What do you mean?" he asked.

Abel breathed through his nose. "I mean exactly what I asked," he said. "Why would either of *us* be afraid of *you*?" Then Abel curled his lips into a sneer and added, "*You pussy.*"

Evan drew back as his eyes widened. He didn't say anything. Izzy was stunned also.

"Why would *anybody* be afraid of you?" Abel asked. "You killed a bunch of innocent children. Defenseless people. Do you think that makes you scary?"

Izzy watched as Abel stood from his seat. Evan, no longer smiling, looked frantically from her to the guard. Neither moved as Abel stepped around the table toward Evan Long, his feet pounding loudly on the cement floor. He stepped beside Evan and leaned down into his face and said, "Do you know who the last person you killed that day was?"

Long said nothing. His eyes bulged in fear as he looked over Izzy's shoulder to the guard behind her.

"It was my twin brother," Abel said harshly. "My identical twin. He was ten years old, and he wasn't afraid of you. He went after you with a baseball bat while you were reloading a semiautomatic pistol. He was tougher than I was, but you know what?"

Long put his head down, trying desperately to bury his chin in his chest as Abel stood menacingly over him.

"Look at me!" Abel shouted.

Evan looked up, tears welling up in his eyes.

"I have bad news for you today," Abel said. "My brother has been with me for twenty years, waiting for this day. And today, he's back. And he doesn't give a shit about your shitty childhood, or how many kids made fun of you during recess. He's here." Abel held his hands in front of him, indicating his brother's presence. Then he said, "And he's going to kick the living shit out of you, you pathetic piece of shit."

In a quick motion, Abel grabbed Evan Long's collar with both hands. Evan screamed for the guard. "I want them out of here!"

Izzy, barely able to process what was happening, turned to see the guard behind her. It was then that Sergeant Greg Burton raised one eyebrow, smiled, and whistled as he slowly turned his back on the cell, closing the door behind him as he did it.

Izzy turned back to see Abel, who was smiling fiendishly, an expression she had never imagined she would ever see. He had suddenly transformed into a predator examining his next meal.

"Please, no!" Long shouted. "You can't do this!"

"Shut your mouth!" Abel shouted. "I'll bet you heard some of those kids yell those words at that campground, didn't you? 'You can't do this!' Who the hell are you to say what I can't do?" He turned to Izzy. "Get the camera," he told her. "I want pictures of this!"

Izzy followed his instructions and began snapping photos of Evan Long's horrified face. Long cried for mercy as Abel continued to torment him. Suddenly, Abel broke into a deep belly laugh, which quickly transformed into a horrific cackle. He let go of Evan and beckoned Izzy to come to the other side of the table. "Get a picture of this," he said smiling.

Izzy stood as Abel stepped aside. She looked down to see that Evan Long had urinated all over himself and the cement floor. With

413

trembling hands, she snapped two pictures of the condemned killer sitting humiliated in a puddle of his own urine.

"We'll have to put that one in the story, right Izzy?" Abel asked.

Izzy said nothing as she sat back down.

Abel listened with delight as Evan Long sobbed uncontrollably, looking from his pants to the guard and back again. When he was able to form words, he said, "How can you do this? You were supposed to interview me!"

"Shut up," Abel said. "That's *her* job. I have different intentions. And you killed my brother."

"God forgave me for that," Evan said desperately.

"Congratulations. I haven't," Abel said. "Neither has Jacob."

Evan sobbed and shook his head. "You're gonna' be in so much trouble," he said. "You can't do this. I have rights. My lawyer will take care of you two. That guard too."

Abel stood again and leaned close to Evan Long, who cowered back as far as he could. "You listen to me, you coward," Abel said. "I want you to know something."

Evan listened.

"Whether you live two more days or fifty more years, you will never breathe a word of this to anybody."

"Yes, I will!" Evan shouted. "You can't stop me!"

"You say one word, Long, and it will all be out there. Sobbing like a three-month-old. Pissing yourself. Crying for help. Pathetic. We have pictures. Is that what you want?" Abel asked.

Evan wept and said nothing.

"You keep your mouth shut about what happened here, and maybe Ms. Buchanan will decide to leave out the part when I scared the piss out of you. And that includes any final statements about being a hero by choosing the rope over the needle. I hear any of that, and I go public with what happened here today." Abel reached and took Long's chin roughly in his right hand, jerking his head toward him so he could see the man's eyes. "And if you win a pardon, guess what? I'll be back every year for a nice little chat, on behalf of my

414

brother. And I'll make sure our good friend, Sergeant Burton, is on duty."

"You can't do this!" Evan pleaded again.

"Your choice, Long," Abel said. "Talk and be exposed for the worthless coward you are, or keep quiet and maybe you can go on pretending to be a martyr to your cause. How do you want to be remembered?"

Evan Long once again buried his chin in his chest and cried.

"We'll be leaving now," Abel said. "I have some pictures to show my mother. She'll love them. And one more thing."

Evan Long slowly looked up at Abel.

Abel smiled as he said, "I hope your lawyer saves your life so we can see each other again."

***

Mike Springer was looking at the serious, stern face of Sheila Avery. They stared at each other for a good minute before she finally spoke.

"Bob's my friend," she said, dabbing a tear.

"Knock it off, Sheila," Mike said. "I don't have time for that."

"For what?"

"Bob is not dead," Mike said. "And stop acting like you're sad about it. His being gone moves you up." He leaned forward in his chair and jabbed a finger in her direction. "And I'm counting on you." It was all true, but Mike wasn't about to tell her that the situation was only temporary.

"I won't let you down," she said.

"I know you won't," he said. "First matter of business. Evan Long. Make sure my comments are ready. I'll release a statement right after he's executed, just like we talked about."

"Yes, sir. Everything is ready."

"His hearing is later today, but that's a pipe dream. He won't get a pardon, but I'm sure you have something ready anyway."

415

"It's all ready," Sheila said with no discernable signs of the tears she had shed a moment ago.

Mike smiled at her. She was a clever one. "Good," he said. "Then all we need to focus on is the Sunday interview. Get out ahead of this thing."

Sheila raised a finger. "There is one more thing, sir."

"What?" he asked.

"Evan Long's final appeal," she said. "It's going to be ruled on today or tomorrow."

Mike scratched his chin. He was aware of this, but he was sure it would amount to nothing. There were no new facts to be considered, as far as he knew.

"There's something new," Sheila said.

She was reading his mind. *That's a good thing*, he thought. "And what would that be?"

Sheila took a breath before she spoke. "The U.S. Supreme Court issued a ruling last week on a case from…" she looked through her notepad.

"I don't need the details," Mike said. "Give me the long and short."

"Okay," she said. "His lawyer was in court yesterday arguing that the ruling disqualifies Evan Long for the death penalty."

Mike leaned back in his chair. "How is that?" he asked.

"It's interesting, actually," she said. "You see the Supremes ruled that only a unanimous jury can sentence to execute. Evan Long's jury was…"

"Eleven to one," Mike said. He swiveled his chair to look out the window behind his desk. He had always grappled with the death penalty. In his heart, he was against it. But the law was the law, he always thought. And he never lost any sleep over the thought of Evan Long being executed for his crimes, even at the end of a rope. This would change things. "Any clue on how they'll rule?" he asked as he gazed out over the skyline.

"Hard to say, sir," she said. "I'll have something ready in case they overturn."

416

He nodded slowly. "Thank you, Sheila," he said absently, still looking out the window. Then he mumbled to himself, "*No shit.*"

***

The hotel air conditioning was blasting cold air through the darkened room. The warmth of Izzy's body juxtaposed against the coolness of the room created a sensation almost as pleasurable as the lovemaking that had ended thirty minutes ago.

It had happened quickly and had taken him by surprise. After the interview, they drove back to the hotel. Abel was at the wheel while Izzy scribbled in her notebook. Very little was said. Abel's hands had been trembling for most of the ride, but they had stopped by the time they parked at the hotel.

When they entered the lobby, Abel pointed to the restaurant and asked if she was hungry for lunch. She shook her head absently and stepped toward the elevator. "Can you meet me in my room in a few minutes?" she asked.

Abel had agreed, assuming they would get to work. Go over the notes and photos. However, after he knocked and she opened the door, she turned toward the window as he entered. After he had made his way inside far enough for the door to close, she turned back around, quickly took both of his hands in hers and kissed him on the lips. It was soft, but it told him everything. She pulled him in the direction of the bed. Things moved very quickly after that.

An hour later, they were both awake, holding each other. Neither wanting to move.

"I better start," Izzy said quietly as she moved from beside him to on top of him. The feeling was exquisite. Warm and cold.

"The story?" he asked.

She lowered her head into his chest, and he felt her head nod against him.

"I'm starving," he said.

"Room service," she said. "Get something for me too."

417

He kissed her head and reached to the bedside table to find the room service menu. She climbed out of bed and walked to the desk where her laptop was plugged in. The sun was coming through the blinds, highlighting her body. "It's four o'clock," she said. "I need to get at it. Do you have notes from when you spoke to your sister and that girl?"

"Yeah," Abel said. "Are you going to use them?"

"Not now," she said, "but if there's any trouble, I'd like to have them."

"I'll get them," Abel said. "Do you want me here while you're working?"

"Yes," she said. "I won't smoke."

"I don't want to be in your way," he said.

"Stay," she said. "I won't get dressed. You can watch me type naked."

"I guess that's worth it," he said.

He lifted the room phone and began to dial when he suddenly felt her next to him. She put her arms around his neck and kissed him gently on the cheek. "I'm glad we did that," she whispered. "It was nice."

He smiled. "It might have been *nice* for you," he said. "For me, it was earth-shattering." He turned to look at her. "You're super-hot. Do you know that?"

She blushed. "I've been told," she said.

"It's true," he said, unable to stop looking at her. "Why did we do that?" he asked.

She shook her head. "I can't explain," she said. "Can you?"

"Not really," he said as he leaned in to kiss her again.

She accepted his kiss, wrapping her left arm around his shoulders and pulling him back to the sheets. "I'm going to get to work," she said. "But checkout isn't until tomorrow." She smiled and started to get up again.

"Go for it," Abel said, watching her climb from bed and walk back to the desk. After she took her seat, he picked up the phone again. He was famished.

418

Will Janicki entered Stanley's Tavern, took a seat at a booth, and ordered a light beer. He checked his watch. It was just after five. A few minutes later, Greg Burton joined him.

Will stood and embraced him. They had never hugged before, and Will was surprised at how happy he was to see the man. It had been more than ten years since they had been face-to-face. Greg was completely bald now, and what hair was left on his scalp was shaved clean. His chin was still solid, and his body was still hard as stone. Will had always been taken by the former Airborne Ranger's physical attributes. Greg had never been a man to be fooled with.

"It's good to see you, Greg," Will said as they took their seats across from each other. Will flagged the waiter and ordered two more. After exchanging pleasantries, Will said, "Tell me how it went, and please tell me that prick broke down into tears."

Will looked across at his old boss and smiled. "It was better than you could have imagined," he said.

Will felt a rush of satisfaction run through him. For years, he had heard from Greg how Evan Long was reveling in his status as a condemned man. He had loved playing the victim, the converted Christian, the martyr. "She got to him," Will said breathlessly. "I knew she would. That girl is fearless."

Greg's beer arrived and he took a long drink of it. He shook his head and said, "It wasn't her."

"What do you mean?" Will asked.

"The dude she had with her," he said. "The photographer."

Will leaned forward, raising his eyebrows in disbelief. "The kid whose brother got stabbed?"

Greg nodded and smiled. "Made him piss his pants. Said his dead brother had come back to life. *I* was scared for a minute."

"Jesus Christ," Will said. "I didn't think the kid had it in him."

"You should have seen him," Greg said. "It was glorious."

Will smiled eagerly. He wanted to hear more.

419

"He really gave it to him," Greg said. "Got right in his face. 'You're a fucking pussy!' It was fantastic."

"Beautiful," Will said. "What did you do?"

"I didn't see a thing," Greg said, smiling devilishly. "The best part was the girl took pictures of the whole thing."

Will's eyes filled with tears. He was overjoyed. He could remember the photographer as a boy now, watching his brother bleed to death. He could still feel the desperate tug of the boy at his leg, begging him to save his brother's life. He had spent every day since then hating the thought of Evan Long sitting comfortably in a jail cell. Three meals a day. Television. Books to read. People to talk to. He was so glad to hear the sonofabitch was finally terrified of someone.

Will had respectfully disagreed with Greg over firearms, and their mutually strong viewpoints had occasionally boiled over into raging, beer-fueled shouting matches. However, they had always agreed that Evan Long should be suffering for what he had done that day, and they both had hoped that he would somehow experience the fear he had inflicted on so many that day. Greg would phone him occasionally to vent his frustration with the conditions of Long's captivity. "They let the cocksucker have T.V.," he had reported about ten years ago. The reports had sickened Will.

He had thought the reporter would get to him. She had a no-nonsense way about her, and Will was amazed at the way she had taken on Father Francesco. He knew she would see right through Long's bullshit. But this was even better. The brother of the boy who stood up to Evan Long making him cower in fear.

"Will you get in any trouble?" Will asked.

Greg shook his head. "He said he would publish them if he ever breathed a word about it."

Will just smiled and shook his head. He was beyond words.

"He told Long he hoped he'd beat the death penalty, so he could come back every year and do the same thing. I'll make sure I'm on duty when he does."

Will leaned back in his chair. This was the happiest he had felt in a very long time. He looked at Greg. "Do you think he'll be pardoned?" he asked.

Greg sipped his beer and shook his head. "No chance," he said. "But…"

"But what?" Will asked.

"The warden called me a little while ago. Said Long's hearing had been postponed until tomorrow."

"What's that mean?"

"I don't know," Greg said. "Could be as simple as somebody on the board got the flu, or it could mean there's something new to consider, so one of the lawyers asked for another day. Either way, Friday will be a long day. He's scheduled to go just after midnight, so those boys will be practicing all day."

"Will you be there?" Will asked.

"Yes, I will," Greg said.

Will nodded. He was glad to hear that, though now his feelings were conflicted. The thought of Evan Long being tormented by a victim's brother for the next couple decades was quite appealing.

"Makes you think, though," Greg said, reading Will's face.

Will nodded. "It does."

Greg placed his beer on the table and looked at his friend. "Will," he said.

Will had been lost in thought, picturing a weeping, pissing Evan Long. He looked back at Greg. "What?"

"Have you gotten past it?" Greg asked.

Will shook his head. "Never," he said. "But this helps. And I told that reporter all about it," he said. "It's funny to say, but that helped too."

"You told her about that morning?" Greg asked. He was surprised. Will had confided in his friend ten years earlier. Greg had never repeated it.

Will nodded. "Then I told her I was going to kill myself."

Greg's face froze for a moment. Then he burst into laughter. "You didn't!"

"I did," Will said, starting to laugh. "I showed her the gun."

Greg's face became concerned. Will raised a hand.

"I'm safe, Greg," he said, waving his hand dismissively. "I'm dealing with it, same as you. Don't worry."

Greg's face softened. "Good," he said. He raised his glass. "Here's to that cocksucker pissing his pants."

"Cheers," Will said, raising his glass. "I'm glad she called you. Think of that: the guy gets executed under a governor who was there when it happened. One of the guards on duty to see him die was there when it happened, and the brother of one of the boys he murdered made him piss his pants just a couple days before. The daughter of the guy who stopped him writes about it in the newspaper. That's something, isn't it?"

Greg tapped Will's glass with his. "Only in Delaware."

Will laughed and sipped his beer. *"No shit."*

***

Raymond Woodson waited for Evan Long to be brought into the meeting room before he took his seat. He pointed to his shackles. "Remove those, please," he told the guard. "We'll be fine." The officer nodded and obliged, unlocking Evan's hands and feet. Raymond always insisted that his clients be unshackled, as long as it was safe and practical. The officers usually didn't give him a hard time about it.

They took their seats.

"Where have you been?" Evan asked, sounding almost out of breath. "I was expecting you hours ago. My hearing has been postponed. Did you even know that?"

Raymond raised his right hand in an attempt to calm his client. "It's been a long day for all of us, Evan," he said. "I know about the hearing. I'm the one who got it postponed. It's actually been canceled, but that's not been made public yet."

"What are you talking about?" Evan said. "Why canceled? Why haven't you told me any of this?"

"I've been busy," Raymond said, hearing the exhaustion in his own voice. "I've been working your case around the clock, believe me. We need to talk."

"Let's pray first," Evan said.

Raymond stopped him. "Not now, Evan," he said. "We need to talk."

"I need to pray," Evan said. "I'm going to be dead soon."

"Just listen to me," Raymond said harshly.

Evan lowered his head and placed his forehead on the table. He began to cry.

"What's the matter with you, Evan?" he asked. He hadn't ever seen his client cry.

"It's been a bad day," he said.

"The interview?" Raymond asked. "I told you not to do it."

"I wanted to," Evan said. "I didn't say anything to get myself in trouble. I promise." He wiped his eyes with his sleeve then lifted his head and looked at Raymond. "I've been waiting all day for you. I need to tell you some things. I've written statements that I want you to publish after I go. I need to tell you some things."

"I know," Raymond said. "Listen to me now, okay?"

Evan nodded.

"The Delaware Supreme Court is going to issue a ruling tomorrow morning."

Evan said nothing. He just looked at Raymond. Raymond reached his left hand and put it gently on Evan's wrist. "It's over," Raymond said softly. "They're overturning your death sentence."

Evan gasped. He started to say something but stopped.

"They're going to rule that your death sentence was unconstitutional. They're going to say the jury should have been unanimous, and they weren't," Raymond said. "If the state's attorneys want, they can retry the sentencing portion of your trial, but I'm sure they won't do that. It's been twenty years."

Evan exhaled deeply. "What's it all mean?" he asked.

"It means they're not going to kill you, Evan. You'll die in jail but not because they kill you. Your life has been spared."

Evan was dizzy. He didn't know what to think or do. This was the last thing he had expected to hear his lawyer tell him.

"What's next?" he asked, barely able to form the words.

Raymond lowered his neck to look in Evan's eyes. "You'll be moved from death row," he said quietly. "You'll be placed in the protective wing, because of the nature of your crimes. But you'll be eligible to work. You can buy things at the commissary. You'll be a regular prisoner."

"So it's all over," Evan said.

"It is," Raymond said. "I will be making a brief statement to the press, explaining that we are pleased with the decision and that I have no further comment. Is that okay with you?"

Evan nodded. "Yes."

"The media will try to contact you after the decision is published," Raymond said. "I recommend you don't make any statement. Just decline all requests and move on with your life. But that's really up to you. Do you understand?"

"Why no statements now? What does it matter?" Evan asked.

"Because however unlikely it may be, the Attorney General could always decide to go for the death penalty again. Don't give him a reason to."

"Okay," Evan said, still thinking of that photographer. "I won't say anything."

Raymond nodded. "Good," he said. He stood and extended his hand to Evan Long. Evan reached up and took it cautiously. Raymond looked at him and said, "This concludes my work on this case, Evan. Good luck to you."

Evan stood quickly. "What do you mean, Raymond?" he asked.

"It means my work is done. I was involved in this case because I wanted to save your life, and I did." He took a step closer to Evan and said, "This is goodbye, Evan."

Evan felt a rush of dizziness flowing through him. For the past twenty years, he had considered Raymond to be his one and only friend. "Well, can I call you if I need representation?" he asked.

"The prison can help you access qualified representation when and if you need it," Raymond said as he made his way to the door. "You won't need me anymore."

As Raymond tried to make his way past him, Evan reached and took hold of his suit coat, prompting the guard in the hall to take a step closer. Raymond raised his hand to tell the officer he was okay. "Please don't go yet, Raymond," Evan said desperately. "I might need you."

Raymond gently took both of Evan's hands in his and pulled them from his coat. Then he quietly said, "You'll make new friends, Evan. My work for you is finished."

"You bastard!" Evan shouted. He felt the guard pull him from behind and force him into his seat.

"Easy, Long," the man said in a loud, but calm voice.

Evan was furious. "All these years, I thought we were friends! You treated me with dignity. Why did you do that?"

"I did it because you're a human being," Raymond said. "Because you were my client."

Evan felt the strong hand of the guard on his right shoulder. He shook his body hard once, trying to shake it free. It didn't work. He looked at Raymond with hatred in his eyes. "You're a liar," he said coldly.

Raymond stared back at the man for a moment, then slowly sat back in his seat. He waited for Evan to calm himself before he spoke.

"Delaware is a small state," Raymond said thoughtfully. "Did I ever tell you that my father owned a construction company a long time ago? He built half of New Castle County. Did you know that?"

"No," Evan said, glad that Raymond was still talking to him.

"It's true," Raymond said. "And one of his first projects was a beautiful campground in the Pike Creek Valley. A gorgeous piece of land."

Evan listened.

"He did it for free, too. All he asked was that Father Francesco provide at least half the material. My dad provided the labor and

425

everything else. All for the church. Father Francesco Antonelli worked very hard. My father too."

Evan looked away from Raymond and fixed his eyes on the table.

"And, as I said, Delaware really is small," Raymond continued. "I know so many of the people whose kids have gone to that camp for the summer. Clients. Friends. Family." Raymond swallowed hard and adjusted his glasses before he continued. "Twenty years ago, I was assigned to defend the man who committed mass murder on that campground that my father built. I took the case. The accused was entitled to a defense, and it was my job to represent him. A lot of my friends decided they didn't like me much after that, seeing as how I was defending the murderer of their children. But most stuck by me. They knew I was a public defender and was simply doing my job. Eight years after that, I left the public defender's office and started a private practice. I could have dropped the killer as a client, but I didn't. I stayed on because I wanted to save his life. Never charged him a penny. You should have seen the hate mail after that. The plastic bags full of shit and urine thrown at my house, and a thousand other lovely gestures of support. I have very dear friends whom I haven't spoken to in years."

He stopped and looked around the small room and smiled. "I don't regret a single thing I did," he said. "I prevented one more person from being killed. But I can't wait to see how my old friends treat me once they hear I saved the mass murderer's life." He smiled at Evan Long and shrugged. "I'll be lucky if I have any real friends left."

Raymond waited patiently for his former client to look at him again. "I've lost a lot of friends because of this case, but I've *never* been your friend, Evan," he said. "I never will be." He stood again and stepped toward the door. Evan stayed put.

"Good luck, Mr. Long," he said as he left, the sound of his footsteps echoing through the corridor. He could hear Evan Long's sobbing as he exited death row for the last time.

***

Izzy Buchanan sat in the office of the managing editor on duty at the *Wilmington Daily News* Dover office. It was just after ten at night. The editor, a bloated and serious woman named Beatrice Novack, stood behind her desk, glaring from behind reading glasses.

"Sum it up for me," the woman barked. "I don't have a lot of time."

"Thanks for seeing me," Izzy began. "My name is Izzy Buchanan, and last year I wrote a story..."

"I know who you are and I know your work, Ms. Buchanan," the woman said sharply. "But don't take that as a compliment. Right now you're wasting my time. What do you have for me?"

Izzy stopped talking and opened her purse. She reached inside and produced a small square computer disk. Holding it up for the woman to see, she said, "You'll want this."

"Why do I want that?" the woman asked, checking her watch.

Izzy smiled. "Because I've interviewed the five people who've never spoken on the record about the shooting at St. Maria Goretti's. They were all there, and they all spoke to me about it for the first time."

Beatrice Novack raised her eyebrows just a bit. "Interesting," she said, hating to admit it. "Anybody who's particularly newsworthy?"

Izzy placed the disk on the editor's desk. "Among the five are Joe Conway's mistress, who gave birth to his baby shortly after his death, the governor of Delaware, and Evan Long, who is scheduled to be executed in about twenty-six hours."

The woman stared at the disk, examining it for proof. She looked back to Izzy. "Is this for real?" she asked.

"I also interviewed the twin brother of the boy who died trying to stop the killer, as well as a groundskeeper who has revealed that he could have stopped the whole thing earlier that morning."

Izzy watched the plump woman slowly maneuver herself into her seat. She picked up the disk in her chubby right hand and held it delicately, removing her glasses to study it further.

427

"Shall we discuss my fee?" Izzy asked.

The woman never took her eyes off the disk. *"No shit."*

Friday, August 6, 1976

Joe Conway folds the note from Shannon Maher and squeezes it tightly in his fist. She wants to meet him in an hour. The game room closet. He knows what that usually means, but he also knows that this time things are different. He knows there is something she has wanted to tell him, and he knows what that something is. He looks at the inside of his locker where he found the note. He squeezes the note tighter, allowing the pain to radiate through his forearm.

Closing the locker door, he comes face-to-face with Abby, his wife. She is standing next to him in the photograph. They are holding hands, and she is pregnant. It has only been two weeks since the photo was taken. It was on a day when he had felt his life was so complete that he wished there had never been a Shannon Maher, or any of the others. He had promised himself that day that he would give up the foolishness that was his personal life. Time to grow up, he had thought. It didn't last.

He closes his eyes and allows the guilt to do its job. He had been a horrible husband. Hopefully, he would be a better father. He pulls the photo off the locker and turns it over. Nothing is written on the back. This is rare, as he loves to write a memory on the back of every photo. He reaches for a pen and quickly scribbles five words on the back before writing today's date. He tapes the photo back to his locker and grabs his tennis racket.

Friday, June 21, 1996

Professor Griffin left his office door open, as he always did during office hours. He had stepped out of the office to refill his coffee and use the bathroom. He could take his time on Friday mornings, especially in the summer. No classes until Monday. Happy hour would start around three. He loved his summer Fridays.

428

When he returned to his office, he was surprised to find someone waiting. She was sitting in a chair, facing his desk, her back to him as he entered.

"Can I help you?" he asked.

"Not at all," came the familiar voice of Izzy Buchanan. "But I do have a few questions, Professor."

Griffin swallowed hard. This was indeed a surprise.

"Good to see ya, honey," she heard the professor say as he entered his office. She could hear the alarm in his voice. "I wasn't expecting you."

"Sorry, Professor," Izzy said. "I've been surprising people all week."

"Part of your job, I guess," he said. "How's the story going?"

"It's finished," she said. "Editor is looking at it. It'll probably run tomorrow."

She watched his eyes as he took in her words. He smiled condescendingly as he fell into his leather chair. "It's running in the fall's first issue," he said, stroking his gray goatee. "I told you that."

Izzy nodded. "That's fine," she said. "I mean if you'd like the school paper to *re-run* it then, but I've already submitted it to the *Daily News*. It will run tomorrow, and probably be picked up on Sunday in Philadelphia, and possibly New York."

Griffin coughed. "What are you talking about?" he said, his eyes darting to the telephone on his desk.

"Do you need to make a call?" she asked, enjoying herself. "I can leave."

"Izzy," he stammered. "What is going on here?"

Izzy leaned toward the professor and smiled as she spoke. "What's going on is that I have sold my story to the *Daily News*. Five hundred dollars. It's pennies, I know, considering all the work that went into it," she said. "But this story is just the start."

"I'm confused," he said. "What about the award? We had a plan here."

429

"You taught me a bunch of things, Professor," Izzy said. "One of them was timeliness."

"Knock it off, Izzy," he said.

"I waited until this week because I wanted the public to hear from all of these people as the execution was approaching. I wanted the story to run as close to the execution as possible. We discussed this for months."

He waved a hand. "Things have changed since then."

"I think *you've* changed," Izzy said.

He scowled at her. "What does that mean?"

"Why do you want it delayed?" she asked. "Did the governor ask you to? Did he offer you a favor?"

"What are you doing?"

"I'm being a journalist," she said. "And I sense a story."

"Stop."

"What did he offer?" she asked. "A scholarship? A grant?"

"Get out, Izzy."

Izzy stopped and looked at him. "I'm close, aren't I? Why would you do that?"

He sighed heavily and looked at the ceiling. "It's more complicated than you think," he said. "There are things at work here, Izzy. Power. Money. Politics."

"All things you've taught me to ignore," she said.

"Sometimes these things can't be ignored. You'll learn that."

She felt a rush of anger. "And this is one of those times?" she asked.

"It is."

"I trusted you," she said. "I *planned* this with you. You supported me."

"I trusted *you*, Izzy," he said. "You told me you were doing this on your own."

"I am," she said.

"Cut the shit, young lady," he said. "First class train tickets to Charleston. Hotel rooms - *plural* - in Charleston and Dover. You have a funding source."

430

Izzy's mind started to race, and she could feel the pressure building in her temples. "I used my own money," she said.

"Bullshit," he shot back at her. "You're nineteen years old. You spend your money on gasoline, Diet Coke, and cigarettes. I know where the money came from."

"What are you talking about?" she said.

He rose from his chair and stood behind his desk. "Your mother financed this story, Izzy," he said angrily. "She's an arch-conservative who donates to every single Republican candidacy and cause that comes along."

Izzy felt her breath shortening. "This story has nothing to do with politics," she said. "I never..."

"It doesn't matter," he shouted. "This story is wrapped in bias, and you know it."

"You haven't even read it!" she shouted back. "My mother has nothing to do with it. It was my money and my story!"

"We're done here," he said, pointing to the door.

"We are," Izzy said, standing from her seat. "I never want to see you again. You're using this as an excuse to protect yourself, and your precious ideals. You are no journalist, Professor."

"Get out!" he shouted.

She walked to the door and turned around to face him again. She jabbed a finger at him. "Before you make your phone call, just remember that story you told me on the first day I met you. When I sat in that lecture hall while you went on and on about our duty to the public to inform them. All that fourth branch of the government bullshit. How you took your story about the drunken football coach to the tabloids because your school paper refused to publish it. This story is running tomorrow, Professor. And I don't give a shit about that award anymore. You print your little college newspaper. My world is bigger than that now. This story will be read all over the country."

The professor slowly sat back down and stroked his goatee again. He took a moment to calm himself. "They're going to sick the dogs

431

on you, honey," he said calmly. "That big world you're entering is going to discredit the story and take you apart. I can't stop them."

"I don't need your help," she said bitterly. "Everything I wrote in that story is true. You can do or say whatever you want."

He chuckled. "*Me?*" he said. "It won't be me that comes after you."

"Yes, it will," she said harshly. "You're just one of *them* now. And it's my job to give people the truth."

Professor Griffin watched as Izzy Buchanan left his office for what would probably be the last time. She didn't slam the door. She was too classy for that. But she was angry. He could hear it in her footsteps.

He reached for the telephone on his desk but stopped himself. He wasn't calling anyone. He listened for a moment and heard her car as it drove away.

He couldn't help but smile.

***

It felt good to be back in Philadelphia. The train and hotel rooms were a nice getaway, but Abel had become a creature of routine, and he was looking forward to settling back in. He knew the next few days would be full of turmoil, but he was determined to watch it from a distance, preferably with a nice beer buzz.

He knocked on the rectory door. A few moments later, a serious-looking young man, a former student of Abel's opened it. "Hey, Mr. Ryan. Go on up," he said. "He knows you're coming."

Abel started to ascend the creaky wooden stairs that led to his friend Father Thomas Patel's room in the rectory of St. Luke's parish. He had walked these steps many times over the past five years, sometimes to spend time with his friend, sometimes seeking spiritual or professional advice.

He had asked the priest for forgiveness many times, but it was about a year ago when his friend had deftly turned the tables on him. "You have asked the Lord's forgiveness many times, my friend. Whom are you willing to forgive that you have not?" It was a difficult question. There were only two people Abel had refused to forgive: his father and Evan Long.

"My friend, Evan Long may not feel any guilt for the evil things that he did," the priest had said in his gentle voice that was softened by his Indian accent. "But your father must have felt tremendous guilt for the things he did - and didn't do - for his family."

"So what?" Abel had asked.

"Don't you believe that if your father were alive, he would ask for your forgiveness? Doesn't that change your perspective a bit?"

Abel had mulled this over countless times, and he knew that he *wanted* to forgive his father. However, his mother's tears and the horrific sleepless nights that he would never forget made it impossible.

"Forgiving is one thing," his friend had told him. "Forgetting is something else. You will never forget, but you must find it in yourself to forgive. You have said to me that your father's addiction stemmed from weakness, yes?"

"Yes," Abel had said. "He was too weak to help us through Jacob's death. He couldn't even help himself."

It was then that the priest pointed out that the weakest among us are the ones in need of the most help. "Who would not forgive a child for taking a cookie from an open jar?" he'd asked.

"Maybe I will forgive him someday," Abel told him. "But Evan Long? How could I ever?"

"Because through God's grace, all things are possible," he had said in the hypnotic cadence his voice took on when he spoke on matters of faith.

"I don't want to forgive him," Abel told him. "Is that the first step? Wanting to forgive him?"

The priest closed his eyes and shook his head. "No. First, you must forgive yourself. You feel a guilt that you should not feel. You sat crying while your brother charged after a killer. You shouldn't feel guilty about this, but you do. You feel guilty that you survived and your brother didn't. You feel guilt over your perception that your father would have preferred your brother survive. You don't even know that to be true, but you are riddled with guilt over all of these things. You feel guilt each time you see your brother's face in the mirror and measure your worth against his.

"You will not be able to forgive Evan Long, or your father, until you cleanse yourself of all of this guilt. You've done nothing to deserve it. You will not be ready until it is your face you see in the mirror rather than your dead brother's."

Even if he didn't agree with it all, the words were welcome to Abel's ears. Growing up, he had not been taught to consider the complexities of forgiveness and guilt. The concept that the power to forgive was something that made humanity more like God was an inspiring one that Abel could apply to many parts of his life. One evening, Father Tom had invited a survivor of the Holocaust, a rabbi, to speak at St. Luke's. Even though the man's wife and two daughters had been murdered by the Nazis, he had found a way to forgive them, mainly because he was tired of surrendering power to them. "As long as I hate them, they have power over me," he had said. "I stopped hating them, and they no longer torment me." Strong words from a courageous man, Abel had thought.

As Abel reached the top of the stairs, he could see his friend waiting in the door of his private room, where he spent most of his free time. The priest embraced him and said, "My dear friend," as he always did when they met. "Come in and sit."

"It's good to see you, Tom."

They sat in the small living area that was decorated with memorabilia of India, the Catholic Church, and the Philadelphia Eagles. The television, tuned to CNN, was muted. Abel was not a tea drinker, except when he visited Tom, who seemed to live on it. They sipped as Abel told him the events of the past week. Father Tom listened with interest, but Abel knew the priest would react with no more than a slight nod, indicating a point they would have to

434

revisit later. Abel started the tale with being ambushed, half-drunk, by a beautiful young reporter in the bar on Main Street, and finished with waking up in bed with the same reporter that morning. "So, I guess I'll need to confess that one later," Abel said.

The priest smiled and said, "Yes, but I have a feeling you are not yet feeling sorry about it. It can wait. Just don't get hit by a bus."

Abel laughed. He had a feeling his reaction would be along those lines. Tom was thirty-three years old, thin and good looking. Abel wondered how a man of his looks and intelligence could maintain a vow of celibacy. He'd asked him once while they were drinking beer. The priest answered, "Through prayer and discipline. It's easier than one would think." Abel didn't believe him.

"But I'd like to discuss this encounter you had with Evan Long," he said as he finished his tea and stood to get more. "You enjoyed this encounter?"

"It was beautiful," Abel said.

"Why?" Tom asked as he stirred his cup.

Abel thought for a moment. "I've pretty much been a wuss my whole life," Abel said. "I avoid confrontations of any sort. You know that about me."

Tom nodded.

"But yesterday, I felt like I finally did something I think my brother would have done. I terrified the man that brought hell to so many people. To so many families."

Tom sat back down on his sofa. "Do you feel like you did what your thirty-year-old brother would have done, or what your ten-year-old brother would have done?"

"Both of them," Abel said.

"Your brother terrified people?"

"No. But he stood up to a killer. That's what I did yesterday," Abel said.

"But your brother stood up to a man who was trying to kill. He was in the act of murder. This is not what you did. You sent fear into the heart of a condemned man."

435

"So what?" Abel asked. "He deserves the fear. What I did wasn't wrong. It might not have been what *you* would have done, but I don't feel bad about it. I know you've said that forgiveness gives a victim power, but you know what? Holding onto this animal and getting in his face and scaring the shit out of him gave *me* power. And it wasn't just for me; you know how many people have fantasized about doing what I did? It felt good. It's probably not what Jesus would have done, but it's what I did."

"Yes," Tom said. "Despite the fact that you took such pleasure in this vengeance, it is what *you* did. What would I do? I cannot say. My brother is alive and well. I have never suffered a loss like that. What would your brother say to this man today? We don't know that either. My point is that, right or wrong, *you* did that, my friend. The memory of your brother may have inspired you, but that was you who did that."

Abel considered this. His friend was making sense, as usual. "Okay," he said. "I guess I should feel good about that?"

"In a way," the priest conceded. "But I am more concerned about what it says about you. You would not have done something like this a year ago. A month ago. No?"

"You're right about that," Abel said.

"What has changed then? What made you do this?"

Abel shook his head and sipped his tea. He didn't know.

"Is it this woman you've been with? Is she the difference?" Tom asked.

Abel didn't answer. Instead, he looked around the room, searching his thoughts as he scanned the items that surrounded him. He thought of the times he had watched in awe as Izzy had stood unflinching in the face of opposition. Will Janicki, Father Antonelli, Shannon Maher. Had she affected the change that drove him to terrorize Evan Long?

"You made love to this woman?" Tom asked.

"I did," Abel said.

"Do you love this woman?"

"I don't know," Abel said. "She's very young."

436

"It's none of my business, my friend, but as your priest, I should tell you that I hope this physical commitment you have made to each other is something meaningful. Something that could perhaps lead to a meaningful relationship. From what you have told me, you may be very good for each other."

"She's good for me," Abel said. "I don't know what I do for her."

"But you say she initiated this physical contact. She is attracted to you, even if you don't know the reasons." He sipped his tea. "But I suspect you might know what draws you to her."

"I don't know what you mean," Abel said.

"This girl, this woman, she is a keen observer of people," Tom said. "Perhaps she desires someone who can demonstrate the strength that her father is remembered for. Someone who is the good part of what her father was."

Abel laughed. "I am nothing like Joe Conway. That can't be it."

"Interesting that you know this man better than she did," Tom said. "She has heard stories her whole life of how he stood to face a killer against all odds to protect innocent lives. But over the course of this week, she discovers that your brother, and then you, did the same thing. It was in different ways, but you all faced him. That must mean something."

Abel scoffed. "It sounds artificial to me," he said. "Either that or I'm back to the same problem: Is she attracted to me or my brother? Or her father?"

The priest smiled. "It was you in her bed, my friend. Nobody else."

Abel finished his tea and sat silently, staring at the television screen as the news of the day poured out of it.

"When will you see her again?" Tom asked.

"Good question."

"You don't know?" Tom asked.

"I might *never* see her again," Abel said.

Tom looked at him curiously.

"You don't know her," Abel said. "She's all business all the time, except when she's not. I've never met anyone like her."

437

"Surely she will phone you once the story is published? Or you will reach out to her?" Tom asked.

"I would think so, but she's very different. I don't get the feeling I'm high on her list of priorities." Abel reclined back on the easy chair and put his hands behind his head. He exhaled and looked at the ceiling.

"What are you feeling?" the priest asked.

"I'm glad the story is done. I'm glad this will all be over soon. I'm ready for the fallout. I won't be going public, even if the press comes after me for comment. Everything I've had to say is in that story. My summer is going to go exactly the way I planned it," he said.

The priest shifted in his seat so he could face Abel squarely. "My friend, forgive me for saying this, but I am worried you are letting something get away from you."

"How's that?" Abel asked.

"This woman. You. Her brother. All of you have lost so much in your lives because of this tragedy twenty years ago. Maybe it is God's plan that you have all found each other, to make up for all of the life and love that has been wasted over the years. Do you think this is possible?" he asked. "Maybe by loving this woman, you can both find peace, and even a measure of joy, in the things you have lost."

Abel closed his eyes and thought very hard. Tom was definitely a "big picture" kind of person, whereas Abel tended to focus much more on the here and now. "I had my summer planned, Tom," he said. "Now you have me chasing a woman."

"And what was your plan for the summer?" Tom asked. "At a bar every day? Passed out by 9 P.M.?"

"I'm not an alcoholic," Abel said.

"I know this," Tom said. "But you have tendencies, and this can be troubling, considering your father."

Abel waved his hand dismissively. "We've had that conversation."

438

"Fine then," Tom said patiently. He waited for the moment to pass before he said, "Evan Long is to be executed soon. Just after midnight tonight, yes?"

Abel began to laugh. At first, it was a laughter of sarcasm, but it quickly turned genuine, to the point that he almost lost control of himself. "I'm sorry," he managed to say.

"What is funny?" Tom asked.

Abel didn't answer. Instead, he pointed to the television screen. A headline had appeared on the muted television screen as a female newscaster spoke to the camera. Abel watched for his friend's reaction, though he knew it would only draw a slight nod.

Delaware Supreme Court: Killer Evan Long's death sentence is unconstitutional

***

"Have you heard?" Abigail asked Izzy, before embracing her tightly. Izzy had just entered their home.

Izzy squeezed her mother. "Yes," she said. "Why are we crying?"

Her mother laughed through her tears. "I don't know," she said. "I don't know if I wanted him to die, or I'm glad he's going to rot in jail."

Izzy understood. She wasn't sure how to feel either. She had heard the news on the radio as she was driving home. She knew their tears were neither sorrow nor joy but naked emotion. The man in their life together had died long ago, and nothing would bring him back. Not a newspaper article, not new information, or the killer hanging at the end of a rope.

"I think I wanted him dead," Abigail said, still squeezing her daughter. "I know I did twenty years ago, ten years ago. I just don't know anymore."

"I know I wanted him dead," Izzy said. "I didn't even know Dad, but I thought he'd want him dead too."

"He would," Abigail agreed. "And you have no idea how much you're like him."

They hugged and cried together while the door remained open, allowing the hot, humid air to fill the foyer. The phone rang endlessly but neither showed any interest in answering it.

It was the first time they had wept together over her father's death.

"Let's sit and talk, Mom," Izzy said. "I'll make some coffee."

They walked hand-in-hand to the kitchen. Izzy made coffee while Abigail figured out how to silence the ringer on the telephone, finally just taking the phone off the hook. Everyone she knew was probably trying to get her on the phone. They would carry the auspice of offering support, but would really be calling to get her reaction to the overturning of Evan Long's death sentence. Family and close friends would be understandably curious. Abby hoped they would be equally understanding in respecting her privacy.

The weather was too hot to go outside, so they sat on a sofa in the sunroom. The brilliant light of the mid-morning sun blazing through the wall-sized windows lit the room as they took their seats and sipped their coffee.

"It's running tomorrow in the *Daily News*," Izzy said.

Abby smiled. "Good for you," she said.

"Shannon Maher," Izzy said. Izzy and her mother's relationship had long ago been established as such that when discussing something difficult, they simply get directly to the point.

"I know about her," Abby said. "And I know there were others."

"Do you know they went to the house at the Shore?" Izzy asked.

Abby sipped her coffee then shook her head. "No, but I suppose you're telling me because the whole world will know tomorrow?"

Izzy nodded. "Did he ever tell you he felt guilty about not serving in Vietnam?"

"Of course," Abby said. "It was my father who got him out of it."

"Shannon said that guilt is what drove him to go after Evan Long. They had spoken about it."

440

Abby's eyes narrowed in thought as she turned to look out the window. "Interesting," she said. She looked back at her daughter. "Listen, you don't need to do this."

"What?" Izzy asked.

"I am sure that Joe and that woman whispered all sorts of sweet nothings to each other during the course of their *relationship*. You don't need to tell me about all of them." Izzy felt her mother's sweaty palm as she reached and placed a hand on her daughter's. "Your father and I married very quickly. Yes, we were in love. But he had not grown up. He was a rich kid who got everything he wanted. He lived a carefree life, one with very little purpose. It drove him to do very immature things. And he had a magnetic personality. It was a bad combination."

"Have you felt this way all along, or have you come to terms with it?" Izzy asked.

Her mother's eyes widened and she smiled. "You are *such* the reporter!" she said. "It's taken me a long time. We'd been married only a few years, and once I discovered what he was up to, I was a wreck. I confronted him a few times, and he denied it. I hoped having a baby would put him on the straight and narrow." She looked in Izzy's eyes again. "Of course, I never knew for sure, but I thought our relationship was getting to a point where he was ready to give up that lifestyle. I never had any evidence of it, of course. But he was really starting to act differently to me. Maybe it was you. But I'm no fool. If he hadn't stopped running around sooner than later, we would have divorced. And my family *does not* divorce. Neither did Joe's."

Izzy shifted uncomfortably before she spoke. "Shannon Maher has a son," she said. She watched her mother's face. There was no reaction. "His name is Conway. She calls him Conny."

Her mother carefully placed her coffee cup on the table and folded her hands in her lap as she sat back on the sofa. "I see," she said. "And I would guess that he would be about your age?"

Izzy nodded.

"Well then," Abby said. She turned to look out the window again, the sunlight illuminating her face. "You met him?"

"Yes," Izzy said.

Abby nodded, still gazing out the window. For the first time in the conversation, her face betrayed her emotions.

"I'm sorry, Mom."

Abby waved a hand at Izzy. "It's not me, dear," she said. "It's just that I've spent a lot of time making sure Joe's family never knew any of this. This will be hard for them. My mother will not be surprised at all, but your father's parents. They will be devastated." She looked back at Izzy. "Oh well," she said. "I guess that's what happens when you go digging into the past, isn't it?"

"That's what I've heard," Izzy heard herself say.

Abby bit her lip and smiled as she gazed out the window again. The two sat in silence for a few minutes as the new information settled in.

"Did you love him, Mom?" Izzy asked.

"I did," Abby said. She ran her fingers through the hair above her ear as she sipped her coffee. "This hurts," she admitted. "First I hear how he shared his heart with her. The idea of these two lying in bed talking softly to each other. Now, you tell me he had a child with her." She shook her head in disbelief.

"He was a hero," Izzy said.

Abby nodded slowly. "No doubt," she said. "I just wish I knew where his heart truly was. Not because I would forgive him for all he did. I wouldn't. I just want to know how much of a fool I was."

"You're no fool, Mom," Izzy said, feeling herself choke up. Her mother was anything but a fool.

Abby gently raised her hand. "I mean I just want to know if his heart was ever truly in our marriage. Did he really want to make things right? He told me he did, many times. I believed him back then. And I always thought there was so much love that we could have shared - all three of us - that was wasted because of what happened. Even if things hadn't worked out between us, he would have loved you so much. And you would have been crazy about him." She looked out the window. "Now we have young Conny. It's hard to know what to believe anymore."

"I know," Izzy said.

"And what kind of a young man is Conway Maher?" Abby asked. Before Izzy could answer, Abby stopped her and said, "Actually, forget it. I don't care at all what kind of a young man he is. I'm not sure why I asked that." She laughed at herself before she found a tissue to wipe her eyes. "What a day," she said. She finished wiping her eyes and looked at Izzy. "Anything else I need to know?"

Izzy nodded. "One more thing."

Abigail exhaled. "Can't wait."

"The picture," Izzy said softly. "The one that Abel, *Norman*, gave you Dad's message about."

Abigail nodded. "It's framed on the mantle," she said.

"Did it say something on the back?" Izzy asked.

"Yes, it did," Abigail said. "Your father wrote on the back of every picture he took."

"I heard," Izzy said. She watched as her mother realized that Shannon Maher knew this as well. One more thing Joe had shared with someone other than his wife. "What did he write on the back of that one?"

Her mother took a deep breath and wiped her eyes again. "For what it's worth, he wrote 'Complete happiness' on the back of that picture," she said. "As far as I know it's the only picture that comes close to having the three of us in it." She shook her head, and Izzy couldn't imagine what her mother was thinking.

Izzy reached out and took her mother's hand in hers. "Then there is one more thing, Mom," she said.

"What?" Abigail asked.

"Did you know that same picture was taped to the inside of Dad's locker at the campground?" Izzy asked.

Her mother's eyes widened. "No, I didn't," she said.

Izzy nodded. "It's still there. They've never taken his pictures down, out of respect."

443

Abigail shifted in her seat. Her eyes wandered around the room, looking for an answer. "Did he write something on the back of it?" she asked.

Izzy shook her head. "I didn't look," she said softly. "And I'm not going to."

"Why?" Abby asked.

"Because that's for you," she said, squeezing her mother's hand. "It was always for you. Journalism has to end somewhere. But the picture is there. I saw it."

Abby turned to look out the window again. "*No shit.*"

***

Raymond Woodson didn't recognize the number that appeared on his cell phone. "Hello?" he said, catching the scornful glare of Jack, his longtime companion, who had been enjoying a celebratory brunch of sorts. So many Saturdays had been devoted to the Evan Long case over the years that he insisted on marking the occasion with something special. They had agreed on brunch at Buckley's, a favorite of theirs. They had been sipping Bloody Marys when Raymond's cell phone rang.

"Congratulations," a vaguely familiar voice said on the other end. It was far from sincere. Sarcastic, actually.

"Who is this?" Raymond asked, making sure the person on the other end knew he was annoyed.

"Has it been that long?" the voice asked.

Raymond concentrated. *Who was this?* he thought.

"Do you know how long I have been waiting to see that bastard hang, Raymond?"

Raymond didn't answer.

"There was a time when I had convinced myself that I didn't care either way," the voice continued. "Let the son-of-a-bitch rot in jail, right? But now that it's official, I'm realizing just how much I wanted him dead."

444

Raymond glanced around the restaurant and tried not to raise his voice. "Sir, whoever you are, you have no right to call and harass me for doing my job."

"I have more right than you will ever know, Raymond," the voice said coldly. "You and I always agreed on politics. Good old liberals, we were. Still are, aren't we?"

"I don't even know who you are," Raymond said.

"But this one is personal, Raymond. You see, I just can't stomach letting this man live when I've been trying to wash the feel of his sweat off my hands for the last twenty years."

Raymond ended the call and quickly turned off his phone. There would be no more interruptions today. "I'm sorry for that," he said to Jack.

"Media?" Jack asked.

Raymond shook his head as he reached for his bloody Mary. "They wouldn't have that number."

"Who then?"

"I'm not positive," Raymond said. "But I have a feeling it was the next president of the United States."

***

Abel turned the familiar corner and he was happy to see the Flat Rock come into his view for the first time in a week. The familiarity of the streets of Manayunk was more comforting than he had expected. As he neared the door, the figure, then the face, of Izzy Buchanan came into view from among the crowds of passersby. She had called him an hour ago and asked if they could meet for lunch. She embraced him warmly, kissing him on the cheek as though they had been apart for days. She felt good. They entered together.

Jackie the waitress, clearly surprised by their entrance, took their orders for a late lunch and winked at Abel as she walked away. He and Izzy made small talk as they waited for their drinks. Dogfish Head for him and coffee for her. "I'll bet she thinks we look older than we did a week ago," Izzy said.

445

"I'm sure I look older," Abel said. "You look exactly the same." He smiled at her and she smiled back. But it was an empty gesture. Abel could see it in her eyes. The experience had affected her. Instead of glowing with the rush that usually comes from the successful completion and publishing of a story, Izzy was tired and conflicted, looking as though she had just completed a long and arduous, unpleasant task.

"I *feel* older," she said, staring at the thick wooden table. Their drinks arrived and Abel drank while Izzy sipped. She reached into her bag and produced a manila folder with papers inside. "That's it," she said, plopping it in front of him. "It's running tomorrow with five pictures."

"Five? Holy shit," Abel said as he thumbed through the folder. "Nice work."

"We'll see," she said. "Shannon Maher was right. A lot of people will be upset."

"That's part of the job."

She shook her head. "I don't know what it's like to lose a child."

"You're doing your job," Abel said.

Izzy shook her head. "It's all about me."

"What do you mean?"

"I wanted to win that damn award," she said. "I thought it was intriguing. Hearing from the five silent voices twenty years later."

"Readers will agree with you," Abel said.

Izzy sipped her coffee and looked at Abel. "A groundskeeper racked with guilt because he could have stopped it; a grown man who feels like a coward because he let a ten-year-old boy do what he should have done; a woman who lost the love of her life." She reached across the table and took his hand. It felt warm from her coffee. Her voice softened as she said, "A boy who watched his brother die trying to save lives."

Abel coughed. "People will want to read it," he said.

"I saw my mom today," she said. "Right after they announced that he wasn't being executed. We just stood in the doorway holding each other and crying. She said she didn't know how to feel."

446

Abel listened.

"Then Shannon Maher called me. She was also crying. Kept telling me how proud she was of me. How proud my dad would be. I cried with her too," Izzy said. She looked into her coffee cup and shook her head. "But the truth is that before I went home, I wasn't really feeling *anything*."

"What do you mean?" Abel asked.

"I heard the news in my car, and the first thing I thought of was how it would affect my story," she said. "Isn't that horrible? It was news that would impact so many people in such profound ways, and I was only thinking about me."

"You were being a journalist," Abel said. "You weren't there. Those people were. Let them feel it."

"I just wish I felt *something*," Izzy said. "Shannon said I'll have to live with how this affects the people who lost their babies that day." She turned her head toward the bar, looking at nothing in particular. "I'm not feeling any of that, Abel."

"You're nineteen years old," Abel said. "You're a rich kid who's never dealt with a major loss. You don't feel anything because you haven't experienced anything in your life that could stir up that kind of emotion. You have a talent for digging up the facts and putting the words on the paper. Understanding emotions that lie beneath a story is something that comes with time. You'll find that."

She looked at him and smiled weakly. "Like interviewing that window washer," she said.

He nodded. "Something like that."

They ordered sandwiches and ate in silence. Abel read through much of the story. His life was outlined for all to see, including how he had changed his name. He wondered how his boss would react. His guess was that considering his unique circumstances, combined with his strong presence in the classroom, she would be rather understanding. He hoped so.

"This is good, Izzy," he finally said. "It might make you famous."

"Good for me," she said.

447

"There are plenty of journalists who'd die for this story. But you got it. Be proud of yourself."

"I am," she said. "What I hate is that pride is all I am feeling."

Abel took her hand again and looked in her eyes. "That's not true," he said. She looked back at him and he could see her eyes fill. "You feel for me," he said.

She wiped her eyes and nodded her head. "That's a start, I guess," she said.

"You feel for your brother too," he said. "And you helped me. I'm trying to stop living to please my dead brother."

She sighed. "Funny how that worked," she said. "I found a brother I never knew I had, and you let go of one you've had all along."

Having made his point, Abel decided to let the moment pass.

"And what's next?" Abel asked. "Wait twenty years to write the next one?"

She smiled. "You know what's next," she said. "Want to help me?"

He shook his head. "You don't need my help. And, no, I don't know what's next." He saw that she was still looking at him, smiling expectantly. He smiled back. "The one juror," he finally said.

"Exactly," she said. "Find him and find out what the hell?"

Abel laughed. "How do you know it was a *him?*" he asked. "You've already started working it?"

"A little bit," she said. "There were only four women on the jury, and they all spoke to the media, making it pretty clear what they thought. So I'm pretty sure it was a man. I'll find him."

Abel nodded. "Good work, as always," he said. "And the other thing?"

Izzy took in his words and leaned back in her chair. "Evan Long," she said.

"Evan Long," Abel said back to her.

She nodded. "The news that had him so upset." Abel could see her thinking. He guessed that she had already started looking into it.

448

"He's a mystery," she said. "Do you think you'll really ever go back to visit him?"

Abel shook his head as he ordered another beer. "Let him rot," he said. "Maybe I'll visit him in ten years. I'll have to go before that guard retires."

"Call me when you do, wherever I am," Izzy said. "I'll come with you."

Soon after, the two said their goodbyes and left separately. However, Abel would continue thinking about Izzy's words for quite some time.

***

"Does this change anything, sir?" Sheila asked quietly. She could see the governor was upset.

He glared at her. "I'm supposed to be asking *you* that."

Her face flushed and she looked back at the television that sat on a table across from the desk in his office. The story was all over the six o'clock news. Legal analysts, citizens, and survivors were all being heard from. Conceivably, the state could attempt another sentencing and try for a unanimous verdict, but it didn't seem practical, considering how long ago the crime and conviction had occurred.

"What in the hell could that one juror have been thinking?" Mike muttered. "Idiot. Delaware is just too damn small. Everybody knows everybody." He looked at Sheila. "This makes Sunday even more important. Big audience. It will be on people's minds."

"Yes it does," she said. "You'll be great, Governor. You always are." She meant it. She knew tomorrow's interview, which would run Sunday morning on national television would be a first for him in many ways. It would be the first time he addressed a national audience, aside from a few sound bites on the news about gun control. It would also be the first time he would ever speak publicly about the campground shooting. Yes, he'd spoken to that damn reporter about it already, but they had been assured that story

449

wouldn't run until the fall. "Just tell your side of the story, sir. People will understand."

He nodded slowly. She could tell he believed her, but she could see in his eyes that he wasn't even sure himself. She put a hand on his arm and smiled. "There is nobody in the world who can say what they would do in that situation," she said. "I don't care who they are." He nodded again.

Outside the office, they could hear the phone ringing nonstop. This was accompanied appropriately by the mantra on the television, *"Delaware Governor Mike Springer, who was present at the time of the shooting, and is believed to have personally disarmed Evan Long, could not be reached for comment."*

He'd made it clear to Sheila as soon as he heard the news: "I didn't discuss it then, and I'm not discussing it now." He had instructed her to write up a brief statement about his respect for both the U.S. and Delaware Supreme Courts, and the rule of law. Then he retreated into his office to be alone.

"What time are we leaving tomorrow?" he asked.

"Eight in the morning, sir," she said. "I'll have the car pick you up." They would be driving to New York for the interview, which would be televised Sunday morning.

"Okay," he said as he stood. "I'm going home. Have them pick me up out back. I'm not talking to the press."

"Are you okay?" she asked.

He looked at her before he left and said, "Between you and me, I feel like that bastard has killed Joe all over again."

Sheila walked with him to the garage and watched him get in the car before she gathered her things and left for the evening.

450

PART 7: CONSEQUENCES

Saturday, June 22, 1996

Father Francesco Antonelli strolled through the entrance of the Wawa convenience store, two blocks from the rectory where he lived. It was just before six in the morning and the daily newspapers were just arriving off the truck. He made his way to the coffee station. It was his daily ritual. He had known for a long time that a man who had taken a sacred vow of poverty probably should not be purchasing premium coffee at a convenience store every day, but the clerk never charged him, only asking him to pay fifty cents for the newspaper, which he shared with the others at the rectory.

He had heard the news about Evan Long yesterday and was glad to have received it in stride. He knew Evan Long had to be suffering through a personal hell for what he had done, and he hoped this suffering would somehow bring him peace in the afterlife. For many nights he had prayed for God's will to be done, whatever it would be, and he was satisfied to know that Evan Long would die in prison, probably many years from now.

He prepared his coffee and waited patiently for the newspapers to be unpacked and stacked on the shelves. The driver must have noticed the priest waiting because he stopped what he was doing and walked over. "Good morning, Father," the man said as he handed him a fresh copy of the paper.

Father Francesco thanked him and began to walk to the counter. Glancing down at the top story's headline for the first time, he found himself stopping and staring at it. He had planned to skip the articles

451

about Evan Long, deciding to put the matter to rest now that his fate had been decided.   Instead, the top story was one he had not expected to see: *Silent No More: Twenty years after the horrific shootings at St. Maria Goretti's, five survivors finally tell their stories.*

He felt the same rush of grief that he had felt when he had heard the news twenty years ago. His camp had come under attack, and people were dead. Children were dead. He hadn't been there to witness it or to offer last rites to the injured and dying. He'd been away, tending to his personal affairs. *Selfish.* That was how he had felt about himself in the months and years that had followed.

Now, his head suddenly felt light and his palms began to sweat. He dropped the paper and reached for his forehead. He was sweating profusely. His body, twenty years later, could not take the grief the way it had back then. He felt the coffee slip from his hand. Dropping to one knee, he heard a voice asking him a question he could not understand. He grasped his chest and fell forward, never feeling his face hit the cold, hard floor.

***

Izzy was leaning against her car, watching the sun come up across a field where construction of new condominiums had just begun. She was holding a copy of the day's newspaper. She hadn't read it, but she did check to see how the photos looked. She was happy. Will Janicki was on the front page standing in front of the monument by the swimming pool. Also on the front page was Shannon Maher, looking sad and pretty, and holding a photograph of herself, Joe, and Mike Springer. Both pictures were in color. Inside, where the story continued, were three more black and white photos, one of Conway Maher holding a pint of beer and looking expressionless into the camera, and another of Evan Long staring out a prison door with a corrections officer looming on the other side, and finally a photo of Abel Ryan on a sofa in a hotel room in Charleston. Izzy had taken this one, which showed Abel holding a camera.

As she waited, Izzy heard the quiet, rhythmic sound of heavy breathing peppered by the soft sound of footsteps that broke the silence of the Saturday morning. She turned to her left and, as expected, saw the lean form of Sheila Avery come into view around the corner. Izzy lit a cigarette, even though she was not at all in the mood to smoke. *This would be her last one,* she thought. She exhaled a plume of smoke and watched as Sheila strode by, decked out in spandex, sunglasses, and earphones. Sheila made an exaggerated coughing sound as she passed, not even recognizing Izzy as she continued on her way.

"Hi, Sheila," Izzy said loudly, hoping her voice would penetrate the jogger's earphones.

Sheila stopped and turned around. Pulling the earphones off her head she barked, "What are you doing?" She was breathing heavily.

Izzy smiled and held the newspaper out for Sheila to take. Sheila made no motion to accept it and just kept looking plaintively at Izzy.

"I would take it," Izzy said. "It's today's paper. That story you're going to New York to get ahead of? It's right here. Top of the fold." She gestured toward the paper. Sheila stared at her for a moment before she snatched the newspaper from her hand. She read the headline.

"You bitch," Sheila said as she read. "You made a deal with him! This wasn't supposed to be printed."

"I still have a deal," Izzy said.

Sheila looked at Izzy with incredulous hatred. "How could you even think that? This was supposed to run in the fall. That was the deal."

Izzy shook her head. "I recorded my entire conversation with the governor, and I never mentioned when the story was running. As far as he knew, it could have run that same day."

"This is bullshit, and you know it," Sheila said.

Izzy smiled and stuck out her chin. "I'm not bound by the arrangements you make with journalism professors behind my back," Izzy said. "However, Mike Springer is bound to every promise he made to me, including when he announces."

"Not a chance," Sheila said, still catching her breath. "You will *never* have access to him again. I can promise you that."

Izzy dropped her cigarette and stepped on it as she moved closer to Sheila. "He will keep every word of his promise to me," Izzy said. "And you will see to it. Or I will be sure the tape I have of you admitting to intimidation of private citizens goes public. How long do you think you'll have a job after that?"

Sheila lifted the paper and held it as if she would throw it at Izzy, or hit her with it, but before she could, her cell phone rang. She fumbled to pull the bulky device from its carrier.

"Hello," she answered.

Izzy tried not to laugh as she listened to one end of the conversation.

"Yes, sir," Sheila said. "I'm looking at it now. Yes, I was about to call you, sir. I just got the newspaper. We can take care of this. I'm already working on it."

Izzy silently blew her a kiss then got back in her car and drove away.

***

Abel's head was heavy. After parting ways with Izzy the afternoon before, he began making the rounds up Main Street in Manayunk. "The Stations of the Cross" his priest friend had once

454

joked of his lonely weekend habit. It had not been a late night. He was too tired from the week's events for that. But it had been a rough one. Full of beer by eight o'clock, he had switched to rum and Coke, then to straight whiskey. This morning he was paying the price.

He shuffled into the kitchen to make coffee and get a granola bar. It was nine-thirty. He turned on the television and fell onto the sofa. CNN was already covering it.

"...and when we come back, an article in a Delaware newspaper is shedding new light on the horrific campground shooting that took place twenty years ago," the deep-voiced anchor was saying. *"The new revelations involve Governor Mike Springer, who may soon be seeking higher office, as well as new information about Joe Conway, the man who died stopping the shooter, and his personal life. Stay with us."*

It went to commercial and Abel stood to run down to the newsstand and buy a Wilmington newspaper. He looked around for his shoes. Before he could find them, the telephone rang. He answered, expecting to hear the voice of his mother or Izzy. It was neither.

"Good morning, my friend," Tom said in his accented voice. "I am sorry for the early call. Have I awakened you?"

"No," Abel said. "I was up."

"Very good, my friend," he said. "I have just read this article in the Delaware newspaper that you had worked on."

"You're ahead of me," Abel said. "I haven't gotten it yet."

The priest laughed. "Yes, I made it a point to go get the *Wilmington Daily News* so I could read about this. It is my first time reading this paper."

"I was about to go get one myself," Abel said.

"I would like to talk to you," Tom said. "Do you think you could stop by the rectory, or I could possibly visit you at your home this afternoon?"

455

Abel detected something unfamiliar in his friend's voice. *Uncertainty? Fear?* "What's this about?" he said.

"I would rather discuss this in person, my friend," the priest said, sounding nothing like Abel's friend.

"Tell me now," Abel said.

"We should meet in person," Tom said again.

Abel didn't respond, waiting instead for the priest to speak again.

"Abel, this is very difficult," Tom said, his voice shaking a bit.

"What is?" Abel said.

"There are things in this article about you," Tom said. "About your personal life. About the way you behaved after the death of your father."

"So what?" Abel said. "It's nothing I haven't already told you."

"You told me these things in the confines of Confession, my friend. "But now these things are public. These things about your having a relationship with a student of yours."

"A *former* student, Father," Abel said. "And nothing illegal happened."

"Yes, I know this, my friend, but you must understand. We have parents who pay money to send their children to our school. To know their children are safe."

"They *are* safe," Abel said.

"I know this," Tom said. "It's just that...this is very difficult."

Abel said nothing. He waited for Tom to continue.

"This business of changing your identity, pretending to be a practicing Catholic, finding personal gratification with a former student who was very young at the time," he said. "I am sure you can understand why parents might feel uneasy with this. I was under the impression that you would be using an alias for this story."

Abel swallowed hard before he spoke. "I changed my mind, Father," Abel said. "I figured that being forgiven by God and the Church would mean something here."

"Of course it does," Tom said. "But it is not that simple, I'm afraid. Our employees must be living their faith by example."

Abel took a breath before he spoke, trying to calm himself. "Since you mention it, I know of at least three teachers at your school who are living with someone who isn't their spouse," he said evenly. "For one of them, it's the same gender. Are you going to call them next?"

"Abel, please try to understand," the priest said. "I am sorry this has all become public, but we will be expected to do something..."

"Is Kathy on board with this?" Abel asked.

"I haven't spoken to her, my friend," he said. "This is my decision, and it is final. You will not return to teach here in the fall. I'm sorry."

Abel bit his lip. He knew Kathy, the Head of School, would never approve of what Tom was doing. She had spent more than twenty-five years in Catholic education, and he was positive that she would stand by him. But Tom was an ordained clergyman, the pastor of the parish. He outranked her, even at his young age.

"I can see where this is going, my friend," Tom said. "So I want to tell you a few things. I hope that you continue to receive the sacraments, even if you don't want to receive them from me. I do hope you find the peace you are looking for. I want to still help you with that, though I am feeling now like you will not allow that to happen. But I want you to keep your faith, my friend. Hold on to your faith."

Abel thought for a moment before he answered. The man on the other end of the phone was the one who had welcomed him to the Church. He had literally baptized him with holy water into a new life. Abel had laughed and cried with him. He had come to know God through this man.

"Father, thanks for calling me," Abel said. "Thanks for everything you've done for me the past few years. I mean that. Before you called me today, I thought I'd be at that school for the

457

next thirty years teaching kids about the three branches of government. Now, I don't know what I'm going to do, or where I'll do it. But I do have faith, Father. I have faith in God and faith in the Church."

"I am so glad to hear that," the priest said quietly.

"But I have very little faith in some of the people *running* the Church."

Abel hung up.

***

Izzy and Abigail had decided to let the phone ring. They were having their lunch, chicken Caesar salad, on the back patio, trying to ignore the near-constant ringing.

"I thought our phone number was unlisted," Izzy said.

"It is," Abigail said. "These damn reporters can find out anything."

Izzy nodded. She knew her mother was right. If she needed to, she could find out how to get in touch with the elusive Abigail Conway without much effort. They had decided the night before that since the story would cause a local media firestorm, especially on top of yesterday's news of Evan Long's being spared execution, they were going to withdraw to their home for the day without talking to anyone but each other. This included Joe's family, who probably wouldn't call anyway.

They had decided they would remain in the house all day together enjoying each other's company, something they had not done in far too long. It was just after noon, and Izzy was craving a cigarette. She and her mother both knew it, but neither would dare acknowledge it. "You are far too young to have an addiction like that," her mother told her a year ago. "Stop now, while you still can." That was Izzy's plan, starting today.

After helping her mother clean up, Izzy decided it was a good time to take a swim. Some intense exercise would do her mind and body some good. She changed into a bathing suit and headed for the pool. Her mother decided not to join her.

The water was colder than she had expected, and it felt good. She was surprised by how much energy she had as she kicked and pulled with long, smooth strokes that grew stronger with each lap. She had always loved swimming, though she had never done it competitively. She was a strong swimmer, but she had known that even with hours of daily practice she could never be as good as the ones who showed up every four years to stand atop a podium and sing along to the national anthem. She didn't have the natural ability to be the best. And if she couldn't be the best at it, then the pursuit would be a waste of time. Always in it to win, Izzy had decided long ago that swimming would never be anything more than a lonesome exercise.

After losing count of how many laps she had completed, she pulled herself out of the pool and dried herself off. Making her way into the house, she heard her mother call her into the kitchen.

"Message for you," Abigail said. "I had to check them. Make sure there wasn't an emergency." She handed Izzy the phone and played back the message. Izzy was surprised to hear the voice of Conny. He had something important to tell her, and she should call him as soon as she could.

"Your brother?" Abigail asked.

Izzy smirked. It was funny to hear her call him that. "I'll call him from your office."

***

Abel wasn't in the mood to drink. He was always somehow glad that when he was depressed or in a bad mood, he didn't crave alcohol, at least not as much as he normally would. It reaffirmed his belief that he didn't have a drinking problem and that he simply enjoyed alcohol more than most people. He was still soberly processing the fact that his friend had fired him and that his teaching career might well be over. *What would he do now?* He could leave Philadelphia and head south. He had enjoyed Charleston. Maybe he could try to survive as a journalist in New York City. For years, he had inwardly thought that would be an adventure worth trying. He would have to find something soon, he thought.

The telephone rang, and he didn't pick up. He didn't feel like talking to anyone. However, whoever was calling had other ideas. It began ringing again immediately. When it happened a third time, he decided he had to answer.

"Abel." It was Izzy. He had been hoping to hear from her. He had been looking forward to talking about the article and any initial reactions either had received. But she wasn't calling to engage in congratulatory banter; that was obvious in the sound of her voice. She spoke his name once when he answered, and there was a long pause that followed.

"What is it?" he asked.

"I just got off the phone with Conny in Charleston," she said breathlessly.

"Okay," Abel said.

"His mother," Izzy said, now choking back tears. "She's dead. She killed herself."

"*Christ*," Abel said.

"I know. I've never felt so terrible."

"Don't," Abel said, trying to wrap his mind around what she was telling him. "The woman clearly had issues. She was a bundle of nerves."

"He said she left a note," Izzy said, still trying to catch her breath. "It said she was ready to join the love of her life, in the next world."

"Dear God," Abel said.

460

"It's all my fault," Izzy said.

"It's my story too," he said. "And it isn't my fault or yours. Blame Evan Long. One more victim to add to his list."

"I don't know what to do," Izzy said.

"Let me see you," Abel said. "I'll go there."

"No," she said.

"Why not?"

"I'll come to you," she said.

"Okay. Come now."

"Maybe," she said. "I'll see you soon. I'm so sorry I brought you into this, Abel. You were right. Digging up the past is dangerous."

He started to tell her it was okay. He was going to tell her that despite all that had happened, he was glad that she had found him and had come into his life. That he loved knowing her, and being with her. But he couldn't tell her. She had hung up the phone.

Sunday, June 23, 1996

Silent No More: Twenty years after the horrific shootings at St. Maria Goretti's, five survivors finally tell their stories.
-By Elizabeth Conway and Norman Suddard

This summer marks twenty years since the worst mass killing in the state's history. It took place on the swelteringly hot, humid Friday morning of August 6, 1976, at St. Maria Goretti's Campground outside of Newark, a camp that to this day welcomes children of all backgrounds.

There are five people who were present when the horror unfolded who, until now, have never spoken publicly about what they witnessed that day.

One of them will never forget the smell of the gunpowder. Another remembers feeling the killer's sweat on the handle of the weapon that he took from him. A third can still hear the screams of the victims, which reminded him of his service in the Korean War. The fourth still thinks of waking up to the taste of his own blood in his mouth. The fifth recalls looking into her lover's eyes for the last time.

One of these five survivors is the killer, Evan Long. Until his execution was overturned, he was bent on being remembered as a tortured soul who had atoned for his sins, ready to accept the honor of being the last American executed by hanging. He wanted to die remembered as a martyr for those who were bullied and abused as children.

The other four see things differently, and they will have the last word. These are their stories.

"You look like hell, Izzy." Izzy looked up from the newspaper to see Professor Griffin poking his head out of the screen door on his front porch. He pointed to the newspaper. "And you're reading yesterday's news," he said. He pointed to the newspaper. "Nice touch. Five senses and five memories. I like it."

Izzy nodded. "It's still yesterday to me," she said. She had arrived at his house just after the sun came up. She hadn't had the nerve to ring the doorbell at that hour, so she decided to sit and read the story that had already cost the lives of two people.

"Been up all night?" he asked.

She nodded without looking at him.

"Well, come in," he said. "Have some coffee."

He held the door for her, and she made her way down the familiar hallway to his den. She took a seat in a cushioned chair that had become her favorite. She listened to him quietly move around the kitchen. Vivian must still be asleep, she thought. He emerged from the kitchen with two cups, one of which he plopped beside her on an end table. "Black?" he asked, though he knew that was how she took it. She nodded.

They sipped their coffee in silence for a time before he said, "You didn't come here because you're pissed at me."

"I *am* pissed at you," she said quietly.

"I know you are, honey, but that is not why you're here."

Izzy frowned and looked at the Oriental rug.

"What happened?" he asked.

"You know about the priest," she said.

He closed his eyes and nodded. "He was an old man, honey. Much older than I, and I'm old. It was his time."

She scoffed. "I'll have to believe that, I guess," she said. "But he wasn't the only one."

He was quiet.

"Did you read it?" she asked.

"Of course," he said. "Hell of a piece. And you used your real name, I noticed."

She nodded. "If it's all going to be out there, then I figured I should."

"Of course, the irony is that even though you've been completely unbiased – as a journalist should – there is no way the public will be able to separate your name from the story."

She shrugged. "I guess I had to be a part of this one. I certainly didn't hold anything back because of who I am."

He nodded his approval. "Bigger so-called journalists have held back for much worse reasons."

"I hate them," she said.

"And they edited it in time to get the court's decision."

She nodded again. "They literally stopped the presses."

"You did good, young lady," he said. "Now tell me what happened."

"Shannon Maher," Izzy said, finding it hard to say her name. "She killed herself yesterday. Slit both of her wrists and her throat." Izzy lowered her head and sobbed.

He stood and stepped close to her, gently placing a hand on the back of her head. "Izzy, I am sorry, honey. You must feel awful," he said.

She did. "I don't know what to do," she said. "I wanted so badly to write this story. I never gave a shit about what would happen to anybody else. But she's *dead*. I could never have known that was going to happen. But maybe I *should* have!"

He found a tissue box and handed her one. She wiped her eyes and nose. She was in bad shape. "Of course you couldn't have known," he said. "You were doing your job."

"Job well done!" she said angrily.

"We call that irony in our business," he said, prompting a smile. She lowered her head again. "Listen, Izzy. What you did was good journalism. Good journalism has consequences, good and bad. *Always*. Good journalism makes politicians resign, or makes Congress pass a new law, or makes the NFL change a rule. Or somebody gets arrested. That's good journalism, honey."

"Or people die," Izzy said.

He knelt next to her and put an arm around her shoulder. "Sometimes," he said. "But it's not your fault. You dug into the past because that's what we do. You uncovered shit that nobody would have ever known. Shit that people *wanted* to know. You did that. You told the story you wanted to tell, and that people needed to hear. You have nothing to apologize for, honey."

Izzy took in his words, crying quietly. In her heart, she knew he was right. She wasn't responsible for what had happened. Shannon Maher had done it, and maybe she had been planning on it for years. That was where the responsibility lay - there and in a jail cell for the rest of his life. But Izzy knew she would never sleep the same again. She would never approach a story in the same way again.

She finished crying as the professor walked back to his chair and sat. She looked up to see him sipping his coffee and watching her cautiously.

"Why did you do it?" she asked him.

He put his coffee on the end table and looked at the floor. "I had to, honey," he said.

"You didn't," she said angrily. "You made a deal with the powerful. You always say that the powerful should fear us. And you bowed to them."

"Well, I'm a pussy," he said. "I was looking out for my college. There are all kinds of things they can do to hurt a public university. And the story would have run anyway. I stopped being a journalist years ago."

"Did you really think you would have stopped me from publishing this thing on time?" she asked.

He smiled and shook his head. "Not at all," he said. "I was just trying to save my own ass, which I did. We don't all have the blood of heroes."

Professor Griffin watched Elizabeth Conway walk through the pouring rain to her car. She was in no hurry, but her strides were determined. She had left the newspaper she'd been reading on his front porch. He picked it up, looked at it again, and smiled. She was fearless and idealistic, very much an old soul, but a teenager nonetheless. He hoped to God she remained a relentless force for truth.

He prayed that she would never become like him.

Tuesday, August 5, 1996

Abel drove uphill on the same winding path that Will Janicki had driven them more than a month earlier, taking him and Izzy to the Joe Conway Memorial Tennis Courts. That had been the first day Abel had worked on the story.

465

He parked his car and looked toward the tennis courts where two others had already gathered. He had received the engraved invitation two weeks prior to today, but he had never bothered to RSVP to Father Bill Johnston. He turned off the engine and saw that Governor Springer and Father Bill had arrived and were embracing. Abel wondered if Izzy would be attending today's ceremony, or whatever this thing was supposed to be. He hadn't heard from her since the day she had told him the sad news of Shannon Maher. In the days that had followed the story's printing, and the fallout that had followed, he had expected to hear from her, but the days became weeks, and he soon realized that she would not be calling. He never tried to reach her either.

Abel had come to realize that he had been used by Izzy Conway. She had spotted his ability as a journalist and used it to her advantage, knowing his insights would make up for her very few weaknesses. He had internalized and accepted this truth. However, he was not willing to believe, or even convince himself, that Izzy Conway had conned him all the way to the end. They had experienced something real together, and he couldn't understand for the life of him why she had shut him out.

He looked at his watch. It was still early and he was not craving a drink. That was good, he thought. He exited the car, still quite unclear what this day would bring.

It was twenty years to the day since the shooting at St. Maria Goretti's Campground.

***

It is exactly twenty years since the day her husband was killed. Abigail Conway squeezes the hand of Father Bill Johnston, then releases it as she walks toward the door of the small shed. She enters the room and immediately sees what she is looking for. The staff room is cluttered, with dishes in the sink and empty

466

water bottles and soda cans strewn everywhere. Empty hot dog containers. Copies of Sports Illustrated. A dirty coffee pot. Worn paperback novels and crossword puzzle books. Youthful idle time at its finest.

But what she is looking for is staring at her from across the hot, smelly room that hasn't been cleaned in days. It is a locker with a piece of tape across the top with the word "Director" written on it. She uses the key that Will Janicki has given her to open the door. As expected, she finds the two photographs taped to the inside of the locker. One of them is of her herself, very pregnant, in the backyard of their home. She cannot remember this one ever being taken. The other is of her and Joe standing arm in arm in front of an ice cream stand in Avalon, New Jersey. It was taken earlier that same summer when she had not been so far along.

She exhales deeply and asks out loud, "Where was your heart, Joseph?" She pulls the photo from the door and turns it over. She feels herself flush with emotion when she sees Joe's handwriting. She reads the words to herself:

Forgive me, both of you. - 8/5/'77

She smiles and speaks out loud. "Really, Joseph?" She places the photograph in her purse and says out loud, "I'll think about it." She begins to close the locker door, but stops. She reaches with her right hand and gently tugs at the corner of the other photo, the one with her in the maternity dress. She smiles again and leaves it where it is.

He can keep that one, whatever it says. She wipes her eyes and closes the door.

* * *

"Thanks for arranging this, Bill," the governor said, probably a little too loudly. It was a clear, hot morning, with very little humidity, a rarity in Delaware in August. Izzy watched the governor shake Father Bill Johnston's hand, then embrace him.

The two men were standing in front of the entrance to the tennis courts named in her father's honor. Izzy watched from a short

467

distance, leaning on the door of her car. Will Janicki was next to arrive, and Izzy was surprised but appreciative to see that he wore a suit and tie. A solemn occasion. He walked to the entrance of the tennis courts and likewise embraced the two men.

Abel was next. He parked his car and emerged wearing sunglasses. He was dressed in a polo shirt and khakis. He scanned the parking lot briefly, landing on Izzy for a moment. She smiled and watched as he turned away and quickly made his way to where the other men stood. *He probably hates me,* Izzy thought, wondering if Abel had had a drink yet today.

When Abigail arrived and made her way over to the others, Izzy noticed how they, including the governor, stood up straighter, almost at attention. Izzy laughed to herself. Her mother was a class act, commanding respect wherever she went.

When her mother joined them, Izzy could hear and see that fresh tears were flowing. She hugged and squeezed all of them. Then she watched as everyone but the priest bowed their heads while he led them in a short prayer. They held hands as they prayed together. Except for Will Janicki, who was too busy wiping his tears with a handkerchief. At the conclusion of the prayer, Father Bill took a step back from the group as the others made their way through the unlocked gate of the tennis court. As the trio began walking to the center of the court, Izzy saw Mike Springer stop and look back. He gestured for both Bill and Izzy to join them. Bill, still standing at the gate, raised both his hands in respectful refusal. Izzy just shook her head.

Very quietly, she said, "You should go."

"Now?" the man asked. He'd been sitting in the passenger seat, watching those gathered on the tennis court. "I wouldn't feel right," he said. "Not now."

Izzy took her eyes off the group, who had now formed a tight circle in the center of the tennis court, and turned around to speak to him. "You were there," she said. "You should go."

She watched as her words registered. The young man nodded and exited the car. Izzy watched the confused expressions of the others as the tall, lean frame of Conway Maher confidently walked through the gate to join them.

It was her mother, of course, who recognized him first. She stepped from the group and greeted him, putting both her hands gently on either side of his face. Izzy could see the storm of emotion in her mother's eyes, even from where she stood. Then Abigail Conway embraced and held the son of her dead husband. She held him for a full minute, neither speaking.

Izzy wiped her eyes as her mother led him to the group, where she introduced him to each of them. Then she watched as the four began to slowly walk hand-in-hand toward the gate.

They would walk across the court, and down the steep hill that led to the baseball field. They would continue, with Izzy and the priest following at a distance, to the pool. Once there, they would pray again, remembering the lost, and celebrating the survivors.

Izzy watched them all as they exited the gate. But it was only her mother's footsteps that she could hear against the hard surface of her father's tennis court.

They were the strong, resolute footsteps that Izzy would hear forever, following them as best she could.

Acknowledgments

Many thanks to Jay Moore for creating the cover. Thanks also to Jude McDonald and Tom Wayock for their time and feedback. Two great Delawareans and one honorary.

KEVIN CONLIN lives in Wilmington, Delaware with his wife and two children.

Made in the USA
Middletown, DE
25 June 2019